back

in the

burbs

NEW YORK TIMES BESTSELLING AUTHOR
TRACY WOLFF

USA TODAY BESTSELLING AUTHOR
AVERY FLYNN

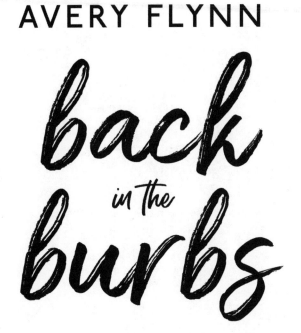

back in the burbs

Entangled Publishing, LLC
10940 S Parker Road
Suite 327
Parker, CO 80134
rights@entangledpublishing.com

Amara is an imprint of Entangled Publishing, LLC.

Visit our website at www.entangledpublishing.com.

Edited by Liz Pelletier
Cover illustration and design by Elizabeth Turner Stokes
Interior design by Toni Kerr

ISBN 978-1-68281-569-4
Ebook ISBN 978-1-68281-591-5

Manufactured in the United States of America

First Edition March 2021

10 9 8 7 6 5 4 3 2 1

an imprint of Entangled Publishing LLC

Also by Avery Flynn

HARBOR CITY SERIES

The Negotiator
The Charmer
The Schemer

HARTIGANS SERIES

Butterface
Muffin Top
Tomboy

ICE KNIGHTS SERIES

Parental Guidance
Awk-weird
Loud Mouth

KILLER STYLE SERIES

Killer Temptation
Killer Attraction
Killer Charm
Killer Seduction

TEMPT ME SERIES

His Undercover Princess
Her Enemy Protector

SWEET SALVATION
BREWERY SERIES

Enemies on Tap
Hollywood on Tap
Trouble on Tap

B-SQUAD SERIES

Brazen
Bang
Blade
Trouble

LAYTON FAMILY SERIES

Dangerous Kiss
Dangerous Flirt
Dangerous Tease

FAIRY TRUE SERIES

Jax and the Beanstalk Zombies
Big, Bad Red

SINGLE TITLES FROM
AVERY FLYNN

The Wedding Date Disaster
Royal Bastard
Attracting Aubrey
Dodging Temptation

To Emily, Shellee, and Sherry
I wouldn't have made it through my dark period without you.
—TW

For everyone out there who woke up one day, unsure of how you got there, don't worry. We've all been there.
What's important is where you go now.
—AF

"Never be so polite, you forget your power."
—"marjorie," Taylor Swift

Chapter One

*H*ow is my day going? Well, I'm thirty-five years old and hiding from my parents in the bathroom at the swanky offices of Lagget, Lagget, & Lagget, Attorneys at Law. So super, obviously.

Sure, it's a classy bathroom, with the wood stall doors that run all the way from the floor to the ceiling and the continual scent of jasmine in the air, but eventually Mom or Dad will find me. And shake their heads before insisting I go *out there*.

I sigh and flush the unused toilet. So many metaphors for my own life come to mind as I watch the water spin around and around before going down the drain, but I'm not feeling especially witty today. Mainly because the *out there* I have to face is the stuffy office of Thaddeus P. Lagget IV—where my aunt Maggie's will is about to be read.

I pull the heavy stall door open and start to pat myself on the back for at least leaving the cubicle. No, I should probably reserve congratulations for after I work up the courage to leave the bathroom entirely.

I sigh again. Ballsy, loud, and always in charge of her destiny, Maggie O'Malley would have never holed up in a fancy bathroom when there was business to be done. She would have blazed in there, rolled her eyes at the snarky comment my dad would inevitably say about the pink tips at the ends of her bone-white hair, and enjoyed the roller coaster of whatever came next.

Then she would have laughed, a great booming sound that could be heard halfway across Penn Station and probably out in the parking lot. It's been four weeks since she passed, and I still wake up every day missing that woman. But she wouldn't want me to dwell. In fact, she'd be angry if she knew I wasted one moment regretting anything about her life—or her death.

And that's the rub, isn't it? Aunt Maggie lived a life without regrets. And me? Well, I regret most everything.

As I walk up to the granite bathroom counter, I go on autopilot and gather the crumpled towel someone left discarded on the counter and use it to wipe up the small puddle of water around the sink before tossing it into the nearby trash bin. Just typical me, cleaning up other people's messes because it's so much easier than dealing with my own.

And what a mess I made.

I'm out of work—note to self, spending the last decade working as the office manager for your soon-to-be-ex-husband's law firm was not the brightest idea.

My bank account needs CPR because not only have I always worked for pennies so more money could be funneled back into building the practice (worst decision ever), I also spent what meager savings I have on a cheap sublet in Hell's Kitchen (yes, irony's a bitch) as I tried to hunt for a new job. Of course, when your ex is your only job reference, well, like I said, worst decision ever…

I finally gave up the ghost and slunk back to Jersey last week. And to my parents.

Now I'm living in my childhood bedroom—because the upscale condo on the Upper East Side where I spent the entirety of my doomed marriage is listed as belonging to my ex's law firm and apparently not a marital asset. Oh wait, no, *that* was my worst decision ever.

My shoulders sink as I stare at my reflection and wonder for the hundredth time how I let this happen. Aunt Maggie would have never ended up in this position.

If she'd found any one of her three husbands going down on his paralegal, she would have pulled some kind of dramatic, awe-inspiring act of vengeance that would probably have involved the bottle of hot honey she always seemed to have in her giant purse and fire ants she would have willed into existence simply from the power of her fury.

Me? I shut the door quietly and waited until I got home to cry. Turns out more than three decades of lectures on the proper way for a Martin woman to behave was too much to overcome.

It doesn't matter. At this point in my life, I am who I am. Of course, I'm not sure exactly who *that* person is anymore.

"Mallory." Dad's voice comes through the closed bathroom door, as low and loud as a foghorn and just as abrupt. "Stop being self-indulgent and get out here. Thad has a tee time."

Golf. One of the three sacred activities of Edward Christopher Martin, Esquire—really, that's the way he's introduced himself to others for my entire life, full name and "Esquire." The only thing I could do that would lower myself further in his estimation after I told him about the upcoming divorce was to make a fellow attorney late for his golf game.

Exhaling a shaky breath, I turn on the gold-plated faucet as if I'm just a hand wash away from being ready to come out. Then I take another thirty seconds to prep for saying goodbye to Aunt Maggie, because that's what this really is.

After the reading of the will, everything will be put back in its place, and any discussion of my great-aunt will be shushed with the admonishment not to make things uncomfortable for others. That isn't just the Martin golden rule; it's the one rule that can't be broken—at least not by me.

Especially never by me, which is why my pending divorce and return home is such a shameful thing. I'm making things uncomfortable.

Unable to put it off any longer, I open the bathroom door

and walk out. Dad is standing across the hall in a black suit, not a strand of his iron-gray hair out of place and with the permanently disappointed downturn to his lips on full display. Maybe it would have been different if I had a brother or sister, but as the lone child, I'm the sole person responsible for Dad's many expectations and Mom's many requirements.

"About time, Mallory," he says, then turns and walks into Thad's office.

A right turn and three steps will get me out onto the street and away from here. I can already feel the sunshine on my face and the summer breeze in my hair. Donello's Ice Cream is barely a walk away—my aunt's favorite place because they always gave her extra cherries on her rocky road double scoop.

Aunt Maggie would have made that right turn.

Me? I go left and follow my dad into Thad's office.

Yeah, I'm disappointed in myself, too.

Chapter Two

"That can't be right." The words come out of my mouth like a squeak as I look from my mom to my dad, trying to force Thad's words to make sense.

Sure, *individually*, I know the meaning of each word Thad just said, but when he put them together in one sentence, it was like when I tried to recall enough of my high school Spanish to understand telenovelas without subtitles. There was drama—but with a toothbrush at a library.

Mom sits still, her face as shocked blank as mine probably is. Mind spinning, I pick up the teacup and saucer resting on the side table between our chairs and hand it to her. She looks down at it, confused for a second, and then gives me a small, grateful smile before taking a fortifying sip from the delicate flower-covered china.

Dad remains silent for once, but there's an all-too-familiar pinched look around his mouth.

Thad clears his throat and pulls my attention back to him.

"I assure you, Margaret left you the house in Huckleberry Hills," Thad says again, handing over an envelope with my name written on the outside. "The property is valued at just over $850,000 with a remaining mortgage of $413,000. Of course, there are currently a substantial number of violations against the homeowners' association bylaws, and you'll need to pay the inheritance tax on the property within six months, which totals roughly $127,500. But the house is most assuredly yours, Mallory."

Again, words making sense on their own but just a jumble of gobbledygook when strung together. I take the envelope, and the sight of Aunt Maggie's handwriting, with its flowing curlicue flourishes, makes my chest tighten.

"There's nothing stopping her from selling it?" Dad asks, the sucked-on-a-lemon expression lessening with each word.

Thad shakes his head. "Not at all. In fact, it's a great way to satisfy the inheritance-tax burden."

"Well then, that settles that." Dad stands up and turns to look straight at me. "You can sell it and, even after paying the taxes, you'll have plenty left to get yourself back on track. Great, Thad, we appreciate your time."

I clasp the envelope tighter in my hands, wrinkling the perfect, smooth pink surface before realizing what I'm doing and loosening my grip. But I don't move. I stay right there in my seat as the flicker of something that feels a lot like defiance warms my belly.

Maybe it's the power of Aunt Maggie's words in my hand, but for one of the very few times in my life, I don't want to do what it takes to make sure everyone else around me is comfortable.

Maybe it's because of our last conversation, the one where I visited her in the active-living facility and told her, and no one else, about how Karl had changed the locks on the condo and left my packed suitcases with the doorman. I was no longer needed. Dismissed.

I thought she'd be disappointed in me, but I should have known better. Aunt Maggie just shrugged and said another door would open, just wait and see. Well, and that Karl is a dinglebutt who never deserved me.

Leave it to Aunt Maggie to mean a literal door—and then give me the keys to it. Am I really going to discard her gift for something better, like *I* was discarded?

Mom must sense a rare intransigence in me because, instead of getting up and going to my father's side, she sets her tea down and looks at me. "Imagine how a personal makeover will have Karl thinking about you again and the idea of what you bring to the marriage beyond a financial boost."

"If only I had a prized dairy cow blue ribbon to go along with it." The words come out before I can think better of them.

By the power of Aunt Maggie's ghost or something.

Okay, fine, I'm not exactly dressing to impress lately. Sure, if someone doesn't know me, they might think that I work at a yoga studio for the potato-chip and true-crime-podcast addicted. I showered. I remembered to put on deodorant and to brush my teeth. I used the time hiding in the bathroom to fix my ponytail that went all wonky. But that's the full extent of my give-a-shit-about-appearances efforts.

"Mallory," Dad says in that tone he uses on me anytime I even consider stepping out of his very narrow lines of what's considered proper. "I do not appreciate your sarcasm." He looks over at the other man. "I apologize, Thad."

I eat the words bubbling up inside me, the ones that Aunt Maggie would have let fly without a second thought—old habits, old dogs, and all that.

Thad shoots me an indulgent smile. "No worries. These readings can often be trying." He nods at the paper in my hands. "Your aunt's will is clear; you must read the letter first before deciding to do anything with the house. So you go ahead and do that while I buzz Grace to come in and take notes for the realtor we use in these situations. I believe there's been some interest in that area by a local developer looking to take out the older homes in these grand neighborhoods and building new."

Dad and Thad go into their usual back-and-forth while my mom stares out the window, her hands clasped in her lap and her legs crossed at the ankles.

Alone in a room full of people, I open the envelope and pull out the single sheet of paper. The forceful, broad strokes of Aunt Maggie's handwriting make me smile despite it all.

Dear Mallory,
Don't feel bad you didn't know I was about to kick the bucket when you visited last. This life—what a ride! I would change nothing. Now, don't listen to your dad. My nephew was never a risk-taker like we are. Let's show everyone you've still got some fight left in you.
I miss you and love you right back. Always.
Love,
Aunt Maggie
P.S. The house could use a little love, but I promise, it'll love you right back if you let it.

A tightness in my lungs has me holding my breath as the tears pool. Damn it. She knew I'd cave to the people in my life. Like I always do. Like I was raised to do.

I shouldn't be surprised.

Leaving me the house isn't just an act of kindness; it's also a dare. The fact of the matter is that I'm not brave like Aunt Maggie or confident *or* a risk-taker, like she said. I always do what I'm told. The one and only time I did something no one expected was when I demanded a divorce from Karl. And then I lost everything.

Each night this week, I slept under the pink canopy of my childhood bed, shame wrapped around me like a suffocating blanket at the certainty that my still-rebellious seventeen-year-old self would have been aghast at the worn-out doormat I'd become. When did it happen? What decision sent me down this path? How did I turn into the woman who teen me wouldn't recognize?

This isn't the life I was supposed to have.

The office door opens, and Thad's assistant walks in.

"There you are, Grace," Thad says. "Can you please get Ethan Restor to swing by this afternoon? We'll need to start the paperwork to get the Huckleberry Hills property on the market. Warn him it's in rough shape, but the location makes it desirable."

There's more back-and-forth, but it all becomes background noise. No one asks me what I want to do. I am dismissed—again—while they just push forward with their own plans. Just like Karl and my dad and every person who has taken one look at me and thought a woman approaching middle-age has no value.

My chest tightens.

"No," I say, the single word coming out as shaky as a cup of Jell-O in a dinosaur park.

Everyone stops talking and turns to look at me. I don't move. I'm not sure I could if I wanted to. Meanwhile, my heart has gone into overdrive, making the blood rush through my body like a racehorse doped up on meth.

"What?" Dad asks, the pinched look reappearing around his lips.

I let out a quick breath. "I'm not selling."

Chapter Three

*O*h my God. I said it. Out loud. Each word. My breath comes in and out in fast spurts, and I'm getting light-headed—I might be delusional, too, because I swear I see my mom smile before she looks over at my dad and her expression changes into one of placid neutrality.

Dad glares at me. "You're being emotional."

"No." I'm not hysterical. I'm not PMSing. I'm not speaking out of turn. I just have a little fight left in me after all. "Aunt Maggie willed the house to me. I'm keeping it."

Tense? Oh, that doesn't even begin to cover it. While my mom is the epitome of stand-by-your-man-no-matter-what steadfastness, my dad is nearly purple. My mom grabs his angina pills out of her purse and hands one to him. He takes it without a word or a drink of water. Once Dad's color dials down from murderous to just completely pissed, Thad lets out a nervous chuckle and shuffles the papers on his desk.

"I'm afraid there's quite a bit more to it than you may realize, Mallory," Thad says once he finally looks back up from the file marked O'MALLEY HOUSE. "There is a sizable inheritance tax to be paid, as I mentioned already. And although the house was grandfathered into the development when the Huckleberry Hills subdivision was built around it, any exceptions to meeting the architectural and appearance standards of the association do not extend to the new owner. As such, you'd have a maximum of six months to bring it in line with the association's expectations or lose the house, according to the agreement your great-aunt signed with the association."

Six months. Half a year. Plenty of time. "I can do that."

"Mallory Martin Bach, stop being unreasonable." Dad sits down in his chair with a huff. "You know nothing about renovations. You haven't even seen the state of the house. Besides, you can't do this alone. You would need Karl to help you with something of this size."

I wince at that—how many times have I not done something in my life because Karl told me I need him to help me with it, even though we both knew he had no intention of helping me? Too many to count—but not this time. Aunt Maggie wouldn't have left me her house if she didn't think I could handle it, so I am going to handle it. And show my parents—and Karl—that I don't need him. More, I don't need anyone.

Thad continues. "I must inform you that it is… Well, a fixer-upper is what I believe the realtors would call it. Remember, your aunt moved into the active-living residence a year before her death. No one has been in it since then. There are currently"—he looks down at a sheet of paper—"forty-seven HOA violations against it. Quite honestly, I believe there are more, but the HOA board took pity on your aunt. Now that it's yours, my understanding is that they expect the changes to be made quickly or they will sue."

I swallow. Okay, that doesn't sound quite as promising. But Aunt Maggie wouldn't have left me the house if she didn't believe I could do it.

"And just how are you going to pay the taxes on it?" Dad asks. "You don't even have a job."

"I can get a job." People do it every day—last two months evidence to the contrary, but I don't mention that.

So what if I went from working for my dad part-time in college to working full-time in Karl's law practice? I have two and a half years of law school and eleven years of experience running a legal practice. I have skills, just not the ones that people like my dad find important.

Dad throws his arms up in obvious frustration. "What you need to be focused on is getting Karl to take you back."

I wince. It isn't something he hasn't said a dozen times this week, but still, it hurts.

My dad loves me and only wants what's best for me; I know that. Sure, divorce is a four-letter word in my family, but really, that isn't why he keeps harping on taking Karl back. I spent the better part of a decade showing everyone that my value began and ended with Karl's accomplishments rather than my own. Why should I be shocked now that they consider my life worthless without him?

And for a moment—just a moment—I almost give in. I almost give up. On the house. And more importantly, on myself. But then I think about Karl's smirk when I told him I wanted a divorce, the pitying looks on my parents' faces when I showed up on their doorstep with three packed suitcases.

And then Aunt Maggie's words.

Sweat beads at the nape of my neck, tickling my skin as I try to take slow and steady breaths so my stomach stops feeling like I'm skydiving instead of sitting in the probate attorney's office, taking a stand for the first time in my life.

"I'll figure it out," I say, my palms sweaty.

"You need to sell, Mallory. It's the right move," Dad says, using the firm tone that means the discussion is over and his judgment rendered. "I know you loved your aunt, but you need to be logical."

Logical. An interesting term. It's the word Dad used when I said I wanted to get a Master of Fine Arts in photography. *There's no money in that—be logical*, he said. So I went to law school instead and met Karl.

"I'm keeping the house."

And I'm going to fix it up and fix my life in the process. Period. I can totally do this.

God, I hope so.

Chapter Four

There's no way in hell I'm going to do this.

Standing on the sidewalk outside of Aunt Maggie's house is like taking a trip down memory lane, but the nightmare version of it.

Where once there was lush, neatly trimmed grass I ran around in barefoot while hopping through the sprinkler, now the grass is nearly a foot tall and strangled with dandelions. The trees and bushes were left to grow hog wild for who knows how long, like the yard is auditioning to be a set piece for *Jumanji*.

I eye the tall grass and shudder. There are definitely snakes somewhere in there, and I shuffle farther away from the grass onto the driveway that looks like protest art with cracks and crevices everywhere. Piles of leaves from last fall have been pushed up into the corners of the wide porch. And the porch swing Aunt Maggie sat on with me as she drank afternoon gin fizzes while watching the sunset hangs lopsided, swaying listlessly in the spring breeze.

But honestly, what really has me gazing at the house in shock is the giant tree limb currently laying in the vee of what used to be the wide wooden porch. It's obvious a storm recently ravaged the neighborhood—well, if you look at Aunt Maggie's house.

I glance around the neighborhood at the perfectly groomed lawns and realize whatever damage anyone else sustained was quickly swept aside and repaired, my aunt's sad house the only evidence that shit happens in the world no one can control.

I'm not the least surprised that all the houses in Huckleberry Hills are perfect. The grass is cut to just-so height. The landscaping is so tasteful, a weed wouldn't even consider making an appearance. Each of the two-story Victorian-looking homes with wraparound porches and quirky little details are like an idealized dollhouse that was supersized. The cars parked in the driveways are shiny. The men and women outside now are totally put together. The kids look Instagram-worthy, and their pets are probably all AKC registered.

I slowly turn back to Aunt Maggie's house and idly wonder how someone didn't "accidentally" torch this eyesore before now. Hell, *I'm* half tempted to do it, and I've only been standing here for five minutes.

It's obvious the other homes were built years later around Aunt Maggie's, which was grand itself when originally built, but now, with peeling paint, the overgrown lawn, and a giant tree in the middle of the porch—well, it needs more than TLC. It needs mouth-to-mouth.

I'm considering getting in my car and going back to…where? My parents' house? Sweet baby Jesus in the manger, please no.

Okay, I have two choices—give up or get to work. So I need to do a little yard work and cosmetic stuff before I can tackle the requirements in the four-inch-thick HOA bylaws Thad gave me that are now sitting on the front seat of my car. I can handle that. It isn't like the inside could be worse, right?

Delusional? Me? Probably. But I have to hold on to something.

Walking around the tree limb and across the front porch is like taking my life in my own hands. The boards are splinter city and jagged, and every squeak grows more B-movie-soundtrack ominous the closer to the front door I get.

I haven't been back to Sutton, New Jersey, in probably

twenty years. Surely two decades isn't enough time for all of this to happen. Why didn't Aunt Maggie say anything to me when we met up in the city—always in the city—for a show or to gawk at all the shop windows or to take a spin on the ice in Bryant Park?

Yeah, well, why didn't you mention the fact that you were married to an asshat who made you cry on the regular?

Good point, self.

I take a deep breath, turn the key in the dead bolt, and walk inside.

Holy. Shit.

The place looks like a haunted mansion on acid. The furniture is covered by sheets in eye-searing blues, greens, purples, and pinks. I flip up the corner of one of the sheets and discover the kick-ass vintage stereo system encased in oak is still where it always was. There is a God—and she has great taste in music, because all of Aunt Maggie's records are in the attached cabinet.

The trip through the dining room and kitchen is pretty much the same. Each room is crowded with knickknacks, piles of books—including five copies of *The Joy of Sex*—and more furniture than needed, all of it in shades that never once were found in nature, but there's nothing a little elbow grease won't fix.

Then I get to the staircase.

It's built to be wide enough for two people to walk up side by side, but that isn't gonna happen until all the stuff stacked up on each step has been moved. There are teapots and egg cups, an entire set of encyclopedias, and magazines—so many magazines—from *Cosmo* to *Good Housekeeping* to what look like twenty years of *Sports Illustrated* swimsuit editions. There are rain boots and snow boots and go-go boots. There are industrial-size cans of ketchup and several issues of the *Sutton Daily Times*, including one dated two years ago that states it was the paper's final printed edition.

Turning sideways, I make my way up the cramped stairwell that's wallpapered in old movie posters, total cult classics like *Blue Velvet* and *Rocky Horror Picture Show*, then pause at the landing only long enough to count at least fifteen coffee mugs where the only thing that matches is the chips they all have. The second flight leading to the upstairs bedrooms is one-foot-in-front-of-the-other territory.

There are four bedrooms upstairs and two bathrooms. And three of the bedrooms are filled, floor to ceiling.

At the first door, I have to press my shoulder to it and really shove to get it open. It's like a consignment store the size of my favorite bodega was squashed into a room barely big enough for a twin bed and a chest of drawers. There are shirts and pants and more—is that a wedding dress?—piled almost to the popcorn ceiling. I chicken out before walking in farther. If I get lost, no one will ever find me.

The next room isn't as hard to get into, but let's just say I've never seen that many VHS tapes in my life. There's a stack of Chinese takeout fortunes in Ziploc bags, and hanging on the walls are dried flower after dried flower pressed between sheets of wax paper. The third room is home to more chipped china, more magazines, and empty glass bottles of nearly every size, shape, and color imaginable.

By the time I walk down the hall, with its starting-to-fall-down floral wallpaper, to the last bedroom, I'm mentally placing bets on what will be inside. Stuffed animals? Will this be where all the world's Beanie Babies went? Or maybe I'll find enough costume jewelry to make a mini crystal palace. The suspense is getting to me—also the fact that I didn't eat breakfast.

I open the door and find what must have been Aunt Maggie's bedroom.

The theme, without a doubt, is "go wild." There are neon zebra-striped curtains, the bedspread is hot pink, and the wallpaper is leopard print—but only if leopards glowed in the dark and probably hung out at a rave held at an abandoned industrial site.

The stacks of stuff aren't as high in here, but there's definitely a lot of it. Programs from high school plays, takeout menus, a *Thunder Down Under* calendar signed by each of the featured dancers. It's a mishmash of the kinds of things people find at the bottom of their purse or in the pockets of their winter coat when they pull them on for the first snowfall.

But the bed is clear, the pillows fluffy, and the room filled with light. Yeah, I can make this work—at least until I figure out how to remove wallpaper.

How hard can it be?

A thousand YouTube searches on my phone later, I find out that it would be a pain in the ass, because of course it would. By then, my stomach is grumbling, and I know I need to go eat one of the two sandwiches I got at Target on the way here. Doing the side shuffle down the stairs, I go back to the main floor and let out a pent-up breath.

I make my way to the kitchen and start shuffling through drawers, looking for scissors so I can open the little mayo packet that came with my turkey club, and that's how I find it. Every kitchen has a junk drawer, the place where single batteries, out-of-ink pens, and random USB cords go to die. Well, Aunt Maggie had that—and she also had a nastygram drawer.

It's the drawer right next to the cherry-red fridge covered in magnets from every state in the Union. I open it up, hoping to find scissors or at least a halfway sharp steak knife, and instead find a two-inch-thick stack of HOA violation notices. Driveway violation. Grass height violation. Paint code violation. Upkeep violation. Shutter violation. Garage violation. Some of them are stamped THIRD NOTICE.

Mayo forgotten, I take a bite of my sandwich. The bread is damp and the shaved turkey dry, but it has crunchy pickles, so

I take that as a victory.

After I inhale my sandwich and have time to take stock of Aunt Maggie's pantry—it's filled with shoeboxes exploding with old receipts but no food—I grab my keys to make a trip to the grocery store for supplies. No one should home renovate without plenty of potato chips. I glance around at the knickknacks on every flat surface and add wine to my mental shopping list. I have my work cut out for me.

Taking my chances, I go out the front door and hold my breath until my Keds hit the cracked sidewalk. As I walk to my car, it's impossible not to notice the picture-postcard suburbia around me. It could be a movie lot—especially compared to New York, where half the beauty of it is the mix of architectural styles in one city block.

There, the glass-encased skyscrapers are within view of the once–Gilded Age homes that are now museums. Here, it's all the same, just in different combinations of the HOA-approved color palate. It's pretty in its own way, but it definitely is not where I saw myself living. Ever.

Across the street, a guy mowing his lawn gives me the once-over. I wave as I open my car door, but he doesn't return the gesture.

Whew. That's at least the level of what-the-fuck-are-you-looking-at friendliness I'm used to in the city. It's kinda comforting, like spotting a rat dragging a slice of pizza down the sidewalk.

I get behind the wheel of the used Ford Focus my parents helped me buy, insert the key in the ignition, and turn it. Nothing happens. I try it again. And again. And again.

Dad insisted I don't need a car—I would be going back to New York soon. When he realized I was serious, though, he begged me to let him buy me something newer. Something from this decade. But pride is a fickle bitch, and I decided this is the right car for an unemployed soon-to-be divorcée. A dented and banged-up, useless shell of its former glory that's now reduced to an anecdotal epitaph. The car, I mean.

I let my head drop to the steering wheel, hitting it just right so that the horn blares and scares the ever-loving shit out of me and sets off half the dogs in the neighborhood. The dude mowing slows down enough to glare at me.

I keep my single-finger salute below the dashboard so he can't see. Then I march back into the house—using the back door, because I have a feeling that the third time is definitely not the charm for me with that porch disaster—to figure out how in the hell I'm going to pay for a tow truck in addition to the inheritance tax and home repairs.

If only Aunt Maggie hoarded hundred-dollar bills.

Chapter Five

I should take the death of my car (melodramatic? me?) as the sign it surely is. An hour later, my dead car has been towed to a garage. Thank goodness Aunt Maggie's car is still in the garage, though I probably need a boating license to drive something that big these days. I decide to not risk another misadventure and instead scour the kitchen for the only thing on my grocery list that really matters—wine.

I find an unopened bottle in the fridge and have it open in five seconds flat. Well, mostly because it has a screw cap, but it's an urgent necessity, too. I just discovered that my HGTV addiction and newfound (and misplaced) confidence has led me to a very dark place.

Literally.

There isn't a single light in the living room of Aunt Maggie's house that works, and the sun is minutes away from disappearing altogether for the night. I toss back the last of the wine in my classy red Solo cup and pour another before I lose all light entirely. Priorities and all. Plus, I already spent forty minutes trying to find the circuit breaker box. It defeated me.

The Property Brothers make it look so easy. Jonathan and Drew are now officially a pair of straight-up lying jerks. I'll still watch them, though. Hell, I swore off men forever after Karl but, no joke, I'd blow Jonathan right now if he showed me where the breaker box is located.

Okay, that might be the wine talking—at least a little. But anyone who has ever tried to find a breaker box in an unfamiliar house in the dark knows my frustration level.

Even more pathetic, I'm doing that alone as I wander onto my death-trap front porch and sink onto the middle step, wrapping one arm around the fallen tree limb like it's a lifeline, and stare out at cookie-cutter Americana.

The only thing that stands out more than Aunt Maggie's ramshackle two-story cottage with its cracked driveway and raggedy yard and porch is the droopy-eared dog of indeterminate breed and age lying in the middle of my jungle-themed front lawn.

I set my empty cup down and slowly approach the sad-looking dog. She apparently has worse survival instincts than I do because she just lays there like this is to be her fate. She is clearly well fed and cared for, so she must have a home somewhere in the neighborhood. I reach for the bone-shaped tag hanging from her collar and flip it over to show her name. Buttercup. But of course no address.

"Nice to meet you, Buttercup." I scratch behind her ear, and her foot immediately starts slapping against the grass.

I wish I felt a tenth as happy as she does. Instead, I'm an anxiety-riddled pretzel who, after way too long staring at my phone today, is now a YouTube-licensed contractor, which is about as legitimate as having a medical degree from WebMD.

Scared?

Yeah, me too.

Of course, being frightened out of my mind and running on panic-fueled adrenaline is pretty much my life right now. To be honest, I'm not sure I ever knew which way I was going besides following the lead of someone else.

A loud three-note whistle comes from down the street. Buttercup lifts her head and looks in that direction but doesn't get up. The sound blasts out again. My girl Buttercup, though, is not interested.

"Butters, come."

A commanding male voice has both of us straining in the dark to gaze down the tree-lined street, lit only by the occasional faux gaslight lamps, at a man jogging toward my house. He runs under another lamp, the soft glow illuminating him enough to pick up that he is a big guy in running shorts with a T-shirt tucked into the waistband. Then he disappears as he moves out from underneath the umbrella of soft light. He shows up a few seconds later under the light of a different lamp. Each time, I take in different details. Wavy brown hair. Broad shoulders. Nice arms. Trim waist. By the time I notice his calves, I realize I'm holding my breath every time he disappears in the shadows.

Yeah, it has apparently been that long since I've even remotely found someone attractive. It's like sometime during the past few years, my libido was turned off. It was there, and then it wasn't. Even worse? I really didn't care.

But suddenly there it is again—tanned, rested, and ready for action like it just came back from vacation on Horny Island. I'm so startled by this revelation that I stumble backward to my porch steps and plop down next to the tree again. Honestly, that's the only wood I want in my future.

I'm so distracted by this change in my hormones that I don't look up at the runner's face until he stops on the sidewalk in front of my house. As soon as I do, my oh-hello hormones become come-and-get-me-tiger hormones. Yeah, I'm embarrassed for me, too.

Buttercup begins thunking the ground with her fat tail; then she gets up, moseys over to the steps, and plops herself down next to me. Of all the dogs in all the world, Buttercup has to belong to the guy I now recognize as the one mowing his lawn across the street, who I flipped off on the down low earlier.

If I could speak, I would. Instead, I just sit there with my mouth half open, because some people really are so good-looking that it's hard to form words around them.

"Getting the place ready to sell?" he asks, his voice low and slow like warm honey in a hot toddy on Christmas Eve.

Words still beyond my abilities, I shake my head.

"I should have known this was where she was going." He nods at the dog as he unwinds a worn leash that was wrapped around his wrist. "I can't seem to keep her away from this wreck."

And just like that, my libido goes back into cold storage. I grit my jaw. "Was that really necessary? My aunt wasn't exactly herself before she got sick."

Unless she was always a hoarder and we just miraculously missed it. I mean, sure, I haven't been back to Sutton once in the past twenty years, but Aunt Maggie and I talked all the time. I would have noticed if she was hoarding at such dangerous levels, right?

Now I feel ashamed that my family just accepted Aunt Maggie's constant suggestions that we meet up at our house, which is two towns and three awful highway interchanges over, or in the city, and we never saw them for what they really were—a strategy to keep us from noticing her illness.

"As if you actually knew her," he says, echoing my own thoughts, the bastard. He gives me a slow up-and-down that manages to stay on the not-creepy side of the line. "So you're the famed great-niece, eh?"

From his tone, it's obvious he's not impressed. And sure, I'm not looking my best these days, but that's intentional. I'm *choosing* not to give a shit. You can't judge a person intentionally fucking off, right?

"You have some nerve just showing up and passing judgment."

He makes a clicking noise, and Buttercup turns her head in his direction but doesn't move.

They always say that dogs can recognize bad people. I never

really believed it, but as Buttercup doesn't even inch toward Mr. Tall, Dark, and Dickish, I'm ready to bet it all that dogs have a sixth sense for sure.

"You're not actually going to live here, are you?" he asks, one brow raised in challenge.

"I am." Against everyone's unasked-for advice.

He scans Aunt Maggie's house, a smile playing on his lips, and then centers his attention back on me. "Good luck with that."

I stand up, needing the extra added height to even out what feels like a weird power differential between us, then cross my arms, going for a self-confident chin raise that still manages to feel awkward as hell. "I don't need luck."

He smacks his palm against his thigh, drawing Buttercup to his side finally, and then snaps the leash to the dog's collar and stands up, a know-it-all smirk on his face. "Glad to hear it. By the way, if you are naive enough to try to fix up this place, I'd suggest starting with the grass. I understand you're on your last HOA violation warning about that."

Wait. How does he know that? Who in the hell is he? And more importantly, do I have "be an asshole to me, please" tattooed on my forehead?

Before I can get any of that out, though, he walks away, appearing and disappearing under the fake gaslight lamps' glow as he crosses the street and jogs up his front steps, then disappears behind a perfectly painted red door. Yeah, I watched. He is a total and complete smug dickwad, but it's still a good view.

Not that it matters. I'm going to show that big jerk.

This is my house, and I'm a new woman.

I'm Mallory Martin, soon-to-be divorcée and already unemployed office manager. I have nowhere to go but toward the light of success—and I will not be mowing the grass until the last possible day now.

Of course, before I can do any of that, I have to find the breaker box.

Chapter Six

*D*awn shoves its way past my aunt's minuscule curtains and bitch-slaps me right across the face the next morning.

It's just my luck that the one thing my aunt apparently didn't hoard was good window coverings. The drapes in here definitely subscribe to the same rules that govern most good lingerie—reveal more than you conceal. And like the sexiest lace teddy, the filmy hot-pink-and-lime-green zebra-print fabric over the east-facing windows do the revealing quite artfully. The concealing? Yeah, not even close to mastering that one.

The clock on the once white, now definitely more tea-stained cream wicker nightstand reads 6:12. Fantastic. Great. Perfect. So much for sleeping in. I could bury my head under the pillow and try to go back to sleep, but with the way my luck has been running lately, I'd end up suffocating myself while getting poked in the eye with the feather quills packed inside it…which might not sound like the worst option in the world right now, except I flat-out refuse to give Karl that satisfaction. I already made things too damn easy for him with this divorce. Death would just be overkill.

Plus, since I've recovered from the retina-searing brightness shining through my window—dear God, how did Aunt Maggie deal with this *every* morning?—my mind is racing with all the things I have to get done today.

Go through the HOA complaints and sort in order of importance.

Find a contractor who will work for magic beans.

Buy about eight million garbage bags to take care of the stacks and stacks of junk my aunt has in every single room in this house. Seriously, who still subscribes to magazines, let alone has multiple copies of the Sears Christmas catalog from the eighties?

Mow the damn grass...though maybe that doesn't have to be today. I'm totally okay with letting my obnoxious neighbor marinate in his own stuck-upedness for a while. I mean, how far up his ass is that stick if he feels the need to whine about the length of my grass? Of course, maybe that's how he got such a perfect ass—he has a copy of *Butt Clenching Your Way to Perfect Glutes For Dummies.* If I encourage him, he'll probably be over here with a ruler to get the exact measurement of my lawn, just to make sure I mowed enough but not too much.

Renewed annoyance sweeps through me like hot fudge over a scoop of vanilla bean, and I push the covers off and all but spring out of bed—and knock over three stacks of magazines. I ignore all the little aches and pains that come with sleeping on a new mattress and mentally readjust my to-do list. Definitely need trash bags *before* HOA regulations.

But first, coffee. Please God, let Aunt Maggie have hoarded the magical brown bean of happiness.

After a quick shower in my aunt's searing hot-pink bathroom, I dry off with one of her zebra-striped towels and slap some expensive moisturizer onto my face. It soaks in and—I swear to all that is good in the world—my skin lets out a relieved sigh. Karl got me the moisturizer for my last birthday. No doubt it was his way of telling me I'm looking old. Sure, I was tempted to hurl the hourglass-shaped bottle at his head, but I controlled the urge. And my skin has thanked me every day since.

A quick brush of my teeth and topknot later, I make my way

down the creaky stairs, doing my best not to trip on everything my aunt piled on the edges of them.

By the time I get to the kitchen, every cell in my body is jonesing for a hit of caffeine. But when I finally open one of my aunt's circus-tent canisters—the one marked CAFFEINE, not the one marked QUAALUDES—it's empty except for a lone coffee bean. Desperation has me searching all the others—CALORIES, CANDY, QUAALUDES, GANJA, GLUTEN, and GLITTER—but to no avail.

I do find small individual snack packs of Oreos in the CALORIES canister, though, and a bunch of Hershey Kisses in the CANDY one, so I take the win. It's okay to chew a Kiss and a coffee bean at the same time, right? Isn't that just a deconstructed mocha?

As I swallow, I do my best to ignore the gummy bears in the GANJA canister. It's *possible* they don't contain marijuana. *Suuuuuuuuuuuure.*

The part of me that is more like Aunt Maggie than my parents can stand is totally curious. I've never smoked weed—or done any other kind of drug—in my life, but that dearth just makes the gummy bears all that much more enticing.

Too bad even thinking about trying one of them is for another day, when my to-do list doesn't involve driving to town for trash bags, coffee, and—I open the door to the very empty pantry—absolutely everything else a human being needs to survive.

Wonderful.

I grab my purse and the keys to Aunt Maggie's purple Cadillac, aka Jimi Hendrix (Jimi for short), and head toward the store, marveling as I make my way downtown that nothing in this place has changed. *Nothing.*

I pull into the local Stop & Shop parking lot—which is packed—and try to find a place to park Jimi. I end up circling the lot for five minutes before someone finally pulls out of a spot all the way at the end of the lot and I manage to squeak in. A guy with wild hair and a wifebeater tank top in a baby-blue minivan waves his fist at me like I didn't just sit here for several minutes with my blinker on for this spot before he turned down the same lane.

As I climb out of Jimi, the guy rolls his window down and yells about my driving, my parentage, and—my absolute favorite (sarcasm alert)—the fact that women shouldn't be able to have driver's licenses at all. I ignore him; a pissed-off dad in the New Jersey burbs has nothing on a New York cabdriver when it comes to creative insults. Plus, it's hard to take him seriously when at least two kids in the van are singing at the top of their lungs about Mickey Mouse's clubhouse and a third is screaming that she wants her My Little Pony.

No wonder he's in a bad mood.

In fact, if I didn't need caffeine so desperately, I might have felt bad enough to give up the parking spot. But there's a Starbucks right next to the Stop & Shop, and inside it is a caramel macchiato screaming my name. Or maybe *I* am screaming *its* name. Either way, right now I need coffee more than he needs a parking spot, My Little Pony notwithstanding.

As I hop out of Jimi, I'm not surprised I'm drawing a few questioning looks. I throw my shoulders back, tilt my chin up in a total yes-I'm-bold-enough-to-own-a-car-like-this move, and head into the store.

I have a date with the coffee shop—or there will be bloodshed. And I have a trunk big enough to hide the body.

Chapter Seven

Ten minutes later, I'm pushing a wobbly wheeled cart through the grocery store with one hand and drinking my venti macchiato with the other. I'm also doing my best to pretend I don't miss the little neighborhood bodega and specialty stores where I used to do most of my grocery shopping. It seems I traded in Effie the bodega cat for a set of four-year-old twins in matching pink outfits and snotty noses. Both are dangerous in their own way, I guess.

On the plus side, Stop & Shop does have an abnormally wide variety of specialty cheeses with samples out, and I decide to try a dozen or so of them, mostly because there's no one around to stop me. Whoever says a woman can't live by cheese alone obviously hasn't met this deli department—or me.

After sampling everything from Brie and gouda to goat cheese and pepper jack, I head to where those with costly home renovations in their futures and anemic bank accounts shop— the cereal aisle.

I have every intention of picking up my usual box of Cheerios—it's heart healthy and eminently sensible, after all— but once I'm standing right in front of the bright yellow boxes, it's the last thing I want. Not when every time I reach for the box, I can hear Karl lecturing me on the importance of fiber—and how much I need him to make sure I eat well—as he pours the little round Os into his favorite black-like-his-heart cereal bowl.

You know what? Fuck fiber.

I drop my empty coffee cup into the cart and grab a family-size box of Crunch Berries in one hand and a box of Froot Loops in the other, throwing them into my cart with wild abandon. Karl doesn't get to tell me what to do anymore. And he sure as hell doesn't get to tell me what to eat.

I toss in a box of Cookie Crisp for good measure and then start to make my way toward the trash bag aisle. But just as I'm rounding the corner, a woman with wild red hair squeals my name.

"Mallory? Holy s-h-i-t! Is it really you?"

She looks vaguely familiar, and as I struggle to figure out how I know her, the toddler she's holding reaches up and yanks on one of her huge hoop earrings. The woman responds with a sound that is half squawk and half yodel as she stops dead and tries to pry his hand off her earring.

And just like that, I place her. Angela Mancini, cheer captain, senior class secretary, and the girl who could shred an air-guitar solo as if she had hopes of winning a college scholarship for it. She was always brash and loud but overall pretty sweet—which is why I step forward and ask, "Can I do something to help?"

"It's okay. I think I've got it," she answers as she finally manages to pry her kid's hand off the gold hoop before he rips it straight through her ear. "It's my own fault. I know better than to wear earrings like this around Joey, but Manny gave them to me for my birthday yesterday, and I couldn't resist."

It takes me a second to realize she's talking about Manuel Perez, her high school boyfriend and—I glance down at her ring finger and find a small but sparkly diamond ring and wedding band—apparently current husband.

She gives me a dazzling smile with even more sparkle than her ring. "It's been a long time, Mallory! How the h-e-l-l are you?"

"Um, I'm good, thanks." It's a lie, but what else am I supposed to say to a relative stranger in the middle of the Stop & Shop? "How are you?"

"Oh, you know. We moved to Sutton about five years ago." She waves an airy hand. "Between Joey and the others, I can barely keep my head above water most days. But honestly, I wouldn't have it any other way."

"The others?" I ask tentatively.

"Joey has four brothers," she tells me proudly. "Jimmy, Johnny, Jordy, and Jeremy. They're a handful."

"I can only imagine." I goggle at her. "You look—"

"Exhausted?" she interrupts with a laugh.

"I was thinking really good for having five boys under the age of…?"

"Ten." She waves a dismissive hand. "You have no idea."

"I really don't." Especially since Karl kept putting off my every attempt to have a family, always telling me to wait a little longer, that it wasn't the right time, that the business needed all our attention.

The women I knew in the city—wives of Karl's business associates—told me not to worry, that *all* men feel like that until they establish themselves financially. But as I eye little Joey Perez gazing up at his mom with adoring eyes, it hits home that it was just one more lie I let myself believe to keep the peace. One more argument I lost without even putting up a fight. Doormat? Yeah, that was me.

The thought makes my skin crawl. More, it makes me want to run and hide before Angela and the rest of the world realize just how weak I let myself become—so weak that buying a box of Froot Loops feels like a massive rebellion. Fuck me. Tears prick at my eyeballs, and I take a step back, put on my sunglasses, and start to make some excuse about having to go. But before I can come up with anything, Angela grins at me. "What are you doing in Sutton? Your parents still living in Brunswick?"

"Oh, um, yeah, they're still there, but, umm, actually, I'm living here now." I stumble a little over the unfamiliar words. "My aunt died a few months ago, and I just found out she left me her house here." I ignore the rest of the disaster that is my current life and say instead, "I've decided to live in it while I fix it up."

"Oh, that sounds fun! Like a mini vacation from your life." She sighs as Joey starts to clap his hands against her cheeks in a rhythm that sounds suspiciously like Queen's "We Will Rock You." "I wouldn't mind one of those every once in a while."

"Well, if I get the place into any kind of decent shape, maybe you can come over for coffee some time."

She laughs again, the rich, rollicking sound of a woman who is totally content with her life. "Make it a glass of wine and it's a deal." Her face turns serious. "Does the place need a lot of work?"

A domestic horror film flashes in my mind's eye. The wild jungle of a front and backyard. The front porch with a tree sculpture embedded in it. The cracked driveway that is threatening to become a mini Grand Canyon. The dying trees that only need one good thunderstorm to finish crashing through the rest of the house. All of it is against HOA regulations. Then, of course, there is the torch fire the inside needs. "Some, yeah."

Joey smacks his mother's cheeks again as he chants, "Go, go, go!"

"Just a second, baby," she answers as she leans down and takes both of his hands in hers before dropping a kiss on each one. "Want a cookie?"

"Coo-kie. Coo-kie!" Joey responds excitedly.

Angela gives him another kiss—this time on his soft-looking brown curls—before she fumbles through the crossbody bag she has slung over her torso. She comes out with an animal cracker in one hand and a business card in the other.

"Here," she says, extending the card to me even as she gives

Joey his cookie. "You should call Mikey. He's Manny's younger brother and he is h-o-t. He's also one h-e-l-l of a contractor. Tell him Angie sent you, and he'll give you a good deal." She wiggles her brows. "And he's totally single and available."

"Available…?" I break off as her meaning sinks in. "Oh, I don't think… I mean… I don't—"

She laughs again. "I'm sorry. Did I overstep? Manny always tells me I'm doing that. Well, Mikey is attractive and really good with his hands, I've heard." She winks at me. "You know, if you're into that sort of thing."

Considering I'm still dealing with the consequences of my last relationship, that would be a hard no. I'm most definitely *not* "into that sort of thing" or any other things that require me getting naked and vulnerable ever again.

No thank you.

"I should probably get going—" I say at the same time Joey finishes his animal cracker and starts screeching, "Go, go, go!" at the top of his lungs.

"Yeah, me too." Angie rolls her eyes. "But give Mikey a call. I swear he's a great contractor." She reaches into her bag and pulls out a pen, then scribbles a phone number across the back of the card. "And here's my number. Call me once you get settled. We'll do lunch or wine or something—without Joey, I promise."

Then, before I can think up a suitable response to her invitation, she gives a quick wave and disappears down the next aisle while Joey continues to scream, "Go, go, go!"

It was the oddest—and sweetest—encounter I ever had in a grocery store, and I can't help but grin as I shove Mikey's card into the back pocket of my jeans. If I'm really lucky, maybe I've found a contractor—and a friend—in one quick trip to the Stop & Shop.

My bodega in the village didn't have that. Maybe big suburban grocery stores really do have everything after all.

Or you know, at least really good deals on two-ply and garbage bags—both of which are necessities as I gird my loins for a trip back to Aunt Maggie's in her giant deathtrap Caddy.

I just pray my obnoxious neighbor will be nowhere in sight when I have to wrestle a metric ton of Hefty garbage bags into the house.

I need another macchiato if there is even a possibility of seeing *him* again.

Chapter Eight

I call Mikey as soon as I get back behind Jimi's steering wheel. It goes straight to voicemail, one of those joke ones where the person makes it seem like they're answering. No matter what Angela said, I'm way too old to hit that—even at my current low point, I have more pride than that.

Still, I leave a message. Not because I'm so anxious to see the h-o-t contractor Angela said was available but because I could use the good deal she mentioned. Bonus point, it's one more thing I can cross off today's to-do list.

I put Jimi in reverse and slowly back out of the parking spot, then head to Aunt Maggie's, still reveling in the joy of actually having accomplished something today.

Normally, I'm not a big list person, but I have to admit that right now, there's something really satisfying about crossing through number one—*get trash bags*. If I can also cross through number two, *find a contractor*, then the day will have a good shot at being a win, despite its inauspicious beginnings.

I could really, really use a win right now.

I decide to bite the bullet and scribble one more item on my to-do list: *find a job*. And immediately wish I hadn't as panic squeezes my chest like a vise. I take a deep breath simply to prove to myself that I can and blow it out slowly—just like all those mindful apps tell you to. It doesn't work. Big surprise. Great, now I have the tightness in my chest *and* feel like a loser—as if I need the help.

Mindfulness is well and good for most things, but I'm pretty sure expecting it to take care of a cheating ex, a broken-down house, a nearly empty bank account, and a lack of job prospects is asking a little much of anything but a fairy godmother. I mean, I'm all for mind over matter, but sometimes the cold hard truth is the cold hard truth. And right now, there isn't enough positive thinking or relaxation techniques in the universe to take away my cold hard truth.

Especially since my mindfulness app is charging me a monthly fee.

And now there's one more thing to add to my to-do list— *cancel my mindfulness app.* And while I'm logged into my autopay subscriptions, I might as well say goodbye to ad-free Hulu.

I take a big sip of my second venti caramel macchiato of the day—I prefer to drink my anxiety, thank you very much— and white knuckle the steering wheel for the traffic-filled drive home.

It isn't that I'm not used to traffic—Manhattan has a lot of it, obviously—but it's been a long time since I had to drive myself in it. There really is something to be said for public transportation.

By the time I get home, my nerves are frazzled—thanks only to the traffic and definitely not the fact that enough caffeine is jangling around in my system to light up Times Square.

After a prolonged fight with Aunt Maggie's extremely finicky garage opener—moving it waaaaaaay up the list of things to get fixed in this place—I pop the trunk and start carrying groceries into the house. I'm on my third trip of just trash bags alone when a red pickup truck pulls into the driveway.

Yeah, someone has the wrong house—the kind of someone who climbs out of his truck with big dick energy and the sexy swagger to back it up. Curly dark hair frames high cheekbones and twinkling brown eyes. Broad shoulders, beefy arms, and very, very large work boots complete the picture. And it's a great picture. If only he weren't also about seven or eight years younger than me.

"Can I help you?" I ask when that long-legged gait finally brings him to a stop right next to me.

"I'm Miguel," he says with a slow grin that might have curled my toes if such a thing were even possible anymore.

When I continue to stare at him blankly, he raises a brow. "Miguel Perez, Manny's brother? Angela—"

"Oh!" I exclaim as it hits me—good Lord, I'm extra slow today, even for me. "You're Mikey!"

He grins. "Yeah, everyone calls me that." Then he holds out a hand for me to shake. "Nice to meet you, Mallory."

"Nice to meet you, too." I shake his hand and reach for another few bags of groceries. "Talk about fast service, considering I only called you about twenty minutes ago."

"Yeah, but Angie texted me as soon as she ran into you in the grocery store and told me to expect your call. And when I got your voicemail, I realized your house was just around the corner from where I'm working now, and I figured it couldn't hurt to drop by and get a look at what you're dealing with."

He takes a couple of steps back and looks the house up and down like a rubbernecker eyeballing a traffic accident before letting out a long, low whistle. "Looks like the answer is a lot."

My stomach drops another three stories down closer to the earth's core, even though I already know the place is a mess. "That's not the answer I was hoping for."

"I know." He gives me a sympathetic look as he grabs the last few sacks of groceries and follows me into the house. "Where do you want me to start?"

"The garage door opener," I answer. "Something is really wrong with it, and I would love to have it replaced. I know, it doesn't seem like a big thing, but I figured it was low-hanging fruit, and I really need a win here. Other than that…" I trail off as I sweep my hands outward, encompassing, well, everything in sight. "Have at it. Though I do have one request."

"And that is?" He pulls his phone out of his pocket, and I watch as he swipes open some kind of construction app.

"Can you work up two separate bids? One for outside and one for inside? I've got to get the outside up to HOA standards and, depending on how much that costs, that may be all I can afford to do right now."

"Gotcha." He gives me a grin that shows off his dazzling white teeth to his advantage. I smile back, even as I wonder vaguely how many women have fallen for that aw-shucks smile before.

Probably a lot, though it does nothing for me except make me wonder who his dentist is. I'm almost due for my next cleaning.

Miguel—excuse me, Mikey—starts making the rounds outside while I put my groceries away. Then, when he still hasn't come in, I eat a whole snack pack of Oreos (for medicinal purposes and science and because I just wanted to and Karl can't say shit about it) out of the CALORIES canister. They are a little stale, but those who are stress-eating out of fear of their construction bill can't be choosy.

He still hasn't come in by the time I swallow the last Oreo, already giving a lusty look at the last two packs in the canister. They really are the food of the gods, and two more packs wouldn't kill anybody. But considering how my day is going, I'm guessing I'll need them later, so I grab the box of trash bags instead. While Mikey comes in and starts assessing the interior, I spend the rest of what feels like an eternity cleaning out the kitchen cabinets, most of which are filled with knickknacks that belong anywhere but in the silverware drawer or mug cabinet.

I'm just about to start on the very scary cabinet under the sink when Mikey finally walks back into the kitchen.

"So, what's the damage?" I ask, trying to be flippant and fun instead of the worried and slightly nauseous I really am.

Then I get a look at his face.

Thank you, baby Jesus, for giving me the strength to hold out on the rest of the Oreos until now. I'm gonna need them.

Mikey looks a lot grimmer than he was an hour ago, and a bowling ball settles in my stomach even before he answers.

"Do you want the bad news or the worse news?"

Chapter Nine

"**N**either." I lean back against my aunt's black galaxy granite countertop and let out a go-ahead-and-break-my-heart sigh.

"Yeah." He grimaces—no doubt as a show of support before bringing down the hammer. "That's what I figured."

Silence stretches between us as I wait for him to break the bad news, and he waits for...I don't know...his own reality show on HGTV where he's the anti–Property Brothers, giving only awful prognostications of construction hell? I shake my head and blurt, "Give me the worse news first."

I figure that way, the bad news won't seem so bad—or at least, that's what I'm hoping, praying, willing to sacrifice a baker's dozen virgins under a full moon to make come true.

He shoves his fingers through his hair and contemplates the weird stain on the granite. "Inside or outside?"

Just shank me in the eye already.

"You mean there's worse news in both areas?" Tears of frustration start gathering like vultures over roadkill, but I blink them all back with steely determination. *I won't cry. I will not do it.*

"Yeah, I get that a lot on old houses like this." He gives me a hangdog look that comes off as totally sincere, which somehow makes it worse. Then he rips off the Band-Aid and starts reading the list of disasters he wrote down on his phone. "The supports on the front porch are almost completely destroyed by the massive tree currently squatting there. Tree roots are what's cracking the walkway up to the porch, so I won't be able to lay new cement until the dead tree still standing is taken care of. On the plus side, once you do that, we can also fix that nasty driveway crack before it gets any worse."

I already feel my bank account gasping for air, and it isn't the only one.

"Is that it?" I ask when I can finally force words out of my too-tight throat.

He gives me a pitying look. "The garage door is warped, which is why you found it tricky to open with the remote. You might be tempted to get away with just keeping it closed, but I'm betting the HOA is going to ding you on it if they haven't already. So that really does need to be replaced sooner rather than later. On the plus side, fixing the door should take care of your problems with the opener, so we won't have to replace that."

Little victories. "How much is a garage door?"

"To match the ones in this neighborhood?" He winces. "About twenty-two hundred dollars."

What in the hell is it made of? Gold?

"What if I don't care about matching them?" *Or can't afford to?*

"Gotta match them. H—"

"OA regulations." I barely resist the urge to bang my head against the granite—at this point that might be just plain old mercy. Truthfully, though, the only thing stopping me isn't manners—it's fear of a concussion. I sure as hell can't afford these repairs *and* an emergency room bill right now. "Yeah, I get it."

"The fence in the backyard needs to be replaced, and I have no idea what kind of magic is keeping that chicken coop out back standing, but that'll have to be demolished, in keeping with the HOA regs. You also need to rebuild the flower boxes out front—it should only be six or seven hundred dollars to do all of them, though. And a lot less if you do them yourself."

I have never built anything in my life—besides Karl's law practice, though that's a different story. But if it means saving a few hundred dollars and also keeping the uptight jerk from across the street off my ass, then I'm all in. If there's an app to remind people to breathe, surely there's an app to teach them how to build stuff—hopefully a free one.

"Is that it?" I ask for what feels like the hundredth time.

"For the outside, yeah." He nods. "Except for the shutters, obviously."

"What's wrong with the shutters?" My stomach pitches as visions of voracious termites dance before my eyes.

He holds up a don't-shoot-the-messenger hand that does nothing to comfort me, even as he says, "Nothing, technically. Your aunt must have had them redone pretty recently because the paint is in good shape and so is the wood."

"Then why would I want to do something to them?" I swear, if he's just trying to jack up the price on me, I'm going to... I don't know what. Something terrible that involves putting a curse on his silky, flowing locks, that's for sure. Or, you know, about three feet south of them. "I've got more than enough to do already."

"Yeah, you do," he agrees, a little too fervently for my comfort. "But I've done a lot of work on houses in this area, and I'm pretty sure..."

He drifts off like he expects me to fill in the blanks for him, but honestly, I have nothing. If he wants me to repaint perfectly good shutters, he better give me one hell of a good reason why.

I guess Mikey figures out that I'm not getting it, because he smiles sympathetically before saying, "The color, Mallory. You have to repaint because of the color."

"What's wrong with blue?" Frustration and fear make my question louder than I meant it to be. "It's one of the most popular colors in the world—"

"Nothing's wrong with blue," he interrupts. "As long as it's navy blue or grayish blue. What you have is—"

"Periwinkle." I narrow my eyes and clench my teeth. Of course I know I'm fudging a bit with the color, but I just need a little break right now. A tiny one. Minuscule, really.

But Mikey has obviously missed the memo, considering his eyes are brimming with amusement. "If by *periwinkle* you mean *violet*, then yes, periwinkle. Which is—"

"Against HOA regulations in this area. Yeah, yeah, I get it." Doesn't mean I have to like it, though. I swear there is a part of me that wants nothing more than to set up a bonfire on the front driveway and burn every copy of the HOA regulations I can get my hands on. Most of the copies likely being digital doesn't change my fantasy in the slightest. Nor does the fact that bonfires are most probably against HOA regulations, too. Honestly, an illicit bonfire seems like exactly what this uptight neighborhood needs.

God, I miss New York. And sweet baby Jesus, do I hate the fucking suburbs.

"Which brings me to the next point. I'm not sure you're familiar with the rules but…" He hesitates before squaring his shoulders like he's going into battle. "You'll have to go through the HOA board approval process for the paint colors you choose before we can actually begin the painting. Could take up to a month to get approval, I'd imagine. So best to start that sooner rather than later."

"Seriously?" I demand when I can finally see past the murderous red haze currently blanketing my vision.

And I have to admit, points to Mikey for not even wincing when it came out sounding more like a shriek than a word. Probably because he knows I'm not mad at him—he seems like a really lovely guy—but this entire situation is enough to make a good woman go bad in the anti–Hallmark movie kind of way.

"Does no one in this godforsaken suburb have anything better to do than get up in everyone else's business? I mean, really? Is there no PTA for these people to terrorize?"

Mikey chuckles, an adorable dimple appearing in his left cheek. "Personally, I like the violet shutters. And after seeing the rest of the house, I'd say the neighbors should count themselves lucky they aren't hot-pink zebra stripes."

I bust out laughing, exactly as he no doubt intended.

"Part of me wishes they were." Visions of my grumpy neighbor's face bright red with the vapors when he spots my zebra-striped shutters make me giggle.

"Me too. I mean, if you're going to rack up the violations, you might as well do it for a good cause, right?" He grins engagingly.

"Damn straight." I think about the kitchen drawer full of violation letters I discovered last night, and the amusement slides away as quickly as it came. "So do you have an estimate on how much all this will cost? And a timeline for getting at least the outside done?"

Some of those violation letters are third or fourth notices. I haven't taken the time to read most of them yet, but I'm nearly certain that means I'm on an even more truncated timetable here than the six months the probate lawyer talked about.

"First, let me say I'll take ten percent off the top, since you're a friend of Angie's."

I almost tell him that I'm not exactly a friend of Angie's—or anyone's for that matter—but the truth is my sad, gasping bank account and I both need every bit of a discount we can get.

"Thank you," I tell him, even though it rankles that I need favors when Karl and his girl toy are living it up in Manhattan in *my* condo, at least according to his Instagram account—otherwise known as Karl's Midlife Crisis—in full color. "I appreciate it."

"Of course. Anything I can do to help, I'm here for. Angie's my favorite sister-in-law, after all."

"Favorite?" We start walking toward the garage door. "How many do you have?"

"Just one. But she's still my favorite." It's a corny line—completely ridiculous and also completely endearing. Just like the rest of him.

Okay, maybe I can pretend I never heard that awful voicemail greeting. Not that I'm thinking about how h-o-t the contractor is, but snap judgments aren't exactly the best, either.

"I've got a crew finishing up a job a couple of streets over. They should be done next week. I was going to give the guys some days off, but I can get them over here instead. We can knock almost everything out in a few weeks—the porch will take the longest but still only a couple of weeks." He gives me another encouraging smile. "As far as the cost, I'll send you a detailed bid later, so you can decide what you want to work on and when. But I'd give a rough estimate of $25,000 in repairs."

As the blood drains from my cheeks, he steers me out of the kitchen and to a nearby couch, and we both sink down onto the floral fabric.

"Now, before you panic, I think the damage caused by the fallen tree might be covered by your homeowner's policy, and that's half the expense. If you can provide me with your aunt's insurance carrier, I can make a preauthorization request, see what we can get covered. It's a long shot but worth a try."

"That would be amazing," I say, already doing mental math, trying to figure out just how far I can stretch my meager savings. The exterior is going to cost a pretty penny, but if homeowner's insurance covers half, maybe it's doable? Not really. And that leaves almost nothing for the interior. "What about the rest of the house?"

"The rest of the house?" He shakes his head. "To be honest, from what I can tell, most of the interior is in pretty good shape. But I won't be able to give you a real, comprehensive answer until you start clearing away the junk. There's so much upstairs that some of the rooms are practically impossible to get into."

He isn't trying to be rude or confrontational, but his words still sting. Mostly because I know he's right but also because I had no idea Aunt Maggie had gotten this bad. Sure, everyone in the family knew she was eccentric, but this level of hoarding is a mental-health issue. Guilt works like battery acid on my insides. Of all the people in our tiny family, *I* should have realized something was going on.

I always thought it was charming the way she gathered up the unopened fortune cookie papers "for souvenirs" after our monthly lunch or how she always asked for the cork from our bottle of wine after girls' night. I didn't know it was just more stuff she felt compelled to save.

How could I not have known? More, how could I not have asked? Or visited? She always said she wanted to meet in the city because it was exciting, and I agreed with her. The last thing I wanted to do was come back to the burbs or, more honestly, back to my parents' criticism.

All of which adds up to it being twenty years since I was here last. Two decades when my favorite person in the whole world kept hoarding and hoarding and hoarding. She never made it to reality-TV bad—the downstairs is mostly clean except for the closets, drawers, and cabinets—but, like Mikey said, the upstairs bedrooms are piled with junk, junk, and more junk.

Knowing this was happening only an hour train ride from my place in the city makes me a shitty niece. More, it makes me a shitty person who took the path of least resistance because it was easier, made fewer waves, and deep down the idea of even a little confrontation makes my bones turn to liquid.

"If you want me to be able to give you a solid estimate on what needs to be done inside, I'd suggest getting a dumpster. You can have one delivered to your driveway, and you can add to it as you sort through each room. When you're done, I'm happy to come back and take a look."

"How much does a dumpster cost?" I ask, because even though I hate the idea of throwing away stuff that meant something to Aunt Maggie, I know I can't live here like this.

"I'll add it to my estimate. In the meantime, look into getting someone in here to deal with the tree and we'll be in business to start as soon as you're ready for us."

"Sounds good." I force a smile I'm far from feeling. This place is turning into as big a mess as my former life, and that sucks, especially considering how much it felt like a potential lifeline when Aunt Maggie's will was read.

"Oh," Mikey says as he turns to go. "One more thing. Stay off that porch until we can fix it. And post a few signs to warn everyone else to stay off it, too. No telling when it's going to collapse completely, but if I were you, I wouldn't tempt fate."

Why do his parting words sound more like an omen than a suggestion?

Chapter Ten

I'm just about to start cooking myself dinner—a chicken breast with a side of roasted asparagus—when the full bid comes through from Mikey. Steeling myself with a large sip of wine from one of the bottles from the awesome collection I just found in Aunt Maggie's basement, I'm not even a little embarrassed to admit discovering my aunt hoarded wine was the highlight of my year.

I open the email attachment and then squeeze my eyes shut before I can actually see any of the numbers.

And yes, I know this isn't going to get me anywhere when I'm the only one around to look at them, but still…I'm scared. Since I walked in on Karl going down on his girlfriend, life has been coming at me extra fast.

No time to catch my breath.

No time to talk myself into whatever has to come next.

No time to hide, even for a second.

Just all crappy reality, all the time.

It's fucking exhausting.

I take another big drink for courage—just because I have to deal with this mess doesn't mean I have to do it sober—then peek one eye open. And nearly have a heart attack. There are more than a few numbers on that spreadsheet. A lot more. And none of them are good.

True to Mikey's original best-guess estimate, the final bid

came in at just over $26,500. He was kind enough to deduct that 10 percent friends-and-family discount, but still... It's almost double what I have left in the bank. If insurance doesn't come through like he thought, I'm screwed.

I shoot back the rest of the wine in my glass—I'm waaaaaay past thinking this bottle isn't going to go fast—and force myself to look at the bid again to find something, anything I can actually afford to do without careful planning.

And the answer is simple. The dumpster. I can afford the $500 a week for the dumpster, even though my HOA doesn't actually give a shit about what the inside of my house looks like. Just the outside with its $12,000 front porch estimate and all the rest.

Fuck it.

I drop my phone on the counter and reach for the bottle of wine. This time I fill my glass all the way up to the tippy top and drink it down in three large gulps. Then I fill the glass up again before wandering into my aunt's family room and up to the old stereo she had, complete with turntable and CD player, under the TV.

When I was a kid, Aunt Maggie used to turn on her favorite Beatles albums and we'd dance and dance and dance around the room before having an elaborate tea party, complete with scones, finger sandwiches, and gorgeously decorated petits fours from the bakery down the street.

When Karl and I got married, I used to dream about having a child—or children—to throw tea parties for.

A daughter to dress up in sparkly dresses and whirl around the room to a special playlist I'd made just for us. A son I could use cookies and cakes and his favorite songs to bribe into dancing with me. Having kids isn't for everyone, and that's totally cool. But I have always wanted to be the mom version of my aunt Maggie—fun, supportive, encouraging, and basically everything I rarely found under my own roof growing up.

But Karl wanted to wait, wanted a little more time before we started a family. And now, here I am—broke, almost divorced, jobless, *and* childless.

Definitely not how I planned to spend my thirty-fifth year on this planet.

Then again, nothing that has happened in the past several months was how I expected my life to turn out. I used to have big plans—law school, partnership in a major firm by the time I was thirty, a solid marriage, kids to spoil with trips to the theater and the beach and maybe even Europe. I refused to settle for less.

I take another long sip of wine, even though I definitely feel the last cup kicking in. Then I open the sliding door that leads out to the patio to let in some fresh air before I drop down on the floor in front of my aunt's incredible and extensive vinyl collection and start searching through it for our favorite album. Part of me expects it to be right in front like it always was, but it isn't.

It's buried deep, about a hundred albums back, behind Cat Stevens, Harry Chapin, and, randomly, a Queen album. I almost put on that iconic album but instead pull out *Abbey Road*—the best Beatles album ever, no matter what the internet says—with reverent hands and slide it onto the turntable. But before the needle gets to "Come Together," my phone rings in the kitchen.

I'm halfway to ignoring it—I'm not expecting a call from anyone right then anyway—but the ringing continues, so I grab my wine and jog into the kitchen. My mom mentioned she wasn't feeling very well when we talked yesterday. Maybe she's feeling worse.

But it isn't my mom. The Caller ID shows the last man in the world I would ever want to talk to again, but years of ingrained habit has me answering.

"Hi, Karl." I hate the way my palms get damp as I wait for him to answer, the way my stomach clenches in dread. He's just a man. Just a total asshole of a man who I used to love.

"Took you long enough," he mutters.

"I could hang up if you prefer and you could call back," I say, barely recognizing my own moxie. "I'll try to answer more quickly." Or not at all, but he doesn't need to know that.

"Why exactly would I do that?" he demands.

"I just thought—"

"Never mind." He talks right over me. "I only have a few minutes, but I was calling to tell you that I'm having the divorce waiting period waiver couriered over. The courier has instructions to stay. Sign the papers immediately and send them right back. I'll file them and all this unpleasantness can be behind us once and for all."

Unpleasantness? That's what he calls our ten-year marriage? Unpleasantness? Even though I did everything in my power to make him happy while, it turned out, he was running around with whatever woman would have him?

The anger from earlier drowns under a wave of regret. Not because our marriage is over—good riddance to bad trash and all that—but because I wasted so much of my time, of myself, on a man who so obviously never gave a shit about me.

It makes me feel naive. More, it makes me feel tired. And small. And sad.

I worked so hard to make him happy, worked so hard to make it work, and now it's just…over. A phone call, a swipe of a pen, done. And all I can think about is that if I'd worked so hard at my marriage only to have it fail so completely, what makes me think I have any chance at all of keeping Aunt Maggie's house?

I slide down the kitchen wall while Karl's voice pours into my right ear, then land with a hard thud on the linoleum floor, all the fight extinguished that damn fast. All I can hear—all I can think about—is him saying that I need him. And maybe, just maybe, he's right.

I have a list of repairs I can't afford. A shitload of junk

that needs to be sorted through and thrown away. Property and inheritance taxes that I don't have the money for. And reality starts to really seep in—like it always does when I'm around Karl.

It absolutely sucks, but my father was right. I need to move back in with my parents, sell the house, and use the money from the sale to pay the inheritance taxes and get back on my feet.

Is it what I want to do? Not in the slightest.

Is it what I have to do? Yeah, it is.

It's the only logical solution. And I'm nothing if not logical—isn't that what Karl always said about me? Boring, logical Mallory who doesn't have an exciting bone in her body? It's exciting to think about keeping this place, about building a life worthy of the great-aunt who used to pick me up at school on a random day once a year and take me to Bloomingdale's to pick out an un-birthday present.

The great-aunt who used to take me to the Strand bookstore and demand that I pick out no less than three or five or seven books to read, depending on what she considered her lucky number that day.

The great-aunt who used to take me for cheesecake at Junior's or hot dogs at Gray's Papaya and then up to the top of the Empire State Building to make a wish as big as the city.

And now I'm such a failure that I can't even afford to keep her house. I can't live the life she tried to give me or the life she wanted for me. All I can do is just…fold.

"Are you even listening to me?" Karl's voice booms through the phone, bringing me back to our conversation. "I need you to sign the papers tomorrow morning."

"I'd like to read them first." Not *I have to read them first* or *I'll have a lawyer read them first*, just "I'd like to read them first." So much for my wine-induced badassery.

"You don't need to read them. They're exactly like we discussed, and I really need to get this done tomorrow."

Anger flares inside me again, and this time there is no sadness for it to get buried in. "Yeah, well, I need a lot of things, Karl. Including twenty-four hours to read the damn papers—which I don't think is too much to ask. What's your rush anyway?"

"I want this mistake over and done with," he says, his voice cold in that way it always gets when I do something to displease him. "You know how you are, Mallory. If I don't push, it won't get done."

"Well, I have no need to set a record for fastest paper signing in history, like you apparently do. Something tells me there's more going on here."

Maybe it's the wine making a comeback or I've just finally reached my tipping point, but I'm not about to be bullied by this man. Not anymore.

A long silence follows my statement, and for a second, I think he might have actually hung up. But then he sighs heavily. It's a long-suffering sound meant to remind me just how difficult and irrational I'm being—per usual. He employed it regularly during our marriage—every time I had the nerve to disagree with him on anything—and the sound of it now, when he's clearly being the irrational one, sets off a wave of anger inside me like nothing I've ever felt before.

Even walking in on him mid-lick didn't make me this angry. Nothing has. It's lava hot and practically sentient, ready for action, to decimate the dick who sparked it.

We are getting divorced because he's a cheating asshole, and he still thinks he has the right to order me around? To *demand* that I do things his way simply because that's the way *he* wants it done? Simply because I've always bent over backward to make him happy before, no matter how unreasonable his demands were?

"I'm not signing anything until you tell me the real reason you're trying to rush me, Karl."

My God, I actually made my own demand. I fist-pump the air. Sure, it took an entire bottle of wine to muster up the courage, but it's a victory nonetheless.

Karl must be as shocked as I am at my tone because for once in our miserable marriage, he tells me the bald-faced truth and leaves out the side order of gaslighting.

"Sasha and I are planning on getting married," he says. "We want to set up an appointment for a marriage license, and we can't do that until the divorce papers are signed."

Chapter Eleven

*I*t takes a second for his words to sink in—probably because my mind went into full-on red-haze mode the moment the words "marriage" and "license" left his mouth. Because what. The. Hell?

I mean, seriously. What the hell?

All the years I spent shaving twice a day so my legs never even held a hint of a five o'clock shadow flash in front of me like a horror movie. And this shithead thinks he can tell me to jump and I ask how high? I swear, at that moment, I hear a lightning bolt in my kitchen and the air crackles around me. Any latent feelings I might have had for him, any tiny hope that maybe deep inside his shriveled black heart he might actually have a shred or two of decency dies right then. I can feel them literally withering inside me.

It isn't that I want him back. I don't and I didn't, not from the moment I got over the shock that he was cheating on me. My sadness at the divorce always stemmed more from my own naivete in staying as long as I did coupled with my abject hatred of failure than it ever did from regret over losing Karl. Which says everything, I know.

But still, no matter how low he goes in this divorce—and he's gone low—a part of me still hoped he wasn't a complete and total asswipe. Not for him but because it really stings to think about how many years of my life I wasted on a guy who has no redeeming qualities besides his wardrobe and his law degree, both of which I helped pay for.

How could I be so clueless? How could I tell myself over and over again that his self-absorption was just brilliance? That his overinflated ego was just well-deserved pride in his accomplishments even as *I* subverted my plans to make sure that he achieved everything he wanted to?

Yeah, well, that stops now. The sadness, the self-doubt, and most definitely the regret evaporate in the heat of my ire. I may have let him bully me our entire marriage—and pretty much our entire divorce, for that matter—but I'm not about to let him bully me about these papers.

I have no fucks left to give, and it feels glorious—so good that I'm ready to break out into a full-on Christmas mass Handel with its eighteen-syllable gloria.

"You know what, Karl?" I interrupt him as he continues going on about how much he and whatever-the-hell-her-name-is want a spring wedding and there are only a few more weeks of spring left to make that happen. "I will take as much time reading—and signing—the divorce papers as I would like. And there is not a goddamn thing you can do about that fact. You'll get them when you get them, which might just be the first day of summer, the way I'm feeling right now."

Karl starts making choking sounds about halfway into my diatribe, and I'd be lying if I said that didn't feel damn good. Whereas the old me might have stopped and checked to make sure he's okay, the new me doesn't give two flying farts.

In fact, the new me ends the call while he's still in mid-splutter, and then I down my nearly full glass of wine in one very unladylike and completely satisfying gulp.

I did it. I hung up on Karl.

I'm a new woman who is broke, yes, and in a world of shit, yes, but I'm a new woman. There's only one thing to do in a situation like this, and Aunt Maggie must be looking down from above because it's at that very moment that the record starts over and the needle hits "Come Together." So I dance right there in the kitchen. All by myself. Drinking straight from the wine bottle. Practically floating on fermented grapes and freedom.

The new me decides to hell with money, to hell with repairs. I'm not selling this house. I'm not moving back in with my parents. And I'm sure as hell not signing the divorce papers until I have an equitable settlement that reflects all the work I put into building Karl's law firm, not to mention paying for his law degree. The shock has worn off, and I'm no longer the little mouse who let that bastard lock her out of her own apartment without even a squeak of protest.

I fucking *ROAR*.

If he wants a quick divorce, he's going to have to pay for it—with my share of what *we* saved and earned in *our* marriage.

I add *find a killer divorce attorney* to my to-do list for tomorrow. I have no idea how I'm going to pay for said divorce attorney, but that's a problem for another day. As is Mikey's construction bid and the piles and piles of junk I have to sort through in this house.

Tonight, I'm going to revel in the fact that for once, I'm on the offensive and Karl is the one who is going to have to scramble to make things right.

The thought cheers me up immeasurably—although, not going to lie, my newfound happiness might also have something to do with the amount of wine I consumed in a very short period of time.

Regardless, I drop my phone on the kitchen counter and open more wine. I meander back into the family room without even bothering with a glass.

I put on "Here Comes the Sun" at top volume and move the dance party from the kitchen to the living room with every ounce of energy and determination I have inside me.

It turns out that there's a lot more than I thought there was, because I dance through half the album—"Because," "You Never Give Me Your Money," "Sun King," "Mean Mr. Mustard," and "Polythene Pam"—without taking a break longer than the few seconds it takes for me to swig another sip of wine.

But when "She Came in Through the Bathroom Window" comes on—my favorite song on the whole album—I stumble to a stop. Holding the wine bottle to my lips like a makeshift microphone, I belt out every word along with Paul, John, George, and Ringo as I twirl and twirl and twirl around the room with my eyes closed.

I don't stop until the song does, and when it finally winds down, I take another sip of wine, push my now-wild hair out of my eyes, slowly open them, and see a man standing right outside my open patio door.

I scream, high and loud. Then an instinct I didn't even know I had takes over and I send the wine bottle soaring straight at his head. And it would have been an impressive toss if not for the fact that I'm tipsy as hell and throw like my grandma.

It ends up just barely grazing his forehead, but he gives a satisfyingly surprised yelp and stumbles backward…at the exact same moment I realize that my late-night—and by *late-night* I meant *nine o'clock*—visitor is none other than Mr. You Need to Mow Your Grass.

I don't mean to giggle—it isn't like I planned to—but it just sort of happens. The kind of out-of-control fit that leaves you gasping for breath and unable to stop.

Maybe I should be ashamed of nearly clocking him in the head, but he's the one skulking around my backyard, after all— probably looking for more HOA offenses he can complain about.

He isn't complaining now, though. In fact, he looks stunned as cheap merlot drips down his forehead.

Oh, shit.

My giggles die an instantaneous death as he stumbles back, his hand going to his forehead and his jaw dropping.

OH, SHIT!

His heel connects with one of Aunt Maggie's many pet rocks at the edge of the small patio, and he goes down to the ground hard enough to jolt his entire body. And then he doesn't move again. I freak out as I race across the room and down the steps. Did I hurt him? Concuss him? *Kill* him?

I drop to my knees by his head and try to see his face, but now that we're on the grass, the light from the house is a lot dimmer, and I can't get a good look at him.

I lean closer until my face is only inches from his, and I realize his eyes are closed—and he's already developing a big, nasty-looking bruise on his forehead from where the wine bottle grazed him.

He groans a little, and I nearly weep with relief. "Oh my God! Are you all right?"

His eyes pop open.

Now that I'm this close, I can see that we have a massive problem.

"Don't move!" I scream right in his face. "Your pupils are really dilated. That's a sign of a concussion. I'm going to go call an ambu—"

His fingers curl around my wrist, cutting off the rest of my words.

"Dilated pupils are normal when it's dark out," he says, his voice deep and rich.

Thankfully, the wine bottle has boo-booed up his head and not his voice box.

"Still, don't you think you should be checked out?" I move in extra close to see if his dilated pupils are the same size in both eyes but instead get distracted by how long his eyelashes are. Why? Because obviously I'm a horrible human being. "You got hit pretty hard."

"One, it was a nearly empty bottle of wine. Two, *you* threw it," he snarls as he sits up, still holding on to my wrist.

Okay, he isn't slurring his speech, so that should reassure me. And it probably would have, except that he's also making absolutely no move to get up off my grass or let me go, and the whole world is growing tingly and hot all of a sudden.

"Because you were skulking around my backyard," I say, holding on to my indignation as much as I can while I slur my words. Hello, two bottles of wine. "Who does that besides creeps and perverts?"

"Are you calling me a pervert?" he asks as he lifts an eyebrow.

My pulse does a pause, thunk, thunk, *thunk* thing, and I might have forgotten how to breathe. I did. Thank God my lungs remember, allowing me to shoot back, "Or a creep. There were two choices there. In fact—"

Abruptly, he releases my wrist and covers his face. He is totally silent, but his shoulders start shaking.

I break off, horror slapping me in the face as he moves on to convulsing.

"Oh my God! You're having a seizure!"

I remember reading that can happen with really bad head injuries. Fear skates down my spine. What if I really hurt him? I have to call 911.

I start to go for my phone, but his convulsions get worse—much worse—and vague memories of CPR start floating through my head. One thought about convulsions immediately comes to mind—I have to get something leather between his teeth before he bites off his tongue.

I drop on my knees again and grab his shoulders, shoving him back down on the grass with superhuman strength. I reach for his belt and have it unhooked in two seconds flat, then start to whip it off as though I'm being timed for a new Olympic event in undressing a man.

He stills immediately. "Stop!" he gasps out and grabs my hands, still wrapped around one side of his belt. "I was laughing." He rolls up into a sitting position, pulling his belt loose from my death grip. "Not seizing."

"Laughing?" I jump to my feet. "I thought I'd hurt you and you were *laughing* at me? You…you…you big jerk."

I consider kicking him out of sheer spite but figure that might be overkill. At least the wine dripped down to his white button-up. Good luck getting that out.

"I'm sorry," he says, still chuckling. "I couldn't help it. You just looked so earnest trying to explain the difference between a creep and a pervert."

"Yeah, well, I've decided you're both, so you can leave now. Before I call the cops and report you for trespassing." I turn and march up the three steps to my patio.

"Wait." He catches up to me easily, even though I had a head start and he was on the ground. "Don't you want to know what I was doing in your backyard?"

"Being a creep *and* a pervert, I assume, as we already established."

"I was trying to let you know that your garage door is still open." He isn't laughing now—not even a superior guffaw. "We've had a bunch of robberies in the area lately, and I was afraid the door leading into your house wasn't locked."

It seems like a more reasonable excuse than the fact that Mr. Subparagraph Three in the HOA Bylaws was trying to get his rocks off looking in my living room window. Still, he's not off the hook that easily.

I narrow my eyes at him. "So why didn't you come to the front door and ring the doorbell?"

"Have you seen your porch?" He shoots me a disbelieving look. "There's no way I'm taking my life in my hands and walking on that thing."

It's a good point, especially considering what Mikey had to say about the porch earlier. But— "Why didn't you knock on the garage door? Wouldn't that be the logical next step?"

"It's what I planned to do, but when I was walking up your

driveway, I heard music coming from the backyard—which you have to turn off at ten o'clock, by the way—and I figured I'd see if I could catch you back here." He holds up his hands in a profession of innocence. "I swear, that's all there was to it. No creepiness or perverted behavior intended."

I totally believe him—it also makes much more sense than any other scenario—but I'm pissed off all over again from his comment about the music. Off by ten. Ugh. All these freaking men with their opinions and rules and *it has to be this way*s that no one actually cares about. "What happens if I don't turn the music off until 10:01? Or worse, 10:05? Do the HOA police come and arrest me?"

His eyes gleam. "I'm pretty sure you get a warning first."

"Well, aren't I lucky?" The words drip with sarcasm.

His smile disappears altogether. "I should be going."

"Finally, we agree on something!" I'm more than fed up with men telling me what to do. Still, I can't send him away without at least offering help. "Can I get you some ice? For your head?"

For a second, it seems like he's thinking about it. "That's okay. I'll get some at home."

"Are you sure? I hit you pretty hard."

"Believe me, I know exactly how hard you hit me." His smile comes back for just a moment. "You know, the neighborhood women's softball league is looking for a pitcher. You'd probably be a shoo-in."

It's my turn to laugh—of course, because of the wine, not because Mr. Music Off at Ten is charming. "I'll keep that in mind."

"You should. The MVP of each game gets free pizza and beer from Salvaggio's."

"Okay, then." I step inside the house before turning to face him. "I'll let you see yourself out."

And then I close the door—and Aunt Maggie's lemon-yellow-and-ecru-colored giraffe-print living-room curtains—right in his astonished (and still merlot-stained) face.

Chapter Twelve

I wake up the next morning to more retina-searing sunlight—and this time, it's about a gazillion times worse, because apparently drinking two bottles of wine is an awful, horrible, no good, very bad idea. Who knew?

My mouth tastes like I spent the night licking rusty scissors and just about every single one of the splinters on the dare-not-walk-on-it front porch was jabbed into my eyes. The single unharmed brain cell in my head is flipping me off, and the bowling ball of bile in my stomach is daring me to sit up and see what happened.

I slam the heels of my hands over my eyes and whimper a little even as I burrow deeper under the covers. I knew I should have pinned a sheet over that window last night, but by the time I got back upstairs, I was too drunk and too tired to hunt down the pushpins I needed to do it.

And that's why I'm paying the price this morning. Well, that and the pounding hangover that feels like someone is taking a claw hammer to my right eye.

Fun times.

I roll out of bed slowly—like dinosaur-stuck-in-tar-pits slowly—and send up a quick prayer of thanks to whoever is the patron saint of alcohol that my stomach clenches but doesn't revolt. Then again, it isn't like there's anything in there, as the dinner sandwich I planned to eat is still in the fridge. Or at least,

I think it is. Everything after helping my neighbor get off on my lawn is a little bit of a blur.

No! Wait!

I helped him get *off* my lawn, not get off *on* my lawn. There is a difference, even if my brain can barely differentiate between the two at the moment.

After stumbling to the bathroom, I make the awful mistake of looking straight into the mirror. Jay-sus. I definitely look as bad as I feel—maybe even worse, considering the never-runs mascara has sprinted away from my eyelids—so I force myself into the shower. I'm not up for the whole serum/moisturizer/ eye-cream circus today, so once I've dried off, I do a quick teeth-brushing/topknot combo and grab the first clothes I see.

I'm soooooo tempted to go back to bed, but I have a to-do list that keeps growing exponentially, and I need to get on it. Besides, I'm not starting the second day of the rest of my life hiding under the covers, no matter how hungover I am.

Once I sidestep down the stairs and get to the kitchen, I take two Tylenol and brew the strongest pot of coffee I can stomach. Three cups of a-spoon-would-stand-straight-up-in-it and one bowl of Froot Loops later, and I'm ready to face the world.

And by *world*, I mean the rest of the kitchen cabinets as well as the bookshelves packed full of paperback romances, biographies of musicians, and at least one copy of every single Nora Roberts and JD Robb book ever published in any language in the family room.

I work through it methodically. One trash-bag pile for the garage sale I hope to have, though I'm sure the HOA will be all up in arms about that; one trash-bag pile for donation; and one trash-bag pile for the landfill.

I'm about halfway through my third box of trash bags—not to mention an entire cabinet devoted to takeout chopsticks, silverware, and condiments—when I decide that Mikey was right. I need a dumpster. There's no way a simple trash collection can deal with all of this.

I leave everything where it is, pausing in my work just long enough to wash my hands and get a second pot of coffee brewing, and then I chase down his card in my purse. I make the call, expecting it to go straight to voicemail like it did yesterday, but instead Mikey picks up on the second ring.

"This is Mikey." His voice is warm and deep.

"Hi! This is Mallory Martin Bach, soon to be just Martin again. You came by my aunt's house yesterday and—"

"I know who you are, Mallory." Now he just sounds amused. "How are you doing today?"

"I'm getting by." Yeah, there is no way I'm telling him I got sloppy drunk after seeing his estimate. That is not the way to conduct a business meeting. "How are you?"

"Better now that you've called."

I have no clue how to respond to that. Is he flirting with me? It sounded like he was flirting, but it's been so long since anyone did that, I can't be sure. I decide to take the safe route and assume that he wasn't—besides, it isn't like I want to flirt back.

"Well, don't get too excited." My cheeks explode with heat when he lets out a startled laugh. "I mean, about the bid." *Way to go, Mallory. You are sooooooo smooth. Like crunchy peanut butter mixed with driveway gravel.* "It turns out the only thing I know for sure I can afford today is the dumpster. I definitely want the dumpster."

"Things are that bad, huh?" He sounds significantly more sympathetic than a contractor should, and I'm not sure how I feel about that, to be honest. It's hard enough dealing with the situation I'm in all by myself. The last thing I want or need is someone else to see how pathetic I am right now.

I can handle a lot of things—Karl being a total dick for one. Finding out that I failed my aunt for two. I can even handle the recriminations from my parents and their plots for me to reconcile with Karl. However, the one thing I can't take right now is someone feeling sorry for me. Just the idea makes me feel a hundred times more pathetic than I already do.

"The quote is okay," I say. "But I need to look at the bid against the most pressing HOA violations. There's no point in doing anything if they levy fines or sue me, as then I won't have enough money to finish the project."

Judging by the tone of the HOA letters my aunt received— letters I spent the first half a pot of coffee this morning sorting through—they are serious as a heart attack that this will be their next step. Turns out the HOA has been on her butt for the last year, everything from length-of-grass violations to four separate notices about her *periwinkle* shutters. And they are done waiting for the repairs.

Not for the first time, I wonder why she decided to leave this house to me. She might not have known before she died that I wouldn't be able to afford it, but surely she had to have known that I would get stuck with all the HOA violations and all the mess.

I'm beginning to think I might not have been her favorite person after all, no matter what she used to say.

"I understand," Mikey says. "But I've got an idea."

"What's that?" I ask warily. The last time a man told me he had an idea, it ended with a wedding ring on my finger and years of my soul and self-esteem being crushed.

"How about I take you to lunch tomorrow? We can talk about the bid, maybe see what absolutely has to be done immediately. We can figure out what we can start with, besides the dumpster, I mean, and a budget you can live with. And of course, talk about a possible insurance claim."

"That's a really nice offer." Not a lie. "But the truth is, I shouldn't waste your time. This is my problem, and I think I can sort through it all with the detailed bid you gave me."

"Let me worry about my time," he says with such confidence, I just want to close my eyes and believe. "I know you're in a pinch, and I'd love to do what I can to help you out."

Pull it back, Mallory! Do not fall for the I'll-take-care-of-you bullshit.

"Why would you want to do that?"

Maybe it's because up until now I spent most of my time around Karl and the people from his law firm, but my experience has been that people don't go out of their way to help you unless there's something in it for them.

He chuckles. "Because I like you, Mallory. So what do you say, tomorrow at Wilma's Diner? It's on Bay Drive. I can send you a link—"

"I know where it is," I say.

An awkward silence ensues as I wait for him to say something else and apparently he waits for me to do the same thing. I don't know what to say, though—this is new territory for me. Someone doing something nice just because? Trust issues? Me? Only a smidgen the size of the Grand Canyon.

Eventually, Mikey must get tired of waiting on me to speak, because he clears his throat. "So tomorrow at noon? Is it a date? Tell you what, I can even pick you up."

"Sure," I say, crossing my fingers in hopes that this isn't a bad decision. "I'll see you then."

"Great! And don't sweat the bid today. I'm sure we'll be able to work something out. We can tackle things in small chunks. I promise."

I'm not nearly as certain as he is—especially since I now need to scrape together enough money to hire a cutthroat divorce attorney to go after Karl. I don't say that, though, not when Mikey is so obviously going out of his way to be nice.

"Thanks so much for all your help with this. I appreciate it."

We say our goodbyes, and just as I'm getting ready to hang up, Mikey adds, "I'm really looking forward to lunch tomorrow."

"Me too," I answer absently, my mind already moving on to the next task on my to-do list—which is to find a place to store all the bags in the trash-it pile until the dumpster comes through.

It isn't until after I've already hung up that Mikey's words hit me in between musings about whether the garage or the back porch would be better to store all the going-to-the-dump bags I'm creating.

But then realization smacks me like a two-by-four, or a wine bottle still half full of merlot, right between the eyes.

Tomorrow at noon? Is it a date?

Because I like you, Mallory.

I'm really looking forward to lunch tomorrow.

Holy shit.

Did I just agree to go on a date with my contractor?

Chapter Thirteen

I didn't, right?

I mean, yeah, he was flirting a little, but he's obviously younger than I am. And obviously hotter than I am. Plus, he knows that I'm broke and living in a junk pile. What exactly screams sexy about that?

I just stand in the middle of the kitchen, surrounded by trash bags, with my mouth hanging open and my brain spinning out into pure what-the-fuck panic mode.

How? How did this even happen? One second I was thinking about trash—definitely not a sexy subject—and the next I became a cougar.

I suck in a breath.

I don't even have anything to wear on a date—and if I did, I don't actually want to *go* on a date. I definitely don't want to go on a date with a younger, gorgeous, smooth-talking contractor who looks like he could strip my panties off as easily as he could strip a piece of wood. Maybe even more easily...

And that's when I realize I need to hand in my ovaries if that whole thought is a negative.

I pour myself a glass of orange juice and contemplate my dead-as-a-doornail libido. Why am I really upset about an innocent lunch date? If Mikey did suggest stripping my panties off, I should climb him like a tree, right? I sigh. I'm not the least bit interested.

There's no denying he is h-o-t as hell. And he seems actually nice, too. Is that it? Did Karl break me from finding nice guys attractive?

I dredge up a mental image of my asshole neighbor from last night, my hands brushing against his hard stomach as I unbuckled his belt, and I get a little dizzy.

I sink down into a kitchen chair and plonk my head on the breakfast table. Fuck. I'm attracted to assholes.

In addition to all my new baggage—which is enough for a year-long cruise around the world all by itself—only dickheads do it for me now. Of all the things my failed marriage has left me with, this is by far the cruelest.

And just like that, I sit up and square my shoulders. My ovaries just need an exorcism, that's all.

I'm going to go on a lunch date with a sexy young contractor. Let him pull out my chair. Make me laugh. Offer me compliments. And if eventually he wants to show me his hammer—I'm going to say yes, please. Pound it harder.

I'm going to do absolutely anything it takes to make Satan get behind me and fucking stay there, because no way am I ever going to end up married to a selfish prick again. I'm going to reclaim my vagina for the side of good, not evil.

I toast the air with my orange juice and giggle. Watch Mikey just want to discuss my home improvements of the nonsexual kind...

Well, either way, that's tomorrow, and today I need to get busy reclaiming the kitchen for eating.

Three hours later, I finally finish the drawers—who knew a person could hang on to that many takeout menus and bottle caps?—and decide to stop to get something to eat. It's only eleven or so, but between the hangover and the panic attack, food has been the last thing on my mind this morning.

I toss together a cheese-and-fruit plate—being single means I can eat whatever I want for lunch, and I'm coming to realize the freedom is a glorious thing—when my phone rings. My stomach goes south. The only people who call me these days are my parents, Karl, and Mikey. Right now, I'm not sure who I want to talk to less.

But when I reach over and snag my phone off the counter, it flashes Angela's name. I texted her yesterday to thank her for recommending Mikey to me, but I didn't expect to hear back from her—especially since my business isn't turning out to be nearly as impressive as I was sure she had hoped for her brother-in-law.

Still, maybe Mikey had an epiphany and tagged her to cancel our lunch date, which might be why I sound a little too hyper when I answer the phone. "Hi!"

Angela gives a startled little laugh. "Hi, Mallory. How are you?"

"I'm good, thanks. How are you?" I definitely want to sound upbeat if she's calling to break my date with Mikey. The last thing I want is for her to feel sorry for me and decide to force him to go anyway.

"I'm good! I'm calling because tonight is the night my bestie is having a Stella and Dot party, and I was wondering if you wanted to come with me?"

Stella & Dot? Am I supposed to know what that means? "Stella and Dot?" I repeat.

"Oh, do they not have S and D in the city?" Angela sounds surprised. "Now you have to come! They make the most gorgeous jewelry."

That's when it hits me. It's a Tupperware party except shiny and pretty. In the city, I went to gallery shows, the Met, jogs in Central Park. Now I'm invited to a home jewelry party. Is there anything more suburban than that?

Is there anything snobbier than you right now?

Fuck.

Inner me is right. It's hard to knock off some of the

Manhattan snottiness, but I of all people know what it's like to have people judge me and find me lacking. That's it. I might be back in the burbs, but that doesn't mean I'm going to act like some kind of city-dwelling snob who never crosses the GW Bridge going west unless forced.

"That would be a totally new experience for me," I say.

"Exactly. A fun one but not as much as dating a hammer-hauling h-u-n-k," she says with a loud laugh. "Just say yes, you'll come to look at jewelry, eat apps, and drink some wine."

Okay, the idea of more wine makes me gag a little, but I say yes anyway and hang up the phone in a kind of daze. I started the conversation with Angela convinced she was going to deliver the news that Mikey wanted to break his date with me. Instead, she doubled down, and now I have a friend date with her tonight and a real date with him tomorrow. I have no idea how I feel about this beyond slightly queasy.

It's been years since I've had any real female friendships. Not because I didn't want them—in fact, I thought I had them—but when the divorce happened, I realized quickly that *my* friends were all part of couples who were *our* friends. And when push came to shove, business won out and every single one of them chose Karl.

Ten years of friendship, in some cases, gone in a blink. Is it any surprise that I figure jumping back into that boat again will end up with me chin-deep in water and treading until my legs give out?

Except Angela isn't Karl's friend. She has no ulterior motive.

I know it's true. Angela is just a really nice girl I used to know who turned into a really nice woman—one who showed up exactly when I could use her most.

Maybe tonight is exactly what I need—sans the push to buy sparkly things, but whatever. Surely I can find a pair of twenty-dollar earrings at this party that won't totally blow my budget.

TRACY WOLFF AND AVERY FLYNN

Besides, it's a small price to pay for the chance to make a friend. Not to mention I could use the time to subtly try to figure out if I should wear my granny panties or not on my date with Mikey tomorrow.

Chapter Fourteen

A horn honks outside my house at exactly six forty-five—apparently Angela believes in Goldfish crackers always in her purse, laughing loud and proud, and arriving right on the dot for friend dates. I, on the other hand, have been running fifteen minutes late ever since I finally looked up from sorting through piles of my aunt's old photographs and had an oh-shit moment.

Honestly, though, the mad dash to get the cobwebs out of my hair and slap on my face was worth it to get a look at those photos. My favorite is one of Aunt Maggie walking across a tightrope at a traveling circus. It isn't a high-wire or anything—just a tightrope the circus put up between two poles, about two feet off the ground, so that audience members could try their hand at doing what the acrobats did, at the bargain-basement price of one dollar per try, if the sign in the picture is to be believed.

My aunt was probably in her late twenties—if her seventies hair and psychedelic bell-bottoms are any indication—and she was about halfway across the tightrope and obviously wobbling. But she had her head tossed back and was laughing at the same time, her eyes and smile so bright that I couldn't help grinning myself despite the years and distance between me and when the photo was taken.

Looking at that photo was like getting a peek at pure,

undistilled happiness—and it rubbed off on me. At least until I realize that what I really want is to be my aunt—sans the hoarding. I want to live my life for me, not for Karl. Not for my parents. And not for some damn HOA who hates periwinkle shutters. They make me happy every time I see them—even if they do hang a bit cockeyed.

I grab my phone and shoot off a quick text to Angie, telling her I'll be out ASAP—the last thing I want is for her to decide I didn't hear her and risk life and limb reaching the front door. Killing my first new friend by porch cave-in is definitely not on my agenda tonight.

With that in mind, I yowl a few more times as I pull a brush through my tangled hair and slide my feet into my favorite pair of red Rothy's. I consider rummaging around in my suitcase for earrings but decide to forget about it. I can buy a pair at the jewelry party and consider my contribution made.

It takes me a minute to find my purse—on a table in the family room behind the pile of worn Time Life commemorative books I promised myself I'd go through tomorrow—and then I'm out the door, kinda-sorta knot-free hair flying behind me.

"Thanks so much for picking me up," I say as I sit down in the passenger seat of Angela's bright red minivan.

"Of course! Honestly, you're doing me a favor. No one likes to go to these parties alone."

She puts the minivan in gear and shoots away from the curb like she's practicing for the Indy 500. As she does, I notice Mr. Stare at You Drunk Dancing in Your Living Room walking back from the mailbox. He has a greenish bruise on his forehead still. Not shockingly, he also has a pinched, disapproving look on his face as he watches us speed toward him on the empty street—not that I blame him this time. I'm all for speed and efficiency, but kids play on these streets. I've seen them.

"Um, Angela—" She hits the brakes as we approach the stop sign at the end of the block before I can get any more words out.

Thank God we end up behind a car going the speed limit right after we made the turn onto the main drag leading out of the subdivision. Do I let out a relieved breath? You bet your sweet bippy I do.

"So how's the house fixing-upping going?" she asks right before snapping her gum. "Mikey says there's a lot for you to do."

"There is." I turn toward her, wondering for the first time if I'm a little underdressed for this party. I didn't think so in my mad dash not to leave the house naked or covered in dusty leggings and an old T-shirt—I went for my dressy-casual night-with-friends-in-NYC look of black pants and black pussy-bow blouse that I always get compliments on.

But Angela is dressed to the nines, complete with huge hair and a full face of makeup, including bright red lipstick that seems better suited for a cocktail party than a casual night at her best friend's—especially when paired with painted-on black jeans and a top covered in so many silver sequins, it looks like the New Year's Ball in Times Square.

"Do I look okay?" I try to keep the worry out of my voice, but we're only a few minutes away from my house, so going back and changing isn't out of the realm of possibility. "Or should I have gotten more dressed up?"

"What are you talking about? You look great," she says as she careens around an Escalade and two Mercedes. When one of them honks at her, she just waves the middle finger back and keeps on talking without missing a beat. "I just overdress for these things. I mean, now that I'm staying home with the kids, when do I have a chance to dress up? Especially since Manny's idea of a date night lately is sending the kids to his sister's and keeping me naked from the time they walk out the door until five minutes before they walk back in." She laughs. "Not that I'm complaining, mind you. I'm just saying that I don't get much of a chance to dress up anymore."

"Well, you look gorgeous."

It's 100 percent the truth, even if I wince at her story. Her life is so different from the life I had with Karl. Not just because we didn't have any kids to send to my parents' for a night off but because when we actually had a date night, it was always about going somewhere fancy so he could see and be seen.

When there was a quiet night at home—which wasn't very often, since Karl was always "working"—it was more of a Netflix-and-sleep kind of night. Or a wham-bam-thank-you-ma'am kind of night, which weren't exactly my favorites. I guess that should have told me something even before the divorce, considering it'd been a long time—if ever—since sex with Karl made me smile the way Angela is smiling and practically glowing.

A little voice whispers in the back of my head that maybe that's why Karl started banging his paralegal. Is it really his fault I wasn't interested in sleeping with him myself in years? I swallow. Hard. And push that thought down. Cheating is never the answer. He could have easily just said he wanted a divorce. *As could I...*

I cough. "Legit, you look amazing, Angela."

"Thanks. Looking hot when I go out without him guarantees Manny is thinking about me all night. Gotta keep them on their toes," she says with a wink.

Maybe that's where I went wrong. I didn't keep Karl "on his toes" with evenings planned to drive him wild with lust, have him wanting to take me against the wall the second I returned. Instead, he was the king of the three-in-the-morning dick poke to my ass followed by a few minutes of pumping, before he came with a grunt and rolled back over, asleep before his head hit the pillow.

"So what do you think of Mikey?" Angela asks when we stop at a red light while she riffles through her voluminous purse.

"I think he's a really nice guy." I scramble for something else to say. "Plus, he can put together a really readable spreadsheet."

"He's the best," she says as she tosses a pacifier into the back seat. "And I'm not just saying that because he's my brother-in-law. It's true. He did all the remodeling on Manny's and my house, and it looks like a million bucks now."

A tiger-print glasses case follows the pacifier into the way back, then a blue toy truck whizzes through the air, and finally one giant purple-feathered earring. The light turns green just as she pulls out a Buzz Lightyear doll. "Here, hold this, will you?" She shoves the action figure into my hands. "Johnny will kill me if I lose his favorite toy."

We inch forward but don't make it through the light before it turns red again, which means Angela is back to digging in her purse. Another pacifier, two more cars, and a hair ribbon are tossed in the back seat before she comes out triumphant with a bright red lipstick that she applies with abandon to her already bright lips—while still singing Mikey's praises.

I'm beginning to think she has some ulterior motives with this party invite, after all—and they revolve around getting me to date Mikey. Since I need Mikey for my new vaginal exorcism plan, I'm more than willing to hear of her plans, too. She drops the lipstick back into her bag and holds it out for me to do the same with the Buzz Lightyear. Then she abruptly changes the subject.

"This party is going to be so fun! I have a ton of people I'm dying to introduce you to!"

"A ton?" I ask, heart starting to pound because I'm really more of a small-group girl. "How many people are going to be at this party?"

"Fifteen? Twenty?" She waves a hand as the light turns green and she starts to drive again. "Does it matter? I've told them all about you, and they are dying to meet the girl who's managed to turn Mikey's head. I mean, there are a whole lot of women who've been trying to do that, but you're the lucky one who finally made it happen."

I have no idea what to say to that, and before I can think

something up, she makes a quick left turn followed by a quick right. Seconds later, we pull into a driveway behind a dark-green minivan that looks an awful lot like the one I'm currently riding in.

"We're here!" Angela announces triumphantly, and then she reaches over and adjusts my bow. "Ready to get your wine on?"

My stomach does the Cha Cha Slide for a million and one reasons—none of them good.

Chapter Fifteen

Angela practically frog marches me up the driveway to her friend's house. "Don't be nervous," she says as we climb a porch that looks very much like mine is supposed to. "They'll love you. Especially Christee—"

"Who's Christee?" I ask.

Angela laughs. "My bestie, of course."

She knocks on the door, then throws it open without waiting for her friend to answer—and we walk straight into a Pottery Barn catalog. Seriously.

And I'm shaken with envy. Not gonna lie. After spending a day surrounded by clutter, this is like a breath of fresh air. Everything perfectly matched and in its place. Nothing extra would dare invade this space. The only nod to personalized items is the enormous oil painting hanging over the fireplace of what is probably her and her husband and their five children of varying ages, magazines about parenting scattered on the large wooden coffee table, and random small, framed photos atop a short bookcase near the front door that features the family doing various activities together.

A birthday party. New puppy. Camping trip. School play. *Paris.*

I swallow the sudden lump in my throat. They took their kids to Europe.

I wrap my arms around my waist and stare at the picture,

their grinning faces in front of the Eiffel Tower blurring as tears well in my eyes. Christee is living my anti-Karl life. The life I naively thought was mine for the taking if I didn't make a fuss, did what was expected, made everyone comfortable.

I desperately want to go home now, but I know I won't. A masochistic bitch has control of my body, and she greedily glances around with a macabre fascination to see what else I missed out on.

A woman whose hair is stick straight, parted down the middle, and as black as the mental hole I fell down rushes up to Angela and pulls her into a huge bear hug before leaning back again and giving me a wide, toothy smile.

"Wine or whiskey?" the grinning woman asks as she loops her arm through mine and guides me across the giant foyer.

My gut—obviously still horrified by last night's bender—gurgles. "Water, please?"

"Water?" She raises an impeccably groomed eyebrow and smooths her fingertips over her shiny hair as if she needs a moment to process. "Tap or bottled or sparkling? Perhaps tonic with just a splash of vodka?"

"You two are going to love each other." Angela squats down and scratches a mop dog who trails behind our host before standing back up and waving an arm between us. "Mallory, Christee. Christee, Mallory. And if she doesn't want that vodka and tonic, I'll take it."

"Nice to meet you?" It comes out sounding way more like a question than I intended. But that's only because Christee is dragging me down her picture-filled hallway like she's a prison guard and I'm the most reluctant inmate in the yard—which, as I think about it, might be a fairly accurate summation of the situation.

As we make our way into the family room, my gaze widens at the massive kitchen in the open floor plan. It has enough French country decor to have been Julia Child's wet dream.

Christee snags a glass of white wine off the makeshift bar on the counter and hands it to me.

"It's so light, it's practically water," she says with a wave of her hand.

After foisting the wine on me, she doesn't even wait for me to take a sip before dragging me into the center of the family room where at least thirty women—not the fifteen or twenty Angela said might be here—are gathered.

"Everybody," she says in a voice loud enough to be heard back in Manhattan. "This is Angie's friend Mallory. She went to school in Brunswick with Angie back in… Well, we don't talk about anything that could give away our age, now, do we?" Everyone chuckles. "She's spent the last several years living in the city, but she's back home now. So let's everybody give her a warm welcome, okay?"

"Hi, Mallory," answers all the other thirty-some women in one breath—which isn't creepy at all.

I wave a little nervously, then step back to hang with Angela as Christee starts chattering to the group about all the great Stella & Dot merchandise her "oldest and dearest friend Valerie" brought to share with us.

A huge "ooh" goes up from the crowd as Valerie opens her trunks. Then Christee announces that everyone gets to pick one piece to take home for free with a one-hundred-dollar purchase and, just like that, there is a high-heeled stampede to the center of the room, with Angela leading the charge. While a few toes get stepped on and more than a few elbows get thrown, it only takes about two minutes before women are settled, shoulder to shoulder, around all four of the different trunks.

I, on the other hand, ease backward a little, until I can find a place to drop my unwanted glass of wine. If I'm lucky, the riot over the jewelry will last awhile, and I can just hang here on my own and observe.

Besides, it's a lot of fun to watch the blonde in the tiger-stripe sequins go at it against the brunette in the red sequins over a heavy gold chain necklace with a multi-stoned pendant. I'm putting my money on the brunette. She's shorter but definitely scrappy, and—

"Looks like I'm not the only one afraid to dip my toes in the Stella and Dot pool," says an amused voice from directly behind me. I turn to see a much younger woman with her hair pulled into a no-nonsense ponytail practically the same shade of brown as mine and, shockingly, there is nary a sequin to be found on any item of her clothing. In fact, she seems a little shy for this group.

"It's a pretty intense group," I say, and we both laugh. "My great-aunt Maggie would have loved these women, though Angela seemed to think she was taking a chance inviting me, since she said the jewelry wasn't exactly Aunt Maggie's style." I thought the comment was odd at the time, but admittedly, nearly everything about Aunt Maggie was a little odd.

"Definitely an intense group. Then again, Christee is intense about everything. She always has been." It's said without an ounce of malice.

Considering Christee is currently involved in a tug-of-war with one of her guests over a silver necklace loaded with rhinestones, I'm not about to disagree.

"How do you know her?" I ask.

"We used to work together at the salon. She managed the place, and I do hair."

"Oh, you're a stylist!" I say. "I've just moved back to Jersey to live in my aunt's house, and I'm definitely in need of a good salon. Plus, I'm thinking about doing something new with my hair. If you're taking on first-time clients, that is."

She smiles, and then a woman squeals in triumph so we both look over at the scrum. The woman raises a pair of dangly earrings above her head like a trophy, and we both chuckle. "Breakup or baby?"

I glance back at her. "I'm sorry?"

She gives me a slow up-and-down, her head slightly tilted. "Your hair looks great. It's healthy and shiny and the style is super flattering on you. So why change it unless—"

"Breakup or baby," I repeat, nodding slowly as realization dawns. "I get it."

She lifts a brow. "So which is it?"

"Breakup." I reach for my discarded wineglass and take a sip, then instantly regret it. "Divorcing my husband, actually."

"Fuck him," she says with surprising vehemence. "You seem like a great person, and if he let you go, then I say fuck him. He's not worth it."

"Oh, well..." I search for something polite to say but end up just grinning instead. "Yeah, pretty much."

She reaches into her bag and pulls out a card. "I'm not taking a lot of new clients right now because I'm super booked up. But I like you, so give me a call, and we'll work something out."

Her card is sleek and black, with silver writing on it. "Sarah Bianchi?" I read aloud.

She raises one brow. "And you are...?"

"Oh, right. Sorry. I'm Mallory Martin Bach. Well, soon to be just Mallory Martin."

"Mallory Martin." For a second, a look of shock flits across Sarah's face, but then it disappears as quickly as it came. "It's nice to meet you."

"It's nice to meet you, too. Thanks for saving me from becoming a wallflower."

She takes a long sip of her wine, eyeing me over the rim of her glass. And in that moment, as her hazel-colored eyes stay leveled on me, she looks really, really familiar. I don't know why, though. I'm 99 percent sure I've never met her before, and yet something about her tugs at something inside me. Most likely, Karl's law office did some work for her at one point—which would also explain her weird reaction to my name.

That has to be it—maybe I even validated her parking or helped her with paperwork at one time or another. I dealt with so many clients through the years that they all blend together. God, I hope she didn't sleep with my husband. That would really be a setback to this whole making-friends thing we have going on. Plus, I really do need a new stylist.

"So," she says as we both look back toward the women and the jewelry chests. "The skirmishes seem to have died down some."

"They have," I agree.

She smiles hesitantly and takes a step closer to the melee. "Want to wade in, see what's left?"

With visions of my meager bank account floating in my head, I start to tell her to go ahead. But then it hits me just how long it's been since I bought anything for myself just for fun. At least a year, maybe—probably—more.

Karl was always the one with the expensive tastes. I got his leftovers when it came to things like phones and computers, and as for the rest? I stopped shopping for myself years ago because every time I spent so much as $100, Karl would lambast me about how much money I was spending and how he had to sacrifice because I couldn't be frugal.

Standing here, I inventory all the stuff my ex bought himself through the years, and just the idea of denying myself anything seems ridiculous. But at the time, I believed him. Every time I tried to argue about anything, he twisted my words and the facts into so many knots that I couldn't keep my own arguments straight, let alone his.

And even though I knew I was right, it was impossible to argue with him because he would just keep hitting me with half-truths, like why did I need a new dress when I really preferred to skip social functions? I mean, it *is* true that I don't enjoy parties. I like trying a new recipe and then curling up on the couch with a glass of wine and the latest show to binge on Netflix. So I would shrug and wear something from my closet instead. But now the blinders are off, and I'm seeing every interaction differently. And myself, too.

Deep down, I know he couldn't have bullied me if I didn't let him. There were two in that marriage, and as much as it pains me to admit, someone can only walk all over you if you let them. I traded my agency for a wedding ring the day I agreed I should drop out of law school and help him build *his* practice instead, agreed it would be harder to get established if one of us didn't already have a job and less student loans. It all sounded so reasonable at the time. And if Karl was anyone other than the selfish prick he turned out to be, I'd still think it made sense.

But tonight—tonight I'm buying some damn earrings, whether it's a smart purchase or not. They are freedom earrings, and I need them more than my next breath.

I just hope I survive the jostling mob of earring-starved women. I know exactly how they feel. This is *Braveheart*-level shit.

Chapter Sixteen

One non-drunk sleep and three brand-new pairs of earrings later, I cleared out the first flight of stairs, ate a killer omelet, and am now checking myself out in the bathroom mirror as I wind my still slightly damp hair up into my usual topknot for my lunch date.

I catch sight of the fun, flirty earrings I bought last night dangling from my ears—the silver chandelier ones with multicolored stones in them—and decide to just give in to the vibe they have going and leave my hair down.

I finally managed to locate the suitcase with my makeup in it earlier that morning—if I'm going on a date with a younger guy in New Jersey, where makeup is practically a religion, I'm doing it fully armored, so I take a few minutes to do my face. It isn't full slap, just a subtle eye, nude lip, and a little bit of shimmer on my cheeks. I have to keep that natural, it's-just-lunch vibe, but I still feel better than I have in a long time—lighter.

I add my favorite pair of jeans, the ones that even Karl used to compliment me on, and a cute cami top in my favorite shade of blue. After a quick spritz of perfume, I'm done.

I glance out the window and realize Mr. Mows With a Sexy Perma-Scowl has pulled into his driveway. A quick peek at my phone confirms that I have fifteen minutes before I need to be ready for Mikey to pick me up, and I sadly know how I should spend that time.

While there is a part of me that doesn't want to ask, I take a second glance out the window at Mr. Damn He Looks Good in a Suit as he opens his car door and know I have to. It would really help Mikey to know the HOA regulations regarding dumpster usage, and I don't have time to search the 150 pages of regulations before he gets here. Plus, I know in my soul that my neighbor already has every line memorized.

I hop up and hurry out to catch him.

Thankfully, he stopped to inspect the flowers on his bushes, probably making sure they're all uniform in petals and diameter, and I manage to get his attention by waving at him before he goes into his house. I hustle across the street.

"Hey! Um…" My brain stops working, but my feet keep moving.

Wow. This is the perfect time to realize I have no idea what his actual name is, and I can't call him Mr. Probably Kicks Puppies for Fun. At least not to his face.

"Nick," he says as he crosses his arms and leans one hip against his sleek silver Mercedes. "Nick Holloway."

Nick. He looks like a Nick. Not in a Santa Baby kind of way, though—well, unless Santa is six-three and has dark hair and the North Pole permanently stuck up his ass.

"Mallory." I stick out my hand as if this is the first time we've met.

He stares down at my hand and then back up at me. For a second, I figure he's just going to leave me hanging, but then he gets this half smile—the kind that should definitely be illegal—and his long fingers envelop mine, sending a sizzle of awareness to all eleven billion of the nerve receptors in my body. And my brain breaks.

"Mallory Martin Bach," I start rambling, the words coming out one on top of the other. "But it's soon to be only Mallory Martin again and—" He lets go of my hand, and my synapses come back online. "You probably already knew that."

"I did," he says as he flexes his fingers.

Okay, this is going about as well as that time I tried to bake a soufflé. "So, um, I need to ask you a question."

He looks a little suspicious—and more than a little grumpy—but he nods reluctantly. "What do you need?"

I open my mouth to tell him, and a fat drop of rain lands right on my nose. Then another. And another.

Nick glances up at the sky, working his jaw back and forth as if the weather gods have personally betrayed him.

"Why don't we do this inside?" He walks toward his open garage, obviously assuming I'll follow. "I've only got a few minutes before I have to head out again for a meeting, and I don't have time to change if I get soaking wet."

"It's not like you're made of sugar, so you don't have to worry about melting," I grumble under my breath, but I still follow him through his absolutely spotless garage—every single tool and box is in its place. Even the floor sparkles like the Swarovski crystals in the earrings last night that I most assuredly could not afford and bought anyway. He has to pressure wash the floor to keep it this level of clean.

He pushes open the door into his house, and my breath catches as I wonder if the inside is as religiously spotless as the garage. Then I walk over the threshold into a large kitchen and just nod. Of course it is. In fact, I'd eat my shorts if you couldn't perform surgery on those gleaming marble floors.

His cleaners have to come twice a day, because for the life of me, I cannot picture him with a mop. Then I close my eyes and force myself to. It's not my best decision, because in my imagination, he is also shirtless as he works the mop back and forth. Imaginary Nick has really good pecs.

I say goodbye to Mr. Clean Neighbor, open my eyes again, and spy Nick staring at me as if I just might be the one who got nailed in the head by a wine bottle.

"You okay?" He comes closer, not touching but near enough

that my girlie parts do the hello-hottie wake up and dance. "Do you need a glass of water or something?"

"Yes. Please. I'm parched."

He heads to the fridge, and I wander into the spacious living room to scope the place out and get my suddenly-alive-again hormones under control. Nick's place is nice. Modern. Lots of windows. Warm leather furniture that looks comfortable but not like you can't eat a cookie on it. There are a couple of paintings here and there on the walls, but the biggest decorative touches are the plants. Lots of them. Everywhere. There are big ones and small ones and hanging ones and drooping ones and flowering ones.

I walk up to the closest plant, a giant thing with split, elephant-shaped dark-green leaves, and can't resist stroking the shiny leaves. I know next to nothing about plants, but I'm pretty sure it's a split-leaf philodendron. My roommate in college had one, and she swore I killed it with all my Red Hot Chili Peppers and Nine Inch Nails music, but I always thought it was because she would water it with the melted ice from her favorite vodka cranberries.

Again, I don't know much about plants, but I'm pretty sure they don't thrive on booze and sugar.

Nick obviously doesn't listen to rock music or water his plants with anything but the purest, most rarefied water, because each and every one of them is gorgeous. Large, glossy, bright green, and full of life. It's impossible not to smile while I wander from one to the next.

As I stroke the foliage of another plant—this one with tiny leaves that I absolutely have no idea the name of—I can't help but think how weird it is to find something so…unruly with life in Nick's orderly house. They are as wild and luscious and unrestrained as Nick is buttoned-up and restrained. It's obvious that he doesn't even try to exert any control over them. He just takes care of them and lets them do whatever they want to do.

Not gonna lie. I am sucked in, wanting to know the why of the one-of-these-things-is-not-like-the-other factor.

I move on to yet another plant—this one a bamboo palm, possibly—and I kind of want to name it. Actually, I want to name every single one of them with ridiculous monikers like Russell and Violeta and Brandywine. Yes, I definitely think the philodendron should be named Brandywine.

Too bad they aren't my plants to name. They aren't even my plants to ask about, despite me dying inside with questions.

Nick walks back in with two crystal highball glasses filled with water and hands one to me.

"Thank you," I say, ignoring the tingle in my fingers where his hand brushed mine. "Where's Buttercup?"

"Doggy day care."

I nod and take a sip of water. "So, um, I just wanted to ask you a question about the HOA regulations."

One of his dark brows goes up, and though his expression doesn't change in any other way, I can't help thinking that he's bracing himself for me declaring the Periwinkle Revolution.

"Anything in particular?" he asks after taking a long, precise sip of his own water. Not a drip slips down his glass, which isn't exactly a surprise. I'm sure it wouldn't dare.

"I was wondering how to go about getting a dumpster. I mean, I know how to get a dumpster. I was just wondering if there are any HOA regulations about renting one and parking it in my driveway for a week or two."

"A dumpster?" Now his second brow joins the first near his hairline. "Don't you think you should start with something a little easier?" he suggests. "Like mowing the grass?"

"What is it with you and my grass?" I ask, setting my glass down on the coffee table. "Yeah, it's a little long, but it's not like it's a jungle or anything."

It is.

"I just know that too-long grass is the number one way to

get a citation in this neighborhood." He walks over, gets two white marble coasters out of a small drawer in the end table, and puts one under my glass and the other his. "Besides, if you deal with the grass quickly, then the HOA might let you slide on a few of the other violations for a little while."

"Like the shutters?" It's my turn to lift a brow.

He sighs. "Okay, yeah. The shutters are going to cause a problem soon enough—if they haven't already."

"Oh, they definitely have. But I have a plan to deal with that." The plan is pretty simple, actually. It involves me, a ladder, and a couple of cans of all-weather paint in the most boring gray I can find.

It's a far cry from periwinkle violet, but it's guaranteed not to piss off the HOA and will keep me from racking up a bunch more fines, and that is all I care about right now. I can afford the dumpster and the earrings I'm wearing, but only if I don't have a ton of extra fees I suddenly need to pay off.

"Why don't you want to handle the grass first?" he says, his voice taking that ultra-patient tone one uses for small children and lost animals. "It's an easy job and will give you a quick win."

The dude is obsessed with Kentucky bluegrass or fine fescue or Bermudagrass or whatever the hell kind of grass lives in between all the weeds that have taken over my front lawn.

"Maybe I don't want a quick win," I shoot back at him.

He rolls his eyes. "Everyone wants a quick win. And a dumpster, while probably necessary, is pretty much the antithesis of quick or win."

Honestly, if he didn't look so cute trying so hard to be something he is most definitely not—in other words, *nice*—I might have found his continued fixation on my grass amusing. But there is no chance I'm going to give him the satisfaction of doing it on his timeline. Partly because I am sick to death of a man telling me what to do or think and partly because mowing the grass just isn't feasible right now. The only mower I found in Aunt Maggie's garage is an old-style push mower without a motor. I cannot replace it with a mower that was built in this century, at least not until I get a regular paycheck.

"You know, the lawn mower is older than dirt and in the garage, stored behind about ten thousand magazines in about twenty different piles. So *if* you want me to mow the grass, you're going to have to step up and help me figure out how to get a dumpster so I can throw away the clutter and clear a path to the world's oldest mower. Otherwise, I'm pretty sure the lawn will just keep growing forever."

Yeah. Take that, Mr. Grass Man!

Whew, I'm all flush and giddy off that little speech. That's right. I can do things my way.

This time, his sigh is more like a groan—a dark little sound from deep in his throat that sends another frisson of something unexpected down my spine. Attraction or annoyance? It has to be the latter, because I refuse to let it be the former, which would be great if I believed it, especially since my hand shakes a little bit as I pull out my phone and prepare to take notes.

Nick doesn't notice, or if he does, he's too staid—or too much of a gentleman—to mention it, for which I am eternally grateful.

Instead, he focuses on the dumpster. "The first thing you've got to do is request the forms. The email address you need to use is at the beginning of the HOA documents—which you should read, by the way."

"I plan to read them," I say, defensiveness creeping into my tone. "I just haven't had time yet, and I want to get a jump on ordering the dumpster."

"Do you even know how to order a dumpster?" he asks.

"Of course I know how to get a dumpster!" There has to be an app for that. "I'm not completely helpless, you know."

"Oh, I know." He rubs at the bruise on his forehead. "After you get the forms, you need to fill them out, and you have to take pictures of where you want to put the dumpster while it's on your property. Once that's done, you submit the forms, and you should have an answer in two to four weeks."

"Two to four weeks?" My voice squeaks as anxiety takes hold.

With all the stuff I have to sort through, there is no way I can wait two weeks.

Nick shrugs. "You can ask them to put a rush on it, but there are no promises."

I'm no more impressed with that answer than I am with any of the other HOA regulations. However, I'm in the suburbs now, and no matter how many times I click the heels of my red Rothy's together, I'm not going to end up back in my condo in the city, where no one cares what I do inside.

"Well, thank you," I say. "I really do appreciate your help."

"Are you *sure* you know how to get a dumpster?" Nick asks as he walks me back out through the garage.

"I mean, I don't exactly know." I glance at the time on my phone. "But I've got a lunch date with a guy who's a contractor, and I'm sure he will be happy to fill me in."

"A date?" Nick asks, sounding surprised, like he can't imagine anyone wanting to take me out.

That shock hits a little close to home. Karl spent too many of the last few years making me feel unattractive, and I snap back, "Yeah, a date. And if all goes well, we're going to come back here and have wild sex in my tall grass."

Then I march away, not bothering to check his reaction, not bothering to so much as glance back at him, even though I can feel his gaze following me all the way across the street just as Mikey pulls his big-dick truck into my driveway.

Chapter Seventeen

I go back in the house and grab my purse before locking up and hopping into Mikey's truck. If I finally glance at Nick's house and note his car is still in the driveway, well, it isn't because I care one way or the other.

Guilt-ridden that I was checking on another man while in Mikey's truck, I give him the brightest smile I can muster and compliment his ride. When his eyes twinkle, though, I realize I may have accidentally flashed him my fuck-I-love-cheesecake smile reserved only for those holy days I indulge in that wicked dessert, and I dial the wattage back.

It takes less than ten minutes to reach the diner and park, and soon we're out of the truck and heading into the restaurant. As I walk through the door, a powerful wave of contentment hits me square in the stomach. There are cracked red vinyl booths, a jukebox playing Motown music, and an oversize pie display case on the wide countertop. I love it all.

Mikey waves to a waitress by the cook station and leads me to a booth in the front vestibule. His face lights up as he slides into the booth opposite me. And if I was still wondering if this is a date-date, he leans back as if to take me in and murmurs, "You look beautiful."

Heat warms my cheeks. "You look pretty good yourself."

It's true. Plus, it isn't like I can just leave his compliment hanging in the air between us.

"Well, thank you." He grins, his brown eyes gleaming with appreciation. It's been a long time since a man looked at me like I was his dessert, and it feels good. Good enough to flash him my cheesecake smile again, in fact, and his grin widens.

I open the giant menu and focus on the rows and rows and rows of options.

"Anything look good?" Mikey asks.

I nod and point to a giant picture of a cookie milkshake. "How about you?"

He raises one brow. "Good idea, but I think I'm going to get a little wild and go for the grasshopper milkshake. It's been years since I've had it, but it used to be one of my favorites here."

"You're a big mint chocolate chip fan, huh?"

"To be fair, who isn't?" He shoots me a mock-censorious glare. "If you don't like mint chocolate chip, you should probably tell me now so we can call this irreconcilable differences and leave before any ice cream gets harmed in the process."

I laugh, because it's hard not to. He's goofy, sure, but also super charming in that funny-friend-of-your-brother's way. In other words, not my kind of charming. At least until the exorcism is complete.

"I have nothing against mint chocolate chip, I swear," I say with a flirty little flip of my hair. "We're in the clear."

"I'm glad to hear that," he says, and the look in his eyes becomes more intense than flirtatious.

It makes my heart catch in my throat—though not in any of the good ways you'd expect. More in a nervous, I'm-not-sure-I-want-to-do-this way. Or more, in a very-nervous, I'm-pretty-sure-I-don't-want-to-do-this way.

"You know I'm not divorced yet, right?" The words come out of their own volition, but when Mikey sits back, the intensity fading from his eyes, I can't say that I'm sorry.

"I figured," he says after several long, quiet seconds. "But divorces take time, and he's obviously not in the picture anymore."

"He's not." I exhale a deep breath. "But it's been a pretty brutal divorce—don't worry; I'm not going to bore you with any of the gory details—but I just felt like I should warn you."

He tilts his head like a sweet, adorable Lab puppy. "Warn me that you're not divorced yet?"

"Warn you that I'm not looking for anything yet—or more likely, ever. I'm pretty sure that part of me died somewhere between filing for divorce and negotiating for who gets to keep what." Or in my case, who gets to keep everything and who gets to keep nothing.

Not that I'm going to let that stand anymore—I am hiring a divorce attorney even if I need to sell all my plasma, and most of my blood, to do it. God knows, with the rates divorce attorneys charge per hour, one meeting would cost me nearly every drop of red blood cells I have.

"Yeah, well, you have to start somewhere, right?" This time, he is a lot less subtle when he reaches out and takes my hand in his, turning it palm-up so he can run a finger over the inside of my wrist.

I shudder involuntarily, and he winks at me. "See, that part of you is definitely not dead."

I don't have the heart to tell him it wasn't a good shudder or that I reacted that way because it's the same spot Karl used to touch me to signal he was horny. Some things dates don't need to know, especially not earnest dates who are doing their best to be nice.

So instead, I just shrug and murmur, "Maybe not."

The waitress comes to take our order before he can say any more. I order a milkshake and a cheeseburger. Mikey one-ups me by getting an order of fries to go with his burger and shake.

After the waitress leaves, he leans back on his side of the booth and teases, "You know, you're not the only one who had a history before we met."

"Oh yeah?" I lean forward, propping my forearms on the table. "Do tell."

"I've actually taken two women here for a first date. The first was Mary Katherine. She was my seventh-grade crush, and I was completely gaga over her curly blond hair and bright green eyes."

"I bet. Mary Katherine sounds like a looker."

"Oh, she was," he says, voice rich with amusement. "Absolutely."

"So how'd it go?"

He shakes his head, a mock frown on his face. "The first time, I crashed and burned. She broke my thirteen-year-old heart into a million pieces."

"That sucks," I say, trying not to giggle. "And the second time?"

"I'll tell you tomorrow." He gives me a cocky grin. "But it's looking good so far."

And that's it. I crack up. I just absolutely, positively crack up. Because— "Did you just *Top Gun* me?"

His grin grows wider, and the gleam in his eyes gets a little bit more wicked. "Maybe I did. Did it work?"

"I don't know." I sit back as the waitress delivers our food. "But so far, it's not looking terrible."

"I'll take that," he says, dipping one of his fries in ketchup.

I pick up my burger and dig in. Mikey is way too nice of a guy for his own good. Which is probably why I say yes to a second date—dinner this time—when he drives me back to my house and insists on walking me to my garage door.

This is the right move. I don't want to like assholes anymore. Been there, done that, and do not want the T-shirt or anything else, for that matter. Plus, it doesn't hurt that not-an-asshole Mikey is hot and built and younger than me.

Even if he does make me crack up all over again when he climbs back in his truck after dropping me off, then starts singing "You've Lost that Lovin' Feelin'" to me through his open window—except he changes the words so that it's more like, "You've Found that Lovin' Feelin'."

A couple of guys walking their dogs nearby join in—just like in *Top Gun*—and I am blushing and grinning like my teenage self by the time I finally walk inside.

My vaginal exorcism is off to an amazing start.

Chapter Eighteen

Am I still grinning a few hours later as the sun starts to set? I am, and I kinda like it, even if my cheeks are gonna be sore tomorrow.

No doubt my back is going to be aching, too, I figure, as I grab another one of the copious trash bags I have to haul to the curb, since tomorrow is trash day. While there is a part of me that's tempted to wait for the dumpster, I can still hear Nick's voice telling me it might be a whole month before I get approval. I am not okay with leaving them around the house or backyard until then—not when I still have so many more rooms and closets and trunks and boxes to clean out.

Fuck my life.

Sometime around trip twelve or thirteen—when I'm hot, sweaty, and red-faced—Nick pulls into his driveway again, except this time he actually parks in the garage. Home for the night, apparently, with a life about as exciting as mine.

I head up the driveway at as fast of a clip as my exhausted body can manage—no one needs to see me like this, least of all one of the most attractive (even if he is one of the grumpiest) men I've ever met. I know appearances aren't everything, but right now I look like I've been ridden hard and put away wet. Very wet, and not in a good way.

"Mallory!"

I freeze right there on the biggest crack in the driveway as

Nick yells my name a second time. Then reality hits that he wants to talk to me—looking like this—and I take off up the driveway at twice the speed. Almost to the door, almost to the door, almost—

"Mallory! I know you hear me!" Nick's voice rings with exasperation at the same time as his hand brushes my elbow. "What's going on?"

A zing works its way up my arm from where he touched me. "Oh, Nick!" I press a hand to my heart and lie my ass off. "You scared me! I didn't know you were there."

Also, how in the fuck did he move so fast? Is his mom a vampire?

The look he gives me says *bullshit*, and I brace myself for him to call me out on my lie. He doesn't, though. Instead, he takes a step back, and I realize two things. One, he looks really, really good in his black pinstripe suit—like, supermodel good. He must have changed into a different hot-guy suit after I saw him this afternoon. And for the first time in a very long time, I'm tempted to reach up and brush an errant lock of hair off a man's forehead.

I resist, partly because I don't want to explain to Nick why I'm petting back his hair and partly because there is no way I am going to let myself touch him in any manner. Not Nick, with his growly ways, surly attitude, and ass that defies description but makes me weak in the damn knees.

The second thing I realize, once I shake off whatever bizarre attack of formerly suppressed hormones almost crippled me just then, is that he's carrying a folder with my name on it.

"What's that?" I jerk my chin toward the folder with the same wariness I reserve for snakes and ex-husbands, which are basically the same thing.

"It's just a folder with the forms you need to fill out for the dumpster." He shrugs off my concern as if it doesn't matter, as if something with my name on it isn't my business. "Why?"

I shrink a little bit inside myself. "No reason, I just—"

Damn, why is it so easy to fall into old habits?

"Just what?" he asks when I don't finish my sentence.

"I don't have the best luck with folders." To put it very mildly. "Especially not when they're handed to me by a good-looking man in a suit."

That was pretty much how Karl had told me every ounce of bad news in our marriage.

Chapter Nineteen

For a second, Nick looks flummoxed. But then his face and his rigid posture relax, and he grins—really grins—for the first time since I met him. And holy cow, it is blinding in the best, most amazing way.

"So you think I'm good-looking?" he asks, and I roll my eyes. Hard. Why do gorgeous people always act surprised when someone notices their stellar gene pool?

"How'd you get the forms so fast? Were they already in the HOA Binder from Hell?" I groan. Leave it to me to ask for something that is right in front of my face.

"No, they weren't, but—" A sheepish look steals onto his face as he continues. "I'm on the board."

I'm not even remotely surprised. It definitely is one of those only-assholes-need-apply boards.

Not that I care. I'm just a homeowner who suddenly has the brilliant idea to bribe the HOA-whisperer-slash-board-member standing in front of me with a couple of glasses of one of Aunt Maggie's fancy French wines. It's shady as hell, sure, but it doesn't mean anything else. It isn't like I'm hitting on him, for God's sake. I'm just loosening him up a little and greasing the wheels to get my dumpster request approved so I can avoid any more citations.

My invitation has nothing to do with his knee-weakening smile and suddenly warm brown eyes and everything to do with avoiding more fees I can't afford.

Or at least that's my story, and I'm sticking to it.

"I'm opening a bottle of wine." I start back to the house. "You coming?" I toss over my shoulder.

"Yeah," he says with what sounds suspiciously like a deep, sexy chuckle. "I'm coming."

"So what has you all dressed up today?" I ask as he walks with me through the garage and into my kitchen. "I like your tie, by the way."

He glances down at his abstract, color-blocked tie in all different shades of blue and green like he's never seen it before. "Thanks. And I was in court."

"In court?" Earth's core? Meet my stomach. Stomach? Welcome to your new home. "You're an attorney?"

It comes out sounding like an accusation, but I can't help it. After being married to Karl for ten years, it feels like it *should* be an accusation. More, it feels like the mother of all red flags against Nick.

"I am," he answers warily. "A tax attorney, which means I spend most of my days in meetings and conference calls instead of actually in court, but today was one of the rare days. Why? Do you have something against my profession, too?"

"No, it's just—" I break off, because what am I going to say? *My ex is an attorney, and he soured me on lawyers for good*? I mean, I'd sound absurd, especially since this guy isn't exactly sending out the I-think-you're-sexy-too vibes. "Never mind." I tell myself I'm overreacting and force a smile I'm far from feeling. "What kind of wine do you like? White or red?"

Mercifully, he drops it. "Whatever you've got going."

I gesture for him to sit down at my aunt's surprisingly elegant patio table outside the sliding glass doors. "The house is still a disaster, so I thought we could sit out there, if you don't mind? It's a nice evening."

"Outside is great," he says, almost sounding like he means it.

"Awesome. I'll get the wine and meet you there." I pause. "Thanks, by the way. I appreciated the help earlier."

He nods, pulls open the sliding glass door, and steps outside. I flip on the patio light—it's nearly dusk, and I don't know how long the forms in that folder, and the wine drinking, will take. Then I rush to my room, splash water on my heated face, and wash off the remnants of my melting makeup in about one minute flat.

I don't bother changing, as the tank top and shorts I'm already wearing are light and cool, if not fancy; then I race back down to the kitchen. Once there, I put together a very quick cheese-and-fruit plate and grab a bottle of Argentinian Malbec from the stash I found in the hall closet. I pause just long enough to rinse two glasses from the still-inundated-with-clutter bar area, then swoop back outside in less than six minutes flat.

Now *that* should be an Olympic sport.

"Want to do the honors?" I extend the bottle opener to him.

"Of course." He stands up to take it, then reaches for the cheese tray. "You didn't have to do all this."

I throw him a sassy grin in an effort to disguise the discomfort I still feel over his chosen profession. "Sure I did. How else can I bribe you into accepting my dumpster request?"

"You don't have to bribe me," he says, all stiff and uptight again. "You just have to fill out the paperwork correctly—" His gaze lands on my face, and he breaks off mid-word. "You were joking."

"Only a little bit." I hand him the bottle of wine before setting the two glasses on the table between us and taking the seat opposite him.

He glances down at the label and smiles. "This was one of Maggie's favorites."

"We discovered it together in a little restaurant in the Village, but how did you know that?"

He gives an uncomfortable shrug. "She must have mentioned it sometime."

"And you remembered? From a passing conversation?" I narrow my gaze and look at him a little closer. "I don't think so."

Nick studies me for a few seconds, like he's trying to figure out what he wants to say. *Just like an attorney*, a little voice in the back of my head warns.

Or a guy who knows he said too much.

Neither is a particularly comforting thought, and I'm getting more and more upset, even though a part of me knows it's ridiculous. Who cares how he knows about Aunt Maggie's wine tastes? It isn't like it matters.

But it *does* matter. It matters to me that he can't answer a simple question. If that's the case, then I don't want him here drinking my wine, eating my cheese, or helping me with my goddamn dumpster request.

Something of what I'm feeling must be showing on my face, because Nick runs a resigned hand through his perfectly coiffed hair before he admits, "Maggie and I were friends."

"I'm sorry, what?" I don't know why, but that was the last thing I expected him to say. Maybe it's because Karl would have never gone out of his way to befriend an eccentric old lady. Hell, Karl would have never befriended an eccentric old lady even if she was *in* his way.

"We'd have dinner together once or twice a week."

For a second, his words make so little sense that I'm convinced he's speaking a foreign language. When they finally do sink in, I'm stunned.

"Wait a minute. You had dinner *here* twice a week?"

I think about the barely contained mess of the first floor versus the ruthless organization of his place and can't help but wonder how that could even be possible.

"Mostly we ate at my place," he says with a sad smile. "But Maggie always brought the wine and the dessert. Her brownies were the best."

"They *were* the best." The salted-caramel drizzle she always put on them was amazing. "And so was her lemon cake."

"God, yes." He lets out a lusty sigh that makes me shift in my seat. "I used to eat her lemon cake for breakfast for the next two or three days after she would make it. For lunch, too, sometimes."

Something about that admission makes him...more human. He seems to do everything exactly the right way according to the powers that be, but the fact that he ate cake for breakfast and lunch...I don't know. I guess it makes him feel more real in all the best ways.

I move over to the chair next to him and pour some of the now-open bottle of wine into both our glasses.

"You ever going to tell me why you were such a dick when we first met?" I ask. I really want to know, as I realize my first impression of him was very far from the person I'm getting to know.

He holds my gaze. "Why didn't you ever visit her, Mallory? You see now she had mental-health concerns. No one ever visited."

I swallow down the bile rising in my throat. Boy, he doesn't mess around, does he? I know I should be upset at the accusation, but honestly, I love the directness. I wonder, if Karl had been this direct, if I'd have risen to the challenge instead of constantly trying to anticipate how he was feeling, what he needed.

So I answer with equal directness. "Because I'm a terrible niece."

There. It can't be said more clearly. And oddly enough, I feel better admitting I let her down. My shame is in the open now, for all to see, and unlike my impending divorce with secrets tucked everywhere, it is liberating. I made a mistake, and I will regret it for the rest of my life—if not for the fact that I know Aunt Maggie would roll over in her grave if I don't forgive myself and move on.

But he deserves to hear the full truth first.

"She always insisted on meeting me in New York, said it was an adventure for her, and I thought nothing of it. And when I was younger, she said she loved leaving her house to come to ours." I shrug. "You're right, though; I should have visited her anyway. I should have known something was up. Suspected something." I wipe at my eyes. "She was my favorite person in the whole world, and I was too consumed with my own shit to see she was suffering. So yeah. I'm a terrible niece."

He doesn't interrupt me once, but as I wind down, he leans forward and places his large, warm hand over mine on the table. "I'm sorry."

My eyebrows shoot up. "Why are *you* apologizing? I was the one who neglected my aunt."

He leans back again, and his gaze softens. "Because I shouldn't have rushed to judgment. Because Maggie had an excellent sense of people, and she adored you. And worse, because I took her to several Hoarders Anonymous meetings, and the one thing everyone mentioned was the secrecy surrounding their compulsions. Of course you didn't know. Because Maggie didn't want you to, Mallory. And I should've realized that."

The wind rustles through the large elm tree above us as we sip our wine in silence, his words settling in my chest. I vow to spend some time tomorrow researching hoarding disorders. Just to feel closer to Aunt Maggie. She obviously felt she needed to keep a big part of her life hidden from me, and even though it's a little late, I want to show her memory that it's nothing to be ashamed of. That I would have understood.

"This is a huge undertaking," Nick says at last. "You shouldn't have to do it alone. I could come over and help a bit, if you want."

I shake my head. "I appreciate the offer, but I can do it on my own."

"She meant something to me, too, Mallory. It wouldn't be an imposition to help."

I shake my head again, my throat too tight to say more. But he seems to get it. I can't ask for help and now, with my history, I have trouble accepting it as well.

I glance at Nick under my lashes and can't help wondering if things had been different, if I had visited, if I had left Karl sooner, would we have become friends? Would we have taken Aunt Maggie to those meetings together? Would the three of us have shared a bottle of wine and laughed into the evening over a slice of lemon cake?

"Thank you," I say softly, reaching for a piece of cheese and nibbling on it.

"For what?" he asks, sounding genuinely surprised.

"For taking care of Aunt Maggie when I wasn't here."

Nick just shakes his head, though, and there is a genuine gentleness in his eyes. "It was no hardship and nothing to thank me for. Maggie took care of me at least as much as I took care of her."

I start to ask him what he means by that when my phone lights up with a text message from Karl—who, apparently, is pulling into my driveway right now.

Chapter Twenty

I can feel all the blood drain from my face even as my heart goes wild.

"What's wrong?" Nick asks, sounding alarmed as he leans over, as if to catch me if I suddenly faint.

"I'm fine." Okay, that's a lie, but I need it to be true.

I don't want to see Karl right now, don't want to have this argument with him before I even get the chance to hire a divorce attorney.

"You don't look fine." Nick reaches out and squeezes my hand.

"Yeah, well, what else is new?" Part of me just wants to ignore Karl—he came all this way without so much as texting me to see if I would be home, so why shouldn't I just hide back here and pretend that I'm out?

It's a good plan, except the last thing I need is for Karl—a very litigious attorney—to get hurt on my front porch. I'm barely keeping my head above water right now as it is. I can only imagine what it would be like trying to do that *and* fight off a lawsuit from my obnoxious almost-ex.

Mikey was right—I need to put some BEWARE/HAZARD signs up on the porch first thing tomorrow. Apparently, not actually expecting company isn't a good enough excuse anymore.

"Mallory," Nick says, his voice tight with concern. "What is it?"

"My ex is here," I say, partly to Nick and partly to myself so it can sink in and I can get control of my suddenly rampaging emotions.

"Here?" Nick's eyes narrow dangerously.

He looks annoyed—really annoyed—and I can't imagine why. I've never told him anything about Karl at all. Apparently, that doesn't stop him from being pissed off, which makes me wonder exactly what Aunt Maggie told him about my ex. God knows, she never liked Karl.

"Did he tell you he was coming?" Nick asks, already starting to get up from the table.

"No." Why start with not being a self-absorbed asshole now? "Then again, it might have just been a sudden impulse. Karl's never been very good at thinking about anything other than what he wants and when he wants it."

I take a deep breath and blow it out slowly as I text my almost-ex back that I'll be out in a minute—and not to walk on the damaged porch under any circumstances.

Karl's only response is to tell me to hurry up. God, how could I have ever been in love with that asshole? And how the hell could I have ever put up with his shit?

Anger replaces my nerves, and this time when I take a deep breath, it's not to center myself—it's to cool myself down.

"Do you want me to go?" Nick asks, looking like he is mentally already halfway around the house.

It's sweet in an I-don't-know-how-to-process-this way, but I don't want Nick to go. I don't want to give Karl any more control over my life—and how I spend an evening—than he already has. "No, of course not. I have a full bribing plan I need to get through." I force myself to smile, even though I'm afraid it turns out more like a grimace. "This shouldn't take long. He's just dropping off the divorce papers."

More like planning on browbeating me into signing them, but I'm not about to let that happen. I caved to that man entirely too many times during our married life. I don't have to do it anymore.

"In person?" Nick takes a step toward the yard and the paved walk that would take him to the front of the house, and I realize *again* that he is an attorney—of course he knows how unusual this is.

"It's fine." We both know it's anything but. I gesture toward the family room just inside the patio door. "Feel free to look through Aunt Maggie's vinyl and find some music to listen to while I'm gone. I'll be right back."

Nick doesn't look happy, but he doesn't contradict me. Instead, he sits back down and pours himself some more wine.

I can't help feeling grateful. No one else needs to see the mess that is the end of my marriage, especially not my totally hot, totally together neighbor who befriends old ladies and eats lemon cake for breakfast.

I hurry around to the side gate, as anxious as Karl to get this over with, though for very different reasons. He's standing in front of the garage, one of his ubiquitous folders in one hand and a pen in the other.

Because of course he is. The jerk really thinks he's going to force me to sign those papers tonight.

Then again, why wouldn't he? I gave him every single thing he ever asked for during our marriage. At first, I fought him over things I didn't want to do, but he'd argue so much that eventually I gave in. Every. Single. Time.

Then one day it wasn't even worth it to argue anymore. I just gave in without a fight, and I forgot what it was to expect—or even want—something for myself.

All that has changed now. Because I want this house, and I want this new life I'm starting to make. More, I *deserve* this new life—just like I deserve half of our marital assets. New York isn't a fifty-fifty-split state, but the law does say the assets must be split fairly between the two parties. Him getting everything and me getting nothing is definitely not fair.

I just need to remember that when Karl starts twisting things around to best serve himself.

"What are you doing here, Karl?" I demand as I walk up to him.

"Well, hello to you, too, Mallory. Charming as always." He looks me over, his expression disapproving.

That only makes me more annoyed. I am well aware that I'm not looking my best right now, but I was in the middle of cleaning out the house and hauling trash. Nobody dresses in designer clothes to do that. Nobody but Karl, anyway. Then again, he has never hauled a bag of trash in his life.

"I don't have to be charming to you," I shoot back. "We're getting a divorce."

"Yes, well, you never were that charming to begin with, were you?"

I grind my teeth together and remind myself that the courts will not look kindly on my petition for half the marital assets if I scratch his eyes out or knee him in the nuts as he so richly deserves.

"If you came all this way to make nasty comments to me, then you've wasted a trip." I turn to go. "I have a lot better things to do than listen to this."

"Wait!" he barks at me.

Even though a part of me has been conditioned to do exactly what he tells me to do, there is a bigger part that is entirely too pissed off to even consider it. So instead of waiting, I walk faster.

Karl hurries along behind me—something that I know really pisses him off. Well, too fucking bad, asshole.

Then he grabs my wrist and yanks me around to face him. "I told you to wait, Mallory." He launches each word at me like a slap. "I have something I want to discuss with you."

"Get your hands off me," I snarl. "Or I'm going to call the police and have you arrested for trespassing and assault."

His eyes widen like I surprised him—and maybe I did. God knows, the Mallory he used to know would never talk to him like that.

"Fine." He makes a little snort of disgust as he drops my wrist. "Just sign the divorce papers and I'll get out of here."

"I already told you I'm not going to do that."

"You don't have a choice," he growls, and suddenly his body language is a lot more threatening.

The thing is, I'm not about to let him threaten me. He's done enough of that to last a lifetime, and I'll scream the whole block down if he so much as touches me again.

"You can say that all you want," I reply, my voice low and quiet even as adrenaline slams through me. "That doesn't make it true."

I take a deep breath and straighten my shoulders, refusing to be cowed by the growing anger on his face. Fear and fury and a decade of repressing every emotion that could even maybe make someone feel uncomfortable builds like a tidal wave inside me.

"I dropped out of law school at your suggestion to help cover our bills and *your* tuition. Then I worked right alongside you to build *our* law practice. From the very beginning, I scrimped and saved and shopped all the auctions to find decent furniture for the firm on a shoestring budget. I spent the first couple of years cleaning the offices—on top of being office manager for a pittance—because you said we couldn't afford to have a janitor come in and clean for us."

"You think because you cleaned a toilet or two, you should be entitled to half of what I built?" He sneers.

"What *we* built."

Karl smooths his palm over his tie and shoots me a patronizing look. "Well, I'm sure that makes sense in your little fantasy world, but you're wrong on so many fronts. Just to take one example, the condo."

"Our home." The one I found, the one I cleaned, the one I made livable.

He shakes his head and speaks in a kind of overly polite and completely insincere tone as he looks around at Aunt Maggie's house, no doubt noting every crack in the sidewalk, chip in the paint, and barely-hanging-on roof shingle. "It's owned by the law firm and isn't a marital asset. The firm, as you'll recall, is mine. My name's on the door, not yours. You didn't even finish law school. The office manager doesn't get half. Maybe you should have finished getting your law degree."

The gaslighting bastard! "Someone had to pay our bills."

His lips curl upward in a know-it-all smirk. "So you admit you freely made your choice."

I'm still reeling from the callous narcissism of his response when I hear the door slam on Karl's beloved Aston Martin.

It's nearly dark, but he parked right beneath the streetlamp, so I can see Sasha perfectly as she gets out of the car. It's just un-freaking-believable. I can't believe his audacity in bringing his mistress here when he's trying to talk me into signing the divorce papers.

It's like waving a red flag in front of a bull, because every time I see her, all I can think about is the way our eyes met in his office that day. The triumphant look on her face as she put her hand on Karl's head and told him how to please her while she looked straight into my eyes. The bitch.

"Get out of here," I snarl at my ex, fed up with him and this entire conversation—not to mention the whole situation. "You can throw the biggest hissy fit in the world, and it won't matter. I'm not going to sign those papers until I hire an attorney and I get a fair settlement. I'm not walking away from the longest decade of my life with *nothing* to show for it. In fact—"

I break off on a gasp as Sasha turns to the side...her hand cupping her slightly rounded belly. She is directly under the streetlight, and its glow makes her obviously pregnant silhouette impossible to miss.

Chapter Twenty-One

*O*h my God.

Oh. My. God.

I've never been hit by a bus, but I imagine it would hurt less. Every part of me is in pain. My bones ache. My head pounds. My heart, oh my God, my chest feels like it's being crushed.

I blink a few times, praying that I'm seeing things, but when I glance back over at Sasha, she looks exactly the same. Breezy sundress, long blond hair, hand pressed against her round stomach.

"She's pregnant," I whisper before I can stop myself.

Pregnant.

Pregnant.

Pregnant.

The word reverberates in my head over and over and over again. Karl's mistress is pregnant. At least five months, by the look of her, too.

"I don't understand," I murmur. And I don't. At all.

I all but begged Karl for a baby for the last half of our marriage. He never wanted one, despite what he told me when we got married: that we just needed to wait.

One more year to get the practice off the ground, Mallory. We can't afford day care yet.

I'm so busy right now and so are you. We should build up the practice a little more first.

I don't have time to talk about this today. I've got to get to court.

There's plenty of time to have a baby. We can talk about it next year, when we have more time.

Next year.

Next year.

Next year.

He put me off dozens of times until I finally stopped asking. And now, we've been separated less than three months, and Sasha is pregnant?

Very, very pregnant from the look of her, actually, but I don't have the energy to consider what that means yet.

I knew he was low, knew he was narcissistic, thought there was nothing he could do to shock me. But apparently, I was naive, because right now, I am shaken to my very core.

The bastard. The unbelievable bastard.

My stomach churns, and suddenly I'm terrified that I'm going to throw up.

"What's there to understand?" Karl growls. "I love Sasha and she loves me. We're having a baby together, and both of us would really like for that baby to be born inside of wedlock. So if you could get over your little fit of hysteria and sign these papers, we can all just move on with our lives."

Once again, he shoves the folder with the divorce papers at me. I am so shaken that this time, I don't even think to refuse. I just take the folder and stare down at it blankly.

Karl sighs, like he's the one who is put upon in this situation, like my shock and heartsickness are major inconveniences for *him*. Then he clicks the pen open and holds it out to me. "Just sign the papers, Mallory, and we'll get out of your hair."

"Mallory's not signing anything without her attorney present." Nick's voice rings out loud and clear through the quiet night, and suddenly he's right next to me, trying to ease Karl's loathsome folder from my death grip. He turns to me and says more gently, "Hey, baby, give me this, okay?"

I know I should say something. I even *want* to say something—the last thing I want is to look pathetic in front of Nick. Or Karl. But as I glance back and forth between them, my brain is still reeling from shock and no words will form—at least no words that I'd want to say in front of Nick.

He must have gotten that, because suddenly his arm is around my shoulders, and he's pulling me into him, sheltering me against the solid, muscular strength of his body.

"Who are you?" Karl demands.

Nick raises an imperious brow at him, and it looks nothing like when he raises a brow at me. With me, it's amused if sometimes annoyed, but with Karl? With Karl, it looks an awful lot like a threat. Even more so when Nick squares his shoulders and pulls up to his full height—an impressive five inches taller than Karl.

"I'm pretty sure I should be asking you that question," Nick shoots back. "Since you are the one standing here, threatening my girlfriend, on *her* property. Which you should probably stop doing. Now."

"Your *girlfriend*?" Karl sounds as astonished as I feel.

He looks back and forth between the two of us while I all but melt with relief. I've looked pathetic entirely too many times in front of Karl and Sasha over the last few months, and I will be forever grateful to Nick for saving me from further humiliation right now, while my head is still spinning and my heart is still breaking.

Not over Karl, of course, but over the baby I wanted so badly and for so long.

"I'll have you know," Karl says, trying to stand taller than Nick but falling woefully short, "Mallory is my wife. I have every right to be here."

"No, you don't," Nick says. "Not after she's asked you to leave."

"Do you really want to get into a debate over the law with me?" Karl's eyes narrow. "I'm an attorney, and I assure you this is perfectly legal."

"Yeah, well, I'm an attorney, too—and apparently, a much better one than you, because I can assure you that you're wrong. And that you're trespassing, which is very much against the law. So"—he waves his hand in a dismissive gesture—"you can scurry on back to whatever hole you crawled out of now."

Karl's face turns so red that, for a second, I actually think he's going to have a stroke. Sasha must think so, too, because she comes awkwardly shuffling up the driveway toward him.

"I didn't know you were dating anyone," Karl says, accusation thick in every syllable.

"And I didn't know you were about to become a father." The words come out of nowhere before I have any idea that I'm going to say them. "Looks like there's a lot we don't know about each other anymore. Then again—" I shoot a look at Sasha, who is staring at Nick with her mouth open and more than a little avarice in her eyes. "That's always been the case. Hasn't it, Karl?"

My ex looks like he is about to explode, which—not going to lie—I would totally be here for. He'd make a big mess, of course, but it's a small price to pay for this whole nasty divorce business being over quickly. Plus, I'd get everything, and as I glance back over at Sasha's burgeoning belly, that feels about right at the moment.

"You don't actually expect me to believe you're an attorney, do you?" Karl spits out.

Nick looks more amused than insulted at the obvious cut. "I don't give a shit what you believe." He squeezes me tighter, his hand stroking up and down my arm in an obvious display of affection meant to make Karl even angrier. "Facts are facts. I'd say that Mallory has a type, except..." He trails off on a derisive little laugh as he looks Karl up and down.

Karl's hands fist at his sides, and alarm shoots through me. "You son of a bitch."

Nick gives him a look that practically dares him to take a swing at him. Even though I'm horrified at the idea, there's a small part of me that wouldn't mind seeing my ex arrested for assault—not because I actually want him to go to prison but because I am apparently vengeful enough to relish the thought of him being disbarred and losing the practice he all but worships. The law practice I worked so many long hours to help him build.

"Karl, let's go." Sasha's voice is high and grating, her eyes filled with fear as she looks between Nick and Karl.

Of course she's afraid—if Karl gets disbarred, she and her baby would lose their meal ticket, not that it's the baby's fault.

It's that thought that has me stepping forward, putting myself a little between Nick and Karl. Whatever else is going on here, the baby doesn't deserve to suffer for choices their parents made.

Nick growls a little at my movement even as his hands come up to rest—warm and secure—on my shoulders. I know this is all fake, that it's just a show for my ex, but I can't help leaning back into the strength and heat of him, just for a little while. It's been so long since I've had anyone to lean on.

"I'm not going anywhere," Karl snaps at Sasha. "Not until Mallory signs the fucking divorce papers."

"If that's the case, then you leave me no choice but to call the police," Nick says. "Because both Mallory and I have told you there's not a chance in hell that she's signing those papers without consulting her attorney. Not when New York and New Jersey are both no-fault divorce states that believe in a fair and equitable distribution of marital assets."

He drops his hands from my shoulders, and I have to force myself not to whimper at the loss. But then I realize the only reason he pulled away is because he has to reach for his wallet.

I step back again and watch as he takes a card out and offers it to Karl.

"I'm not Mallory's lawyer," he says. "But she is at my firm. I expect you to contact us by Wednesday with a full accounting of all marital assets—or I'm sure my partner will be more than happy to see you in court. And I think we both know that the judge won't look kindly on an adulterous ex trying to cheat his former wife out of her fair settlement just so he can pay for his pregnant mistress—a mistress who, by the looks of it, got pregnant before the separation even took place."

Nick puts his arm back around me—but this time, it's around my waist—and smiles down at me with twinkling eyes. "I hope this hasn't put you off dinner. I have plans for you later, and you're going to need all the energy you can get."

And I can't help the cheesecake smile I lay on him. Full wattage, no holds barred. How did he know Karl showing up with his pregnant mistress would make me feel undesirable? Like I'm not woman enough to satisfy my man or some other archaic feeling that I really shouldn't be having right now but am? The next words are out of my mouth before I can stop them. "I hope those plans include that wild thing you did with your tongue last time."

Like a switch has been flipped, the teasing glint in his eyes turns to molten lava in point-two seconds flat. As though he completely forgot Karl was even standing there, he leans down and whispers against my cheek, "You can count on it."

A shiver of anticipation skates along my skin as Nick pulls me tighter into his side and steers me back to the patio, Karl and Sasha dismissed.

"Looking forward to hearing from you," Nick tosses over his shoulder right before he opens the back gate and ushers me through.

Chapter Twenty-Two

As the gate closes behind us and I settle back into the hard metal patio chair, the loss of Nick's warmth and strength is immediate. The cold seeps into my bones so fast, I shiver.

There is a part of me that wants to ask Nick what the hell just happened. There is another, bigger part that knows I should thank him. But then there is the biggest part—the one that is still reeling from everything. Everything I just found out. And that part wins.

My shoulders sag in defeat. I wanted to be a mother my entire adult life. I mean, yes, for a long time, I also wanted to be an attorney, but even then I wanted to be a mom, too. A mom like my aunt Maggie would have been, not my own mom. Fun and loving and full of life.

All those years with Karl, I let that dream fall by the wayside because he seemed so sure he didn't want to start a family yet.

Except that was obviously not true. It wasn't that he didn't want kids; he just didn't want them with me.

Could I possibly, *possibly* have been a bigger fool? I really don't think so.

I am aware, in a very vague way, of something cold being pressed against my hand. I look down and am a little surprised to see my wineglass from earlier resting against my palm.

"Thank you." I don't know if I'm thanking him for standing up to Karl or for taking care of me or for handing me my wine.

Maybe all three.

Either way, Nick doesn't exactly seem inclined to ask me what I'm thanking him for. Instead, he just kind of nods before awkwardly sticking his hands in his suit pants pockets.

I can't believe this. I just can't believe this.

I know I should be grateful that I don't have a kid with Karl, that I don't have to try to co-parent through what looks like it's going to be an incredibly contentious divorce.

But I'll be grateful tomorrow. Tonight…tonight, I just want to grieve.

For what was and for what could have been if I'd just been a little bit stronger. If I'd just walked away all those years ago.

I gave away my youth, my hopes, my dreams to a man who would never appreciate the… I start to think *sacrifice*, but that isn't right. Because at the time, I didn't view it as a sacrifice. I willingly gave him everything he wanted, and when he didn't seem fulfilled, I gave him more. I convinced myself if I just kept giving, eventually he would be satisfied. Eventually, he would love me enough to fill the gaping hole in our marriage that I couldn't fill by myself.

"Mallory," Nick says, still standing beside the table and obviously unsure whether to sit or sprint home as fast as he can. "I don't know what to say."

I laugh, a strange, broken sound that makes my ears hurt. "Then we're even, because I don't know what to feel."

His big hand comes down on my shoulder. "What can I do?"

"You've already done far more than anyone else in my life ever has. Thank you." I let out a shaky breath that's already thick with unshed tears. "But right now, I need to soak my ovaries in wine. Alone."

Nick gives my shoulder a squeeze and nods. "Absolutely." But instead of walking out the gate, he walks into the house.

I know I should follow him, but I don't have the energy right now. I don't have the energy to talk, to think. Hell, if I'm honest,

I don't even have the energy to *be*. Keeping my heart beating and my lungs filled with oxygen seems like too much effort.

Nick comes back a minute later with another bottle of wine. He opens it in silence, then leaves it on the table next to me.

"I'm across the street if you need me."

I nod, even as I answer, "I won't."

"I know."

I close my eyes and rest my head on the edge of the table as I breathe. I just breathe.

I don't know how long I sit there like that, just trying to survive the pain and the regret ravaging my soul with razor-tipped claws.

Long enough for night to settle around me completely.

Long enough for the still-unfamiliar sounds of the neighborhood to quiet down.

More than long enough for the pain to change to ice-cold rage. Ice-cold resolve.

When I finally open my eyes and lift my head, Nick is long gone, just as I thought he would be. I reach for the glass of wine I poured a lifetime ago and drain it in one long gulp.

A lot of people might have condemned Nick for leaving me alone when I'm this messed up, but not me. It's been a lot of years since someone listened to a decision I made without questioning it or ignoring it. Nick not only listened to what I wanted, but he respected me enough to give it to me without question.

Right now, I think it's probably the nicest thing anyone has ever done for me.

Chapter Twenty-Three

I should have just drunk the damn wine. It's what a more rational person would have done, after all. They would have drunk themselves into bed and then fallen into a stupor. But oh no, not me. I sat in the backyard wallowing for a good half an hour. Then I just said fuck it. I wasted more than a decade of my life on that son of a bitch. I'm not wasting one second more.

And I've been cleaning ever since.

Because while I can choose not to waste my time getting drunk over him, I'm not quite evolved enough *not* to waste my time being pissed. And since I can't sleep with all that angry energy, I use it to clean the entire laundry room, top to bottom.

My back may never forgive me, but on the plus side, I can now wash—and dry—my clothes, something that was impossible before because, it turns out, my aunt stored her rice and pasta in the dryer. Because that's normal, right?

I finish hauling the last of the bags to the garage for the next monthly bulk pickup day—because my back totally needs the extra work—then promise myself the longest shower in existence *after* I fill out the HOA paperwork for the dumpster so I *never* have to do this again.

The paperwork isn't hard, just time-consuming, because of course they have to know every little detail down to the kind of garbage that will end up in the dumpster. It takes two cups of coffee to finish it. All I need is a picture of the driveway, and then I can upload everything via digital documents and send it on its way.

Thank God.

I am so tired that it takes me a good minute to remember where my camera is on my phone, and I'm just snapping the first photo when a call comes in. My mom's number pops up on the caller ID, and I let out a groan. No. Just no. After everything else I dealt with in the last twelve hours, there is no way I can deal with her, too.

I swipe Decline and head back inside, only to realize that my mom's voice—her shouting "Mallory! Mallory!"—is coming from my phone.

Damn it! I must have swiped Accept instead. All the bleach fumes have clearly gotten to me.

I'm so tempted to hang up and pretend that I have no idea she called, but it's too late. My mom has a special gift for torture, and if she thinks I am deliberately ignoring a phone call from her, she will absolutely find a way to make me suffer for a long time to come.

With that cheery little thought from hell in my head, I do the only thing I can do. I bring the phone to my ear and tell a fib. "Sorry, Mom. I dropped the phone. How are you?"

She sighs heavily. "You always were clumsy. It used to drive me to distraction when you were younger. I know it bothers Karl, too."

Yeah, well, Karl can trip and fall over every one of the no more fucks I have to give about that.

"Look, today's not really a great day to expect me to care what Karl thinks, Mom, so…"

"What happened?" she asks. "What did you do now?"

"What did *I* do?" I can't believe what she just said. "Are you serious?"

"Karl is an eminently practical man. If he's upset, it only stands to reason that you did something to upset him."

At this point, I should be worried that my eyebrows are going to merge with my hairline.

"You can't actually believe that, right?" I'm ready to hang up right now, but I just don't have the spoons to deal with the shit she'll heap on me if I do. "Don't you want to know what he did to upset *me*?"

She sighs, the sound loud and long-suffering, and it gets my back up like nothing else can. "What did he do, Mallory?"

"You mean besides get his girlfriend pregnant?" I say, dropping the news like a live grenade. "And from the size of her, he didn't even wait until I was out the door to do it."

My mother doesn't answer. In fact, she's silent for so long that I pull the phone away from my ear to make sure we weren't disconnected. She's still there, according to the call timer that just keeps ticking away. Still, she doesn't say anything. Finally, I break because I can't deal with the silence—one of her favorite torture techniques—anymore. "Mom?"

"Maybe if you apologized, Mallory."

"For what?" I nearly choke on the indignation that swells inside me. "He cheated on me, Mom. He got his girlfriend pregnant while we were still together. How is any of that my fault?"

She makes a *tut-tut* sound. "I'm not saying it's your fault. I'm simply saying that maybe if you took better care of yourself, none of this would have happened."

The fire of a thousand suns bursts out in my chest. What. The. Ever. Loving. Hell. "Maybe if I took better care—"

"I was always after you to let me take you to the spa with me," she says, her tone so calm it borders on creepy. "A man has the right to expect his wife to be well-groomed."

"I'm not a troll, Mother. I just didn't add blond streaks to my hair or wear fake nails."

"Or get facials to take care of your skin. And you almost never go to the gym—"

"Our building had a heated pool! I did laps three times a week."

She scoffs. "It's not the same as a good cardio workout."

"Oh my God!" I have to clench my fists to keep from tearing my hair out or throwing my phone across the room when I can't afford to replace it. "Swimming is literally one of the best cardio workouts there is. Plus, it uses every muscle in your body!"

"But it dries out your hair." She lowers her voice as if sharing the deepest secret. "And you know how yours likes to frizz at the best of times."

I am so tired that angry tears burn the backs of my eyes. I can't deal with this right now. I just can't. I've had to listen to these same I-just-want-to-help diatribes of advice ever since Karl and I broke up. It's almost like she considers my failure as a wife a personal slight against her parenting. And I just can't go there right now. Not without sleep and not with everything that's happened.

"I need to go, Mom. I've got—"

"Why do you keep insisting on running away from this conversation, Mallory?" She lets out a huff of disapproval and frustration—oh, I know that sound way too well. "I've been trying to talk to you ever since Karl left you, but you just won't listen."

"*I* left *him*! He didn't leave me, Mom. I left him after finding out he was cheating on me." I will not scream. I will not scream. I will not scream. "Doesn't that matter to you at all? Doesn't it matter more than whether I have frizzy hair or—"

"Of course it matters to me. He needs to apologize for what he did. But, Mallory, baby, marriage takes hard work. It requires sacrifice. Besides, you need him."

Those three words—the same three words Karl has thrown at me from the very start of our relationship—zap the air from my lungs. I nearly give up, nearly just let my mother prattle on, but then force myself to take a deep breath instead. Force myself to take back the air, and everything else Karl has stolen from me as I respond, "Yeah, well, maybe if I hadn't given him everything he'd ever wanted, he might not have taken me for granted. Ever think about that, Mom?"

She just continues. "Maybe if you wore more makeup or went to Victoria's Secret every once in a while…"

And I am done. Her suggesting I wear sexy lingerie to keep my husband from cheating on me is the last freaking straw. "Karl cheated on me because he is an asshole, Mom. He is an entitled douchebag who thinks the entire world owes him everything and that he can have everything—including a wife and a girlfriend at the same time."

"Yes, but—"

"No buts!" I cut her off for maybe the first time in all of recorded history. "Karl is the asshole here, Mom. Not me. *Him*. And all the makeup and sexy lingerie in the world won't change that fact. If you keep harping on me about it, I'm going to boycott makeup. And sexy lingerie—no, not just sexy lingerie but all lingerie. I will burn every freaking bra in my suitcase and throw away every lipstick I own. So for everyone's sake, you should probably just stop."

Whew. That felt *good*! Like first-day-of-summer-at-the-beach good or coming-home-and-ripping-off-my-bra good.

"Mallory!"

She sounds shocked, but I don't care. I'm tired of everyone in my life telling me that everything is my fault. I know I'm not perfect. I know I make mistakes. A part of me even acknowledges that I wasn't entirely blameless in the failure of my marriage. Still, everything that went wrong didn't happen because my fucking underwear wasn't sexy enough.

"I have to go, Mom. Someone's at the door." And then I hang up the phone before I can change my mind.

I am so annoyed that I end up eating my weight in Oreo cookies before going upstairs and taking a shower, where I do everything I can to scrub and exfoliate my frustrations away.

I don't get it. I just don't get it. Why is my mom so hung up on me going back to Karl?

I mean, I get that our family doesn't believe in divorce, but come on. Does that mean our family believes in cheating? Talk about a bastardization of decency or normalcy.

Does she really want me to stay with him and be miserable, knowing that I can't trust him? Knowing that he's out there fucking other women? Knowing that he has at least one child—if not more—out in the world while I stay home, longing for my own baby? A baby I will never ask him for now and that he wouldn't give me if I did?

It's absurd. More, it's hurtful. Really, really hurtful.

I know my mom and dad are all about appearances, but I always assumed there was some substance underneath it. Now I'm finding out that there really is no substance. There is just them caring so much about me not having the stigma of divorce attached to their name—like there is even a fucking stigma around it anymore—that they want me to be miserable for the next forty or fifty years of my life.

I'd rather scrub toilets with my toothbrush.

I'd rather sleep in that damn pink canopy bed forever than go back to Karl for one more second.

I'd rather be alone for the rest of my life than lay awake at night, staring at the ceiling, wondering where he is and who he's with.

I just don't know how to get my mom to understand that.

I dry off quickly, tying my hair up in a topknot so it doesn't get my pajamas all wet while I get dressed.

Mom hasn't always been like this. There was a time when she would have torn apart anyone who broke her baby's heart. A time when she would have taken me out for pancakes and trash-talked with the best of them about whoever had hurt me.

I know when that changed, but I don't know why. The

second I got old enough for boys to be interested in me—and for me to be interested in boys—her attitude shifted. Suddenly, it was all about me making sure not to rock the boat, making sure not to upset the boy in my life, making sure not to stand up for myself if it meant disrupting my relationship. Not just with Karl but with every guy I've ever been the least bit serious about.

As I climb into bed, sliding between the cool cotton sheets, I put thoughts of my mother and her bizarre behavior out of my head. After all, it's been going on for nearly twenty years, and there is no reason to think it'll stop now.

Besides, I have more important things to think about when I wake up. Like how to thank Nick for stepping in with Karl tonight. And where the hell I'm going to get the money to sue my ex, as Nick all but promised I would.

Chapter Twenty-Four

I manage to wake up around three o'clock in the afternoon, sunlight be damned, to the to the sound of my doorbell ringing over and over again.

I'm tempted to ignore it—I'm not expecting anyone, and after my last surprise guest, I'm not in any hurry to see who's out there. But just as I start to drift back to sleep, I remember. The porch!

I jump out of bed and go racing down the stairs as my phone starts to ring and Dad's photo pops up on the screen. "Sorry, Dad, I can't talk right now. I have to—"

"I'm downstairs, Mallory, and I know you're here," he says. "Please come—" He breaks off as I throw open the door.

"Come in!" I all but pull him off the porch. "You shouldn't be out there! I haven't had a chance to have the porch repaired yet—"

"Don't you mean you don't have the money to have it repaired?" he asks as he casts a disapproving look at my pajamas.

"Well, yeah, that too." I turn and head toward the kitchen, happy that I at least have the family room and kitchen done, so that—as long as I keep him in this part of the house—he won't be able to speak badly of Aunt Maggie.

"Has it occurred to you to get a job?" He follows me toward the kitchen. "Since money is such a problem for you?"

I clench my jaw. As if looking for a job isn't exactly what I've spent the last several months trying to do. Up until I inherited Aunt Maggie's house, I was doing nothing but circulating my résumé, trying to get a bite.

"Yes, Dad. I'm looking for a job." And if something doesn't come along in the next couple of weeks, I'm going to forget about office managing and put my name in at a few temp agencies for office workers. The pay will suck, I'm sure, but something is better than nothing. I just need to get Aunt Maggie's house in any kind of decent shape first. And by decent, I mean livable.

"By sleeping until three in the afternoon?" He settles himself at the head of the kitchen table.

Counting to infinity, I walk straight to the coffee maker and start brewing a pot. Silence reigns in the kitchen for a couple of minutes, which is so unusual for him that I can't help glancing behind me to see what's up. I barely stop myself from snickering when I see him staring in horror at Aunt Maggie's canisters—particularly the ones marked QUAALUDES and GANJA.

I'm tempted to offer him a gummy bear—he definitely looks like he needs to relax—but I'm not up for the fight that would probably ensue.

"Your addition?" he asks when he catches me looking.

"Oh, yes. Definitely. I have so much extra money to toss around that I decided to spend it on a thousand dollars' worth of canisters." Yes, I looked them up. And yes, they really do cost more than a hundred dollars each.

He shakes his head. "My aunt always did have her problems."

"Maybe so, but being a drug addict wasn't one of them, Dad."

He harrumphs his disagreement. Or maybe it's his disapproval. Since I announced my divorce from Karl, it's gotten harder and harder to tell the difference between the two.

The coffeepot starts brewing. "Do you want a cup?"

He looks around the kitchen. "Do you have something stronger?"

"Stronger?" I lift a brow in mock surprise. "At three o'clock in the afternoon, Dad?"

He shrugs but doesn't say anything else.

I don't have any hard liquor, and I haven't found Aunt Maggie's stash yet—if she had one—so I grab one of the open wine bottles from last night and pour him a glass.

"Thank you." He grabs the glass like it's a lifeline and takes a deep sip. Then he sighs and looks around the room. "I hadn't realized things had gotten this bad."

"What things?" If my mom told him about Sasha being pregnant, I really don't want to talk about it. I don't even want to think about it—not now. Not until I absolutely have to.

"With Aunt Maggie." He gets a pinched look around his eyes, and the muscle in his jaw twitches. "The house is a disaster."

I have no clue what to say to that. If he thinks this is a disaster, I can only imagine what he would have thought if he saw the place a couple of days ago—or the upstairs right now.

"I saw all the bags down at the curb," he continues. "My parents used to talk about Maggie's tendency to 'collect' things, but it wasn't until I was much older that I understood what that meant. She did so well for so long, I hadn't realized she'd fallen back into her old habits."

He turns his face away from me, his lips pursed together, and if it hadn't been broad daylight, I never would have believed for a second that the man's cheek was wet before I watch him wipe the single tear away.

"I should have checked on her more," he admits.

I plop down into the chair next to Dad's, my knees no longer willing to hold me up with the sudden and totally out-of-character reveal.

"She was always something. I mean, I didn't understand her. Ever. She was flighty and wild and more than a little bit of everything a Martin shouldn't be, but I couldn't help but be amazed by her. She never did what was expected." He drains the rest of the wineglass in one gulp. "The last thing I would have expected was for her to leave you the house. I guess that's why I should have expected she'd do it. She always did love cheering on the underdog."

Wow. Okay, that hurts even if it's true.

But where Dad saw a flighty woman who didn't meet expectations, I saw a woman who bowed to no one. Ever.

Dad twirls the glass around on the table. I figure he's thinking about Aunt Maggie some more, and I stand up to get more coffee and give him a little bit of time to collect his thoughts.

But then he totally surprises me by asking, "Why didn't you tell me you hired some law firm to represent you in the divorce?"

"How do you know that? I haven't told anyone." I whirl around, shocked, until it dawns on me. "You talked to Karl."

"He *is* my son-in-law, you know."

"Your soon-to-be-ex-son-in-law," I shoot back, wondering how coffee would taste with a wine chaser.

"My soon-to-be-ex-son-in-law," he repeats, sounding defeated. "I just can't figure out why you wouldn't ask my firm to represent you once you decided you really wanted to go through with the divorce."

"Dad, I decided I wanted to go through with the divorce the moment I found out Karl was cheating on me. I can't live like that."

"Maybe so." Somehow, he looks even more pained. "But I wish you'd come to me, to my firm."

"I didn't think you'd want to represent me."

More, I don't want him to represent me. One, because I don't want to mix my family up in this any more than they already are. And two—and this is the kicker—after everything he and my mom said about Karl and me, I don't actually trust him to represent my best interests—not once Karl starts spinning tales about how hard he worked to establish the firm and how most of it should thus, rightfully, belong to him.

"I'm still your father, you know."

There is a wealth of emotions in those words and at a different time, I might want to explore them and what they mean. But that isn't today. I'm just too exhausted. Everything that happened over the past couple of days has taken the last of my emotional strength, and I don't have anything left for the complicated mess that is my relationship with my parents.

Someday, I will talk to my dad about everything that happened since I told them that I was leaving Karl. But someday is definitely not today. Not even close.

"I know." I drop a kiss on the top of his head.

And then I change the subject to lighter things.

We talk for a few more minutes, and then my dad pushes back from the table. "If you're in a pinch, I can hire you at the firm. You can be an assistant office manager—I know it's a step down from what you were doing for Karl, but we've got Lottie, who handles all the big managerial tasks. Still, we can always use—"

"No, Dad," I say firmly, even as I take his hand in mine.

Going from Karl to my dad feels like a definite step backward, and I can't do that right now, not if I want to be able to keep looking at myself in the mirror. Not if I want to keep telling myself that I really am moving forward.

"There might be a time when I have to take you up on that offer. I hope there isn't, but I'm realistic enough to admit that there might be," I say. "But I'm not there yet. I appreciate the offer—and no matter what happens, I will always appreciate it. But I've got this."

He looks around the kitchen, which is now clean but still needs a good coat of paint and probably a new floor.

"You've got this?" he asks doubtfully.

"I do."

And as I say the words, it hits me. *I do have this.* Somehow, some way, I'll figure things out—with Karl, with the house, with myself.

It's gonna take a while, but the best things always do. Besides, who cares? Right now, it feels like I have nothing but time.

Chapter Twenty-Five

I walk my dad out through the backyard—no way am I letting him on that death trap of a porch again—then sit down at the patio table and try to figure out what I want to do next.

I could go over to see Nick, but I figure he isn't home from work yet.

I could spend some more time going through my aunt's photo cabinets so I can finish up the family room once and for all.

Or I could pick a random room and start going through it—God knows, there are way too many left to do.

In the end, though, I decide to start with a late lunch—avocado toast and a sparkling water consumed over the sink. Then I snap the pictures of the HOA dumpster request forms that I meant to handle last night when my mom called. It takes a few minutes, but I finally get all the HOA documents submitted.

Now all I can do is wait.

With nothing left but to procrastinate from the real work inside, I decide to skip the pictures in the cabinet—I'd rather do them when I have the time and can actually enjoy sorting through them instead of just trying to sift all the clutter out of the boxes. That means only one thing: it's time to start on the dining room.

The table is big enough for ten, even without the leaf, and has several boxes of stuff at either end. That won't take that long to go through. I do a tight spin because of the many shoeboxes on the floor and give a hard look to the china cabinet that is completely full of Wedgwood and another cabinet half full with Mottahedeh I spotted years ago at Neiman Marcus. Knowing Aunt Maggie as I feel I do not, I figure it isn't just china inside the cabinets. There's probably a Costco-size amount of tropical drink umbrellas or something, too.

After grabbing a box of trash bags from the newly cleaned shelves in the laundry room, I pick out one of my aunt's albums at random and put it on. Jim Croce's voice fills the house with its folksy calm.

Aunt Maggie loved this album. Not as much as she loved the Beatles, but it was a pretty close second. Right up there with Johnny Cash's *Man in Black* and ABBA's *Super Trouper*.

As "Bad, Bad Leroy Brown" pours out of the stereo, I bite the bullet and open up the first china-cabinet door. Then I close it and weigh the option of selling the china on eBay and throwing the rest of the cabinet and the untold number of toothpick boxes, drink stirrers, and purloined diner sugar packets into the dumpster when it gets here.

Still, there have been important papers and other things in every single cabinet I've sorted through—except the chopsticks cabinet—and the chances are that behind everything else, there are documents stuffed in the back, so tossing it all is not really a viable option. Plus, I love this dining set with its wild swirls and curved edges, and the thought of throwing it away makes me sad.

Which means no more whining. It's time to get to work.

I clean all the way through the first half of the album, then pause just long enough to grab a glass of water and switch sides on the record before diving back in.

I've just finished the first cabinet and am about to start on the second when there's a loud knock on my back door. It startles me, and I let out a little shriek before peeking my head around the corner.

Surprisingly, and yet not, Nick stands there. As I walk down the hall to the door, he gives me an impatient look, which seems a little out of place. He's the one standing in my backyard, after all.

"What's up?" I ask as I slide the back door open.

"I figured I'd pick up the dumpster forms."

Awww, that is really...hot? Kind? Sexy? Neighborly. I settled on neighborly. "Thank you, but I already emailed them in."

He nods and walks inside and to the family room, his eyes going immediately to Aunt Maggie's record collection. "Well, then we can focus on your case."

Distracted by the way he looks with the top button of his crisp white shirt undone and his tie hanging loose, I miss most of his words except that last one. "My what?"

"Your case." He pulls his tie free, rolls it up, and sticks it into his suit jacket pocket. "Remember that slimy little shithead in your driveway, the one you're going to take for every penny you deserve? One of the attorneys at the firm specializes in divorce and would like to meet with you."

My case. Divorce. Driveway. My body pressed up against Nick's. The way his steady heartbeat and strong hands felt against me. The fact that I spent last night dreaming about him shirtless and pantsless and— *Oh my God, Mallory. Be in the moment.*

Inner me is a joy sucker, but she's right. The last thing in the world I need right now is another man—and an attorney, no less—in my life telling me what to do and how to do it. Plus, there is the little issue of M.O.N.E.Y.

"Look, Nick," I say as I move in front of him and stand there clasping my hands together, because I don't trust myself with where my thoughts keep going. "I really appreciate your help, but there's just no way I can afford the fees your kind of practice probably charges. I've seen the car you drive, and the art on your living room wall wasn't a lithograph—it was the real thing."

He scowls at me while taking off his suit jacket and laying it over the back of a chair. Then he continues to do so as he rolls up the sleeves of his shirt like he's doing a striptease but only of his forearms. By the time he's done, I have no clue if he's still glaring because I'm staring at his perfect sinewy forearms.

"Give me a dollar," he says and holds out a hand, palm up.

Sure, a tip is reasonable—and wait, what? "Why?"

"Because then you will have paid our firm the going rate for neighbors who pet my plants—speaking of green things, you'll have to mow your lawn, too. Do that and consider your retainer paid."

I don't believe him but walk over to the couch and grab my purse off the cushion anyway. "My lawn mower is trapped behind a zillion old magazines stacked almost all the way up to the garage ceiling, remember?"

"So you can use mine." He crosses the room and stands next to me. "Do we have a deal?"

I get it. The grass is long enough that a toddler could get lost in it. The time has come. Ugh. I hate that Mr. Green Grass Police is right.

I scrounge around in my handbag until I hit pay dirt—a single crumpled-up dollar bill.

"Deal." I give him the cash. "I'll get to it this week."

"So does Thursday work for you to meet with the attorney to discuss next steps and give background on that numbnut?" he asks.

"Sure. I hope they have a free afternoon. There's a lot of background."

"Don't worry." He places his hand on the small of my back. He doesn't try to guide me away from the couch; it's just the weight of his palm against me, like a transfer of power. "Don't worry about a thing."

"Like that's possible." The idea of it is so ridiculous, I start pacing from one wood-paneled wall to the other. "I'm barely able to afford the dumpster the HOA better approve, I owe a ton of back property taxes, I have to come up with more than $120,000 for the inheritance tax, and even if I shake the couch cushions in hopes of finding enough to cover home repairs, I still haven't been able to find a job." I wrap my arms around my middle and keep marching one way and then the other. "And why is that? Because I've spent my entire adult working life dedicated to making sure Karl's practice became a success. I worked seventy-hour weeks for minimum wage because he said the practice needed the money more to continue to grow—but I have my doubts now." I take a deep breath and look Nick square in the eyes. "Really, does it make sense to you that the firm would own our condo? It doesn't, does it?" It's like a series of lightbulbs is going off in my head, illuminating just how screwed I am. "Oh my God, what was I thinking?"

By the time I'm done, I'm out of breath, my hands are shaky, and I have a million more thoughts going a gazillion different directions. Nick? Not so much. There isn't even a flicker of emotion or panic or freaking the fuck outness on his too-handsome-for-real-life face.

"So you need a job?" he asks. That's what he wants to focus on? Not the fact that I've been such a child with my finances?

"Yeah, that would be a good start."

He nods. "And you have experience as a law firm office manager?"

"Eleven years' worth." Working at not even close to my value. The frustration of it all has me pacing again, right back to the couch and next to Mr. Lotsa Plants.

"Give me until Thursday," he says. "I think I have a lead on the job situation."

Something unfamiliar and bubbly fills my chest. It's been about a million years since I felt it, but the old-old Mallory, the teenage one who spent way too many nights staring at her canopy and dreaming of her future, recognizes it right away.

Hope.

"Why are you doing this?" I ask, wariness seeping in.

He pivots, the move bringing us face-to-face. Okay, more like my face to his top button—did I mention it's undone?

"I like to help," he says.

"Says who?" I scoff, trying to distract myself from the shadow of chest hair I can almost see. "Your mom?"

He hooks a finger under my chin and tilts my face upward. "Are you trying to imply that my mother would lie?"

"Maybe." Not really. I don't know. Wow, are his eyes gorgeous and intense and pulling me right in.

"At this moment, my mom is somewhere laughing her head off and she doesn't know why." He pauses, his gaze searching my face as if he's trying to figure out why he can't look away. "She's gonna love you."

"What, you want to introduce me to your mom? Does she have a grass obsession, too?" Oh yeah, immature jokes in the face of uncomfortable feelings. Classic Mallory.

God, inner me is such a bitch sometimes.

His thumb traces the line of my jaw. "You do love to give me a lot of crap for following the rules, don't you?"

"I've committed the rest of my life to a no-bullshit-rules mantra." I try to make it come out all cocky and confident, but even to my own ears, it's all soft and breathy and take-me-now. "I'm the new Aunt Maggie."

"Funny," he says, taking a step forward and eliminating any space between us. "You don't look a thing like her."

"That's a lie; we have the same eyes and the same Martin family mouth." One that I, all of a sudden, have no idea how to keep quiet.

"I can assure you that you do not, because I never wanted to…" His words fade away as he dips his head lower.

My breath catches.

My brain checks out.

My hormones give a loud cheer.

And then—he pulls away, dropping his hands to his sides and taking a quick step back. He rubs his palm across his neck and works his jaw back and forth. "Anyway, I gotta go."

He leaves without another word, and what in the hell am I supposed to say after that? I have nothing besides yearning. My phone vibrates on the dining room table—a text from Mikey asking me if we're still on for dinner. I can't type *yes* fast enough. This is exactly what I need.

Being near my h-o-t contractor is perfect, because unlike with my uptight neighbor (and much to Angela's disappointment, no doubt), I do not want anything more from him than a new porch.

There. Man situation sorted. Now, if I can just figure out the job situation, the house situation, and the tax situation, everything in my life will be perfect. And I almost believe it.

Chapter Twenty-Six

A boycott on makeup seems like a not-so-great idea, I decide a few days later as I stare at myself in the bathroom mirror—especially after another nearly sleepless night.

I didn't get it. Early-morning wakeups notwithstanding, I'd been sleeping like a baby since I got here—despite the towering amount of crap I have to sort through, the repairs I have to get done, and the no-money situation. Something about being in this house just felt freeing and made me conk out as peacefully now as I did as a kid.

Until the last two nights, when I tossed and turned for hours.

Yeah, sexual frustration will do that to a girl.

"I was not sexually frustrated," I say aloud and then slick a soft rose lip gloss on my lips. I mean, yeah, Nick and I almost kissed last night, but we didn't. And when he pulled away, I didn't care at all. Would I have done that if I were sexually frustrated?

Well, yes, if you are sexually frustrated and *a chicken. What a catch.*

Oh my God. I close my eyes and barely resist banging my head against the mirror. Inner voices are not supposed to have this much snark. There should be a rule.

I finish putting on my makeup, then dress in real clothes for the first time since my lunch date with Mikey. And unlike with Mikey, this time I bust out the real shoes—a pair of black heels that, when I combine them with my favorite black dress pants, make my legs look really long.

It isn't that I'm trying to impress anyone. Law offices have a certain dress code. I can't just show up at Nick's place of work looking like a total slob, especially when he's offered his firm up to do this whole thing pro bono for me—no, the squashed-up dollar and lawn I eventually have to mow anyway don't count. I need to project the right attitude.

Half an hour later, I'm standing in the middle of the reception area at Holloway and Murphy, wondering why I even bothered. Nothing here is projecting professionalism, save the heavy desks and giant floor-to-ceiling bookcases covered with law books.

The only person I've seen so far is the receptionist, who has green-and-purple hair, an addiction to her AirPods, and absolutely no knowledge of how to deal with clients.

"Oh, right." She gives me an enthusiastic nod that sets the fifty or so bells she has tied into various locks of her hair jangling. "You're Nick's eleven o'clock. I'll take you right back."

"He's not with a client?" I ask, surprised. It's only ten forty-five, and the whole reason I came early today is because Nick texted that he could squeeze me in around his other clients for the day at eleven; then I'd meet with his partner, Gina, who'd actually represent me. I didn't want to keep him waiting when he was obviously doing me a favor.

Maybe his last appointment ended early. It's possible. AirPod Girl escorts me down a long, lawyerly looking hallway with warm wood paneling, gorgeous landscape paintings of calm meadows, and bookshelves lined with more law books—and an abundance of plants, very similar to Nick's house.

It's not what I expect out of a law firm, but I like it. It has a warmer, more serious feel than Karl's slick, flashy offices, and I can't help feeling at home here. My shoulders, and the rest of me, relax amid the deliberately soothing decor.

We wind our way past a pretty impressive-looking conference room, as well as an office with what looks like a couple of paralegals in it. I grow more confident in Nick and his firm's representation. Except for the less-than-with-it receptionist, everything else looks spot-on.

"Hey, Nick!" The receptionist throws his office door open with abandon. "Your eleven o'clock is here."

Nick whips his head up from the document he was studying on his desk. A man in a crumpled suit across from him—obviously a client—shrinks back into his chair, his eyes wide and looking from one possible exit to the other.

"I'm so sorry." I grab the doorknob and start to pull it closed.

The last thing I hear before I shut the door is the client complaining about a deadline being missed and the need for a restraining order. He looked completely worried and pissed off. The last thing Nick needs is for the two of us barging in on the obviously already tense meeting.

I turn to AirPod Girl with raised brows, but she is already bebopping her way down the hall.

"Is there a place to put together a cup of coffee here?" I ask her retreating form.

She shrugs and says over her shoulder without breaking her stride, "There's an employee break room down the other hall."

"Show me."

Something in the iron tenor of my voice must get through, because she backpedals and walks me to the break room. In less than five minutes, I have a tray put together with a pot of coffee, some cream and sugar, and a small plate of what looks to be homemade peanut butter cookies. I do all this completely on my own, as AirPod Girl grows bored the second I reach for a coffee mug.

There are ten minutes left before my appointment when I knock on Nick's door again.

"Come in," comes his slightly aggrieved response.

"I'm sorry to bother you," I say as I carry the tray in and place it on the top of Nick's neat credenza. "I just wanted to offer you a cup of coffee. Light and sweet?" I ask the client.

"Just sweet," he says, sounding a lot happier than a few minutes ago.

I fix him his coffee, set a couple of the cookies on a plate, and hand them both to him. "I'm so sorry for the interruption earlier. Usually the office runs like a well-oiled machine, but it's been a busy morning."

"We're having a few hiccups," Nick jumps in. "Our office manager went into labor last Friday—a few weeks early—and since Viola is indispensable around here, we're all trying to play catch-up. But I can assure you, everything is under control, and we'll have the final forms for you to sign next week."

"We'll courier them to your home or office, so you don't need to come back," I add as I walk toward the door. "Just let us know where you'd like them sent."

Twenty minutes later, Nick walks his much happier client to the reception area. The man even grins at me on his way out the door.

Nick, on the other hand, looks positively frazzled now that his client is gone. "I'm sorry that took so long," he says as he ushers me back to his office.

"Don't worry about it. I was early," I say, while most definitely not noticing how good he looks in his suit.

It's charcoal gray, and he's wearing it with a black shirt that really sets off his dark eyes. Plus, he smells fantastic—not that I'm sniffing him or anything, but still. He smells really, really good—like bergamot and everything crisp and sexy and male.

I ignore the thought, and his scent, and push both to the back of my head—which is easier said than done. "I'm sorry we interrupted when we did."

"Not a problem." He waves my concerns away with a grin. "Vic is just an old curmudgeon who likes to be pampered a little bit. Viola always got him coffee, too, and he seemed a little disconcerted that no one was around to do that for him today. I should have offered, but I didn't think about it until you brought in the tray. Thank you for stepping up like that."

"Of course. Anything I can do to help." I wait until we're back in his office with the door closed before I continue. "Speaking of which, no offense to your super-helpful receptionist, but you look like you could use some temporary help around here. Lucky for you, I know a very competent office manager looking for work."

Chapter Twenty-Seven

"Well, about that," Nick starts as he pulls his desk chair out and sits down, motioning for me to take the seat across from him.

I don't give him time to say no. "I *am* overqualified for the position, considering I've been doing it for pretty much my entire life," I say, keeping my tone breezy even as my heart starts to beat faster with excitement and fear.

This could be the answer to my prayers, at least for a little while.

"Besides, I owe you one, don't I?" I lean forward, giving him the full weight of my detail-oriented attention. "Considering you offered to represent me for a dollar and a mowed lawn?"

His face gets that pinched look that takes it from worried to truly concerned. "So you're volunteering to work here for free?"

Part of me thinks I should—legal representation adds up to the thousands or even tens of thousands very quickly—but I don't have that luxury right now. I have a massive property tax bill along with a scary renovation looming over my head. Plus, the sad fact that a person can't live on wine alone.

"I was thinking more along the lines of we meet in the middle."

"The middle?" he repeats, brows raised.

"How much do you normally pay Viola for this position?" I brace myself for a number even less than what Karl paid me.

Even though I knew I wasn't paid my full wage, his law firm was a lot bigger than Nick's, with larger clients than a simple family law firm would have.

"Eighty-four thousand dollars."

I nearly choke on my own tongue.

"Eighty-four *thousand*? I can't work for that!"

I collapse back against the chair, all my airy coolness gone. I couldn't have heard him right. Karl paid me thirty thousand a year. In Manhattan!

Nick grimaces, toying with one of the royal-blue fountain pens on his desk. "Fine. You drive a hard bargain. I can't pay you more than Viola; that just wouldn't be right. But I can pay you the same salary. I can even throw in helping sort through Maggie's belongings a few hours a week to sweeten the deal."

My eyes widen. "I wasn't asking for *more* money, Nick." This is going to be embarrassing to admit, but he'll find out anyway when we start discussing the details of my case. I take a deep breath and woman up, laying it all out there. "Look, Karl never paid me more than fifteen dollars an hour. Granted, I managed the office of his successful law firm with fifteen associates for ten years, so I know I'm a valuable asset, but jumping up to forty dollars an hour just doesn't seem fair to you. I'm obviously willing to work for less, and we both know it."

Nick's jaw clenches as he stares over my shoulder for a minute. Then nods. "You're right. You're worth more than Viola; you have more experience. I'm sorry—I just really don't think I can afford someone as qualified as you."

Wait, what just happened? "But I explained, I'm willing to work for less." Shit. I really need this job.

But Nick shakes his head. "I can't in good conscience pay you less than you deserve, Mallory. I wouldn't feel comfortable with my firm's integrity if I did."

I roll my eyes at him. "If you're going to insist on paying me what I'm worth, you should help clean every day. Plus at least four hours on the weekends. And lift all the heavy stuff. Oh, and definitely find what died in the kitchen and take it out." I'm on a roll. "Honestly, that means a lot of shared meals, too, so you should probably provide dinner at least every other night as well." I raise one brow at him in defiance. "Or you could negotiate like a civilized person and we could—"

Nick interrupts. "Deal." Then he leans forward and holds out his hand.

I place my hand in his, more out of habit than anything else. Hell, I'm still grappling with what just happened. I mean, I know what happened, I was a part of it, but seriously. What just happened?

As I take in his widening grin, it finally sinks in. I was outsmarted. Did he plan this all along?

"I adore Tessa, who by the way is Gina's niece and doing us a favor, but I cannot tell you how excited I am to have a real professional as the face of this firm again. Thank you so much for volunteering, Mallory."

Volunteer, my ass. I was bamboozled. And I am not the least bit upset about it. I have a job, at least until Viola returns from maternity leave, that pays forty dollars an hour! And on top of that, I'm getting free manual labor, too. But I still have a trump card to play.

"Well, I'm glad you'll find my presence so valuable. Just as valuable as I believe your firm's assistance will be with my divorce. And of course you will deduct all associated legal fees from my salary. Let's say, fifteen an hour? I know the bill will be more, but we can work out a payment plan for the balance after Viola returns." Ha! Take that, Mr. Smarty-Pants.

"There won't be a balance. Employees who work here get our legal services for free," he says, his self-satisfaction evident in the cocky grin that widens his mouth.

I narrow my eyes at him. "Did you just—"

"Make that up for you?" he asks and shakes his head. "No.

We've done wills, custody agreements, any number of things for our employees and their families through the years—all pro bono. Of course we'll do the same for you."

Well, hell. I was outsmarted again. But honestly, all ego aside, I'm also relieved. I really need every dollar I can earn right now. This job is temporary—Viola will return eventually. So this one time, I'm going to graciously give in and accept that maybe, just maybe, Nick is trying to look out for me. It's a new feeling but one I shamelessly admit isn't unpleasant. I also have a strong feeling he wants to help settle Aunt Maggie's things as much as I do, take care of her all the way till the end.

So I say the only thing I can in this situation. "Thank you."

"Of course," he says, then leans against his desk and crosses his arms. "Now, how about you tell me what's going on with your divorce so far. Gina should be back from court in a few minutes, and she'll join us when she gets here."

I am barely through the "early years" of my marriage when Gina arrives a few minutes later like a hurricane in a teacup. She is short enough to make *me* look tall, with long, dark wavy hair, and she has a laugh we hear from half the hallway away. Once inside Nick's office, she takes one look at the coffeepot on Nick's credenza and lets out a heartfelt "hallelujah." She pours herself a cup—black—as Nick takes care of introductions.

"I really appreciate your help," I say, looking down and noticing I have a white-knuckle grip on the arms of my office chair.

I force myself to loosen my fingers.

"Nonsense," Gina says as she struts across the office and sits down in the chair next to mine. "Anytime I get to go after one of these creeps, it's a good day for me."

My gut does that shimmy-shake thing at the memory of Karl standing on my driveway. "Yeah, the whole mess with him showing up at my house the other night was bad."

"That was bad, but what he's done to you up until then is

even worse. Your soon-to-be-ex is a real piece of work, and there's really not an insult worse than that." She takes a long sip of coffee before launching into her report. "According to the preliminary information I was able to get from Nick and the total joke of a financial report he sent over, I have no doubt that he's trying to hide your marital assets. The numbers just don't add up at first glance."

I'm not shocked, but it still isn't what I want to hear. "How much?"

She shoots me an evil little grin and damn, am I glad to have her on my side.

"Honestly?" she asks rhetorically. "Not to get your hopes up, but his firm is worth millions alone. Half of which should belong to you."

I swallow the lump in my throat, afraid to even hope. I mean, I knew the firm was massive. I could see the clients, was aware of the billing rates. But I'd never bothered with the accounting department. Why would I? We had a comfortable life, and I thought we were building the firm for our future. And he'd always said New York office rents were exorbitant, the cost of staff and other things outrageously high. No, I corrected. What he'd said was that the firm was our future. *Our* future. And I'd just completely believed him.

"I want to pay the property taxes I owe on my aunt's house and get the tree off my front porch—that's it." My voice sounds shaky even to my own ears.

Gina sets her coffee cup and saucer down on Nick's desk, pivots in her chair, and looks at me head-on. "Girl, I'm going get you that and so much more. Karl is racking up debt to make the firm look insolvent on paper and making sure your name isn't on any paperwork, ever. Too bad he doesn't realize that no one fights for a Jersey girl like another Jersey girl. This is real fuck-around-and-find-out shit, and Karl is about to find out."

"Do you think you'll be able to prove he's trying to defraud

Mallory?" Nick asks, leaning forward as if he's as invested in the outcome as I am.

"Is rum cake delicious?" Gina asks. "You can count on it."

If I were a better person, I wouldn't have images of Karl chasing after ambulances for the rest of his miserable life dancing in my head, but I'm certainly not going to feel bad about it after the news I just got. And for the first time since I came back to Jersey, it seems like I finally have the world on my side.

Chapter Twenty-Eight

I step outside Nick's office flush with triumph and excitement. One, I have a divorce attorney. Two, I have a job. And three, Nick agreed to help me out around the house a few hours a week. With the extra body and strong arms, I might actually get everything organized and livable in half the time.

As I climb into Jimi, though, I'm not thinking about my new job or redecorating plans. Instead, I am laser-focused on the white-hot fury I've been holding at bay for the past hour. Any doubts I had about fighting Karl in the divorce crumbled like ashes as Gina continued to explain exactly how much money Karl has been robbing me of over the years.

I totally understood getting paid so little in the beginning, when we were trying to get the firm off the ground. But to have kept me there for years even when the firm was making money hand over fist and there was no reason for it? It made me want to tell Karl off all over again—and myself for never following up or taking the time to look at comparable salaries. Then again, who expects your husband, the man you love, to screw you over so incredibly?

I vow right then and there that I will *never* give another man power over me again. I might be a lone boat in the ocean, but at least it's my choice if I sink again.

By the time I get home, I have to force myself to stop thinking about how pissed off I am. I pour myself a well-deserved glass of wine, then wander up to my bedroom to take off my makeup and change into yet another pair of leggings.

I consider taking a nap—the bed looks so inviting after a night of tossing and turning—but I am supposed to report to work bright and early Monday morning. That means I only have the rest of today, Friday, and the weekend to make serious inroads with my cleaning plans.

I still have the remainder of the dining room, living room, and Aunt Maggie's office to do downstairs, but since I'm up here, I decide to take the day off from the main floor. Seriously, it will be really nice to wake up in the morning and not nearly die if I step an inch off the path I've managed to carve to the bathroom on my first day here. Which means it's time to start cleaning out Aunt Maggie's room.

Just the thought makes me a little sad, because clearing out in here means clearing out everything that made Aunt Maggie who she was. Her feathered boas, her sparkly shoes, her magnificent clothes, and the boxes upon boxes of costume jewelry she had forever.

When I was a kid, she'd bring me up here before our tea parties and let me pick out whatever jewelry I wanted to wear. Inevitably, I would drape myself in faux diamond bracelets and colorful necklaces and earrings—anything that made me feel beautiful. It seems sacrilegious to just throw it all away now.

Still, I can't keep living out of suitcases. I'm starting a new job in three days. I have to get my own stuff unpacked and my own space under some kind of control if I have any chance of getting—and keeping—my life together.

I decide to start in Aunt Maggie's closet. Besides all her clothes that are hanging in there—and there are a ton—there are also hats, scarves, purses, and dozens upon dozens of pairs of shoes. And that doesn't include the boxes full of items she has lining the top shelf that go all the way around the closet.

I start with the shoes, partly because there are so many of

them and partly because they're fun to look through. And we're pretty close to the same size…

I'm in the middle of trying on a pair of thigh-high boots that I'm pretty sure date back to the 1970s—because why not—when my phone buzzes with a series of texts.

Yanking it out of my hoodie pocket, I glance down at the caller ID and can't help grinning.

Nick is texting me. He asked for my number before I left the office, and I assumed it was so he could reach me about work.

Nick: Are you busy?

Nick: I'm downstairs. Can you come let me in?

My smile slides off my face. Downstairs? What is he doing here?

After unzipping the boots and pulling them off as fast as I can, I hurry down the stairs to the family room—and the back door that he has been showing up at more and more lately.

The fact that I've started looking forward to his impromptu visits has not eluded me. But just because I recognize the feeling doesn't mean I actually have to deal with it. Denial isn't only a river in Egypt, after all.

"Hi!" I slide open the back door and nearly swallow my tongue. While he definitely looks amazing in dress pants or a suit, he looks *AMAZING* with all the exclamation points in ripped jeans and a black V-neck T-shirt. "What are you doing here?"

And why is he dressed like that? Not that I'm complaining, but still. It's definitely a different look.

He lifts a brow. "I was under the impression that I was being pressed into service. I'm here to help you clean."

"Oh, right!" I step back to let him in. "I didn't mean you had to come by tonight. It's Thursday."

"Do you have other plans?" he asks, his eyes suddenly intent on mine.

"No, of course not." Heat blooms in my cheeks. "I guess I

just assumed that you did."

"Nope," he says with a grin. "I'm free all night. So where do you want to start?"

"I've been working in the bed…room…" My voice trails off at the end as I realize what room I just invited him into. And what people normally do there. In half a heartbeat, my bra feels too tight as warm desire winds through me. I clear my throat and will my suddenly out-of-control libido to settle down. "I got started on the master closet a few hours ago, but there's just so much to get through."

"Well, then I guess we'd better get back to it, right?" He takes off up the staircase, expertly dodging the piles stacked on every step.

"Yeah, of course." I start up behind him. "But I feel like I should warn you. Things upstairs are a lot worse than they are downstairs."

He glances back at me while I talk—which I appreciate, considering it used to take a full tap routine and long periods of nudity to even get Karl to focus on me, let alone with such concern and intensity.

"You okay?" The caring is implicit in the question—and his tone.

It has me ducking my head so he can't see how much a simple question like that means to me. How long has it been since someone asked me that question? And how much longer since someone paid attention to the answer?

"I'm good, actually. A little sad, sure, but as I'm sorting through all of Aunt Maggie's things, it's hard to ignore the fact that she had a good life."

He smiles. "That's all that matters, then, isn't it?"

"Yeah." We get to the top of the stairs, and I lead him toward the master bedroom. "I think it is."

Aunt Maggie was a hell of a woman. Hoarding, no hoarding, it doesn't really matter in the grand scheme of her life. She was the type of woman who wore thigh-high go-go boots for fun.

The type of woman who dyed her hair bright red just because it was August.

The type of woman who glued sparkly glitter all over her face to prove to a little girl that magic existed.

The type of woman who lived her life with complete abandon.

As I lead Nick into her bedroom, I can't help dwelling on how much I want to be that kind of woman. The no-holds-barred, take-no-prisoners, do-and-say-and-wear-what-I-want kind of woman.

Somewhere along the way, I lost that dream. I lost all my dreams, actually. Whether I had them stolen by Karl or gave them away myself because it was the easier path, it doesn't really matter now. What matters is that I'm beginning to reclaim them, one small step at a time.

And if those steps happen to be in thigh-high go-go boots, who the hell is anyone else to judge me anyway? Besides, life is always more interesting in stilettos.

An hour later, the bedroom that seemed plenty big earlier feels like a shoebox. There's room for a king-size bed, a six-drawer dresser, and piles upon piles of books and bric-a-brac. But after spending sixty minutes, 3,600 very long, very slow seconds with Nick in a room dominated by a giant bed, it's become teeny tiny.

Every time I pick up a pile of Sherlock Holmes mysteries and turn so I can put them in the box on the bed, I have to slide by Nick.

My arm brushes against his firm chest as we pass each other in the skinny path between the window and the door. Over and over.

My ass grazes his hard thighs as I carry a tower of adult coloring books that go up to my chin over to a donation box.

My gaze snags on his at least forty-five times a minute as we work in companionable silence—except of course I'm not feeling very companionable about Nick. No, the more matchbooks for lighting candles that I pick up, the more naughty thoughts I deposit in my spank bank.

Seriously, a woman can only see a T-shirt stretch across that man's broad shoulders or see the way his jeans cling to his ass when he squats down, lowering a heavy box of books to the ground, so many times before having thoughts. Does that make me a bad person for ogling my neighbor who is just helping me out? Yes. Does that fact stop me? Nope.

New Mallory has gotten her hormones back. My stomach growls. I've also seen the return of my appetite.

I take out my phone and pull up a food delivery app. "How do you feel about Thai? Or are you more of an Indian guy?"

He takes a trash bag filled with two decades of holiday cards and ties it off. "I like it all."

Yeah, we both know that isn't the case. "Mr. Easy? You? No way. You, sir, are a stickler."

"Then Indian," he says. "How about some *pav bhaji* from Chowpatty in Iselin?"

Honestly, I've kind of been craving Thai all night, but my mouth starts watering immediately for all the Indian-prepared mixed vegetables simmered in spices. "*Naan* or *rotli*?"

He grins at me. "Both, definitely both."

Finally, something we can agree on without a fight first. A few thumb clicks later and our order is in. We finish up the last corner of spiderwebs and old Christmas cards by the time the food arrives.

I randomly grab an ABBA album and have it queued up on Aunt Maggie's record player by the time Nick has dinner spread out on the coffee table in the living room.

I can barely hear "Waterloo" over the sound of our *mmmmmm*s and *yummmmm*s as we eat. Afterward, we both lay down on the floor, our stomachs way too full to do anything else. We're almost cheek to cheek, staring up at the ceiling, happy, satisfied, relaxed.

"I have no regrets," I say, my palm on my belly.

"In general, or when it comes to all the *pav bhaji* we inhaled?"

I chuckle. "All of the above."

Nick rolls onto his side, facing me, and props his head up in his hand. "So do you want me to mow the grass tomorrow after work?"

Friday. Why does that sound familiar, like there's something—oh yeah. "Nah, I have a date tomorrow."

His jaw tightens as he notices a few crumbs on his shirt and swats them away. "The contractor?"

I nod. "What is it with you and things that are green? I mean, tell me about all your house plants."

He rolls back so we're both staring at the ceiling again. "That would be because of my mom."

"You guys are close?" I try to picture what Nick's parents would be like and get nothing. Every time I think I've figured him out, he does something like sing along to every word of "Fernando," so no, I can't imagine who raised this mysterious guy, but I strangely want to meet them.

"Yeah," he says, a smile obvious in his tone. "She's pretty awesome."

"And she gives you plants?"

"For every birthday and Christmas."

Now it's my turn to roll onto my side so I can see his face when he answers my next question. "Why?"

He chuckles. "She seems to be under the impression that I need to take care of things to feel personally fulfilled."

"Okay, in all fairness, I can see your mom's point." And I can. "Look at how you've been with me, how you were with Aunt Maggie, and even your grumpy client today. You excel at all the white-knight stuff, you just like to pretend you're a big grouch."

"Is that how you see me, as a big softy?" he asks as he rolls onto his side again.

Now we're practically nose to nose, and it's suddenly getting very hot in here. "'Soft' is not a word I associate with you."

His eyes darken. "What is?"

I swallow. "Does 'friend' work?"

Wow, Mallory. You have Mr. Hot in a Suit and a T-Shirt flirting with you, and that's what you come up with?

He drops his gaze for a second, and when he brings it back up, there's an intensity shining in his eyes that takes my breath away.

"It will for now," he says and then gets up and reaches down to help me stand. "I gotta get back home. The house plants are calling."

I nod and walk him to the sliding glass patio door. We stand there, him on the outside of the open door and me on the inside, both leaning against the doorframe. Neither of us moves. The hint of chlorine from a nearby pool floats on the air, and somewhere a neighbor is barbecuing, sending the scent of mesquite into the atmosphere. All of it mixes with the feeling of promise and more than a little buzz of attraction, giving me thoughts I should not be having about my temporary boss and permanent neighbor.

"Mallory?" His gaze takes me in, from my usual messy topknot, to the stain on my shirt from dinner, to the dust clinging to the hem of my leggings. Instead of giving me a disapproving look like Karl would have, he gives me a look that could probably burn all my clothes off by sheer will if he wants. "Have fun on your date tomorrow night."

Then he is gone, disappearing around the side of the house while I stand there blinking and wondering why in the hell a lingering disappointment has settled in my stomach. It has to be nerves. After all, Monday is my first day at my new job, which would make any woman feel a little off.

Yeah. That has to be it.

As I close the sliding glass door and lock it, I can't help wondering what color suit and tie Nick will be wearing to work next. Good Lord. Am I developing a suit fetish?

Chapter Twenty-Nine

I spend most of Friday cleaning out the rest of the clutter in my bedroom that Nick and I didn't get to. It feels less sad today and more a celebration of my aunt's life. And also, cathartic. I cry more than once as I pack her favorite hat or dress or earrings into boxes for charity to pick up.

But at the same time, no matter how sad it makes me to see her things and know she will never use them again—to know she is well and truly gone—it also feels like a proper goodbye in a way that the staid, boring funeral my father insisted on giving her never did. She left money for the funeral she'd wanted, along with plans about how to cremate her and what to do with her ashes—I'm pretty sure Bora Bora was involved.

Instead, my father ignored all her wishes and buried her in the ground in a plain black casket that was as different from her as she was from my father. At the time, I was too distraught to do more than put up a cursory argument, but now that a few weeks have passed and I'm more clearheaded, I'm ashamed.

Ashamed of my father for doing it, ashamed of my mother and myself for allowing it, and ashamed of everyone who stood around my parents' house after the funeral talking about what a beautiful service it was.

There was nothing beautiful about that service, and as I fold her favorite shawl, her favorite dress, and her favorite gloves just to put them in a box, I can't help thinking that she deserved more. And that maybe, just maybe, I can find a way to give it to her.

Around four o'clock, I stop cleaning and wolf down an apple and some water before jumping into the shower to wash the grime off me yet again. Mikey said he'd pick me up at seven for our date tonight, and while I'm looking forward to seeing him because he is a sweetheart of a guy, that's about it. There isn't even a hint of a zing that tells me I'm hot for this guy.

Instead, all I can muster is a pleasant anticipation—as if a friend were coming to visit—but that's it. No spark. No excitement. Nothing.

It's too bad, not because I want anything to happen with him, because I don't—and I'm not lying to myself about him. Seriously, the last thing I'm ready for right now is a man in my life on a regular basis. But the spark would be fun. And exciting. And maybe even hot.

As soon as I think it, an image of Nick shirtless and mowing my lawn dances through my mind. He might be—okay, he totally is—a bit of a curmudgeon, but apparently it isn't just assholes I'm attracted to anymore. I have to add eighty-year-old men trapped in thirtysomething-year-old bodies to that list as well.

After my shower, I take my time picking out what I want to wear and put on my makeup. Hey, there is nothing wrong with a little extra va-va-voom to make yourself feel good. Anyway, if I look like a million bucks—or at least as close to it as I can manage—maybe Mikey won't notice that I'm glancing at my phone instead of hanging on his every word.

Guilt about that thought trips me up as I walk over to get another pair of Stella & Dot earrings. I had a great time with Mikey on our lunch date, but the truth is, there's a part of me that wants to like him just to prove to myself that I can. But I don't. I just don't. And that sucks because the man really is adorable.

I've just slipped my new earrings into my ears and done

a little fun and flirty headshake when there is a knock on my back door.

Mikey's probably a few minutes early. After a quick spritz of perfume and a final look in the mirror, I head down the stairs.

But when I get to the family room, it isn't Mikey on the other side of the sliding glass door. It's a woman with her back to me, but from the way her shoulders are shaking, it's obvious she's crying.

I have no clue when my backyard became a gathering spot for the neighborhood—especially since I know, like, five people in the entire town—but it seems to be true.

As I get closer, though, I realize it isn't a stranger on my patio. It's Sarah, the woman I met at Christee's party. I have no clue how she ended up on my doorstep, but she obviously needs a friend.

"Hey," I say as I slide open my back door. "Are you okay?"

"I'm sorry." She looks up at me with tear-soaked eyes. "I didn't mean to just drop in on you like this. And I'm sorry I came to your back door. I saw the signs on your porch about it being unsafe and I started to leave, but I knew if I left without talking to you, I'd never come back again. And I really, really want to talk to you."

There's a lot to unpack there—in words and in emotions—but I try to do it anyway, even as I steer Sarah toward my aunt's Victorian-style purple couch.

"It's okay," I say as we sit down a few feet apart. "Can I get you some water or some tissues?"

She holds up her right hand, and it's filled with a clump of half-used tissues. "I'm okay."

"No offense, but that's a big ol' lie." I reach over and pat her back as softly as I can.

The contact only makes her cry harder, which is absolutely not what I intended. I pull my hand back, hoping it will calm her down. But it doesn't. It's as if the floodgates have opened and nothing is going to stop the onslaught. Seriously, she starts to sob like her world just ended.

And since I know very well what that feels like better than most, I don't interfere. Instead, I walk to the kitchen and get her a glass of water and some more tissues.

I feel bad for her, this woman I barely know, but I'm also curious as to how exactly she ended up on my couch. Did Angela tell her where I live? And if so, why?

Her sobs wind down to occasional soft whimpers by the time I get back to the family room, so I silently extend the tissues and the glass of water.

She takes both with a murmured "thanks," then doesn't say anything else until I'm sitting next to her. "I'm sorry," she finally whispers.

"It's okay." I offer an encouraging smile. "How can I help?"

She sniffs. "I didn't want to tell you this way."

Every nerve ending in my body goes on red alert, and if I had antennae, they'd be standing straight up, too. "Tell me what?"

"I'm—I'm—" Tears start to fill her eyes again.

Meanwhile, my heart rate is so jacked up, I might start hovering over the couch. I stand, needing to do something, anything, at the moment as nausea climbs its way up my throat.

Please God, don't let this be another one of Karl's cast-offs. Please God, don't let me have one of his ex-girlfriends sitting on my couch right now, about to pour her heart out to me. I can take a lot, but I'm pretty damn sure I can't take that.

Sarah gets herself together enough to lift her chin and look me square in the eyes.

And my whole body goes cold in one of those moments when you know what's going to come next will hurt—a lot.

"I'm your…your…your…sister."

Chapter Thirty

And just like that, the already shaky foundation beneath my favorite pair of high-heeled boots dissolves, and I collapse onto the couch beside her.

"I'm sorry?" I must have misheard her. "What did you say? You're my—"

"Sister." She starts crying again. "I'm your sister. That's how I knew where to find you, because Aunt Maggie was my aunt, too."

And then the sobs start up all over again, but I'm too flummoxed to comfort her. To be honest, I'm too flummoxed to do anything but sit here with my mouth open and my head on the verge of exploding.

Because if she's my sister and Aunt Maggie was her aunt, too—and that smarts, considering that means my aunt lied to me about something this hugely important—and it's obvious that she's younger than I am by at least five years and maybe even more…

Okay.

I take a deep breath.

Okay, okay, okay. I can deal with this. I can totally deal with the fact that my father is a dirty, lying cheat.

I blow out the breath, and that's when it happens. A sob that I was totally unprepared for comes out right along with it. Because no matter how much I want to deny it, no matter how much I want to pretend that Sarah is just pulling a cruel, cruel trick—or worse, is some kind of con artist—there is one thing I can't ignore.

From the moment I first saw her, I thought Sarah looked familiar. And now that I'm staring at her in the middle of my very bright family room, I realize why that was. From the tips of her streaked brown hair to her ocean-blue eyes to the tiny little cluster of birthmarks on the side of her neck, she looks *exactly* like my father did when he was young.

All those times he lectured me about the sanctity of marriage even during hardship… All the times my mother told me that I needed to go back to Karl because a woman belonged with her husband no matter what… They hadn't been talking about me at all. They'd been talking about themselves.

They'd wanted me to stay with Karl so they could feel better about themselves—about what they'd done and the choices they'd made.

And all the time my father had been lecturing me on what a good man Karl was, about how adultery didn't have to mean the end of a marriage—all the time my mother had told me to wear sexier underwear and more fucking makeup—they'd been carrying around this secret.

The secret that not only did my father cheat on my mother with at least one woman—though my very angry gut says there were probably a hell of a lot more through the years—but that he fathered a child with her. And he kept that child a secret for more than two decades.

What the hell am I supposed to say to that? Except, "Welcome to the family."

The poor woman.

That only makes her bawl harder and—not going to lie—for a second, I think about bawling right along with her. I've never felt more betrayed in my life, and that is saying something, considering the way my last few months have gone. By my father, by my mother, by my favorite aunt. What the hell is even happening right now?

My phone buzzes with a text—Mikey messaging me to let me know he's looking forward to seeing me in a little while. I have to bite my lip to keep from laughing because oh my God. Am I living in the middle of a farce right now? Or just a really intense episode of some practical-joke TikTok? Because how the hell am I supposed to go on a date when my long-lost baby sister has just shown up at my door?

"I'm really sorry," Sarah says. "I wouldn't have come here if I had anywhere else to go. I even tried to talk to Dad—"

She broke off when my gaze snaps to hers. I've been an only child all my life—or so I thought—and hearing someone else call my father "Dad" shakes me to my already trembling core.

"What do you mean you tried to talk to him?"

Sarah sighs. "I went to his house, but he shooed me off the porch, then texted me to go away. That he would see me on Tuesday evening, just like he has every Tuesday evening for my entire life. But that I'm not to contact him other than that. I tried to tell him that I need help, that I'm in trouble, but he just stopped answering my texts."

Jesus. I close my eyes, and the horror washes over me. From the time I was eight years old, Tuesdays were poker nights for my father. Every Tuesday night, he would come home from work early. He'd change his clothes, check on my mother and me, and then leave for the rest of the night to hang out with his buddies from law school and play a ruthless night of poker.

Every Wednesday at breakfast, he would regale my mother and me with tales of the cutthroat games he'd played the night before. I looked forward to those stories every week, even when I was a teenager. I shake my head, so annoyed that I hadn't been a sucker just with Karl. I'd been that way with everyone my whole life.

The lying son of a bitch. I don't know how I'll ever be able to look him in the face again. Hell, I don't know if I'll ever even *want* to look him in the face again, because right now I am about ready to say good riddance to bad trash, as my aunt Maggie always said. And she was right about that, even if she was wrong to keep such an important secret from me.

"My mom was your babysitter, just barely in her twenties, when you were a kid," Sarah continues in between sniffles. "She died last year. She said she regretted the affair but never regretted having me."

"Why are you telling *me* this?" I mean, yeah, I want to know, but why now?

"History seems to have a way of repeating itself, at least in some ways." Sarah lets out a shaky breath. "I'm pregnant and the baby's father doesn't care, doesn't want to be a part of the baby's life, doesn't want to be a part of mine. I don't have anywhere else to go. I lost my job and a place to live all in one fell swoop. You're my last hope."

This is a lot to process. A lot a lot.

My dad had an affair. I have a half sister. Does Mom know? Does it matter at this point?

"Sarah," I start, prepared to say what, I have no fucking idea, but then I look at my sister and what I see is a woman alone, without someone like Aunt Maggie to pull her in and wrap her arms around her—without someone who will tell her they'll figure everything out. Together.

So that's what I do. I throw my arms around her shoulders and squeeze her tight. "It's gonna be okay. We'll figure this out. Together."

Sarah lets out another huge torrent of tears. "Really?" She presses the crumpled-up tissues to her face. "I don't know what to say. I'll be out of your hair as soon as I get an apartment."

"There's no hurry. There's plenty of room here, and she was your Aunt Maggie, too. I'd love to have you stay as long as you want—as long as you don't mind a mess." As soon as the words are out of my mouth, I realize just how much I mean them.

"I don't mind at all," Sarah says.

I laugh. I can't help myself. "You haven't seen the upstairs yet."

We're both still sniffling messes when Nick walks in through the patio door and comes to a dead stop. "Is everything okay? What happened?"

I look at Sarah. She looks at me. And we both burst out laughing at the thought of even trying to bring him up to speed.

Chapter Thirty-One

Nick looks from me to Sarah and back again and, going by the crinkles around his very serious eyes, he's trying to figure out how we're related. I have a feeling that's going to be happening a lot.

"What are you doing here?" I ask, glancing down at the stack of papers in his hands that isn't contained in a panic-inducing folder.

"Wow." He shoves a hand in his jeans pocket. "Temper your excitement. I could be dropping off paperwork for Gina."

I lift a brow at him. "Are you?"

"No," he says with a crooked grin.

The second he smiles, Sarah let out a tiny squeak and, believe me, I get it. He looks hot as fuck when he's doing his flirty-but-still-kind-of-grumbly face. When he smiles? Well, the only thing holding up my panties right now are my super-tight jeans. The man has game—even in a room full of women who are currently disgusted with the entire male species.

"So what brings you all the way across the street?" I ask.

And yes, I am aware that in some circles, my question—and the tone I am asking it in—might be considered flirtatious. Which I sorta, kinda meant, God help me.

I could be imagining this, but I'm pretty sure his eyes go a few shades darker as he looks at me, if that's even possible. For long seconds, he doesn't say anything and neither do I. We just kind of watch each other, and I have to admit that watching him is a lot better than dealing with the bombshells my sister just dropped on me. Even if it is just for a minute or two.

Sarah clears her throat. "Do I need to give you guys some space?"

Way to make it weird, Mallory.

"No," we both say at the same time.

Nick holds up the papers. "I got the committee to fast-track the approvals for your dumpster. I figured I'd bring them by personally instead of making you wait to get them in the mail."

He offers them to me. "They said yes."

"Oh, that's amazing." I take the papers, ready to start crying again but this time out of happiness. "Thank you so much. I owe you."

I can't believe he thought to make a special appeal to the board. I didn't expect it, but then again, it isn't like this is the first time he's gone above and beyond. From sticking up for me to Karl to helping me with the house to giving me a job and free legal counsel, Nick isn't nearly as gruff as he wants people to think. Truth be told, there's a lot of softness underneath.

Exhibit forty-two in my case? Even as he stays near enough to me that I can smell the scent of his soap, he glances over at Sarah, and the heat level between us just drops.

He dips his head down so his lips are practically touching my ear. "Is everything okay?"

Wow, how in the hell do I start? "Not really. This is my s—" I nearly choke on the word, even though none of this mess is her fault.

I clear my throat and try again, and this time I finally manage to get the word out. "My sister, Sarah. Sarah, this is my…"

This time when I fumble for words, it has nothing to do with angsty familial relationships and everything to do with the fact that I have no clue what to call Nick. My neighbor?

My friend? My boss?

"Friend." Nick fills in the awkward silence for me with an easier smile than any he's ever given me. "I'm Mallory's *friend* Nick."

Sarah peeks up at him, her lips almost curled into a tiny smile, and not for the first time, I realize how fragile she looks. So different from the woman I met at the Stella & Dot party. "Nice to meet you, friend Nick."

Some of the tension in the room eases right in time for Mikey to show up at my back door, dressed in his date-night best dark-rinse jeans and gray Henley. Ugh. In all the confusion, I forgot to text him that I want to cancel tonight. Damn it.

Smoothing a hand over my now-ruffled hair—nothing like finding out you have a long-lost sister to mess up twenty-five intense minutes with a straight iron and hair gloss—I step through the open door. *Oh yeah, Mallory, standing on the other side of a sliding glass door is gonna give you two plenty of privacy.* Nick and Sarah stay in the family room, watching unabashedly.

"Wow," Mikey says with an appreciative grin. "You look gorgeous."

"Thank you." I tuck an errant, and obnoxiously frizzy, hair behind my ear. "You look nice, too. But I'm afraid I've got a problem."

"What kind of problem?" His smile stays in place, but his eyes dim a little. Not that I blame him—Mikey's not naive. He knows I'm about to break the cardinal rule of dating by canceling on him when he's already arrived for the date.

"My sister showed up out of the blue, and she just broke up with her boyfriend. She needs a place to stay, and she's really upset, and—"

Right then, the sound of Sarah's full-bodied laugh about something Nick said carries out to us.

"It's okay," Sarah says as she gives Mikey a wave. "The

last thing I want to do is disrupt your night. Especially since Nick just explained you're the contractor who's going to bring this beautiful house to life. I just love the mahogany staircase and the built-in bookshelves." She makes a sweeping gesture. "Besides, I can leave if—"

"You don't need to leave." No way. I just found her—okay, really, she found me—but either way, I'm not letting her go now. "I just didn't think you were in any mood to be alone right now."

"I can stay," Nick volunteers, easy-breezy. "Sarah can veg out with Netflix, and I can clean a few closets."

"You don't have to d-do that," I splutter.

Mortification has me doing a gut clench for some reason I don't understand. It's not like he hasn't seen the inside of my house.

"Sure I do." His eyes meet mine. "A deal's a deal, after all, and I'm officially your helper every day, remember? Go enjoy your date."

"Yes, but—" I break off because I don't know what I want to say. Why does it feel so wrong on a gut level to leave him here, working on my house, while I'm out on a date with some other guy?

It's absurd. I mean, it isn't like it matters. Nick and I are... friends. That's all. Nothing more. In fact, we're barely even that. Why should either of us care if one of us goes on a date with someone else? Why should either of us care if one of us encourages the other to go on said date?

I mean, yeah, we had a moment yesterday, and we had a moment the other evening, when I thought for sure he was going to kiss me. But he didn't. He left, and I need to remember that. Need to realize that when he tells me to go on a date with Mikey, he means it. There's nothing for me to feel guilty about.

Or to feel *any* way about, for that matter. We barely know each other.

"Go, Mallory," Sarah says, and it's obvious she's trying to

be as nice. "Go on, have fun."

"Sounds like your sister has made up her mind." Mikey's face is made even hotter—who would have thought that possible?—by an enthusiastic grin. "Think you can handle it?"

I sneak another look at Nick. Who is already gathering trash bags and telling Sarah a joke. Mr. Uptight has jokes now?

Fine.

Perfect.

Wonderful.

I give Mikey my most dazzling smile. "Yes, let's go have a blast."

I slip my hand into the crook of Mikey's arm, and we follow the path around the house to his truck. And I don't even look back at all—not even once—which is exactly what I want out of this moment.

Really.

Chapter Thirty-Two

Bella Bella's is a neighborhood Italian restaurant that has white tablecloths, votive candles floating in a bowl surrounded by fresh flowers, and a hostess dressed in all black who never smiles when she seats you. In other words, it is the fancy date-night place that stays on the right side of too expensive but has great food and no one brings their kids.

Mikey and I have gone through all the small talk by the time my chicken Parm and his lasagna arrive. The weather. The way Sutton changed but still stayed the same. Angela's kids, the amazing renovation he's working on for the Jhaveris a few blocks over from my place. Now I'm chewing each bite a million times to keep my mouth full so I don't have to come up with any more chitchat. I mean, honestly, my mind is still going a million miles an hour about the whole "secret sister" thing anyway.

It sucks because he's so nice and hot and an absolute gem of a guy—but for someone else. There's no way to avoid it; I'm just not ready for dating. I might never be.

"So," I say, drawing out the word. "Talk to me about dumpsters."

Mikey wriggles his eyebrows and gives me an exaggerated leer. "You wanna talk dirty, huh?"

I let out a squawk of amusement that has several other diners turning to stare. Oops.

"Well, I actually already got approval from the HOA, and I can afford it, so what do I need to know?"

"You want to consider a lot of things. Placement. Size. What you can't put in there. Exactly how much you can put in. Oh, and how much it's gonna weigh when you're done filling it. Landfills are gonna weigh that sucker before you can empty it, and that bill can be a shock."

Great. Just what I need—another bill.

"Did you save room for dessert?"

Always. Who doesn't save room for cannoli? Too bad I just can't do another half hour of dumpster talk, and I've exhausted everything else.

"I wish; that chicken Parm was too good not to eat it all."

"I understand."

I'm pretty sure he does. In addition to being a fantastic guy, he's smart as hell.

He stands up. "Shall we?"

I nod. I insist on leaving the tip when he won't let me split the check, and after he pays the bill, we walk out into the parking lot. He doesn't try to hold my hand or even walk so close that we're almost touching. I spend most of the ride home asking questions about the renovations Aunt Maggie's house needs.

The running convo in my head, though, is all about what a sweetheart of a guy he is. Really, he deserves someone better than a woman with enough baggage to start her own luggage company. No. What I need—when the time is right—is a guy with as much baggage as I have. Then we'll be equals, at least.

Nick probably has baggage. Why else would he be so uptight? He might even own his own luggage line full of more emotional BS than I have.

"So that's when I switched my lifelong allegiance from the Yankees to the Mets."

I jerk my head around and stare at him. "What?"

He snort-laughs. "I figured that would get your attention.

I almost went from being a Devils fan to a Rangers fan, but I can't even kid about that."

Way to go, Mallory. You are such a keeper.

"I'm sorry, Mikey. It was a long day clearing out another room of Aunt Maggie's stuff, and I'm about to drop." Not a total lie.

"Sure," he says, keeping his tone light even as I see the truth in his eyes. "That makes sense."

He pulls to a stop in front of the house, and I'm opening the door before he's even turned off the ignition.

"Thanks so much for everything," I say as I do the short-people maneuvering it takes to get out of a big truck. "Next time, though, I'm picking up the bill."

"You got it." He glances over at the other side of the driveway. "That's where I'd recommend putting the dumpster. Enough room to get your car in and out of the garage but easy for the truck to drop off and pick up."

"Then that's where we'll put it." I step down from the runner under the passenger door. "Night, Mikey."

He nods, an easy smile on his lips. "Night."

I shut the passenger door and take the path around the back to the sliding patio door. The lights in the family room are dim as I walk inside, but there is no missing Nick. He's half lying, half hanging off the couch that's barely long enough for me and definitely not for his long legs.

"Hey there," I say, keeping my voice soft so I don't startle him.

Sleepy-eyed, he smiles up at me, his usual firm lines and determined set to his square jaw softer now. "Sarah crashed about half an hour ago after we finished *Kill Bill*. I told her to take your bed, figured that's what you'd want." He sits up and rolls his neck. "She really liked that movie."

A movie about a betrayed bride out for revenge? Yeah, that definitely tracks. "With our family's history, when it comes to men, wouldn't you? And yes, I'll definitely take the couch. Poor girl. She needs sleep."

Nick nods. "She's coming by the office tomorrow. I'm going to help her get palimony and child support arrangements made."

Awwww. That hits me right in the soft and vulnerable spots. "Always looking out for the Martin sisters, huh?"

"Someone has to, because it seems like you two look out for everyone else but yourselves."

I want to argue, but I can't. Instead, I plop down on the couch next to him. "Apparently, it's our fatal flaw."

We sit there for a few minutes in silence but, unlike during my date earlier, this is comfortable. Neither of us seems to feel the need to fill the quiet space. My eyes, though, are getting heavy. I wasn't lying about being exhausted. They're half closed when Nick moves beside me, getting off the couch and holding me by the shoulders as he maneuvers me so I'm lying down. He tugs the afghan blanket from where it's draped across the back of the couch and lays it over me, tucking the edge under my chin.

"Night, Mallory."

My eyes flutter shut. "Night, Nick."

Then he's gone and I'm alone on the couch, exactly like I want to be, need to be. But for some reason, it feels lonelier than ever before.

Chapter Thirty-Three

There's nothing quite like waking up and feeling as though you're dead—or wishing you were. First, there was the hangover from hell the other day and now, after a single night on Aunt Maggie's Victorian-style sofa-slash-torture-device, I'm seriously wondering if my neck will ever work properly again. I turn all the way to the left just fine, but if I look to the right? Oh, that is very much not happening unless I suddenly become very into pain and the idea of paying for a chiropractor.

If Aunt Maggie had been a different kind of woman, I'd be worried she's haunting the place. Of course, if she was, her ghost would be putting on David Bowie records and leaving a trail of Quaaludes everywhere she went.

I let my eyes flutter shut. Really, what's the hurry when I can just lay here and enjoy my own demise under a super-soft brown-and-tan afghan blanket? I let out a deep breath, and the moment I inhale, it hits me. The beautiful, life-giving scent of heaven itself—freshly brewed coffee.

The lightly caramelized and almost nutty scent teases my lids open half a second before the meaning hits my still-half-asleep brain and I jackknife up to a sitting position. My right shoulder blade pinches, the nerves in my neck cry out with a bitch-what-are-you-doing, and I let out a yap that sounds like it comes from Christee's little dog. It's worth it, though, because someone is making coffee in my kitchen and, at this moment,

I love them with all my heart.

Moving a little more slowly this time, I get up off the couch and shuffle past the stacks of old lampshades heaped one on top of the other and toward the kitchen.

"Are you sure this is safe to drink?" Nick asks, his voice carrying down the hall.

I nearly trip over my own feet. Nick? He's here? Already? I catch a glimpse of my reflection in the mirror hanging from a nail by a pink ribbon and cringe. I definitely look like I spent the night face-planted on an unforgiving couch.

Frizzy hair? Check.

Pillow line etched into my cheek? Check.

Supposedly sleep-proof eyeliner on only one eye anymore? Check.

I hold a cupped hand to my mouth and breathe into it. Whew. Morning breath is a triple check.

Yeah, I'm totally not prepared to go see Mr. Knight in Shining Armor. But there is coffee...

Sarah chuckles. "What's wrong, pretty boy? Are you scared of a little caffeine?"

I continue down the hall toward the big yellow kitchen, tiptoeing as if I'm a burglar in my own house—at least it would be mine if I could actually pay off the inheritance taxes, back property taxes, and HOA fines. Well, and the mortgage, but luckily I don't have to start paying that just yet.

"No one would call this *a little*," Nick says. "You doubled the recommended amount."

"Come on, live a little," my sister shoots back. "Take a drink. Dooooooooo it."

Nick laughs, and it's warm and rumbly and makes me think of roasting s'mores over an open fire. Of course, that could just be because, judging by the scent wafting out from the kitchen, Sarah used the Oh Fudge beans. Usually, I can't help but smile when I get a whiff of the chocolate-flavored coffee, but not this morning. Instead of a silly giggle at the punny name, I can't work past the jealous pang in my belly.

He doesn't laugh with me that way. Actually, I don't know if I've ever heard him laugh around me. Chuckle? Yes. Epileptic-seizing quiet-laughing *at* me? Okay, that too. But a real, deep-in-your-belly, happy laugh? No.

But he does around Sarah.

Pull it together, Mallory. This isn't a Karl and Sasha situation again. This is your sister and your neighbor. That's all. Stop trying to make overthinking your mission in life.

Yeah, this is definitely a case of I-don't-like-myself-all-that-much-when-I'm-hangry. It's time for peaches-and-cream oatmeal and enough coffee to power a nuclear submarine. Kinda mean but totally on the money pep-talk complete, I walk into the kitchen.

Nick is standing with one hip leaning against the big oval kitchen table. I allow my gaze to flick over to him for 3.6 seconds. Any longer and I'm afraid I'd melt into a puddle of early-morning want right there in the middle of the linoleum floor. What can I say? Mornings are always my let's-go time. It must have something to do with the fact that the day hasn't beaten me down yet, making morning sex forever the best sex.

"About time you got up, sleepyhead," Sarah says when I finally tear my eyes away from Nick.

She shoots me a teasing smile as she pours me a cup of coffee and holds it out to me as I walk into the light-filled room.

Nick scoops up the Kill the Bingo Caller mug before I can make it anywhere near my sister at the coffeepot and meets me halfway. "I'm reporting for duty."

He's in jeans that cling to his thick thighs, a T-shirt with sleeves that end right at that perfect spot on his biceps, and he—unlike me—has obviously showered that morning. Ugh. It isn't fair. The man not only looks good this early but he comes bearing coffee.

I take a sip and then let out a contented sigh. "Oh fudge."

One side of Nick's mouth curls upward in a half smile that does funny things to me. Discombobulating things. Tingly things. Definitely I'll-be-thinking-of-this-later-tonight things.

"Yeah," he says, looking straight at me, his gaze dipping down to my mouth. "Early-morning coffee is the best, isn't it?"

Oh. My. God. My skin feels flush. Forget funny things. That look from him has my toes half curled, and a greedy little groan, hungry and needy, escapes my lips. Why doesn't real life come with a rewind button? My hands start to tremble and I set my mug on the counter before I drop it.

Forget oatmeal. I need to get out of here stat.

"I'm gonna go shower." I shuffle backward. "Then it's all about the green guest room. After that, we're going to burn that ridiculous couch."

I'm halfway up the stairs before I realize I left my coffee on the counter.

"Oh fudge."

Chapter Thirty-Four

"Oh wow." Sarah stops at the doorway and stares into the first of my aunt's guest rooms. To be fair, it isn't like any of us can get beyond the doorway; the room is so packed with clutter anyway.

Boxes, sewing mannequins, piles and piles of books, bolts of cloth, and baskets of yarn and ribbon cover every available spot.

"You sure you guys want to do this today?" I ask. "We could go downstairs and make margaritas and chocolate chip cookies instead."

"It's nine o'clock in the morning," Nick says.

"Is that supposed to mean something to me?" I joke.

Nick takes a step closer, and the nice, wide upstairs hall gets a whole lot narrower. "Nope, just noting the time."

"How about we make a plan to clear half the room today?" Sarah says. "We uncover the bed and tackle the side of the room closest to the door. Once we've done that, lunch—and margaritas at the Mexican restaurant down the street—is my treat. I found out a couple of weeks ago that they make really good virgin piña coladas."

"Margaritas for lunch it is," Nick says.

I look from them to the stacks and stacks of stuff crammed into every nook and cranny, then back again. "Or dinner…"

"Or dinner." Sarah laughs as she turns in the doorway and takes a step into the hallway and a deep breath. "But I say we all take a box of trash bags and do our worst between now and one o'clock. Whoever manages to fill the most bags wins."

"What do they win?" Nick asks.

I peek into the room—well, as much as I can because it's just *stuff* from the floor to the ceiling.

"Winner gets their pick of whatever treasures we uncover in here." I spot a pyramid of yarn in a million different colors. I've cleaned out so many rooms in the last week that standing here, trying to come up with a plan of attack for this room, feels overwhelming.

"Oooh, good idea!" Sarah does a little clap-dance move. "I want the hat."

She points at the giant Kentucky Derby–style hat on the mannequin in the farthest corner of the room. My jaw unhinges. What in the hell? It's hot pink (Aunt Maggie seems to have had a favorite color) and covered in pink roses and two nearly life-size flamingos that are also wearing flowery hats. It's a monstrosity. It's amazing. It's soooooo Aunt Maggie.

"Sorry, I want that hat," Nick teases her with an easy grin that makes my heart go pitter-patter even as I wonder what's up.

He's never been as easy around me as he is with Sarah. He smiles at her, laughs with her, and teases her while he's all tense and grumpy and smoldering whenever he and I are alone together.

He is helpful, absolutely. Even thoughtful. But there's definitely a lot more grump and smolder when he's dealing with me. Then again, as I watch him literally reach up and tweak her ponytail, I admit that maybe I'm okay with the differences.

If Nick is going to tweak something of mine, I definitely don't want it to be my ponytail.

Not that I want him to tweak anything, I assure myself. The last thing I want to do is add a new man to my life before I'm even officially divorced from the old man.

I clear my throat—and my mind—then say, "So it's agreed. The hat is the prize." I give Nick the side-eye. "I've got to admit,

I'm kind of dying to see you in it."

"Hot pink *is* my favorite color," he shoots back.

"Mine too!" Sarah rubs her palms together and squeezes her way into the room. "So get ready to lose, buddy."

He rolls his eyes in response, but he's grinning, too, even before my newfound sister starts the countdown. "On your mark, get set, go!"

I'd like to say we leap into the room and get to work at the word "go," but the truth is, beyond Sarah, we can't get into the room. Instead, Nick and I each bend down and start grabbing stuff and pulling it into the hallway while Sarah does the same just inside the doorway. In an unspoken agreement, Nick and I make sure to grab the heavier stuff, leaving things like pillows and small material bolts for Sarah to lift.

I'm all for getting help cleaning out this room. But I draw the line at letting the pregnant woman lift anything heavier than her purse. Apparently, Nick feels exactly the same way, because anytime Sarah reaches for anything bigger than a shoebox, he magically gets there first.

Twenty minutes later, we have a ton of boxes and other things piled in my hallway and we've—kind of—made a path to the bed in the center of the room.

"Now what?" Sarah asks as she looks around with wide eyes.

I get it. It seems like a lot when it's all piled up in one room. Now that it's spread out, it's completely overwhelming. But if the last week has taught me anything, it's that you just keep sorting and pitching. Sorting and pitching. Eventually you get to the bottom.

"I say we sort," Nick says. "Trash in one pile. Things for charity in a second pile. Things that need to be saved in a third pile. And everything we're not sure of in a fourth pile that we can look at once we've got the first couple of rounds of items clear."

"Sounds like a plan to me." I open the lid on the first small box I get to and let out a yelp.

"What's wrong?" Nick rushes to my side and pulls the box away.

He takes one look and nearly drops it entirely.

"Not so brave now, huh?" I say as we look down at dozens of dismembered dolls' heads staring back at us with blank eyes.

"I thought it was a rat or something." He starts to close the flaps back up on the box. "This is so much worse."

Sarah comes over and stops him to look in before taking a step back, her palm pressed to her chest. "Sooooo much worse."

"I say trash," Nick decides, careful not to look inside the box again.

I can't blame him.

"Like there was ever a doubt?" I hold open my half-filled trash bag so he can empty the box into it. "What in the world could Aunt Maggie have possibly had planned for those?"

"Uh, sorry to break it to you, Mallory." Sarah takes the now-empty box from Nick and starts to break it down. "But I'm pretty sure she didn't have a plan for *any* of this stuff."

I stare down into the bag full of disembodied heads. "I'm not so sure that's a bad thing."

A few of the items are total what-were-you-thinking-Aunt-Maggie, but honestly, we try to treat everything as special to her. With kindness regarding her hoarding compulsion while we decide what to do with the item. After all, these things meant something to her. I can even pick out various collections as memories of things she did over the years, memories she couldn't bring herself to part with. But the disembodied baby doll heads? That's just straight-up creepy. *Sorry, Aunt Maggie.*

"Definitely not a bad thing," Nick agrees as he holds up what looks very much like a stuffed raccoon. And not of the fluffy stuffed-animal variety, either.

"Was that—" I break off in horror, taking as many steps back as possible before I'm butt-to-headless-torso with a mannequin.

"Once alive?" Sarah lets out a squeal of glee instead of horror. "Oh, yeah. Mr. Buttons here is definitely the result of a taxidermist."

"Mr. Buttons?" Nick and I ask at the same time.

"That's what Aunt Maggie used to call him when she brought him out for our breakfast dates. She would make him dance on the kitchen counter."

Nick and I exchange vaguely nauseated looks.

"Because that's not weird at all," I say.

Sarah shrugs. "It didn't seem weird when I was little."

"I'm not even sure what to say to that," I tell her. "Except here." I take the raccoon from Nick and hand it to her. "My gift to you."

"Should she even be carrying that thing when she's pregnant?" Nick's brows hit his hairline.

"It's not a litter box," I answer with a roll of my eyes. "It's not going to give her toxoplasmosis."

He leans in closer. "You sure about that?"

"I thought I was sure," I say as doubt creeps in. "You know what? I'll hang on to him until you have the baby. Then I'll give him back."

Sarah laughs, but she dutifully relinquishes her hold on Mr. Buttons. And I dutifully add him to the brand-new pile for saved items. I'm proud I don't toss him, even if I do hold him out as far as my arms will allow.

Nick gives me an amused grin before diving into the closest box to him. I grin back before doing the same.

We work pretty much nonstop for the next hour, the only sound being one of my aunt's Cat Stevens albums drifting up the stairs and an occasional squeak from one of us.

At least until Nick opens up the top of a large, fancy chest and then drops it right back down with a muttered curse. Several seconds go by before he bends and opens the chest again; then he stands over it, peering into its depths as he laughs and laughs and laughs.

Chapter Thirty-Five

"**W**hat's so funny?" Sarah asks as she maneuvers around one of the piles between them so she can also peer into the box.

A shocked look comes over her face for a full fifteen seconds before she, too, busts out laughing.

I'm really hoping to finish the basket I've been working on for the last ten minutes, but now my curiosity is totally aroused. I toss the items in my hands—a giant bag of what looks to be used batteries—into the trash, then walk around the clutter until I can see into the box.

And like Nick and Sarah, it takes me several seconds to comprehend what I'm seeing. "Is that…?"

"Yeah," Nick says with a wide grin. "It definitely is."

"Huh." I bend over to get a closer look. "And the blue one is—?"

"Yep. It's definitely what you think it is," Sarah says like she's got some kind of insider knowledge.

And what do I know? Maybe she is an expert in sex toys—like apparently Aunt Maggie was. Because inside this chest is what has to be a lifetime supply of vibrators, fur handcuffs, and just about every other kind of sex toy one can imagine. Like, *every* kind. I had no idea vibrators came with a glitter option.

"Did she make these dance around at your breakfast dates, too?" I joke as I swipe a clump of hair out of my eyes.

"Now, that would have been a sight to see." Sarah cracks up all over again. "What do you think we should do with them?"

"Um, throw them away?" I suggest in my most obvious tone. "I mean, do you really want to hang on to a vibrator Aunt Maggie used?"

The second the words leave my lips, all three of us start laughing again, because it's not actually that big of a surprise to think about Aunt Maggie having a chest full of sex toys. What is a shock, though, are the breadth and variety of her selection.

"Honestly, most of these don't even look like they've been used," Sarah says, reaching down to pick up a giant veiny purple vibrator with an extra enhancement for clitoral stimulation. Which, not going to lie, are two words I never thought I'd use in a sentence when thinking about my aunt. "This one is brand-new."

"Thank God," Nick mutters from beside me.

I shoot him an incredulous look, but he holds up a hand in a wait-a-minute kind of gesture. "Don't give me that look. I have absolutely nothing against female self-pleasure. Nothing. But I don't want to imagine my friend, your sweet, old Aunt Maggie, having anything to do with that."

I have to acknowledge that he has a point. "Yeah, I don't really want to think about it, either."

"Well, I think it's cool," Sarah says, picking up a bright blue anal plug—also still in its original packaging. "I mean, Aunt Mags lived the life she wanted to live. She traveled where she wanted to, hung out only with the people she wanted to, only did the things she wanted to. And if that included giving herself a whole bunch of regular orgasms with a pink vibrator—"

She grabs the vibrator in question—a long and slender wand, with balls of varying circumference placed at adjustable intervals along its length. "Then I say, more power to her."

I snicker. "I take it you mean that literally."

She giggles as she tosses the unopened vibrator back in the

chest. "At least now we know what Angela meant when you mentioned she took a chance inviting you to the Stella and Dot party, since it wasn't really Aunt Maggie's style."

My eyes go wide as I remember puzzling over the strange comment. "You don't think this is what she meant, do you?"

"I think it's *exactly* what she meant," Sarah answers. "I've been to enough bachelorette parties in Newark to recognize Lovewinx and Pure Romance as two different at-home-sales brands."

"And Maggie went to enough of these that women in the neighborhood knew to invite her?" Nick asks, his dark-brown eyes looking slightly bemused.

"There's a couple thousand dollars' worth of products in here easy," Sarah says as she bends down and picks up a giant gold vibrator that looks more like an ancient scepter than it does an instrument of female pleasure. "So my guess is yeah."

I look more closely and realize my sister is right. There are a lot of products in this trunk, and all the ones I can see are completely unopened. "You don't think she went to those parties just because she was lonely, do you?"

"Ummmm, she has a trunk full of sex toys to prove just the opposite."

"Yeah, but even you said they aren't used. What if she just bought them so people would keep inviting her to the parties, so she wouldn't have to be on her own all the time?" Suddenly I feel incredibly guilty for all the weekends I planned to get over here to see her and then couldn't because something came up with Karl or the firm or the life I built for myself in New York.

"I said most of them weren't used," Sarah reiterates. "Not all of them. Because judging from the state of these two—" She holds up a short, fat vibrator in a vivid green and another, longer one that sparkles. "They're very well used."

"Good on her, then," Nick says.

No one is laughing now, and I find myself nodding along to

Nick's pronouncement. Hey, it's kind of cool to realize a woman as old as Aunt Maggie still thought of herself as a sexual being. Especially since I felt like that part of me has been dead for longer than I'd like to admit—right up until someone started to bitch about the length of my grass.

"So what do you think?" Sarah asks after she tosses the used vibrators in the trash. "Should we donate the brand-new ones or throw them away?"

I have no idea. Is it even legal to sell or give away someone's sex toys? Forget the HOA; do I really want the police on my front porch? That would definitely make the tristate local news and kill any chance of getting a fair divorce settlement.

"Don't stress, sis. I'll take them," Sarah says, sweeping several sex toys still in their original packaging into one of the empty boxes. "I've sworn off men, not orgasms."

I have absolutely no idea what to say to that. Judging by the amused but still wide-eyed look on Nick's face, neither does he. The universe, however, finally smiles on me and my doorbell rings, rescuing me from having to say anything more.

I hustle down the front staircase, eager to get to the door before the porch ends up eating a human sacrifice. Who would ignore all the signs I left? Prepped to yank the person inside, I throw open the door. My mom stands on the other side in a pale-pink sheath dress and matching bolero jacket. On her face is a stiff almost-smile. In her hand is the extra-large roller suitcase sitting next to her.

"Really, Mallory," she says as she walks inside, leaving her suitcase on the porch—no doubt for me to bring in. "You're going to scare your visitors half to death if you answer your front door like that."

Fuck.

So much for the universe being on my side for once. Part of me figures that at least it can't get worse, but I know better than that.

Chapter Thirty-Six

"So, Mom," I say as I roll her suitcase inside. "Any particular reason you brought a suitcase with you?"

Please let it be because she wants to lay claim to something of Aunt Maggie's. I don't care what it is—cooking magazines, hair clips, her entire sex-toy collection. She can have anything she wants, just please, please, please let it be that my mother needed a convenient way to pack something up. Not because—

"Don't be ridiculous, Mallory," she says as she stands in the middle of the front room and looks around disapprovingly. "Obviously I'm moving in."

And the hits just keep on coming.

Of course she's moving in. I mean, why wouldn't she be? After spending the last however many weeks haranguing me about the sanctity of marriage and how important it is for me to go back to my husband, she's left hers.

The irony of the situation is almost more than I can stand... especially since it seems to be completely lost on her.

For a second, I think about hitting my head against the nearest wall until I knock myself out, but that'll just lead to a lecture on my very non-ladylike behavior, which must be the reason I can't keep a man. And while such lectures are always a barrel of laughs, the truth is I'm just not up for it today—or ever again.

"Is there any particular reason you've decided to move in

here?" I ask.

Mom surveys the room, which I admit is still a work in progress. "I haven't suddenly gone senile, so I would appreciate it if you wouldn't treat me as though I have."

Her gaze lands on Sarah as she walks down the stairs with Nick, and Mom's mouth puckers up like she's just sucked a five-pound bag of lemons. "You must be the mistake."

"Mom!" I am so mortified that the volume it comes out at is close to a yell. But I'm also astonished, because how did she even know Sarah was staying with me? "Don't talk to her like that!"

I turn to apologize to Sarah, but she's already fleeing to the kitchen. I start to go after her, but Nick puts a hand on my elbow.

"I'll make coffee," is all he says, but his expression shows that he'll take care of her.

That leaves me out here with my mother—exactly where I don't want to be.

"I have to say, I don't really like what you've done with the place." She looks around. "I know you've never been a fastidious housekeeper, but really, this is pretty bad even for you."

"Yes, well, maybe if I'd known you were coming, I could have made more of an effort," I answer, tongue totally in cheek. Because, seriously, what else have I been doing for the last week and a half but busting my ass on this damn house?

"A lady's house should always be prepared for company." She wipes a finger over a window ledge, then wrinkles her nose at the dust on it.

"Yeah, and a lady's husband probably shouldn't father offspring with another woman, but we're pretty much oh and two for that, aren't we?" The words pop out before I knew I was going to say them, but as my mother's spine stiffens and her eyes widen, I can't say I'm sorry.

I've spent my entire life tiptoeing around her feelings while she shredded mine, which—now that I think about it—is exactly what I did with Karl as well. It felt good standing up to him the other night, and I'd be lying if I said I didn't feel some satisfaction at standing up to my mother as well. I'm sick to death of always worrying about everyone else's feelings when they never worry about mine.

"I don't know why you insist on being so crude," Mom snaps at me right before she marches into the kitchen with her nose in the air.

Part of me is tempted to just let her stew for a few minutes, but Sarah and Nick are in the kitchen and neither of them is prepared for prolonged exposure to Elizabeth Martin when she is in a snit. And while I'm annoyed as fuck at my mother right now, it isn't fair to leave them alone with her.

By the time I make it to the kitchen, Mom is sitting at the table while Nick makes coffee. Sarah is leaning against the counter on her phone—as far from my mom as she can get and be in the same room. Not that I blame her. That's pretty much how I've spent my entire adult life.

But since that's not an option now, I sit down next to my mom. Nick plops cups of coffee in front of both of us and I'm impressed he's remembered that I like mine with cream. Then I take a sip and nearly choke on the burn making its way down my esophagus. Nick must have figured out where Aunt Maggie kept her alcohol because there is a *whole* lot of whiskey in this coffee. I turn toward him, gasping for breath.

He just shrugs. "It seemed like coffee by itself wasn't going to cut it for the two of you right now."

Truer words have probably never been spoken. I swear, if my mother weren't here, I would kiss him for that alone.

Then again, if my mother weren't here, I wouldn't need to be drinking whiskey anyway...

Speaking of, my mother is drinking her spiked coffee with nary a peep, but that just might be because she's too busy staring at my sister to notice. Sarah, on the other hand, is doing her best to pretend my mother doesn't exist.

And she almost pulls it off. But she makes a rookie mistake when dealing with Mom—she looks up from her phone and makes eye contact.

Which is pretty much a declaration of war in my mom's book—and always has been.

"So you're staying here now?" my mother asks in the snootiest tone I've ever heard come out of her mouth—which is saying a lot.

I drain my coffee and hand the mug back to Nick with a low, "Can I have another, please? Hold the coffee this time."

Sarah must be getting sick of Mom's rudeness, though, because she stands up straight and gives Mom a very impressive fuck-you glare. "Yeah, I am. What of it?"

And just like that, my strong, indomitable, never-show-weakness mother crumbles. She drops her head on the kitchen table and starts to cry as if her heart is breaking wide open.

"One more coffee, please." I shove her mug at Nick, too.

He responds by plunking the whiskey bottle down in the middle of the table along with three glasses. Then he settles into the chair on the other side of my mom and gives her a hug. And he never even winces when she lets loose with a tortured wail and buries her face in his shoulder and cries and cries and cries.

I grab the whiskey bottle and pour us all a stiff drink. We're going to need it before this day is over, of that I'm sure.

Chapter Thirty-Seven

*M*om sets down her now-empty shot glass. "After he finally came clean to me and told me about Sarah, I told him that he did you girls a great disservice." She looks from me to Sarah. "To never let you know each other when you're family. It was the last straw. I packed up and left while he sat there in his chair by the big front window doing his damn crossword puzzle."

"This calls for a drink." Nick gathers the shot glasses from in front of him, Mom, and me.

"Another one?" Sarah asks from her spot at the head of the kitchen table, the only sober one in a room full of adults having a much-needed medicinal moment.

"Yes," Mom agrees. "Page sixteen."

I thumb through Aunt Maggie's *My Drinking Buddy* book that was tucked into the cabinet with the liquor. We've been playing this game for the past hour, ever since Mom apologized to Sarah for their initial meeting. One of us would call out a page number and someone else would pick a drink to try from that page.

"Banana Bombers." I concentrate on the letters in the middle of the row of three in my immediate vision. "Triple sec, grenadine, and banana-flavored schnapps."

Nick scoots his chair closer to mine and looks over my shoulder at the page. "Who has banana-flavored schnapps?"

Sarah gets up and goes to the built-in liquor cabinet, hunting around for a minute before crowing in triumph and turning, holding a bottle aloft. "Aunt Maggie!"

Mom throws both her arms up in the air and lets out a loud "wooooooo." My mom is a woo girl; who would have thought.

"I might regret this later," she says. "But I'm beginning to think that old bat was onto something with this hoarding thing."

"Mom!"

"Come on," she says. "Margaret would have laughed at that and you know it."

It's true. She would have. Aunt Maggie loved to laugh at herself and everyone else.

"Ready, bartender?" I ask Sarah.

She nods. "Ready."

"One ounce of schnapps, three-fourths ounce triple sec, splash of grenadine. Shake it like a Polaroid picture and put it in a— Oh shit."

"What?" Nick asks, his words a little slower than usual like the rest of us—well, except Sarah. "Do we have to put it in a pineapple or something?"

"Worse." I look up from the page. "A chilled shot glass."

Nick grabs the shot glasses, gets up, then puts them in the freezer and slings the door shut. "Give it a minute."

"Booooo," Mom says, obviously drunk.

Really, we all are, well, except for Sarah. It's the only thing that can explain why we're willing to try banana-flavored schnapps. There's no way it's going to taste good. We munch on chips and salsa delivered by a bored teenager from the world's best Mexican restaurant this side of the Hudson.

"So you really think I could carry off longer hair?" Mom asks Sarah, picking up the conversation they'd had ten minutes ago as if no time had passed at all. "I thought once I hit forty, I had to cut it all off."

"No way." Sarah shakes her head. "With your bone structure, you could do anything you want with your hair. Have you ever considered going auburn?"

"Red?" Mom blushes. "Oh no, I couldn't. That's very…in your face."

"Come on, Mom, live a little." I cheer her on. "You're sixty-three, not dead! You can do whatever you want."

"I can't believe I left," she says as she fiddles with the bent corner of the *Drinking Buddy* book. "I wonder if he sat at the dining table expecting dinner to magically appear in front of him."

I sigh. "That is how it's worked for the past forever." True story. I don't even know if he knows where the kitchen is in their house, but he definitely doesn't know where to find the pots and pans.

"I have to make a confession." Mom looks around at us, her gaze hazy as she weaves a bit in her chair. "I tossed out all the leftovers before I left, and you know how he abhors delivery food. He'll have to make something from scratch or break his own rules and go out to eat by himself."

We all stare at her in an impressed silence.

"Mrs. Martin," Sarah says. "You are an evil genius."

"Thank you, Sarah. Call me Elizabeth or Liz or Bet; that's what my friends growing up called me because I always won everyone's milk money when we played Jacks."

Who would have thought that my mom was a grade-school hustler?

"Bet it is," Nick says as he opens up the freezer and gets out the shot glasses. "Ready?"

"You bet," the rest of us call out in one voice and then break into laughter.

Sarah pours the Banana Bombers out of the shaker and hands us each a shot glass.

"To fresh starts," I say, my glass held aloft.

Nick, Mom, and I clink our shot glasses and Sarah adds her water glass.

I close my eyes, gird my taste buds, and throw back the shot. That's when I know I'm really past the point of no return— because it tastes delicious. Oh shit. I'm definitely going to regret this in the morning.

Chapter Thirty-Eight

I wake up with a hangover for the second time in a week—which is saying something, since it's been more than a decade since my last one before this week. I really, really want to do nothing more than pull my pillow over my head and stay exactly where I am. Except now that I'm awake, it's impossible to ignore how uncomfortable this couch is. And how much my neck hurts in my current position.

The first thing I'm going to do when the divorce is settled is burn this damn couch and buy another one. And when I do, I'm going to make sure it's the most comfortable one on the market. If I have to spend the next God only knows how many nights on this couch, I freaking deserve it.

In the meantime, I'm going to get myself off this one and get dressed. It's Sunday, which means…I have a lawn to mow.

I force myself to stand up. The room goes up, down, sideways, and then does some kind of undulating diagonal-wave thing. I flop back down and bury my head in my hands. Correction, I'm going to get myself off this couch as soon as my head doesn't feel like the slightest move will make it shatter into a million pieces.

"Mallory?" my mom calls out from the kitchen. "Is that you, dear?"

"Yes, Mom." Just getting those two words out makes me wince with pain—in part because all the brain cells I didn't kill off yesterday are crying in agony and partly because my voice sounds like a frog has not only taken up residence in my throat but has actually died there.

Lucky frog.

"Well, come in here, then," Mom says. "Sarah and I are making blueberry pancakes for breakfast."

Shit. She sounded closer that time. I pry my hands away from my eyes and force myself to turn and look back toward the kitchen.

Sure enough, my mom is standing in the doorway between the kitchen and family room, dressed in her favorite apron and brandishing a spatula like a weapon. "You're not going to get any better sitting there. I have hot coffee and Tylenol waiting on the table for you, and the pancakes and bacon will be ready in just a minute. We'll get that hangover fixed up in no time."

Then she disappears back into the kitchen.

And if I ever need—more—proof that my mother is an alien, today is definitely supplying it. She had way more to drink yesterday than I did, yet she's acting like she's perfectly fine. That isn't human.

Still, I spent enough of my life under Elizabeth Martin's thumb to know that the clock has started. If I don't get my ass to her table—I mean, my table—in the next three minutes, she will come drag me there by the ear. And since my ears are part of the head that feels like it will shatter at any moment, it seems like a bad move to let that happen.

I make a quick stop in the half bath and splash water on my face and wind my totally unruly hair up into a topknot before I drag myself to the kitchen table. I shove the Tylenol my mom has waiting for me into my mouth, then swallow it down with scalding-hot coffee.

The shot of caffeine is totally worth the pain.

I take another long sip, then turn to look at my mom and Sarah, who are working the stove in perfect harmony. It's a far cry from "you must be the mistake," but apparently several rounds of Banana Bombers can cure anything.

Except this hangover.

As my mom drops a stack of blueberry pancakes on my plate, I get my first good look at her. I can't believe it. Her hair is wild around her shoulders and her face is devoid of makeup. Considering my mom doesn't even leave her room in the morning without being fully done up, this is one of the few times in my life I can remember seeing her like this.

Figuring it's because she is devastated about leaving Dad, I brace myself for more tears. But instead of looking sad, she looks resolute. Not happy necessarily, but like she knows what she wants to do. And, more, is at peace with it.

It's that peace, and the fact that she's obviously trying—with Sarah, with me, and with the universe—that has me moving over to hug her. It isn't something I do often, so I'm not sure who's more startled by the action, my mom or me.

Still, she hugs me back and even pats my arm. "Eat your pancakes before they get cold."

It's pretty much as close to an *I love you* as my mother gets on non-holidays, so I take it.

Breakfast is a lot more subdued than most of yesterday, but once my stomach is full and the Tylenol has kicked in, I feel a million times better. Which is a good thing because, even though I have a hangover and the mother of all cricks in my neck, I still have a job to do. A job that starts with raiding Nick's garage for his lawn mower and ends with my grass actually getting cut.

A deal is a deal, after all, and he stuck around through way more yesterday than I would ever have asked him to. And since I start work in the morning, it's time I keep up my end of the bargain.

After taking care of the breakfast dishes—Sarah and Mom cooked, so I cleaned—I run upstairs and change into a red tank top and my most comfortable pair of shorts. Then I grab my phone and head out the door and over to Nick's.

Before he left last night, Nick mentioned that he'd be running errands most of the morning. I insisted he text me the code to his garage so I can get the mower, and he humored me—even though the look on his face said he didn't expect me to be in any condition to mow the yard.

I may not be in any condition to mow, but I am going to do it anyway. After pulling up the text on my way across the street, I get into the garage without a problem. And since I'm braced for it, I'm not even surprised by the obsessive neatness of the space, complete with printed labels above each of the tools he has hanging over his large workbench.

I am, however, shocked by the size of his lawn mower. And sadly, that isn't even a euphemism.

To begin with, the thing is a Honda, and forget a lawn mower, the engine on it looks like it could probably power a small SUV. Plus, it's wide. Like really, really wide. And I know it says it's self-propelled like my vacuum, but I'd be lying if I admitted I don't have a few doubts about how I'm going to control this thing.

I glance over at my grass. Each green blade looks like it has somehow managed to grow another six inches overnight. Maybe it's good that he has a giant metal beast like this. I'm not sure anything else would get through my mini jungle.

The only problem? I have no clue how to get this bad boy to move.

Still, Google exists for a reason.

After I roll the mower across the street to my yard, I pull out my phone and technology teaches me how to start the beast and how to keep it revving afterward. Thank God for YouTube parents who post how-to videos.

Following the steps Ed from Topeka showcases in his video, I turn the fuel valve, move the flywheel break control to the run position, and then yank the starter cord. Nothing happens.

Not a thing. I try again. And again. And again. My right arm is jelly now, so I try with my left until it is marshmallow fluff. I'm mentally running through every curse word I know, but I refuse to let this beast defeat me.

My breath is coming out in hard puffs when I turn back to Ed, saving a few curse words just for him. Forty-seven seconds into the video, I spot my mistake. I turn the fuel valve, adjust the choke throttle lever, move the flywheel break control to the run position, and pull the starter cord. The sound of the beast's motor coming to life almost makes me pass out in joy.

It's a helluva lot better than actually pushing the mower through my unruly grass. After three feet, though, I realize pretty much nothing is cut. What the actual fuck. So I turn back to Ed, who it's clear now has left out some pretty important steps.

After scrolling through a few videos, I discover that I can't mow my grass like they do on the Home Depot commercials. It's too long. Instead, I have to do some circus-act routine where I lean backward so the front of the mower lifts up and then lower it onto a small section of grass slowly. I try the maneuver. It's awkward and hard and my sorry excuse for arm muscles are aching like a bitch, but it works. Thank fucking sweet baby Jesus, it works.

An hour later, I've sweat out my brain—it's totally possible— and even more of the stinky wet stuff is rolling down my face, my back, my generous-size thighs. It's gross and miserable and all of that has to count for something, so with my last ounce of energy, I put the finishing touches on my message to the HOA, cut off the mower's engine, collapse onto the section of still-to-be-mowed grass, and close my eyes.

If there are snakes slithering around in here, they can have me.

I am too damn tired to fight.

Chapter Thirty-Nine

I'm not sure how long I lay in the hot sun, waiting for the snakes to attack.

Long enough for the foot-long grass to prick me through my clothes in every uncomfortable place imaginable.

Long enough for sweat to drip from every pore in my body.

More than long enough for me to wonder if I can hire a lawn service that takes sexual favors as payment. At this moment, I am happy to give as many blow jobs (condoms required) as necessary if it means I never have to do this again.

I've just begun contemplating whether I have the strength of will to crawl to the door in the back of the house or if I'm just going to die right here—not going to lie, the fact that dying on my front lawn is probably against HOA regulations makes the second option oh so much more appealing. I'm about to decide if I'm going to expire while flipping off the neighborhood or not when something moves between the burning sun and me.

"I'm impressed." Nick's warm, gravelly voice interrupts my final plan to stick it to the Huckleberry Hills HOA. "That had to take some effort."

I open one eye (because two seems like too much investment) and look up. "It did. A lot of effort. And now I'm going to die."

I close my eye again and would have totally tried for final death throes, but I'm afraid it will only make me sweat more.

"You are the strangest woman I have ever met," he says with a bemused laugh.

"That's not true." This time I don't even bother to open my eyes. "You knew Aunt Maggie, queen of the psychedelic vibrators."

"True. But she left them to you, so you've inherited the title." He doesn't sound the least bit upset about the fact that I'm a little odd, not the way Karl would have been. Back when we were first married, he always complained when I danced a little in line at the post office or sang my favorite song while shopping in the produce aisle or wore my favorite red shoes anywhere.

At first, I stopped doing those things around him because I didn't like making him feel uncomfortable. Eventually, I stopped doing them at all. It wasn't a conscious decision to stop. I just got out of the habit of being happy.

Now, I realize as Nick takes hold of my hands and pulls me into a sitting position, I'm beginning to remember what happy feels like—so much so that when he lets go of my hands, I let myself fall backward onto the grass again just to make him laugh.

It works.

At least until he crouches down beside me and strokes a wayward, sweat-soaked curl out of my face. As the pads of his fingers graze my skin, we both stop laughing.

My eyes meet his warm brown ones, and suddenly I feel a little light-headed.

Heatstroke must be setting in, so I sit up abruptly. This time when Nick grabs on to my hands and starts to pull me to my feet, I let him.

"So what made you decide to go with SOS as your message?" he asks as we stand surveying my lawn and the three giant letters I mowed into it.

"The universe wasn't answering my texts, so I went for something a little more in its face."

He laughs again. "The universe really must not be paying attention, Mallory. Because everything about you is pretty much in your face."

"Yeah, well, I'm taking that as a compliment." I grin up at him.

"It was meant as one."

Before I can think of something to say to that, he moves back out over the grass to the mower. "Why don't you go inside and take a shower to cool down?"

"I think I'll do that," I say, grabbing on to the handle of the mower. "If you don't mind, I'm going to park this around back for now. I'll give it another go after dinner, when it doesn't feel like Dante's seventh circle of hell out here."

"There you go, exaggerating again." He shakes his head. "It's really more like the fourth or fifth circle."

"Says the man who hasn't been trying to mow a jungle for the last hour and a half." I roll my eyes and use all the strength I have left to push his behemoth of a lawn mower over to my side gate.

"Can I help you with that?" he asks, walking behind me.

"Nah." I set my shoulders and do my best not to sound like I'm out of breath. It turns out it's even harder to push the beast over grass when the motor is off and the self-propelling feature isn't engaged. If someone tried to tell me that an hour ago, right before I gave up and mowed my first S, I wouldn't have believed them. "I've got it."

He eyes me skeptically. "You sure?"

"Absolutely." I pause to catch my breath but pretend it's to flex my muscles. "Wonder Woman's got nothing on me. I mean, except big boobs, long legs, and a really great ass."

I expect Nick to laugh along with me as we walk around

to the side of the house, but he doesn't. "You were more right the first time."

"What first time?"

He lifts a brow. "When you said Wonder Woman had nothing on you."

And then he turns and walks back down the driveway toward his house, leaving me staring after him with my mouth wide open.

Chapter Forty

*E*ventually, I rally and manage to push the lawn mower through the gate. I leave it right there in front of it, though, unwilling to move it one inch farther than I have to. Besides, it isn't like I'm not going to have to push it right back out in a few hours.

I'm soaked in sweat by the time I make it into the house. My mother takes one look and her eyes go wide. I wait for the inevitable comments about how unfeminine I am or how no man wants a woman who can sweat like I've been wrestling with oiled pigs, but she doesn't say anything.

However, she does press her lips together really hard, like she's having to fight to keep the words in. I almost want to hug her, sweat and all, for making the effort.

Instead, I start shedding clothes as soon as I get upstairs, leaving a trail of stinky, soaking-wet garments from the door of my bedroom all the way to the shower. The fact that I'm going to have to pick them up in a little while doesn't excite me—the only thing worse than sweaty clothes are cold sweaty clothes—but I seriously can't stand having them on my body for one more second.

I get right into the glass cubicle and turn the water on full blast, only yelping a little when the cold spray hits me. Then I just stand there until my body temperature settles back into some kind of normal range.

Eventually I'm revived enough to actually clean myself—shampoo, conditioner, body scrub—but it takes a while. I haven't felt this hot since I caught the flu about seven years ago and ran a temperature close to 105.

Normally, I'm not a water waster—I try to keep my showers in the seven-minute range because water is a precious commodity—but today, I blow that all to hell. I stay under the spray long after my hands turn pruny and every goose bump on my body becomes activated. Then—and only then—do I turn the shower off with a sigh of regret and finally step out.

I know I'm just going to have to get hot, sweaty, and nasty again later, but I decide to hell with it and take my time doing the whole girlie routine. I start by slathering my entire body with my favorite Jo Malone lotion, which I promised myself I'd only use on special occasions, since I definitely can't afford to buy more. It's a nice follow-up to the full-body sugar scrub I did in the shower. Then I do my whole skin-care routine—something I've been pretty lax with since I moved into the house—and I don't even skimp on the products. Some days, a girl deserves to treat herself.

After a blowout that leaves my hair in shining waves—again, something I haven't bothered with in quite a while—I slip into my most upscale pair of yoga pants (which isn't saying a lot, but still) and my most flattering rose tank top. A slick of lip gloss across my lips and a touch of mascara on my lashes, and I figure my mom won't have much to complain about over lunch, even if she wants to.

Satisfied and feeling pretty damn good, I head downstairs. My stomach is growling like an enraged bear.

I'm barely halfway down the stairs when I hear Mom and Sarah chattering amid the clanging of pots and pans. Even more surprising is the fact that Nick's deep voice sounds like it's coming from right in the middle of the action—which, it turns out, it is.

The three of them are in the lemon-yellow kitchen like they all belong there together. Sarah and my mom are setting the table, and Nick is sautéing chicken in a pan.

"I thought you were going home," I say. He *was* walking to his house when I went inside.

Nick doesn't bother glancing up from the frying pan. "I did go home. And now I'm here. Some people can do more than take a shower in an hour and a half."

"Yeah, well…" I walk farther into the kitchen, getting the glasses out of the cabinet while I scramble for a witty comeback. "Sometimes efficiency is highly overrated."

Oh, girl, that's what you're going with?

Ignoring my snarky inner voice, I make eye contact with the back of Nick's head, expecting him to argue with me. Everything about him screams that he's the most efficient person on the planet, after all. But instead of coming back at me with facts and figures, he looks up with an amused grin that kind of freezes when our eyes connect.

And suddenly, that weird breathless feeling is back. It's the one that makes me feel like all the baggage from my broken marriage is sitting squarely on the middle of my chest.

"What's wrong?" I ask when he continues to stare at me without saying anything.

"Nothing. You just—" He breaks off and blows out a long breath. "You look nice."

"Yeah, well, when you last saw me, I was at risk for drowning in my own sweat. Anything is an improvement over that."

"Nothing wrong with working up a little sweat," he says, turning his attention back to the chicken.

There's something in his tone that has my heart beating too fast, even as Sarah lets out a little snort.

My mother is surprisingly quiet.

I'm in the middle of trying to think of another comeback—I'm fast like that—when my phone dings. I glance down at the text from Mikey, asking if I want to meet for a drink around two.

It's pretty much the last thing I want to do—I'm tired and grumpy and it's way too hot outside right now—but I make the mistake of mentioning the invitation to my supporting cast.

"You should go," my mom says. "He sounds like a nice guy."

"He's a very nice guy." I sit down in the empty chair next to her. "I'm just not sure I want to go anywhere right now."

"You should totally go," Sarah chimes in. "You look super hot and besides, what else do you have to do?"

What *do* I have to do? The only things that come to mind are drudgery, followed by hard labor, followed by chores. "Clean out another room so that maybe, maybe I can get my ass off that miserably uncomfortable couch. Plus, I still have the lawn to finish."

"The lawn?" Sarah looks confused. "But—"

Nick places the four perfect portions of chicken on a platter in the middle of the table and sits down across from me. "You should go."

It's pretty much the last thing I expect him to say. On the plus side, it makes the breathless feeling go away really fast.

I'm trying to process the why of that when I happen to glance out the window with a view of the front yard. Then I'm breathless for real, because all the air in my lungs whooshes out in one big angry breath. My entire front lawn has been mowed.

"What did you do?" I demand.

"What do you mean?"

He tries to look innocent, but I've gotten to know him well enough now to see a hint of *something* lurking behind his eyes. The big jerk. We had a deal. Just because I'm broke doesn't mean I need his pity.

"You. Mowed. My. Lawn."

"Oh, that." He serves Mom a piece of chicken, then passes the tray to Sarah. "I thought it would free up the rest of the day for you—"

"So I can go on a date with Mikey?" Acid that has the distinct hint of hurt burns the back of my tongue.

"That wasn't my first choice, no." He shrugs. "But, like I said, you should go if you want to."

Oh wow. Isn't that just fucking big of him to allow me to live my life. "Thanks for the permission."

He sighs. "That's not what I meant."

"I don't actually care what you meant." Heat stirred up by frustration and annoyance and bruised feelings makes my whole body tingly in a very bad way. "We had a deal. I give you a dollar and mow the lawn, and your firm will represent me in my divorce."

He shrugs again. "Yeah, well, I decided to renegotiate after you almost gave yourself a heart attack today."

"That was not your decision to make," I snap. Doesn't he get that I don't want anyone taking care of me anymore? Men. I swear.

"Sorry, I didn't realize you were emotionally invested in the lawn." He holds his hands up in surrender. "I was only trying to help."

"Oh, no." I narrow my eyes at him. "You don't get to do that."

He looks mystified while Mom and Sarah are both watching the happenings as if it is the best reality show ever.

"Do what?" he asks.

I'm not buying it. I've had men do this shit to me over and over in my life—the whole time acting as if I'm the one with the problem or that my concerns or feelings aren't valid. Karl was an expert, and now that I think about it, so is my dad.

"You did what you thought was best for me," I say, forcing myself to keep my voice steady even as my knee is jiggling under the table to let out some of the angry adrenaline rush. "But you never even bothered to ask if I agreed. You did what you wanted to do and didn't care at all if I wanted help."

"Are you kidding me?" He looks incredulously from Mom

to Sarah as if they'll back him up against the overreaching, hysterical, probably PMSing woman.

They're now looking at every single spot in the kitchen except the two of us, and I can't blame them. Part of me feels guilty for putting them in the middle of this, but I'm not backing down.

"No, I'm not," I say. "I didn't ask for your help—"

"You literally mowed SOS into your lawn." Nick leans forward on the table, his entire body strung tight. "It's the universal call for help. Pilots flying into Newark from all over the world probably think you're asking for help, so how the hell was I supposed to know you weren't?"

"Because," I say, my temper on the precipice of going Mount Vesuvius. "If I wanted help, I'd ask for it."

My phone buzzes again with another text from Mikey. I don't think about it. I don't even read his new text; I just started thumb-typing that I'd love to go out and get a drink. Right. Now.

Chapter Forty-One

Maybe I should have thought it was strange when Mikey suggested we meet somewhere instead of picking me up, like he did for our other two dates. But truth be told, I'm just excited to have my own transportation—that way I can leave after one drink without feeling bad.

But the minute I see him sitting at a barstool nervously thumbing through his phone, I know there's going to be trouble. I mean, he didn't even bother to get a table. No man does that if he's hoping to have an intimate, private date with a woman.

Sure enough, his smile when he spots me is a little dimmer than usual. He does get up, though, and even drops a kiss on my cheek before pulling away and waiting for me to sit.

"How are you?" he asks as we both get settled.

"A little frazzled, actually." I give him a wary smile. "But nothing a cold drink won't cure."

"Right?" He laughs somewhat awkwardly even as he flags down the bartender. "What are you drinking?"

After last night, the last thing I want to do is pump more alcohol into my system. In fact, I'm good with not drinking again for a long while.

"Can I have a club soda with lime?"

The bartender nods and makes it up right on the spot.

Mikey raises a brow when I take my first sip, but I just roll my eyes.

"Yesterday I had enough alcohol to last me a year," I say without breathing a word about drinking games and Banana Bombers.

"Oh." He looks concerned. "Are you drinking because of the divorce? Because that's understandable, but still something to worry about if—"

"What? No!" I start laughing. "I was drinking because my mother and my long-lost—and by long-lost, I mean secret—half sister have both moved in with me since the weekend started. And since my mom didn't know about my sister until Saturday—which is why she left my dad to come live with me—it's been exciting. That's why we got drunk yesterday." I pause for breath and take in his shell-shocked expression. "And I realize, saying it out loud makes it sound just as bad as it is." I take a long sip of my club soda and wish that I'd gone for a wine spritzer instead. "Maybe even worse."

"Not bad," he says, taking a big pull from his beer. "Just a lot."

I nod, the writing on the wall becoming a little clearer with every second that passes.

"That's actually why I wanted to meet today." He rubs away a nonexistent stain on the bar, looking at it instead of me. "You know, Mallory, I think you're a really great girl. I just—"

"It's okay, Mikey." I smile at him. "I get it."

"I don't think you do." He gives me his full attention, and he looks more serious than he has since he first gave me the never-ending renovation list. "Just let me finish, okay?"

Honestly, it's not okay. I'm done with my club soda and more than ready to get out of here before my soulful contractor gives me a list of all the reasons he's not interested in me. I mean, I'm not interested in him, either—the abject and total lack of chemistry is something that can't be fixed.

But that doesn't mean I need to sit here and listen as he gives me a list of all the things that are wrong with me according to him. I don't know why guys do that—why they feel the need to list our faults like they're doing us a favor—but most of them do. And frankly, I already spent way too much of the last few years feeling bad about myself. The last thing I need now that I'm finally getting my life and self-esteem back together is for someone to try to tear it all down again, no matter how well-meaning.

"We're in different places right now," he says with a soft smile.

I know it's meant to take the sting from the words. It isn't his fault they didn't sting in the first place.

"That's no one's fault," he continues. "It just is. Your plate is really full, and it seems like you don't exactly have time to date. I don't want you to have to feel like I'm one more ball for you to juggle."

Wow. I can't help but be grudgingly impressed. Maybe I misjudged him. He seems self-aware and kind and not very egotistical *at all*. I feel a little guilty, honestly, considering I was so certain that he was one of those guys who was basically decent but who also—

"Plus. I know what I want in life," he says. "And frankly, the last week has shown me that you really don't."

And there it is. My grip tightens around my glass, and I try my best to keep the fuck-you off my face. Looks like he isn't so different after all. Even worse, even knowing everything I do, his words sting—not because they aren't true but because they are. I *don't* know what I want out of life right now. Not just because of the divorce but because of everything else that has come at me so fast over the last few weeks.

My mom. My sister. Karl and Sasha's baby. My dad. My new job. Nick— I cut off that last thought before it goes any further. Nick isn't just my boss and my neighbor and the guy who is going to help me get a fair settlement from my divorce. I mean, maybe he's gotten to be a friend, too, but he doesn't really belong on the list of things in my life that are in flux. I mean, we've only known each other a short time. There's nothing there to be in flux.

And now that that thought is up there in the front of my brain, there's no time like the present to move this whole thing along.

"Well, thanks for dinner the other night, Mikey. And the club soda—" I hold up my empty glass. "It was really nice getting to talk with you."

I start to get up, but he reaches out and snags my hand before I can do much more than grab my purse. "Hold on, Mallory. Please. I wasn't trying to offend you."

"I'm not offended." And it's true. I'm not offended. What I am is a little embarrassed that I let my life get to this point and a lot ready to figure out what comes next. "I do have a lot on my plate. And I am in the middle of a contentious divorce, so you're right. I don't have a lot of energy left for other things. Which I actually think is okay—just like I think it's okay that I don't know what I want from my life at the moment. For the last decade, I've thought—expected—my life to end up one way. And now I'm finding out it's going to go in a whole different direction. I think it's okay—no, I think it's better than okay—for me to take a little time and figure out what that direction is."

And whoa. That was a mouthful. Even more, it was a brain full—and something I had no intention of ever saying to Mikey or anyone else. But now that I've said it, now that it's out there in the universe, I don't feel bad about doing so. In fact, I'm proud of myself. Proud of myself for speaking my mind and even more proud of myself for taking ownership of my shit.

"I'm really not offended," I reiterate when Mikey continues to look a little like a deer caught in the headlights. "And I'm not angry. I'm just telling you where I'm coming from—which I feel like I already did when we met for lunch."

He inclines his head. "You did. I just…"

"Thought you could fix everything?" I tease with a grin.

He nods, shifting on his barstool. "Maybe something like that. I am a contractor, after all." His grin fades. "Speaking of which, I ordered the dumpster, and it'll be there in three days. I hope this whole thing doesn't change us working together."

"No, of course not." I stand up and grab my purse from the hook under the bar. "You're a good guy, and the references I called all said you're a great contractor."

"I'm glad to hear that. I would love to help you bring that house back to its original glory." He pauses and drums his fingers on the table as if he's trying to figure out how to say something.

I'm about to tell him to just spit it out—no need to be delicate at this point—when he finally looks back up at me.

"I know you're having a rough time, so I can cut my bid by twenty-five percent to try and give you a break," he says. "It'll be tight getting everything we need to do it at that price, but I think if we're creative—"

"No." I shake my head emphatically. "I really appreciate you wanting to help me. I do. And it'll take me a little while to get the money together, but I will get it together. And I'll pay full price just like any other customer you took out on a couple of dates. Well, except the Angela discount—I'm totally taking that."

He looks embarrassed. "Mallory—"

"I'm teasing about the dating part." I reach over and squeeze his hand. "But I really do need to go now. I've got a house full of people, and I'm afraid they'll run amok if I leave them alone too long."

He laughs, as I intended him to. "Like I said. A lot on your plate."

"A lot a lot," I agree and push in my stool, tossing him a smile before I walk out of the cute wine bar with a great guy in it, knowing neither was for me.

I climb back into Jimi, feeling pretty good about myself, Mikey, and the future construction on Aunt Maggie's—no, on *my*—house.

I'm actually glad he ended it, because I was never actually interested in him—something I should have told him from the very beginning. I knew there was no chemistry, but I wanted there to be. I wanted to fall for a nice guy who was just a nice guy. Uncomplicated, loves his mother, does what he says he'll do when he says he'll do it. Simple.

But apparently, I don't like simple. Or, to be more specific, my libido doesn't like simple. In fact, my libido appears to only be attracted to guys who have an asshole streak in them. Guys who don't say what they mean, who always have more than one agenda going on, who can't be trusted to keep the deals they made, because they think they know better.

It is annoying as hell.

By the time I make the turn onto my street and then swing Jimi into my driveway, I have myself all worked up again about men who think they know everything. Then I catch sight of my perfectly mowed grass and the top of my head feels like it's going to come off.

Yeah, the guys who really rev up my ovaries are more than annoying. They are positively infuriating.

I'm sick to death of Nick doing things without consulting me. From running his mouth off at Karl to getting me signed up with Gina as my lawyer to befriending my sister and my mom to mowing my grass. He did it all without consulting me and I am done. Just. Done.

I get out of the car in a huff, slamming Jimi Hendrix's door hard enough to rock it back on its wheels. I start to march across the street, then decide—before I do—to do the one thing that will make Mr. HOA Rules Should Be Laws' head spin.

Chapter Forty-Two

My outrage propels me up the driveway and even gives me the strength to wrestle with the warped garage door. Because the last time I was in here, I'm positive I spotted— Yep, there they are. Right behind the stacks of empty picture frames. Two dozen lawn flamingoes.

Hot damn.

It takes me three trips and fifteen minutes, but I finally get them arranged on my freshly mowed lawn in the shape of a penis. Then I march across the street to Nick's house.

He answers about three seconds after I ring his doorbell for the fifth time. Not that there is a lot of time in between the rings, but still. I'm annoyed as hell when he finally pulls open the front door.

"Mallory?" He looks confused—and also more adorable than I can take in his checkered pajama bottoms and black V-neck T-shirt, with his damp hair falling over his forehead. "What are you doing here?"

"Were you sleeping?" I ask incredulously, though I have no room to criticize anyone about their sleeping habits. "It's three o'clock."

"I just got out of the shower, actually." He glances over my shoulder, and a look of shock flits across his face. Followed by an adorable smirk. "Nice flamingoes."

It's not the reaction I was counting on. "Nice?" I all but screech.

He shrugs. "Maggie used to make funny pictures with them, too. I always liked seeing what she dreamed up next. Maggie would have been proud of your artistry." He grins and steps back. "Come on in."

"Oh, no. I'm not coming in. You're not going to soften me up with your plants." I poke him gently in the chest for emphasis. "I've got a bone to pick with you, mister!"

That ridiculous eyebrow of his goes up as he looks from my face to my finger, then back again. "A bone to pick with *me*?" he repeats, and when he says it in that ridiculously sexy voice of his, it sounds both absurd and hot as fuck.

Which only infuriates me more. "Oh, don't you play innocent with me. You know exactly what I mean. And now my contractor has gone and dumped me because my hormones can't behave and it is. All. Your. Fault." I poke him again for good measure.

"Am I supposed to have any idea what you're talking about?" He cocks his head to the side as he stands there, filling up the entire doorframe. "Though I'm taking this diatribe to mean you and the contractor won't be seeing any more of each other?"

"What I am talking about is that I have had three very nice dates with a very nice man and my ovaries—and the rest of me, for that matter—couldn't give a shit. Apparently, there is something wrong with me, and I'm only attracted to guys like you!"

Oh, shit. The second the words are out, it's like a bucket of cold water was dumped on my head. Anger fades, reason returns, and I want nothing more than to turn and crawl back to my house to nurse the utter humiliation of this day in peace.

I mean, Nick has shown almost no interest in me—a few sizzling looks don't count, considering he's been shoving me out the door at Mikey every chance he gets—and here I am, standing on his doorstep, all but screaming that I have the hots for him. It's beyond embarrassing.

But Nick doesn't look like he cares about my embarrassment as he steps over the threshold and gets right in my face. "Guys like me? What exactly do you mean by that?"

"You know exactly what I mean." I wave a hand up and down to encompass his gorgeous physique and even more gorgeous face.

"Yeah, actually, I do know what you mean, and I'm not exactly impressed. You think I'm just like your ex, right? An asshole who has an agenda every time he does anything."

The ice-cold annoyance in his voice sets off a similar annoyance in me.

"Are you saying you don't have an agenda?" I shoot back at him.

Now both brows are up and he looks an awful lot like an enraged ancient god about to smite the inconsequential people—and by inconsequential people, I mean me. Too bad I'm too worked up to care right now.

Even when his mouth firms into a straight line and he leans forward and down so that we are eye to eye. "Exactly what agenda am I supposed to have, Mallory?"

"Oh, I don't know," I grumble. "How about the fact that you've been judging me and telling me what to do from the first time we met."

"I have not—"

"Oh, yes you have." I make my voice deeper as I mimic, "Mow your lawn, close your garage, don't roll over for your ex, fight for a fair settlement, go out with the contractor, fill out these forms, give me a dollar because my partner and I will represent you, go out with the contractor again, take a shower—"

My voice breaks on the last one because his eyes narrow to slits. And yes, I am more than aware that I am being ridiculous. Because all those things that pissed me off along the way—all those things that made me feel like he was trying to boss me around like Karl used to—actually sound pretty decent when

I lay them out in a list like that.

Maybe not the mow-my-lawn part, but the close-my-garage-because-I-might-get-burgled, let-me-help-you-out-of-this-mess-with-your-ex stuff...that all sounded pretty good. It certainly sounded better in retrospect than how I was taking it earlier today.

I blink several times as realization dawns. Well, hell. I'm not mad at Nick at all. I'm mad at the universe, but *it* doesn't handily live across the street so I can cuss it out.

I finally want someone again, crave him actually, and he pushed me toward another man. A man who just spent our date telling me exactly why I'm not date material. Apparently, my hormones have been in cold storage for more years than I can count, and my thawing ovaries are not enjoying this party at all.

And just like that, the fight eases out with my breath, my shoulders hanging low.

I'm about to be reasonable and apologize when Nick takes another step forward. "You're a real piece of work, you know that?"

Um, ouch. Okay, buddy, no apology for you. The muscles tic in his clenched jaw, and I don't even care if he breaks a molar now. There was no call for that low blow. I know I'm damaged goods right now. No need to rub it in, Mr. Perfect Pants.

"I'm going to take that as a compliment." I lift my chin.

"Go ahead and take it any way you want," he snarls. "God knows, you will anyway."

"What is that supposed to mean?"

My eyes widen as he takes one last step forward. Now his chest isn't the only thing that's close to me as we go toe to toe on the front porch in front of God and all of Huckleberry Hills. His mouth is as well. And even though he's mad as hell right now, there's a part of me that recognizes something even more important. Nick is not unaffected by me.

It's been a while since I've seen real attraction this up close, granted, but it's hard to miss the signs. His pupils are blown out, his breathing is ragged, and his eyes... His gorgeous eyes are fixed on my lips. I can't help wondering what would happen if I just leaned forward a little more. What would happen if I just pressed my lips to his?

He draws in a deep breath and brings his gaze back to mine. "It means that maybe your ovaries know what they're talking about, and you should listen to them for once."

The breathless feeling I always get around him is back—about ten times worse than usual. A confidence I didn't know I had has me asking, "Oh, and do what exactly?"

"The same thing I've been wanting to do for days now." He takes one last step and eliminates the small sliver of space I left between our bodies. "The same thing I've been thinking about every fucking second of every fucking hour of every fucking day since you moved in across the street from me."

"Yeah?" I barely get the word past my suddenly dry throat. "What's that?"

"This."

His hands come up to cup my face seconds before his lips slam down on mine.

Chapter Forty-Three

Oh my God is Nick a great kisser. It's like everything that was building up inside—all the want and the need and the gotta-have—got to the point where it couldn't be locked down any longer, and the relief valve has been well and truly flipped open.

His hands are on my hips, his mouth is on mine, and I can't get enough. I've never been called greedy in my life, but right now—right now I want everything I can get and more. His mouth nips and licks and sucks at mine, devouring me so completely, I feel dizzy.

Suddenly, the world tilts, and I chalk it up to his kisses being just that powerful before I realize he's scooped an arm under my legs and is carrying me inside. His foot slams the door closed behind us and a molecule of wariness pricks along my skin. Not because of Nick, per se, but because the last time I gave my body to a man, he took my soul instead.

If this is going to continue, and God I hope it does, I need to set some boundaries. I'm not ready for a relationship or anything like that. I just want to have an orgasm that makes me forget my name. That's reasonable, right?

"This doesn't change anything," I say as I touch every part of him that I can while he carries me into the living room.

In a heartbeat, my feet are on the floor again, but I still can't stop touching him.

He pauses his journey of kissing his way down my neck. "What won't change?"

I reach out, grab the hem of his shirt, and slide my hands underneath so I can glide them across the hard ridges of his abs. And God, he feels good. "I don't need a man to help me with anything but orgasms."

Nick pulls back at that. Takes a few steps away. Then we stand there, both breathing heavily—from my words? From the kiss? From both?—staring at each other in the middle of his living room. The only illumination is the soft light coming in from the foyer.

He crosses his arms over his chest, the move drawing my attention to his biceps straining against the short sleeves of his T-shirt. "You don't need my help?"

"No." I don't, and he needs to learn that, but maybe now isn't the best time for the lesson. Not when we could go back to kissing.

"So that means you can take your shirt off all on your own?" He punctuates the question with a dare-you smirk that makes my breath catch.

I didn't think it was possible to want him more, but I do. A man who hears what I need and gives it to me is the sexiest thing in the world to me. All I want in that moment is to feel Nick's hands on my bare skin, so I grab the hem of my filmy red tank top and slowly pull it over my head, then drop it to the floor.

"Guess you really *didn't* need my help," he says, his gaze sliding over me with an intensity that leaves every part of me burning.

He takes a step back and then, without a word—not a single word—he reaches behind his neck and tugs his T-shirt off over his head.

Holy. Fuck. Just holy. *Fuck*.

All those dreams about him mowing the lawn without his shirt were woefully inadequate. It isn't just the abs or the hard wall of his chest or the dusting of dark hair that goes from his belly button and disappears behind the button of his jeans. It's that I want this man. Badly. It hits me like a crosstown bus, the lust and desire. I. Want. Nick. Holloway.

And for one of the very few times in my adult sexual life, I am going to experience the satisfaction of getting exactly what I want. With that thought in mind and his abs firmly in my sights, I walk slowly and deliberately over to where he stands.

"Is there something I can help you with?" he teases, his eyes hot as I stop in front of him.

I don't answer—at least not verbally. Instead, I glide my fingertips straight down the center of his abs, from the hollow of his throat to his belly button.

He shudders at my touch, his eyes blazing even hotter as I tangle my fingers in his belt loops and tug him close. He comes willingly—eagerly—and the moment his body meets mine, everything inside me shuts down but the want. The need. The have-to-have.

He's big and strong and warm—so warm that I want to burrow into him and just breathe. So I do. For long seconds, I press my body tightly to his and relish the feel of him against me. More, I relish the feelings inside me—the fact that I can want like this after years of feeling nothing with Karl. Of feeling less than nothing, if I'm honest.

Eventually, Nick slides his hand up to cup my jaw and I turn into it. I press a kiss to the center of his broad palm. And then I tilt my head, raising my lips to his.

I expect him to slam his mouth down on mine, to repeat what happened earlier when he said that he wanted me. Instead, he's gentle as he brushes his lips against mine. As he slides his tongue along my lips. As he tangles his hands in my hair and tugs my head back just a little to give him better access.

For several seconds—minutes—he devours me, his lips and tongue and teeth ravishing me in a way I didn't know I wanted to be ravished. A way I didn't know I *could* be ravished. I love every second of it. So much so that I ravish him right back, loving the way he responds to me—like he can't get enough.

Eventually, though, he pulls back, and I would complain, except his hands are skimming along the sensitive skin of my lower back, and it feels good. So good.

It's been too long since I've been touched like this. Not just since I asked Karl for a divorce but for months—maybe years—before that, when sex had become perfunctory, just a box to be checked off whenever Karl was in the mood instead of something hot and desperate and intimate.

As Nick's fingers dance across my skin, it is all of those things. Hot and desperate and intimate—so intimate—as his mouth slides along my jaw and down the soft, exposed column of my throat.

"I'm going to take these off now," he tells me as he takes hold of the button on my jeans. It's a question as much as it's a statement, and I appreciate the care, the concern, even in the middle of all this heat.

"Yes," I answer, my hands clutching at his hair. "Please. Yes."

Seconds later, my jeans are gone as I stand in front of him in nothing but my navy-blue satin bra and panties set. For a second, it doesn't matter—nothing does but the way his hands feel sliding along my arms and over my back.

But then it hits me.

Nick is the first non–medical professional not named Karl to see me this naked in ten years. I'm not in my twenties anymore. There's a definite pooch above the waistband of my panties. When my bra comes off, my boobs lower a few degrees. And there's cellulite on my hips that just appeared one morning and never went away.

The heat starts to curdle in my stomach, discomfort turning all the sensations inside me to something else as Karl's voice plays in my head, picking every single inch of me apart over the days and months and years of our marriage.

I start to turn away, to cover myself, but Nick is looking at me like a desperate man. And like he very much loves what he sees.

And that's enough—more than enough—to bring me back to myself. To the moment. Karl has already taken so much away from me. No way is he going to take this moment, too.

So when Nick draws me closer and runs his lips over my shoulders with soft, sweet kisses, I don't stop him. I don't do anything but tilt my head back and enjoy every second of it.

His mouth never leaves my skin as he finishes stripping me—and himself. But then he's kissing his way down my body, his mouth sliding lower and lower until my already shaky knees threaten to give way.

I clutch at his shoulders and he laughs, moving lower still, pulling one leg over his shoulder and kissing me more intimately, his tongue stroking against me as though I were his only sustenance. And just like that, my body breaks like the ocean against the shore. Pleasure rolls over me—through me—in waves that sweep me under...and away.

I'm vaguely aware of what happens next—of Nick reaching toward a side table and grabbing a condom out of his wallet before pulling off his pants and boxer briefs, then sinking down on the sofa and pulling me over him.

"You can still change your mind," he whispers against the sensitive skin behind my ear.

"I'm not changing anything," I answer. Not here, when Nick is pressed hot and hard against me and not now, when I finally feel good. When I finally feel more like myself than I have in a very long time.

"Good." I feel the upward curve of his lips against my skin. And then his hands are on my hips—soft and urgent and desperate.

I lift onto my knees, then lower myself slowly, relishing

the way the heat and strength and power of him fill up parts of me I didn't even know were empty before tonight—before this moment.

"I want to hear you," Nick says, his voice harsh and breath coming way too fast. "Let me hear you."

I can't deny him—or myself. Not on this. For once, I don't have to stay quiet while I come all by myself in the bed next to a snoring husband. I can moan and sigh and talk dirty and whatever the hell else I want.

So I do.

It feels amazing, just like everything else about this afternoon. And this man.

My fingers tangle in his hair.

My hips move against his.

My lips slide over his.

Electricity. Power. Need. They sweep through me all at once—sweep through us both—and take us up, up, up. Until I can't think. Can't breathe. Can't do anything but feel.

I'm drowning in sensations, drowning in a need I've never felt before, and just when I'm certain I can't take any more—that *we* can't take any more—I shatter into a million tiny pieces.

Nick breaks with me, and it isn't until long minutes later, when I'm finally able to remember my own name and how to do something more than tremble and cling, that I can't help wondering how many of his pieces have gotten mixed up with mine.

And how I'm supposed to give them back.

Chapter Forty-Four

I wake up with a hand cupping my breast and a long, warm body pressed against my back.

I'd like to say it takes me a few seconds to remember where I am, but the truth is, I know where I am as soon as I drift into consciousness—maybe even before. I'm in Nick's house, in Nick's bed, and every single muscle in my body is aching just enough to remind me of what we spent most of the evening doing.

I moan a little—in horror, not pleasure—as images from last night flash through my brain at high speed.

Nick slamming into me against the wall as I dug my nails into his back and begged for more.

Nick dropping me down on the edge of his bed and then falling to his knees between my legs.

Nick turning me over while a third orgasm still had my knees shaking and plunging inside me until I screamed myself hoarse with pleasure.

Nick touching me, kissing me, fucking me, over and over and over again.

Nick throwing his head back as he came.

Nick smiling wickedly.

Nick.

Nick.

Nick.

He's all I can see against the black backdrop of my closed lids. All I can feel wrapped around me in this warm, toasty bed. All I can smell or taste or hear as I try to get my galloping heart and rampaging imagination under control. What happens next? It's hard to have a one-night stand with a guy *who lives across the street*!

I take a deep breath in an effort to tamp down the panic sliding around inside me, but it doesn't work. Partly because I'm too freaked out and partly because Nick is waking up, his long, lean, hard body moving against me even as his fingers stroke and squeeze my nipple.

Heat that never really went away flares to life, and there's a part of me that wants nothing more than to roll over and kiss him. To graze my hand along his body until he's trembling against me. To shift down the bed and take him deep inside my mouth, my throat.

But there's another part of me that is screaming about the fact that I'm supposed to be walking into his office to *work for him* in less than two hours. And before that, I have to do the walk of shame across the street to *my house* in front of the *entire neighborhood*.

What am I supposed to do? This is a mess. A huge, giant mess, and I've no idea how I'm supposed to fix it.

Nick's hand drifts lower, down my rib cage and across my stomach, and I stiffen as all the worries in my head come roaring over me.

His hand stops immediately.

"Hey," he says in a voice that is even lower and sexier and more gravelly than usual. "Everything okay?"

"Yeah." The word sticks in my throat as I roll over to climb out of bed. "I should probably get going—"

"Going? Now?" He sounds surprised, and maybe even a little concerned.

"It's okay," I say. "Everything is—"

"Wait a minute." He tugs me onto my back so that I can't hide from him, then props himself up onto an elbow.

He's pulled away and isn't touching me anymore, and there's a wariness on his face that makes my stomach churn even as it exacerbates every fear I have deep inside.

"What's going on inside that head of yours?" he asks.

"As opposed to outside this head of mine?" I snark.

Nick sighs, even as he reaches up to brush a few strands of hair out of my face. "I'm sorry. I probably should have said this before we ended up in bed last night, but the moment just got away from us both. We should discuss boundaries, you working for me right now and all. So there are no misunderstandings, yes?"

Oh God. The only thing more embarrassing than the walk of shame for all of Huckleberry Hills is for the guy, whose house said walk begins with, to first tell me this was a onetime thing.

"I get it," I tell him, shoving away and out of bed. "You don't have to spell it out."

"Spell what out?" he asks as my gaze darts around for a blanket or towel. Or hell, a dirty sock on the floor.

My clothes are in the living room, and I've never been more embarrassed being naked in my life. It's one thing having Nick look at me yesterday, when everything was couched in a sea of lust. It's another altogether to have him staring at me with clear eyes in the harsh glare of the morning sunlight. I head toward the door in all my un-glory.

"That this can't happen again," I clarify. "That we're about to start working together and are neighbors and need to stay friends." I toss a wave over my shoulder and try to make it out the door with my last shred of dignity. "Like I said, I get it."

Except Nick is around the bed before I can even get to the door. "Hey," he says, grabbing my hand. "That's not what I was going to say."

"Yeah, well, it's what I was going to say, so you don't need to bother with trying to let me down easy."

He's nicer than Karl and probably wants to get out of this without hurting anyone's feelings, but I don't have it in me to listen to him fumble around trying to be a good guy.

Things are what they are—better to just lay it out there so there are no hurt feelings or misconceptions. The last thing my pride can take right now is another man thinking I'm going to shrivel up and die without him.

I'm not, and it's important that both of us know that.

"Okay," he says after a second of studying my face. "If that's all that needs to be said, then I'm going to catch a shower before work. I'll see you in the office at eight."

He smiles tightly, then turns and walks straight into the master bathroom without a backward glance.

Seconds later, I hear the shower start, just like he said. And though I suddenly want to stick around and try to figure out why he went from warm and amused to cold and distant so quickly, the clock is ticking. I need to head home, fend off my mom and sister, and grab a shower of my own before getting dressed for my very first day of work.

But as I rush naked around his living room, gathering up my clothes and looking desperately for my missing pair of underwear, I can't help thinking that this really is the only time I'm ever going to get to have sex that fantastic in my life— especially if that fantastic sex is supposed to happen with Nick.

Because he might be the kind of guy to have sex with me and ask questions later, but he's not the kind to want anything to be uncomfortable afterward. Just look at his house, for God's sake. He likes his life neat and orderly. Two things a relationship with me would definitely not be.

Which I'm pretty sure means everything is going to be completely platonic and completely businesslike from now on—and that he'll never make another move on me again.

Which is a good thing—I know it is. What I can't figure out

is why, as I let myself out of his house to start what feels like the longest walk of my life, it doesn't feel so good.

And that's before I run into three neighbors who are out walking their dogs. I tell myself they don't actually know what I'm doing or why I'm out this early with a serious case of bedhead and what I'm sure is mascara running down my cheeks.

But it feels like they know, feels like I have a giant scarlet *S* for walk of Shame plastered across my chest. A nice old lady with a poodle compliments me on my va-va-voom tank top and I just kind of smile and wave at her.

And then I run—all the way up my driveway, through the gate, and around the back of the house. My only saving grace is that it's barely six a.m. and there are no lights on in the house that I can see. Which—please God—means Mom and Sarah are still upstairs in bed.

The last thing I want to do right now is see anyone else, let alone my mom as I wobble in on shaky legs after the best, most confusing sex of my life. She hasn't been as judgy since our hours of drunken abandon two days ago, but I'm pretty sure the judiness will roar back, full force, if she catches me sneaking in at six in the morning. And I'm just not up for that.

I slide the back door open and start to tiptoe inside, only to find myself face-to-face with Sarah and my mother, both of whom are sitting on the couch drinking coffee. And watching me sneak in with raised brows.

Fuck.

I close my eyes and pray for the ground to open up and swallow me whole. When that doesn't happen, I decide I might as well look on the bright side. At least I got one last fantastic orgasm before I died of total and complete humiliation. Okay, several orgasms, but that's not the point right now.

Fingers crossed that this won't be as bad as I think it's going to be.

I smile sickly at them and give a little wave—kind of like

how I treated the neighbors—before I make a beeline for the stairs.

"From the look of you, I'm guessing the contractor knows how to swing his hammer," Sarah says with a grin.

I give her an are-you-kidding-me look. "I, umm—"

"Don't be ridiculous, Sarah." My mother gives me a knowing look. "Mallory wasn't with the contractor. The car's been in the driveway since three yesterday afternoon."

"Well, then, who was she—" Sarah's eyes go huge, and she claps her hands as she squeals, "Really? Nick?"

"I don't—I mean—"

"Stop dithering, Mallory," my mother says with a roll of her eyes. "Of course it was Nick, Sarah. The two of them have been dancing around each other since I got here."

"She's right, isn't she?" Sarah says, watching my face closely. "That's awesome. Nick's a great guy. And super hot."

I don't know if he's great, but he's certainly not a bad guy—despite our awkward morning after. "He's very nice," I agree as I creep toward the stairs. The last thing I want—or have time for—is a bunch of questions about last night.

"Do you want some coffee?" my mom asks.

"I've got to take a shower and get dressed. I have to be at work by eight." I remind myself to smile at her. "But thanks for the offer."

I'm almost at the stairs, thank God, but as I all but make a running leap for them, my mom says, "I'm proud of you."

"For..." I trail off, not willing to say out loud to my mother that I had sex with Nick, no matter how chill she seems to be right now.

"For going after what you want. It's been a long time since either of us did that," she murmurs. "But watching you, I find myself inspired."

"Me too," Sarah says. "I've been feeling sorry for myself for the last few days, but I'm done with that. I mean, I may not be able to go out and find myself a guy as awesome as Nick—at least not yet—but that doesn't mean I can't get the rest of my life in order... Starting now."

"There's no time like the present," my mother agrees. "Especially with inspiration like Mallory around."

I have no idea what that means, but I want to know—just not when I really do have to get ready for work. Making a mental note to ask her later, I give her and Sarah my first real smile of the day.

"Thanks, Mom."

And then I race up the stairs and dive straight into the shower. As I rinse the shampoo from my hair, I can't help wondering if anyone at work will be able to tell I just had the best sex of my life with the boss or not. I feel like it's tattooed on my forehead. Or vagina, at least.

Chapter Forty-Five

I totally regret the thong—especially since it keeps crawling way too far north as I walk a potential client down the plant-lined hall at Holloway and Murphy to Gina's office. I grit my teeth to deal with the pinch between my cheeks.

"As you can see," I say, gesturing toward the conference room where several of the paralegals are meeting, "while we're a boutique firm, we have the ability to meet all of your needs."

"I just want someone who will fight for me," she says, her grip tight on the strap of her black handbag.

"Well then, you are most assuredly in the right place." I knock on Gina's door, wait for three full Mississippis, and then open it. "Ms. Washington, this is Gina Murphy. Now, can I get you coffee or a sandwich? I know you had to use your lunch hour for this appointment."

She smiles, her short, natural-styled hair perfectly framing her face. "I couldn't bother you."

"It's really not," I say. "How about a turkey and Swiss from the deli down the block?"

After she agrees and Gina puts in her own order, I walk back to the break room, where Tessa is dancing along to whatever is playing in her AirPods while compiling the staff's lunch order. Turns out Gina's niece isn't a bad kid, she just got thrown into the deep end with absolutely no training when Viola went out on maternity leave. Now she's working as the office intern, and I'm showing her the ropes of office management.

"Can you add another turkey and Swiss for Ms. Washington? She's Gina's noon. And Gina would like a turkey on wheat, hold the mayo."

"You got it." Tessa snaps her gum and gives me a thumbs-up. "Do you mind getting Nick's?" she asks. "I have to go ask Steve if he wants onions or no onions."

I nod, trying my best to ignore the buzz of anticipation skimming across my skin. I haven't seen him all day. In fact, I haven't seen him since I did the walk of shame this morning.

"Sure, I can do that." I can. Really. Maybe.

Suck it up, Mallory.

I stop in the bathroom for a quick thong adjustment and lipstick refresh while I'm there—it means nothing—and then walk down to Nick's office at the end of the hallway and knock. After his muffled "come in," I let out a nervous breath and walk inside.

His gaze only flicks up to me for a minute before going back to his computer screen. "Hi, Ms. Martin."

Ouch. That stings. Okay, that's how we're doing it. Fair enough. It isn't like we were planning on a repeat or a relationship or anything.

"Tessa is leaving in a minute to get the lunch order from the deli," I say. "Do you want her to get anything for you?"

"You're a godsend. I've been fighting for the past thirty minutes with this ridiculous spreadsheet for payroll to send to the accountants and haven't even gotten to think about lunch."

Spreadsheet? Payroll? Does he not realize why I was hired?

"Here, let me." I walk around to his side of the desk. My hands are halfway to the keyboard when I realize what I'm doing. "That is, if you don't mind a little help."

He waves toward the screen. "Go ahead."

I lean down and scan the information. "Ah, I see what's wrong."

A few keystrokes later and everything is adding up again—at least in the spreadsheet. For me, not so much. Rational, logical, boring me knows this is the workplace and Nick has made his position clear. Still, being this close to him, inhaling the scent of his aftershave, and trying—and failing—to ignore the way my body responds to him, I am having a really hard time remembering we aren't having a thing. Then he pivots in his chair, turning so that we're face-to-face and definitely within kissing distance. My breath catches and the world slows down to molasses-in-February speed.

"So, Nicky." Tessa barges in mid-sentence. Her wide gaze goes from me to Nick and back again, her eyebrows inching upward with every second.

I start, rearing back. My cheeks burn with embarrassment after almost kissing my temporary boss and nearly getting caught. For his part, Nick seems completely unflustered. It isn't fair.

"Sorry." Tessa looks down. "Am I interrupting? I just wanted to get Mallory's order, too."

"Not at all," Nick says, covering for me because I can't quite form words. "Ms. Martin was helping me with my spreadsheet."

Wow. What a great way to make a first impression at my brand-new job. Way. To. Go. After Tessa takes down his order of a pastrami on rye with extra mustard and mine of another turkey on wheat, she skedaddles out of his office, giving me a curious look on her way out.

"Thank you, Ms. Martin," Nick says, picking up a deposition from the stack of paperwork on his desk. "The entire staff has you to thank for making sure they get paid."

I know all too well what that kind of formal thank-you means. I'm dismissed.

Fine with me. I'm here to work anyway.

The rest of the day is one fire after another, but that's pretty much life in a small law firm. Clients show up late, some pop in without appointments, and there is the huge amount of paperwork flowing in and out of the office that has to get to the right judge, filed in the right order, or double-checked for errors.

During my downtime, Tessa and I go over her career hopes. It's actually pretty fun to talk to her. The whole world is still out there waiting for her to conquer it. In a way, I'm a little jealous of her for having that opportunity, but at the same time, whew, I'm not sure I'd want to go through my twenties ever again—with or without Karl.

By the time I'm the last one in the office and thus tasked with turning off the lights, I've reorganized the inventory ordering system so the office won't run out of toilet paper every three weeks, had a chat with the payroll company about how we can update the software on our end to be more efficient, and lined up three private investigators to come in for interviews next week. All in all, it was a pretty damn good day.

"Burning the midnight oil?"

I scream and jump about a mile high only to see Nick when I land. "I didn't realize you were still here."

Truth is, he spent the entire day locked up in his office. According to the paralegal pool, that's not his usual procedure, so obviously he was avoiding me. Fine. I can deal with that. Whatever.

"I hope you had a good day?" he asks as we make our way out of the office and into the elevator. "How about dinner to celebrate?"

That sounds an awful lot like a date. "Is it an employee benefit, like the legal advice?"

He shakes his head. "It's a neighbor benefit."

I should say no. Going to dinner with Nick is not what I

need in my life. We've gotten each other out of our systems—probably just rebound sex. Don't they say that everyone has a post-divorce wild phase? Maybe this is just the beginning of mine.

What will wild Mallory do? I have no clue. What would Aunt Maggie do? She'd definitely choose dinner.

"Dinner sounds perfect."

Chapter Forty-Six

One text to my mom and an hour later, I rinse off a soapy but clean dish and hand it to Nick. My belly is full of the best thing in the world to eat after a long day at work—breakfast for dinner.

I'll admit, when he asked, I didn't think he meant dinner at his place, but honestly, it just felt perfect. No awkward silences over a restaurant table while waiting on our orders to be taken or dinner to be cleared away. We were both too busy sorting out who would make what and where to really pause long enough to feel weird.

"You've got to be kidding me," he says as he dries off the plate and puts it in the cabinet over the wine fridge. "You haven't ever seen any of the Lord of the Rings? Frodo? The Shire? Gandalf? One ring to rule them all? We have to fix this. Tonight."

Temptation, thy name is Netflix and chill with my superhot neighbor who kisses like it's his job and loves what he does for a living. Speaking of which…

"I have work tomorrow."

"Amazing, so do I." He tosses the tea towel over one shoulder and leans against the granite counter. "We'll only watch the first one."

I pull the sink drain and watch the suds disappear along with my willpower. "How long is it?"

TRACY WOLFF AND AVERY FLYNN

"Good movies aren't about how long they are."

That is definitely a lie, but the kind that I want to believe. I have no idea what it is about this man, but he just gets to me. Every. Damn. Time.

"Nick." I hold out my dripping hands for the towel.

"Fine." Instead of handing over the towel, he starts to dry my hands. "It's nearly four hours. But it's worth it." He hangs up the towel and walks me out of the kitchen into the living room. My purse is on the coffee table. My heels are still by the front door. "Come on, I have a big screen, a really comfy couch, and I won't even say all of Sam's lines during the movie."

"Is this just an excuse to sit in the dark and make out?" I'm not saying I'm projecting, but yeah, I am totally projecting.

"That is an extra added benefit."

I lift an eyebrow. "For friends with benefits and only friends with benefits?" Confirming that last bit for myself? Absolutely. So what if I just decided over soapy dishes that it was time I sow some wild oats, be free, roll with it. "Okay. I'll stay."

We settle in on the couch, with me tucked into his shoulder, and he turns on the movie. We don't even make it through the opening title sequence before Nick has lost his shirt and my pants are in danger of coming off. Without a single protest, he scoops me up in his strong arms and carries me upstairs. In any other circumstance, it would be ultraromantic, but I'm not looking for romance. I'm not looking for love. I'm definitely not looking to fall for anyone.

This is just for fun. I have absolutely nothing to worry about.

And if my ovaries are taking bets on which one of us is lying, well, that's nobody's business but my own. They're traitorous bitches anyway.

I sink my fingers into his hair, nuzzle his neck, and tell him all the things I want him to do to my body tonight, a list of demands that it's apparent he's more than willing to deliver as he starts taking the stairs two at a time.

He drops me onto the bed, and I bounce with a giggle that gets stuck in my throat when he unbuckles his pants and climbs onto the bed over me, his strong arms caging me in.

His eyes twinkle as he grins and says, "Oh, we're definitely going to do that second one you mentioned."

That one is my favorite, too, so I grin right back.

Then he leans forward and shows me all the ways the things on my list of demands can make me scream an orgasm, and I'm practically hoarse by morning when I tiptoe home and get dressed for work with a silly, satisfied smile on my face.

The next two weeks follow a similar pattern.

At work, I find more and more ways to make myself useful and ensure Nick's office runs smoother. It's an incredibly satisfying job. And Nick is the epitome of professional there, never crossing a single line. But when the clock strikes five, by some unspoken agreement, we meet up at my house for some light packing, then dinner with my mom and sister, or we head to his place for an evening of cooking and teasing and walking the dog.

And always, every night, Nick suggests we watch a Lord of the Rings, which is code if I've ever heard it for *wanna fuck?*

I'm not ashamed to admit the hobbits never make it out of the village as far as I've seen.

In fact, it's gotten to the point that my heart starts to pound with desire every time I hear Sauron's name in the opening scene. I don't think that's the reaction Peter Jackson, the director, had in mind at all when he made the film, but all I can say is kudos, Peter. Kudos. I fucking love your movie.

Chapter Forty-Seven

*N*ick and I have a rhythm in the kitchen that almost feels like we've practiced it all our lives. I place pasta into the boiling water on the stove just as Nick finishes chopping basil and turns to toss it in the saucepan as he puts the finishing touches on the alfredo sauce.

Everything has been going so smoothly, I hate to rock the boat with an uncomfortable question, but it's been bugging me for a while now. I hesitate, and almost decide to wait and ask tomorrow instead, but then remind myself that's what Old Mallory would do.

New Mallory squares her shoulders and just asks, "So, umm, I've been wondering something."

Nick turns the burner down as he continues to stir the sauce slowly. "Mm-hmm. What's up?"

"If you and Aunt Maggie were so close, why didn't you ever do anything around her house or mow the lawn or anything?" The question has been gnawing at me for weeks. I've really gotten to know him, or at least I think I have, and he's a great guy. I just can't reconcile the Nick I know with the Nick who wouldn't do something as simple as occasionally mow an old lady's lawn.

He holds my gaze, as though he's trying to decide how much to say, and my stomach sinks. I'm not going to like his answer, I'm sure, but I have to know. "Just tell me. I can take it."

His eyes soften. "Oh, hon, it's nothing bad. Not really." He walks over and pulls me into his arms. "I used to do all the things around her place. That's how we met, actually. I knew she was having trouble with her lawn guy being reliable, so I walked over one day and offered to mow it for her. I just got into the habit of coming over a few times a week, changing her light bulbs, fixing her dryer, whatever she needed. Even after she went to live in that active-living facility, I tried to continue to keep the house up for her."

My eyes widen. "Then why did you stop?"

His mouth turns down. "I was mowing the lawn one day when her solicitor came by, and he threatened me with trespassing. Said if I went onto her property again, it was an insurance liability and he would be forced to prosecute. Nobody ever came to take care of her house after that. When the tree fell onto her porch, I decided enough was enough." His jaw clenches. "I had the HOA send her notices of violations."

My heart pounds. "*You're* the one who reported Aunt Maggie?" I try to slide out of his arms, but he's not having it.

"Hear me out first, Mallory," he begs. "I was trying to get the attorney to see that her house needed upkeep and to let me take care of it. But he simply ignored the notices at first. So I sent more. And more. At some point, I kept thinking, surely they will take care of the property. Surely they'd rather let me take care of it than let it fall into disrepair and mired in legal issues."

I shake my head. "But Aunt Maggie got all the notices. They were in a drawer in her kitchen."

"I never sent a notice to Maggie, not before she left and not after. I sent every single one to her attorney's office. He must have come and put them in the drawer at some point, maybe after realizing you would be taking possession. I swear to you, Mallory. I would never do anything to intentionally hurt Maggie."

And I believe him. "I just can't believe Thad Lagget would neglect his duty to care for the property."

"Her attorney wasn't Thad Lagget." Nick narrows his eyes. "Her attorney who handled her estate was Lester Stills. I think someone else took it over for probate, but I'd bet my law degree Mr. Stills was with a management firm pocketing her money every month. But what could I do? I couldn't risk trespassing."

A pained expression flits across his face, and I know it must have been hard for him, unable to help Aunt Maggie. I hug him to me, rest my head on his chest. "You did your best, Nick. She would have appreciated that."

But then I lean back and ask, "How come the notices stopped when I took over the property? I mean, the porch is fixed now, thank you, Mikey and my first paycheck, but I've still got periwinkle shutters and a number of infractions."

Nick's cheeks sport twin spots of red. "About that, well, I've been meaning to tell you...I'm not just on the board. I'm the president of the HOA."

Oh my God. I can't help the belly laugh that has me doubled over. When I can catch my breath, I notice Nick has his arms crossed, staring down his nose at me.

"Hey, now, we're not all bad. You know there have to be rules and order, right?"

I laugh again. "I can't believe I've been *sleeping* with the president of the damn HOA all this time."

He walks back over to the sauce and gives it a few more quick stirs. "That's not the only thing you've been doing with him."

So true. Delicious thoughts of other things I want to do to him tonight, and calling him *Mr. President* while I did them, make me full-on blush. Totally adding that to tonight's demand list.

I grab a set of tongs and pull out a strand of linguini, testing it for doneness. It still needs a bit more time, so I hop onto the counter and cross my legs. "How did you end up living in the suburbs in the first place? This isn't normally where hot, single men tend to congregate."

He stops stirring for a second but then begins again as though nothing happened. He doesn't turn around to look at me before answering. "Oh, I'm sure you don't want to hear about that."

My antennae are up, and I know in my marrow that it's important how he ended up living here. So I say as nonchalantly as possible, "Of course I want to hear this story. Spill, Nick."

He flips the burner to warm before leaning against the stove. "It's not a friends-with-benefits sort of story, Mallory."

My heart is pounding in my ears because I know what he's saying. What he's asking. If I want to get to know him more, to learn his secrets, I'm going to have to admit there's more going on between us than just hooking up.

A part of me knows I'm not ready to take this any further, that I'm just starting to figure out who I am outside of my marriage, what I want in life. But another part wants to know everything there is to know about Nick, wants to know what he was like as a child, what he dreamed of being when he grew up.

Which is why I'm not shocked when I hear myself whisper, "So tell me."

Hello, relationship line, don't mind me as I try not to freak the eff out as I mosey across you.

Nick holds my gaze for a beat, maybe two, then nods. "I was engaged when I was in college."

My breath hitches. Of all the things he could have said, I would never have guessed that. I can't say anything, the parallels between our lives whizzing through my mind at warp speed.

"We were both in law school together…" He pauses, clearly

trying to gauge how I take this information, again so similar to Karl and me, but I don't even blink. I am a stone. "We planned to head to New York and start our own firm together."

The hits just keep coming. My throat feels scratchy and tight, and all I can do is nod for him to continue.

"But then we got pregnant just before graduation and, well, New York was no longer important to either of us. Instead, we planned to buy a house in the suburbs and start a family, build a much smaller law practice so we could spend more time with the kids."

I manage to drag in a shaky breath and ask, "You're divorced? With kids?" I never saw Nick with any kids, and we'd practically been living in each other's pockets for the last several weeks. There were no pictures of a family in his offices. No one mentioned a family... My eyes widen. Oh God, no.

"I wish I were divorced with kids," he says, and I shatter. I just break into a million pieces. "She died in a car accident, pregnant with our first."

I can barely see, tears blurring my vision and wetting my cheeks, but I manage to get off the counter and find him, wrap my arms around him, pull him against me. And sob.

When I think there are no more tears left to cry, I lean back and wipe the wetness from his face, too. "Were you—"

"Driving? No. She was. But I was sitting beside her."

I squeeze him again. I can't even imagine what that must feel like, sitting next to your wife and child as they die before your eyes. He survived a nightmare, a literal nightmare, but he found a way to move on, the strength to heal.

"Is this the house you bought together?" I gesture at the space around us. "Is that why you're always so neat and tidy, everything in its place? Like she would want?"

I feel like that's a reasonable question. I mean, really. Why else would anyone be *this* neat? But Nick lets out a bark of laughter. "Sorry to disappoint, but this is all me, baby."

I smile back at him. As flaws go, I can live with neat freak. Especially one who can cook…

"Oh no! The pasta!" I pull away and grab the tongs, but I know even before I've pulled the first noodle out of the water, it's overcooked and ruined. We both stare at the sticky mess. Then each other.

And say at the same time:

"Popcorn?"

"*Lord of the Rings*?"

Chapter Forty-Eight

We barely make it through something about a ring before we're half naked and racing each other up the stairs. We get to the door of his bedroom in record time, and I expect him to toss me down on his bed and rip off my clothes—or better yet, let me rip off the rest of his clothes. But instead, he carries me straight past the bed and into the bathroom.

"What are we…" I ask, wondering if he's got some kind of mirror fetish or something. Not that I'm complaining, mind you. I can definitely get on board with seeing both the front and the back of this man at the same time.

"It's been a long day," he murmurs as he slowly slides my body down his, making sure as he does that all the good parts of me touch all the *really* good parts of him. "And a long night. I thought we could both use a hot shower."

"Oh, right." I let out a slow, uneven breath at the thought of being able to touch him as warm water sluices over all his smooth, gorgeous skin. I'll have to save the mirror fantasy for another night—or at least another round.

"You feel good," I tell him as I lean into the pleasure.

As I lean into him.

"You feel better than good," he answers, his fingers moving to the buttons of my blouse.

"I can do that," I tell him, but he just grins.

"I know you can do it, but I want to do it." His smile turns soft. "Okay?"

I nod as his nimble fingers make short work of my buttons, then sigh a little as he slips the blouse off, his finger skimming across the skin of my shoulders and arms as he does.

I rest against him now, relishing the feel of his body touching mine, and he holds me for long seconds, his hands stroking over my skin and down my back. But when I reach behind me to take off my bra, he stops me with a hand over mine.

"I've got you," he whispers, and there's something in the words—something in his eyes and his hands—that has my heart trembling in my chest just a little.

I ignore it, tell myself it's hunger, since we never finished cooking dinner, and focus instead on the way his big, warm hands feel sliding over my lower back and up my spine until he reaches my bra clasp. He flicks it off one-handed in about two seconds flat, and I almost tease him about his prowess, but before I can say anything, he's sliding my bra off and cupping my breasts in his hands.

He toys with my nipples for just a moment and I gasp, all thoughts of teasing him—all thoughts of everything—slipping right out of my head. And when his lips brush against mine, once, twice, I fall headlong into sensation. Headlong into him and the fire that burns between us even before his fingers move to the buttons of my suit pants.

Within seconds, they're pooled on his travertine floor—along with my underwear.

He wraps his arms around me then, presses soft kisses to my cheeks, my jaw, the hollow of my throat, the sensitive spot where my neck meets my shoulder.

It feels good—amazingly good—but it's not enough.

"I want your mouth," I tell him, my hands smoothing over his warm, naked chest.

He answers by pressing a string of openmouthed kisses to my neck and jaw that has my knees weakening and my heart beating fast and hard.

But when I drop my hands to his belt buckle to return the favor, he stops me.

"What's wrong?" I ask, confused.

Nick grins as he steps back and opens the door to one of the most decadent showers I have ever seen. When he turns on all three water sprays, the environmentalist in me has a heart attack, but the hedonist is completely on board. Even before he drops his pants and completely distracts me by my first unadulterated view of his beautiful body tonight.

But when I reach for him, he takes my hand and tugs me gently into the shower.

Unlike at Aunt Maggie's, the water here heats up almost instantly, and I nearly moan in delight as the hot water hits muscles still sore from my mowing adventure. Nick laughs, then wraps his arms around my waist as I relax against him.

We take several breaths while he does nothing but hold me, his body strong and heated and aroused against mine. I wrap my arms around his waist, too, then start to kiss my way across his chest.

And for a moment, he lets me. Then he moans, his arms tightening before he eases away.

"What—" I start, but before I can ask him what's going on, he slides his fingers into my hair and tugs softly until I tilt my head back and let the water cascade over me. Then he reaches for a bottle of shampoo and squirts some into his palm.

No one has ever washed my hair before. When Karl asked me to take showers with him, it was just a euphemism for a quick blow job. But with Nick…with Nick it's anything but quick and it is focused entirely on me.

Gently, he massages the shampoo into my hair, his fingers making small, thorough circles against my scalp. It's a slow, sexy process, one that feels so good, it turns my entire body to mush. I collapse into him, more out of necessity than choice, and he takes my full weight with a grin that lights up his face.

When he's done with the most amazing scalp massage of my life, he guides my head back under the water and painstakingly washes out the shampoo.

He repeats the process with the conditioner, and by the time he's done, my entire body is on fire. My hands are on his hips, my nails digging in as I press hot, desperate kisses to every part of him that I can reach.

But just as I start to drop to my knees, he stops me with a gentle hand to my jaw. Then he leans forward and kisses me until I can barely remember how to breathe, let alone how I thought this was supposed to go.

He reaches for his shower gel then, squirting some into his palms, then running his hands over my shoulders and down my back before sliding over my ass. He circles around to the front, his fingers toying with my belly button for long seconds before slipping over my rib cage to my chest and lowering his mouth to mine.

I twine my arms around his neck, pulling him closer. He lets me for one second, two, before settling me on the bench that runs the back length of the shower. Then he drops to his knees in front of me.

My heart is going wild now, my whole body in sensory overload even before he soaps up his hands and strokes his way slowly, painstakingly from my ankle to my thigh.

And then he takes hold of my right ankle and does the exact same thing to that leg, too.

By the time he reaches my right thigh, all worries about whether my body is good enough for him, all plans for sowing my wild divorce oats, all thoughts of anything and everything but Nick, have disappeared from my head completely.

I'm drowning—in sensation, in Nick, in the overwhelming power of my own emotions—even before Nick presses his mouth to the very heart of me, taking me up and over so fast that my head spins out, right along with the rest of me.

I haven't even caught my breath when he's turning off the shower. Lifting me up. Carrying me out. Setting me down in front of the sink—and the mirror.

He dries me off slowly, carefully, his fingers skimming across my shoulder, my hip, the sensitive spot on the inside of my elbow. By the time he's done, I want him again, even before he reaches into the nearest drawer, pulls out a condom, and puts it on.

And then he's turning me so that my back is against his front.

"I need you, Mallory," he whispers as he slides inside me.

I need him, too, but the words stick in my throat.

He leans forward, his body covering mine so that we can be as close as humanly possible, and as his wide, vulnerable eyes meet mine in the mirror, I can feel the words—and the emotions—rising inside me. Getting bigger and bigger and harder and harder to tamp down.

So that when I'm right there, my body drowning in a whirlpool of emotions and sensations, there really is only one choice. "I need you," I whisper as pleasure pours through me, over me, dragging me further and further into the abyss. "I need you, Nick."

It's the most amazing—and the most devastating—feeling in the world, and for a second I'm caught in the whirlpool, every part of me spiraling wildly out of control.

Fear rises right along with the pleasure—what have I done, what have I done?—but Nick is there to catch me, to hold me, to shelter me through the storm.

And nothing has ever felt so right.

Chapter Forty-Nine

*I*f Nick doesn't fall asleep soon—and I mean soon—I am going to go from panic attack to actual heart attack. And sadly, I'm pretty sure that isn't even an exaggeration. The human heart is not meant to beat more than 130 beats per minute for extended periods of time, and mine has been pounding like an acid rock drummer for way too long.

Add in the fact that the room is spinning and I can't catch my breath, and I would have thought I'm already *having* a heart attack if all of this wasn't clearly a result of me absolutely, positively freaking out…and have been since Nick carried me out of the bathroom and laid me on this bed nearly an hour ago.

We talked for a little while before he turned out the light, but now we're curled together under his thick down comforter—and by curled together I mean he is wrapped around me like he's the tortilla and I'm the stuffing. Which also would probably be fine at any other time, considering normally I like being the little spoon.

But right now, after everything that happened in the bathroom, it feels like the room is closing in on me.

It isn't Nick's fault—none of this is his fault. It's my fault for stepping outside my comfort zone and doing something I knew I wasn't ready for just because I was strung out on desire. I can't believe I told Nick I needed him. I can't freaking believe it. I made it what, a month, after vowing to never need another man again? *Way to stay strong and independent, Mallory.*

And I can't believe he said he needed me, too. We've known each other less time than it takes to grow a tomato, for God's sake.

He can't need me. I'm a freaking mess. Broke, in the middle of an existential crisis and a messy divorce, currently living with my mother and my sister...both of whom are also in the middle of messy relationship drama. What about this scenario makes me sound like a good relationship bet?

And I know, Nick hasn't actually asked me to be in a relationship yet, but men don't do what he did in that bathroom if they plan on keeping it casual. I may not be the world's leading expert on relationships, but even I know that much. And earlier tonight, in the kitchen, I know we were taking friends with benefits to a new place. It just went from fun and games to overwhelming me in the span of a breath.

All of which has led to me lying here in his bed, freaking out, as I wait for him to fall asleep. Is it a coward's move to sneak out while he's unconscious? Absolutely. Am I going to do it anyway? Abso-fucking-lutely. Not because I don't like Nick but because I do. More than I want to. Definitely more than I should. And after what he shared tonight about his wife and child, I know I have no choice. I can't put him through more heartache.

"You okay?" he asks as he pulls me closer, nuzzling in.

"Yeah, I'm good." I don't know what else to say. Plus, there's a part of me that wants it to be true, a part of me that wishes I was okay with all of this. Because this is definitely a case of it isn't him, it's me.

No matter how much I want to paint him with the asshole card because of our first meeting, the truth is, he's a good guy. A very good guy. One who helps out his neighbors, serves in the community, rescues stray dogs, and gives divorcées who are in over their heads really good legal advice and representation.

And me? I'm a woman who still needs to work on her shit. I've gotten a lot of it together since I first told Karl I wanted a divorce, but there is more than a little left to go. And until I get that shit figured out, there's no way I'll be able to give Nick what he deserves...and what he apparently wants, as well.

Eventually, his breathing softens out a little bit, becomes more rhythmic, and the arm around me grows heavier and more lax. And still I wait a couple more minutes before rolling gently—oh so gently—away.

His arm flops on the bed between us and he startles a little—which also startles me. My heart begins beating even faster and it takes every ounce of self-control I have not to freak out and just run. But since I'm pretty sure that will just make Nick chase me, I stay where I am, facedown on the bed, and hyperventilate pillow fuzz for a while.

When nearly ten minutes go by and he doesn't so much as move, I finally decide it's safe to start inching toward the edge of the bed. As my fingers and toes eventually touch nothing but air on my side of the bed, I just go for it.

I roll straight out of bed and land on the floor with an *oompf* that knocks the air out of me—and settles out my hyperventilating at the same time. Nothing like a few bruises for the win.

I think about trying to get my clothes, but they're still in the bathroom and there's no way Nick will sleep through all that. And if he doesn't, what am I going to say? I have a crawling fetish? I'm sleep-crawling? No, nothing good can come from that, so it's going to have to be every pair of lace underwear for herself in this situation. Besides, I never liked that suit anyway.

Inch by inch, I stealth-crawl to the door, feeling more and more like a special-ops soldier moving through enemy territory. The bedroom door is open, thank God, and I'm out and in the hallway when I hit my second booby trap. Buttercup.

She must be a night dog, because suddenly she's right next

to me—and she's wide awake. Also, apparently, feeling the love tonight.

I get a face full of enthusiastic doggie kisses and end up having to take every single one of them, since she's determined not to be dissuaded. Eventually, she eases up a little and I take my shot, power-crawling to the stairs as fast as my hands and knees will carry me.

Yes, I am aware that I am a thirty-five-year-old woman who is sneaking out of her lover's bedroom because she got cold feet.

Yes, I am more than aware of how pathetic that is.

No, I really don't give a damn about my pathetic quotient right now. Frankly, I don't give a damn about anything but getting out of here before Nick wakes up and decides we need to talk.

I have to put up with Buttercup's kissing and dancing around me all the way to the top of the stairs. Once there, I jump to my feet before bolting down the steps two at a time. I'm so freaked out at this point that I almost make it to the front door before I remember that I'm naked. And while it's late, it isn't middle-of-the-night late, and somehow I bet my neighbors will freak out if it comes to light that I was streaking through the neighborhood at midnight.

Their loss, but still.

A quick search of the living room yields one of Nick's shirts—and my phone, thankfully—and I shrug it on before racing for the door. I button two buttons, which is more than enough for decency in my book—though I'm pretty sure I lost my own decency somewhere between Nick's bed and his bedroom door. Then I make a break for it and head straight down the driveway, across the street, up my driveway, and—force of habit—through my gate and around to my back door.

I run the whole thing as if I'm angling for a gold medal in the sprint of shame and don't let myself slow down until my back-door handle is actually in my hand. Then and only then do I breathe a sigh of relief at finally being safe.

But as I go to open the door, I realize my sigh of relief is more than a little premature. Because my mom and sister—being two savvy women who are now living on their own in New Jersey—were smart enough, or diabolical enough, to lock the door before they went up to bed.

Fuck. My. Life.

Chapter Fifty

I text Sarah, and when that doesn't work, I call her. But she
doesn't answer, which means I could try calling my mom, but
I would honestly rather wax my bikini line myself than end this
walk of shame with my mother's raised brow. So unless I want
to run back across the street to Nick's, I am stuck out here for
the rest of the night.

And since I can't actually think of anything I want to do
less than go back to Nick's... Who knew life in the burbs could
be this completely random?

With an annoyed sigh, I flounce over to one of the lounge
chairs my aunt had set up around her mermaid sculpture
fountain in the center of the backyard. I used to tell her she
should get a pool, but she'd just take a sip of her mai tai and
tell me that anyone could have a pool. It took a woman with
style to have mermaids.

And she wasn't wrong. No better site for my shameful
demise, I suppose.

I pull the lounge chair several extra feet away from the
sculpture's splash zone before settling down on it for the night.
The chair is still damp from the last few times the sculpture
spit on it, but it's a warm night, so it's no big deal.

And thankfully, the lounge chair is as comfortable as I
remember, so sleeping on it won't be that big of a deal. If I
can sleep, which I'm not sure I can—not when visions of that

moment in the bathroom keep running through my head.

Nick's eyes locked on mine in the mirror, his body thrusting into me, my heart falling wide open at his feet as I admit the one thing I swore to myself I would never tell another man. The one thing I swore to myself I would never let happen.

I need you.

Just the thought of having said it out loud gives me the heebie-jeebies. I can pretend it was no big deal, can pretend that I was just talking sexually, that I was just saying I needed him in that moment. It's a valid argument—he did have me totally drunk on desire—but I know the truth. In those moments, when we were both so open, so naked, so vulnerable with each other, those three words—"I need you"—meant a whole lot more than for a simple orgasm.

They meant everything I've been fighting against, everything I've been trying to prove to myself I could do without since the divorce.

Apparently, when push comes to shove, I really have learned nothing. I'm not even fully out of from under the mess I made with Karl but determined to stand on my own two feet. Determined to build a life for myself. And within a month, I ended up totally wrapped up in another guy. And not just any guy. Nick.

He's not having my baby, obviously, and I'm not having his, but am I really any different from Karl? Or am I just the same, hitting thirty-five and determined to give my life meaning by any means possible, including sleeping with—and worse, falling for—some guy I didn't even know existed a month ago?

Can I get any more pathetic?

No. No, I can't.

And now I'm going to have to come up with some reason as to why I snuck out in the middle of the night that won't hurt his feelings or make me look like a total asshole. Then again, I left my clothes piled on his bathroom floor and my shoes kicked off under his dining room table. The ship has probably sailed on that last one. I *am* a total asshole.

But at least I'm an asshole whose heart is safe. And who still has a chance of building her new life the way she wants it, not the way anyone else wants it. Surely that has to count for something, right?

And honestly, after what Nick shared tonight, can he blame me? How could I possibly be in a relationship with him, knowing how fucked up I still am and what it would do to him if things ended badly? Hasn't he been through enough agony for one lifetime? I can't add to his pain, I just can't. It's better that I end things now, before he's any more invested, than realize six months from now that I'm just not relationship material anymore.

I roll over onto my side and try to pretend that I'm not worried about being eaten alive by mosquitoes all night.

Besides, how can I ever learn to fix the mistakes I made with Karl if I jump right back into a relationship with another guy? I know Nick is nothing like Karl, but I'm still me. And I can see all the old traps looming in front of me. I've spent a long time blaming Karl for our divorce—and yes, he is the one who cheated on me and he is the one who's trying so hard to screw me over financially—but I'm the one who let him do that to me.

I'm the one who gave him my power. I'm the one who spent all those years swallowing my tongue, not rocking the boat, letting him have his way because it was easier, even when I knew it was wrong.

Is that on Karl?

Hell yeah, the man is an asshole who wouldn't know how to shoot straight if his life depended on it. But it's also on me and I'm willing to own it. But owning it means I have to work on it. I have to solve the problem. I can't just jump into another relationship unless I want to make the same mistakes with Nick that I did with Karl.

And I don't. I really, really don't.

All evidence to the contrary, though. Hell, even ordering dinner that one night, I let him choose what we ordered. I mean, yeah, I was fine with Indian, but honestly, I'd had a craving for something else. Why hadn't I said something then? What is it about me that's so willing to make everyone else happy over myself?

Nick deserves someone who can stand up for herself, who is treated like an equal because she *is* an equal. Nick deserves better than a doormat. And honestly, so do I.

Giving up on my side, I roll onto my back again and stare at the sky above me. In Manhattan, there are way too many lights on at all times to ever be able to see the stars. But out here at night, when the whole neighborhood is in bed around me, it's hard to miss them up there.

They're bright and beautiful and shiny, and I want nothing more than to reach up and grab one. Obviously, I know that's impossible for about ten million different reasons—the first and foremost one being science—but knowing that doesn't make me want to do it any less.

Aunt Maggie used to tell me falling stars were falling because they'd lost heart and that's what made them drop out of the sky. She warned me never to do that, made me promise to never give up, to never fall, to stay burning bright in the sky forever.

I tried, but I failed. And now, here I am, with a perfect view of the stars and no way to get back among them.

If I give up now, if I just fall for Nick, how am I ever going to find my way back to the sky—back to the stars—again? Even more important, how will I ever find my way back to myself? He's a great guy. I have absolutely no doubts about that. But am I the great woman he needs by his side when I'm still such a work in progress?

It's a question I'm still contemplating when the stars begin to disappear and dawn streaks across the sky. And I still have no answer. To that question or what I'm going to say when I see Nick at work again today.

Chapter Fifty-One

I wake up to the sound of a throat being cleared above me, and I freeze before I even regain consciousness, convinced Nick has found me and that I'm going to have to explain everything.

But when the throat clearing comes again, my galloping heart gets a reprieve because I would recognize that exasperated, disappointed sound anywhere.

My dad is here.

I open my eyes slowly, feeling like I passed out a minute ago. A quick glance at my phone proves the feeling isn't completely inaccurate. It's barely six o'clock, and I only fell asleep about an hour ago.

My dad is standing over me, arms crossed at his suited chest and a distinct frown of disapproval on his face. I brace myself for the worst when our eyes meet.

But all he says is, "Rough night?"

"You have no idea." I sit up slowly and try to get my shit together.

Matching wits with my father is always a dangerous affair—he isn't one of the tristate area's best litigators for nothing—but doing it when you're half asleep and groggy as fuck is guaranteed to be a disaster. Then again, so is showing any kind of weakness, so I refuse to shake my head or rub my eyes or do anything that will tip him off as to how tired I actually am.

"What's up?"

"Obviously not you," he answers acerbically. "Despite the new job your mother says you started recently."

"Wait a minute. You talked to Mom?"

"I've talked to your mother every single day of our thirty-eight-year marriage. You didn't think I was actually going to stop just because she moved out, did you?"

"*Actually*, that's exactly what I thought," I tell him. "I mean, isn't that the point of her moving out?"

He shakes his head as he walks over to the patio table and takes two paper coffee cups out of the cupholder he must have placed there. He holds one out to me, and I nearly cry with relief as I wrap my hands around it and breathe in its heady aroma.

"For a woman who likes to pretend she has everything all worked out, you've still got a lot to learn," my father says after a few seconds.

My laugh is harsh when it comes. Is he really going to lecture *me* on having my life together? We haven't spoken since I learned of Sarah, so it doesn't take long for me to dig back into that raging cesspool of hurt. "I think you're confused. I'm the first one to admit that I have nothing worked out."

"That's where you're wrong." He takes a sip of his coffee as he sits down on the lounge chair next to mine and kicks up his legs. "You like to say that you don't know what you're doing, but the truth is you've made very conscious decisions that have gotten you to this point in your life, Mallory. You decided to quit law school to support Karl. You decided to help him build that law firm into what it is today without taking any credit for yourself. You decided to leave your husband without so much as consulting me before you did it—"

"So you could try to sell me on the sanctity of marriage as you see it?" I snipe before I can stop myself.

"No, so I could have helped you protect yourself. Karl is a bastard, no doubt about it, but he's a damn good lawyer. Instead of remembering that, you went off half-cocked, and look at where that got you."

"It's pretty hard not to go off half-cocked," I tell him, "when you walk in on your husband giving oral sex to another woman. It's one of those situations designed to make people go off half-cocked."

"Maybe so. But you should have known better. You're the daughter of a lawyer, the wife of a lawyer. I could have helped you protect yourself."

"Maybe I didn't want or need your protection," I say. "Did you ever think of that? Maybe I needed to do this on my own."

"Which is why you're sleeping with your new boss, right?" my dad asks, brows raised. "Who also happens to be your lawyer? Because you want to do things on your own?"

"First of all, his partner is my lawyer. And second of all, my relationship with Nick is none of your business."

"Nothing about you is my business," my father snaps back. "You've made sure of that."

Guilt rears its ugly head, but that's exactly what he was aiming for, so I tamp it back down. He's the one who has made so much of this divorce so difficult for me. Is it any wonder I didn't ask him for advice? Not to mention the fact that he's made a pretty big mess of his own life—and my mother's. It isn't my fault I don't want to end up like her.

"And you want me to apologize for that?"

"What I want is for you to listen. And to think about what I'm saying," he says, looking more concerned than I've ever seen him. "Because you're heading down a path that will lead you right back to where you were. You know that, right?"

"That's not true," I say. "I'm doing everything differently now." I think about Nick and my desperate crawl out of his bedroom last night. "Maybe everything I do isn't great," I admit after a second. "But I'm trying—"

"Are you or are you not sleeping with your boss?" he

demands, his normally steady voice rising in anger or excitement or I don't know what. "I just don't want you to end up single in a few years, without a reference again, and without Aunt Maggie to bail you out by giving you a house this time."

Fury rips through me, digs into me with razor-tipped claws. "You may be my father, but it is absolutely ludicrous for you to sit there and give me life advice," I tell him. "Considering the absolute disaster you've made of your life—and of my mother's."

"I just want you to protect yourself, Mallory—"

"The way you've protected yourself all these years?" I ask. "By fucking over anyone who didn't do exactly what you wanted them to do? And even some who did. That's the real message here, right? Nick can't be trusted because you can't be trusted. I can't be trusted because all men will do what you did—"

"That's enough, Mallory!" His voice cuts like glass.

"No," I say, openly defying my father for the first time in a long time. "It's not enough. You hurt my mother. You hurt Sarah. You probably hurt Sarah's mother and you definitely hurt me with your behavior. So for you to stand there and tell me that I need to think ahead, that I need to make sure I don't let some man hurt me again, is insulting. It's beyond insulting."

I put the cup of coffee he gave me back down on the table where I got it from. "And if you think I'm so bad at choosing men, if you think I'm destined to let them treat me badly and hurt me over and over again, maybe you should look at my role model," I say. "Maybe you should ask yourself why it is I chose Karl and who he reminded me of. Believe me, if I've done nothing else over the last couple of weeks, I've figured that much out."

By the time I'm done talking, my father looks pale. Gray even. But his eyes are the same as they've always been when he looks at me—filled with a cold annoyance that says he's not really interested in anything I'm saying. More, he isn't even really interested in me.

So when he turns on his heel and storms out of my backyard, it isn't even a surprise. What is a surprise is the fact that once I'm alone, I realize that a part of me—though I am loath to admit it—knows there is some truth in what he said. And if I don't want to make the same mistakes I already have, then I'm going to have to do something to change it.

Chapter Fifty-Two

Thank God Sarah wakes up and sees my text not long after my dad leaves, because I've barely sunk back down on the lounger when the door opens and my sister stands there grinning.

"Aren't you a little old for the walk of shame?"

"Apparently you're never too old," I tell her as I follow her inside. "Or to get caught by your dad."

Her eyes widen. "Dad was here?" She looks outside as if he might materialize right in front of her.

And fuck if that doesn't make me feel more awful than I already do. "He's an asshole." I hate saying that about my own dad, but when it comes to Sarah, he really is. "And he shouldn't treat you the way he does. He shouldn't treat any of us the way he does."

She shrugs, but the look on her face says she appreciates the acknowledgement. "Maybe that's why we're so messed up. Maybe we let our previous guys treat us the way they did because it's what we were used to seeing from him. I know how he treated my mom, and I've guessed he treated yours pretty similarly if she's hanging out here. It's what we knew."

"Maybe so," I agree, thinking back on how many times during our marriage Karl reminded me of my dad. "But fuck that."

She laughs. "Damn straight. I'm done begging a man for attention because my daddy wouldn't give me his."

"And I'm done worrying about what's right and proper."

"Obviously." My sister wiggles her brows even as she reaches over and pulls one of my strands of knotted hair. "Because I've got to say, you've done the walk of shame proud this morning."

"Yeah." I think back to crawling out of Nick's bedroom on my hands and knees like a commando. "But that's about the only thing I've done proud."

"What do you mean?"

I shake my head as I turn for the stairs. "Long story and I've got to get ready for work."

"You'll tell me later?" She narrows her eyes at me in a way that says it's more a demand than a question.

"What are sisters for?" I tease, even though I'm not sure I'll be up to talking about it later. Or ever.

But right now I need to get ready for work, so I put Nick—and everything that happened between us last night—out of my mind as I shower and get dressed.

During the drive, my father's words are a tight ball in my stomach. Because, while I knew from the moment I crawled out of Nick's bed last night that I was going to have to break up with him—and even before, if I'm being honest—I didn't think I was also going to have to leave the job that I've already fallen in love with. The job that I happen to be really good at and is the one thing, besides Nick, currently helping me keep my head above water.

I stop on the way to work to pick up some cookies for the office—we have a full day of clients planned on both sides—and to drop Nick's shirt at one of those twenty-four-hour dry cleaners. It's going to cost more than it should, but I feel like making sure I get his shirt back to him pressed is the least I can do.

I plan on quitting early, more because I can't stand the knowledge that I'm going to have this hanging over my head all day than because I'm actually anxious to get it over with.

But the second I walk through the door, one crisis after another starts and I don't even have the chance to breathe until lunch.

First, Mr. Kinickey, who it turns out is extremely difficult on his best days, shows up an hour early for his appointment, though he absolutely will not admit that he got the time wrong. I get him settled talking to one of the paralegals, Marigold, because she's really sweet and has a way with him, then bring him a cup of coffee and some cookies to keep him busy.

I barely drop off the tray when Gina starts yelling in Italian and, when I go to investigate, I find it's because she's at war with the laser printer over documents she needs ASAP—and obviously losing. I get her settled with a cup of coffee and some cookies before her first appointment, then spend fifteen minutes troubleshooting the laser printer before I figure out what the problem is.

It takes me another ten minutes to fix it—finicky machine—and I make a mental note to talk to the partners about replacing it before I leave. Thinking about having to talk to Nick about quitting depresses me, so I stop by Marigold's office to check on her and Mr. Kinickey. They're having a grand old time as he regales her with tales from his days of being a writer in Paris.

I relax and head to finally—finally—get my first cup of coffee of the day. But before I actually make it to the break room, Gina's at it again, this time with her laptop.

"I'm sensing a pattern here," I tell her as I ease the machine out of her death grip.

"Always," she answers with a dramatic wave of her hand. "But usually it doesn't happen all in one day."

I get her login credentials, then look at her over the top of the laptop. "Your first appointment for the day is in fifteen minutes."

"I know." She sighs grumpily. "That's why I was trying to go over my notes from last time."

"My laptop is on my desk." I write down my login credentials and hand them to her. "Why don't you use it to look up whatever you need in the client files? Hopefully, by the time the client gets here, we'll both be back to our regular computers."

"You are a godsend, Mallory," Gina says, blowing me a big, smacking kiss on her way out the door. "Whatever we're paying you, it isn't enough."

Ten minutes later, I trade laptops with Gina—after making sure to pull up the client docs she'll need for the meeting—and I bring her an extra cookie because she looks like she needs it.

After getting both her and Nick's nine o'clock clients settled in their offices, I head back for that cup of coffee—and get waylaid by Marcus, one of the first-year associates, who has an irate client on the phone yelling at him about billing errors.

I head to my office, where I find out that Gina has somehow completely screwed my computer up in the ten minutes that she had it—and end up having to borrow Marcus's laptop to look up any discrepancies in billable hours.

By the time I finally get off the phone with Mrs. Hart, Marcus and I both need a cookie. And then it's back to my desk to try to figure out what on earth Gina managed to do to my laptop.

The whole day goes like this, so I manage to avoid Nick without even trying. Unlike last time, he actually makes it out of his office once or twice, but every time he stops by my desk to talk, I end up getting pulled into another emergency. He watches with bemused eyes several times—each time while he shoves a handful of cookies into his mouth before heading back to his office.

By four thirty, I feel like I've run a marathon and I'm pretty sure I look like it, too. My hair is a mess because I ran my hands through it so many times during the day, my feet hurt from all the running I've done back and forth to everyone's offices who had a problem, and my stomach is churning—a combination of nerves and way too many cookies.

When Nick sticks his head in, the churning stomach turns into full-blown anxiety, something that the smile on his face and the softness in his eyes only makes worse.

"Can you stop by my office sometime before you head home?" he asks. "I want to talk to you about something."

The anxiety ratchets up another ten degrees. "Yes, of course."

I give him the best smile I can muster, which must not be that great because the softness in his eyes turns to concern. "How was your day?"

"Good so far." I force a smile I'm far from feeling. "Give me about ten minutes to finish what I'm working on and I'll be in, okay?"

"Absolutely." He starts to walk away, then stops and takes a couple of steps backward. "Are there any more of those cookies—"

"No," I say and raise one brow at him. "There are no more cookies, mainly because you ate more than a dozen of them yourself today."

"In my defense, they were really good cookies." He gives me his most charming grin.

"Of course they were good cookies. They're from Garimbaldi's bakery. But now they're gone, so..." I shoo him away.

He just laughs, but he takes the hint and heads back to his office.

I finish dealing with the access problem Marigold mentioned she was having, then log out of my laptop and lock it up in my desk drawer before heading back to Nick's office. Once I get there, I take a deep breath and try to center myself as much as I possibly can.

Then I knock on the door.

Instead of telling me to come in, Nick pulls the door open and ushers me inside. The second we're alone, he wraps his arms around me and pulls me into a hug.

"I've been wanting to do that all day," he murmurs. "I missed you when I got up this morning. What time did you leave? And—if you don't mind my asking—what did you wear when you left, considering your clothes were still all on my bathroom floor?" He wiggles his brows at me and it's so charming and sweet that I kind of want to crawl into a hole.

"I couldn't sleep, so I left a little after one. And I didn't want to wake you, so I just grabbed your shirt from downstairs. I took it to the dry cleaner this morning, by the way, so you should have it by tomorrow morning."

"Wow." He rocks back on his heels a little. "Well, that's very efficient of you."

"I'm nothing if not efficient," I answer with a grin I am far from feeling. But when he bends down to give me a kiss, I duck out from under his arm and make my way to the chairs in front of his desk—ignoring the sudden wariness in his eyes as I do. "Is there something specific you wanted to talk to me about?"

"Actually, yes." He clears his throat and walks back toward his desk as well. But instead of sitting behind it—in his chair—he perches on the edge right in front of me.

"I got a call from Viola today. She's still got a few weeks left on her maternity leave, but she's decided she wants to stay home with the baby, so she quit. Which means," he says with a grin, "we have an opening for a full-time office manager. And since you happen to be an amazing office manager, Gina enthusiastically agrees that if you want it, the job is yours. Permanently."

Chapter Fifty-Three

*S*hort of saying that he loves me, it's pretty much the worst thing he could tell me right now. Because I am already in love with the job. I love the people here, I love what I do, and I'm good at it—no matter what my father thinks.

But I also know my father is right about some things, too. Including the fact that taking a job where I am fucking the boss is a definite step backward. I'm determined to take my life back—to turn myself around—and falling into the same pattern I had with Karl would be a mistake. A big, giant mistake, one I would have no excuse for making. Not when I can see the problems coming from a mile away.

"Nick," I say after several long, awkward seconds go by.

He lifts a brow, and now he does move to sit behind his desk, like he knows that, whatever's coming, he's not going to like it. "Mallory," he responds in kind.

"I appreciate the offer, I do. But I'm going to have to pass on it. In fact, I came into work today planning to tell you that I'll stay until you find someone to take my place but that I think it would be best if I don't work here." Meeting his eyes when I say that is one of the hardest things I've ever had to do.

But I'm not the same Mallory who never fought with Karl, the same Mallory who spent so much of her time running away from conflict that she couldn't tell if it was there or not half the time. I'm working too hard to put that woman behind me. No way am I going back to her now.

So I meet Nick's eyes when I say this—and because I do, I see the quick flash of surprise and the even quicker flash of hurt that he manages to bury as fast as they come.

"Is this because of Karl?" he asks, his tone even and eminently reasonable. "Because I would never behave like he does, Mallory. Your job is safe here no matter what happens between us."

I take a deep breath and blow it out slowly, because this is the part I've really been dreading. "Actually, I wanted to talk to you about that, too."

"That?" he says, arching a brow. "When you say *that*, you mean us, right?"

"Yeah." I clear my throat. "I've been thinking—"

"So it wasn't a matter of you not being able to sleep last night. You left—so worried about facing me that you didn't even take the time to get dressed—because you were freaked out."

"I wasn't freaked out," I lie. "I just thought we should have some space, and I didn't want to wake you."

"More like you didn't want to face me." He leans back in his chair and stares at me through narrowed eyes. "I'm curious. Were you so desperate to get away that you would have run home naked if you hadn't found my shirt?"

"No! Of course not," I tell him, ignoring the fact that he's managed to hit uncomfortably close to what my thought process was. "I'm pretty sure I'd get a really big fine from the HOA for that."

He ignores my attempt at levity. "What's really going on here?"

There's something about the way he says it—and the way he's looking at me—that gets my back up. I'm not sure what it is, as he's being perfectly polite and reasonable, but there's something there that pisses me off and has me snapping back at him, "This isn't working."

"Really?" He lifts a brow. "Because I thought it was working pretty damn well."

"But you're not the only one in this relationship. And I happen to think it's a really bad idea for me to be fucking the boss."

His eyes narrow even further at my deliberate crudity. "Is that what you think this is? You fucking the boss? Me fucking a hot employee?"

Again, there's that tone—direct, demanding, brooking no argument—and it makes me want to throw something at him. And then it hits me. It's his cross-examination tone.

"Don't talk to me like that." I spring out of my chair.

"Like what?" The second brow goes up.

"Like I'm some witness for the other side and it's your job to poke holes in my story. Karl used to talk to me like that, coming at me like a lawyer every time I disagreed with him. I hate it."

"That's not what I'm doing—"

"That's exactly what you're doing. I put up with it from Karl for our entire marriage because I didn't think I deserved better. There's no way I'm putting up with it from you, too."

"Don't." Nick's voice cracks like a whip. "I am nothing like your ex-husband and you know it, so don't you dare use some bullshit comparison between us to justify what you're doing here."

"What I'm doing here?" I repeat, incensed. "Please, Nick, tell me what it is I'm doing besides objecting to being talked to like some kind of criminal."

"I'm not that kind of attorney, Mallory," he growls. "I don't fucking cross-examine witnesses. I file tax paperwork and write letters. And how the hell did I suddenly become the bad guy? You're the one breaking up with me here—and comparing me to your limp-dick sleaze of an ex-husband while you're doing it."

"Yeah, well, you're acting a hell of a lot like him right now," I shoot back. "Do you always throw a fit when you don't get your way?"

"I do when the woman I'm falling for hands me a line of bullshit a mile long and expects me to buy it." He comes out from behind the desk so that we are standing nose to nose and toe to toe now. "You want to know what's really going on here?"

"Oh, please." I gesture magnanimously. "Enlighten me,

oh wise one."

"You're scared."

"Scared?" I squawk even as my heart beats thunderously. "Of what? You?"

He nods. "Damn right, of me. And of you feeling something for me whether you want to or not. But because you haven't learned nearly as much from your bad marriage as you think you have, you've decided to blow everything up instead of sitting down and having a conversation with me like a normal person."

"Excuse me? Are you saying I'm not normal?" I demand.

"Are you kidding me?" He snorts. "Honey, you are a lot of things. Normal isn't one of them."

"Don't call me honey in that tone."

"Oh, sorry. Did Karl do that, too?" he asks.

My head threatens to explode. "You're a real asshole, you know that?"

"Maybe." He inclines his head. "But I'm also a pretty decent guy, which you'd know if you ever let yourself talk to me without an agenda. But you're too busy running away from whatever you think this is to bother asking me what I think it is. Or what I want from you."

The weight is back, pressing on my chest like a bad marriage and the thousand mistakes that killed it. "So what do you want?"

"Too late and not enough, Mallory." He walks over to his office door. "But I'll tell you one thing. It probably wouldn't be to fall for a woman who comes with an entire eighteen-wheeler full of baggage attached. Someone who makes you realize that—before her—you weren't really living. That you've just been existing in a world without color since your wife died. Or one who's too scared to turn all that color into a real, authentic, beautiful life."

His words are still hanging in the air between us—painting pictures in the empty spaces of the room and the even emptier spaces of my soul—when he yanks his door open. "Goodbye, Mallory. Have a safe life."

Chapter Fifty-Four

I spend the next two hours after Nick kicks me out of his office driving around aimlessly. It's probably not one of my better moves, considering Jimi Hendrix doesn't get the best gas mileage. He does, however, have a fantastic compilation of CDs to wallow to, and I'd be lying if I said I wasn't taking full advantage of that during my drive.

Eventually, though, I have to go home, and as I turn onto my street, I can't help glancing over at Nick's house to see if the lights are on. They are, which means he's home, and for a second I can't help wondering what he's doing.

But that's not my business anymore—if it ever was—so I force myself to stop guessing and look away. On the plus side, the full dumpster appears to have been replaced with a new empty one, so at least I know what I'll be doing tonight. Purging the final guest room and my messed-up head at the same time.

I'm wondering about dinner—and whether or not I'm going to need to cook something or if my mom or Sarah did—but when I make it around to the back door, it's to find my mom's and Sarah's suitcases lined up right outside. And the two of them sitting on the couch drinking lemonade.

"I'm going back to your father, Mallory." My mom says it quickly, like she's ripping off a Band-Aid. Which maybe she is, because God knows, I feel the sting. "And I'm taking Sarah with me."

"Sarah? Why?" I glance between the two of them, and I can't help noting that they both look...hopeful. How can that be possible after everything that's happened?

"Because it's high time your dad gets to know his daughter. Compartmentalizing her to one evening a week for pretty much her entire life is not an acceptable way to treat his daughter and it is not any way for him to get to know her," Mom says crisply. "So she'll be moving in with us for a while. I'll be able to help with the baby after it's born, and we are all going to work on being a family. Something we should have been doing for a long time now."

She gives me an arch look, like I'm part of the problem. Which...whatever. I've already had Nick dump all over me today about my emotional unavailability. My mother might as well climb on board, too.

Then again, it's not like she's got much room to talk.

As my divorce from Karl and my fling—or whatever it is we had—with Nick has taught me, it usually takes two people to ruin a relationship. And while my relationship with my mother hasn't been great for a lot of years, it's not all my fault. She has more than played a role.

Speaking of which, I don't get it. "How could you possibly take him back, Mom? He cheated on you and lied to you for twenty-seven years. I don't get how you could ever forgive that."

"I can forgive it because"—she makes air quotes with her fingers—"'we were on a break.' Was I angry that your father went right out and slept with someone else the second we decided to separate? Absolutely. Do I understand that he was as hurt and broken as I was by the state of our marriage and that men—especially of your father's generation—tend to deal with their emotions differently than women? Also absolutely.

"I never blamed him for cheating on me—" She breaks off with a sigh. "That's a lie. I totally blamed him for cheating, but I never said it out loud to him. I kept it buried inside me, thinking if I talked to him about how angry and hurt and violated I felt, it would ruin any second chance we had to make things right."

She sighs. "But what I didn't realize was that not talking about it was doing just as good a job at ruining us as talking would have—probably an even better job. Your dad didn't bring up that time because he didn't want to hurt me, and because he was afraid I would leave him if he rocked the boat too much."

"Which is why he never told you about Sarah?" I ask, brows lifted incredulously. "Because he didn't want to hurt you?" I can't keep the skepticism out of my tone.

My mother's eyes narrow in warning. "You don't have to believe your father, but you don't get to bad-mouth him to me."

"Yeah, well, I'm happy to tell him to his face."

"You know, Mallory, if you could ever stop casting blame, you'd probably get a lot further in life." My mom glances in the direction of Nick's house. "And probably a lot further in relationships as well."

"Don't, Mom." I get up and storm into the kitchen to pour myself a glass of wine. "Don't get on the same old tired loop about how Karl and my marriage breaking up was all my fault. That if I'd worn lipstick more or worn prettier dresses, he wouldn't have screwed his twenty-three-year-old paralegal. Because that is bullshit and I am sick to death of you putting it on me." I take a big sip of wine for courage and then say what I should have said a long time ago. "It's not fair and it hurts. A lot."

My mother puts her lemonade down on the coffee table and then crosses to me. "You're right, Mallory. It's not fair for me to have done that, and I'm sorry."

"Are you kidding me?" I ask. "That's it? You harangue me for months about how Karl's cheating was my fault and now you say you're sorry and I'm just supposed to forget it ever happened?"

"Not forget," she tells me. "But I hope you can understand.

I told you those things because they are what I've been telling myself for the past twenty-seven years. That if I had just been prettier or better put together or made better meals or never argued with your father, then he wouldn't have cheated on me."

Her voice breaks on the last word, and I hate that it makes me feel sorry for her. And I hate even more that it makes me forgive her. "Mom, you don't have to—"

"Yes, I do." She puts a hand on my cheek. "I appreciate that you're trying to spare me this, my dear, beautiful girl, but I do have to do this. I do owe you an apology of epic proportions. And I do need to talk about it with you because I need you to understand."

Again, she glances over toward Nick's house. "I don't want you to make the same mistakes with Nick that you made with Karl and I made with your father."

"Karl cheated on me, Mother. When we most definitely were not on a break."

"I know. And he is scum of the first order. I won't even try to tell you otherwise anymore. He deserves whatever he gets and more." She tries to pull me into a hug, but I'm still too raw to accept the embrace. "But you stopped being honest with yourself a long time ago, Mallory. Long before you found out he was cheating on you."

"What do you mean?" I ask her.

"You were unhappy for years," she answers, her gaze steady on mine. "But you had a terrible role model in me of what a real marriage should look like, and for that, I'm sorry. I should have shown you how to stand up for yourself, how to ask for what you need"—her voice breaks—"how to love yourself enough to not be afraid to rock the boat. And how to know when to leave."

Tears slide unchecked down my cheeks. She's right in that my marriage just repeated the mistakes of hers. I did what I thought I was supposed to do. But it's not entirely our fault, and I can't let her take the blame for everything. "You were great, Mom. In the end, I married a selfish prick. I didn't want to quit law school. He made me feel guilty if I didn't. I didn't want to just build his practice, but he made me feel like it was how we were a team. And I sure as hell didn't want to work for beans and have to ask every time I spent *his* money. But he was a master at making me feel that my wants and needs were just me being selfish. I can take the blame that I let him treat me like a doormat and should have fought for myself, and I probably would have acted that way even if he'd been a great guy. Sacrificing for your man *was* my role model." I give her a shaky smile. "But at the end of the day, sometimes you just married an asshole."

"This guy sounds like a tool beyond measure," Sarah adds. Then she winks at me. "Do you want me to tell his girlfriend he gave me herpes?"

I chuckle. She's totally kidding, obviously, but I love what her words really mean. My chest tightens. I have family in my corner. I have a *sister.*

"Thanks, sis, but I say good riddance. Hell, his girlfriend will someday *wish* his worst trait was herpes."

We all chuckle for a minute, but then my mom is zeroing back in on me again. "So what are you going to do about Nick?"

I shrug. "There's nothing *to* do. I broke up with him this afternoon, told him I'd work until he found a replacement for me at the office."

Sarah's eyes go wide. "Now, why on earth did you do that?"

"Really, Mallory." My mom shakes her head. "Are you ever going to learn?"

Well, what the fuck? I thought we'd just had this beautiful moment and now she's back to telling me I don't know what's best for me. I square my shoulders. "Yes, *Mother.* I'm quite capable of learning. I've learned that I too easily give up my power to men, let them take control of my life. And what I need right now is a little alone time to figure myself out and then a nice, healthy relationship with a man who listens to me."

"Oh, I had no idea Nick was such a controlling man." She makes *tsk*ing noises.

I can't let that stand, though. To be fair to Nick. "He isn't a controlling person. Not really. I mean, yes, he did sometimes just take charge, but only to help me and never in a way I would object to. He also pretty much always gave me time to say no to his help, too."

"Well, then he shouldn't have made you feel weak, dear. That's never good in a partner."

And again, I feel myself rising to Nick's defense. "He didn't make me feel weak at all. In fact, if anything, he made me stand up for myself and gave me the power to do it myself." And he did. From letting me try to mow that devil lawn by myself before answering my literal SOS in the grass to letting me interview Gina before deciding to work with her. He gave me options but ultimately, everything was my decision. How did I not see that before?

"Then I don't get it," Sarah says. "What's so bad about Nick?"

"He said he needed me." I swallow. Hard. Then admit, "And I said I needed him back."

My mom's face lights up with a smile. "That's wonderful, Mallory! It's good to need someone and be needed in return."

"Umm, no, it's not. After Karl, I never want to need another man again." Fact.

"Honey, then you're going to be alone for the rest of your life."

Her words are like a kick to the stomach, stealing my breath. "Wh-what do you mean?"

She leans over and squeezes my hand. "Because, dear, everyone needs love. With someone who loves them back just as much."

"What does love have to do with needing someone? I don't want to be with another man who needs me to do things for him, Mom. Like, seriously, ever again."

"What has Nick asked you to do for him? That man actually seems pretty self-sufficient, if you ask me."

I open my mouth to list all the things—but nothing comes to mind. In fact, the only thing I can think of that Nick needs from me is the same thing I needed from him…his company. I just liked spending time with him. Cooking dinner. Watching movies (well, almost watching). Talking about Aunt Maggie. Even working together is something we want to do, not need to do.

Something he said in his office comes back to me… *Someone who makes you realize that—before her—you weren't really living. That you've just been existing in a world without color since your wife died.*

That's what he does for me, too. My world was gray before I met Nick. And I'm afraid of what I would give up of myself to stay with him, to never go back to that gray existence. That's the real power he has over me—and it's so much more than I ever gave Karl. If that doesn't just scare the bejesus out of me, I don't know what would.

"It's okay to take your time, Mallory. You deserve that. But don't give up on love. You deserve that, too."

I swipe at the tears on my face but don't even try to speak again. I can't. My throat is choking with sadness and fear and regret and what feels an awful lot like hope, too.

This time, when my mom goes to hug me, I let her. At which point Sarah jumps in on the hug and squeezes us both so tightly that it makes me laugh. More, for the first time in a really long time, it makes me grateful to be part of this specific family, with these specific women. Because there's nothing in the world quite like finding a couple of women to like, or love, who understand you better than you understand yourself.

Maybe that's why it's so hard to watch Mom and Sarah leave a few minutes later. I carry their bags to their cars for them—it's not like I'm going to let my pregnant sister or my sixty-some-year-old mom carry their own bags if I can help it. And then I stand on the driveway and wave as they drive away.

I really hope my mom is right. And I really, really hope she knows what she is doing for her and for Sarah's sake. Once their cars are out of sight and I have no reasonable excuse for being out here anymore, I turn to go—determined not to look over at Nick's house at all.

Of course, I lose that battle with myself. I stand there staring at his place, willing him to come into view for just a second—or better yet, to walk out of his house and across the street to my driveway so we can have a second chance at our discussion from earlier.

But he doesn't come outside and I never get that glimpse. Eventually, I head toward the backyard again, determined to do something to take my mind off the mess that is my life...and the punches I keep throwing at myself.

Chapter Fifty-Five

A month later, it's just me, myself, and the few remaining stacks of Aunt Maggie's hoarding. Work still hasn't replaced me, but soon my job will be gone. My mom is gone. My sister is gone. Nick is gone—or at least he hasn't come by to help clean, not that I can blame him. Oh, he's in the neighborhood, all right. The lights are on at his house. I even spot him walking past the windows watering his plants once or twice.

Not that I'm watching.

What do I care if he waters the same one four times?

I'm just making a natural observation as I stand at my own front window, staring at my neighbor's house like a stone-cold stalker because of *reasons*.

I spend a whole ten minutes watching people pull into their driveways after a long day at work, only to be greeted by bounding dogs and happy families when they park and get out of their cars. Then I can't take it anymore and go back to handling the last stack of Aunt Maggie's things.

At the bottom of the stack of nineties *Elle* magazines is a small wooden jewelry box. I pick it up and open the lid, then stare at the contents. Plastic rings. Not just any plastic rings but a bright red one and a bright green one that are overly large and gaudy as fuck. We won them when we went to the fair when I was twelve. We giggled and joked about each of the Prince Charmings who must have given us the ring, telling stories about what they were like and how they loved us so completely. Aunt Maggie had kept our fairy-tale wedding rings.

I think back to that day, to my description of the Prince Charming who was going to sweep me off my feet... He was brave and kind and smart and loved animals (especially dogs because I wanted one badly and my parents had told me no) and loved Aunt Maggie and most importantly, he loved me just the way I was. That last one was very important because even then I was annoyed by how often my father pointed out everything I could do better. But my Prince Charming, he was going to love me just the way I was. I ran my finger along the smooth edges of the plastic ring, my eyes misting. Nick is literally my damn childhood dream hero, and I threw him away. But what can I do about it now?

My mom's words play over and over and over again in my mind. *I deserve love, too.*

And suddenly I'm done letting my reactions—the fear, the panic, the insecurity—control me. If I deserve love, then surely I have the strength to fight for it.

Of course, that means I have to go apologize—something no one in the world likes to do. But Nick is worth that and so much more.

I get to my feet and shove the ring in my jeans pocket, grab my favorite cherry-red Rothy's, and take off, making a beeline for Nick's house. Ignoring all the neighbors working out in their yards or hanging out on their front porches who are watching me as if I'm the evening's entertainment, I walk up to Nick's front door and knock.

He opens the door, his expression wary. "Hey."

I clasp my sweaty palms behind my back and try to take a relaxing, mindful yoga breath without being obvious. "Can I come in?"

He doesn't say anything, just steps back and lets the door swing open so I can walk inside. His house is spotless. His shoes are lined up by the door. His keys and wallet are in a small wooden bowl on the coffee table. There isn't a speck of dust, stray takeout menu, or crumpled receipt to be found. How in the world can someone so together ever want to be with someone who is as big of a mess as I am?

Nick stands a few feet away from me, his arms crossed, looking way too good for my heart.

"Why are you here, Mallory?" he asks, sounding as tired as I feel.

I let out a deep breath, straighten my shoulders, and lay out my plan. "To say I'm sorry and to see if there's a way that we can work something out. Maybe a friends-with-benefits type of thing again."

There. It's all out there. So why hasn't that prickly nugget of misery disappeared from my belly?

He lets out a low chuckle that sounds anything but amused and shakes his head in disbelief.

"Let me get this straight," he says, stalking toward me. "You came over here to offer up a quote friends-with-benefits situation unquote, and you think that is not only a solution but also an apology?"

I hold up my hands palms-first and he halts his approach. Okay, when he puts it that way, it doesn't sound so great.

"I don't want to lose you, but I just want to take things super slow," I say, grasping for some way to be able to explain my idea without it sounding so cold and impersonal. "I'm still learning how to live this new life, and I can't afford to get into another situation where all I'm doing is trying to please another person no matter what it costs me."

"All of that seems fair," he says, the muscle in his jaw throbbing. "But how does that get to us not being able to be more than a neighborly booty call?"

My chest tightens and it's everything I can do to get the answer out past the emotion clogging my throat. "I can't afford to fall for another Karl."

Nick's entire body goes slack, his shoulders drop, his gaze loses its intensity. The Nick I know, the one who cracks jokes and fusses about HOA violations, who has carried me up those stairs two at a time, has been replaced by a stranger.

"That's what you still think of me?" He stares at me as if he's looking at someone he wrongly thought he knew, too. "Really?"

"Nick. You know I don't. Not really. But I can't afford to be wrong—"

"Yeah?" He cuts me off with one harsh syllable. "I can't, either, Mallory. I can't afford to get involved with someone who is only willing to see the worst in me. I can't afford to be in a relationship with someone who can't see past her own baggage. I can't afford to fall for someone who is never going to be able to trust anyone again—especially not herself."

I stumble back, his words hitting me harder than a Mack truck and my whole body aching.

"That's not me," I croak out.

"How long are you going to lie to yourself about that?" he scoffs, walking to his front door. "Look, I was all in. I was more than ready to take a relationship—not a fuck buddy—slow, to get to know each other, to really give the idea of us a chance. But you aren't there. You aren't ready. I don't know if you ever will be. So I'm going to do what you can't." He opens his door wide and stands to the side, leaving me no illusions about what he wants me to do next. "I'm gonna have the courage to watch you walk away because you don't."

Shell-shocked, hurting, and lost, I walk out the door, trying to process what in the hell just happened.

He shuts it behind me without another word.

I make it halfway across the street, going back to my house, fired up on indignation and pissed-off-ness, muttering "how dare he say that" and "what in the hell was he thinking" and "oh my God could he be more wrong?" before I shove my hands in my pockets and discover the ring again. And realize that he's right.

I stop dead in the middle of the street and suck in a deep breath.

Shit.

Shit.

Shit.

Really, is there anything worse than being the wrong one in an argument where you let your ass hang out there in the wind like a chump? In reality terms, yes, there is, I know that. I don't have to have a Kim-there's-people-that-are-dying moment, but in the circle of my little world, it's pretty cataclysmic.

Hands fisted at my sides, I throw my head back and let out the mother of all angry groans at the perfect, cloudless sky. The anger in my gut fizzles like Pop Rocks until there's nothing left but sticky-sweet regret. It isn't fair of me to demand he do exactly what I want in terms of having a relationship. Have I learned nothing from being with Karl? I have to be able to unbend the stick up my own ass enough to be able to bend with the wind at least a little. Otherwise Nick will never be anything more than my neighbor across the street who makes my heart speed up, my toes curl, and actually gets me to watch (someday anyway) three really long movies about short guys with huge, hairy feet and some possessed jewelry.

I know what I have to do.

I have to turn around, go back to Nick's house, and make a real apology—not the half-hearted, self-protective one I offered up before.

I've lived through trying to mow my jungle of a lawn with the beast. I can do this.

Turning, I set my shoulders and march back across the

street, right up the sidewalk to Nick's porch, up the stairs, and—finally—with a please-God-don't-let-me-fuck-it-up-again sent heavenward, I knock on his front door.

Nick whips open the door. Jaw set, he's listening to someone on the other end of his phone talk really loudly. His entire body is tense and stress wafts off him in waves as he paces from one end of his living room to the other. Despite the truly epic volume of the person on the other end of the call, I can only catch a few words.

Trouble.

Jail time.

Had enough.

Need an ambulance.

He hangs up without a goodbye and stands there in the middle of the room, staring at his phone and looking more alone than I've ever seen another human being. Witnessing him like that turns my insides out.

"It's my mom." He rushes out of the house, heading toward his car in the driveway. "I gotta go."

I follow at his heels.

"Not by yourself." Whatever is waiting for him at the end of this drive, he's going to need a friend—and whether he likes it or not, that's going to be me.

I'm his friend no matter what. That connection between us is stronger than my bullshit—stronger even than the friendship, I am willing to admit to myself, but that's for figuring out another day. Right now is about being there for Nick the way he's always been there for me.

My apology—and it's going to be a big fucking one—will have to wait. He needs me more than I need to clear my conscience.

I've barely gotten my seat belt clicked when Nick throws the car into reverse and the Mercedes's tires squeal as he peels out of his driveway. I have no idea where we're going, but even as he drives like a Texas cheerleader's mom on the way to take out her daughter's rival, I know I'm with Nick and I trust him completely.

His driving? A little less. That has me sending up a few Hail Marys as we merge onto the parkway at light speed and head for his parents' house and God knows what disaster is waiting for us there.

Chapter Fifty-Six

*N*ick's car needs an oh-shit handle. As it is, I'm using all three of my butt muscles to hold on to the supple leather passenger seat, wondering if I missed my opportunity to tell him, to apologize, because it seems like there's a damn good chance he's about to launch us into space. He makes a sharp right into a neighborhood so fancy, it has an actual security guard sitting in a little building by the functioning gates instead. Mercifully, Nick slows down as he approaches.

A woman with the bearing of someone who has spent time in the military and raised at least six boys who caused all kinds of good trouble comes out of the guardhouse.

Nick unrolls his window. "Hey, Ms. Geraldine."

"Mr. Holloway, you going to see your parents?"

"Yeah," Nick says with a grimace. "Mom's about to start World War III."

"Knowing your mama, she's gonna end it, too." Geraldine chuckles as she writes a note in her clipboard marked VISITORS. "Don't take that turn by Mrs. Lauder's house too fast; you know she'll complain."

"Yes, ma'am," Nick says.

Geraldine hits the button that raises the gate and Nick drives through at a slower speed—only making me use two of my butt muscles so I don't go flying. All I can see are trees with lone driveways disappearing between thick coverage, with names like Springsteen and Bongiovi on the mailboxes, but not a single house in sight.

Then Nick hooks a left down another densely tree-lined street and hits the brakes so hard, the seat belt is gonna become practically a new layer of skin between my boobs for the foreseeable future.

He jerks his chin to the right. "The Lauder place."

Well, that's one word for it. I would have called it the Lauder freakin' estate. It looks like someone took a castle out of Disney Paris and plopped it down in Jersey. It's huge and stone, and I get to stare at it with my mouth hanging open for about six seconds before the Mercedes rounds the corner and Nick guns it.

There are more visible homes on this stretch, and all of them have three things in common. One, they are massive places where a person can say "her room's in the south wing" and it wouldn't be ironic. Two, the yards are pristine and landscaped to look like formal French gardens. Three, there isn't a single solitary sign of life in any of them. No kids playing outside. No homeowners puttering in their flower boxes. No cars sitting in the circular driveways.

Except for one place and, of course, that's the one that Nick whips the Mercedes into, pulling to a stop right beside a bright canary-yellow old-school Camaro. It has white racing stripes going down the hood, which has a cowl scoop that sticks out from the hood like a nose—or a giant yellow middle finger.

On the other side of the car stands a short woman who is maybe five-two on a tall day, in her early sixties with mahogany hair cut in a bob that hits her right in the sweet spot of her jawline. She's surrounded by a handful of people towering over her in full diamonds at ten in the morning, who look about to pop while she has the look of utter boredom and distance I know I've seen before. Pivoting in my seat, I look at the man who used the exact same look to great effect on me earlier today.

"*That's* your mom?"

He lets out a long sigh and turns off the engine. "The one and only Victoria Holloway."

"Is that her car?" It's a monster. A badass, classic muscle-car monster in a loud enough color, the astronauts can probably see it from the space station.

Nick opens his car door as he says, "I have my suspicions."

We get out of the Mercedes and make our way over to the scrum.

"You know the rules, Vickie. We expect things to be held to a certain level in Woodhill Estates, and you have been keeping this"—the woman points a manicured nail at the Camaro—"thing parked in your driveway for four days. The community rules clearly state all vehicles have to be stored in the garage."

"Maude, don't you *ever* call Limoncello a thing again. She is a fully restored 1967 Chevrolet Camaro with a 6.2 liter LS3 engine with a six-speed transmission, a cold-air intake, speed injectors, and a Brian Tooley stage-three camshaft. And when Limoncello hits the street, she's going to blow the shingles right off your roof, so treat her with some respect because she deserves it."

Maude's high-boned cheeks turn red with anger. "I don't care what this *thing* is, if it's out here one more hour, I'm going to have it towed."

Victoria—I can't even imagine ever calling this woman Vickie unless I felt like getting my ass kicked—doesn't make a move toward the other woman. She doesn't have to. One lift of a single dark eyebrow does the job. Maude takes two big steps back. Who'da thought Maude was smart enough for that?

"I'd love to see you try, Maude, darling," Victoria says.

Wow. Go Victoria.

Nick clears his throat and each of the four people surrounding his mom turn to look at him. Only Victoria smiles.

"Now, now, Mrs. Crews," he says in an aw-shucks tone as he holds up his hands in supplication. "We both know that you have no such authority to step on private property, HOA violation or not. The neighborhood guidelines allow you to file a complaint. I'll help you with the paperwork."

Yeah. That's the softy hidden underneath all the prickly layers.

The realization hits me so hard, I nearly stumble back. I've never been more wrong about anything—and I've been wrong about sooooo much stuff—as I've been to think that Nick would ever secretly be hiding a side of himself that's even on the same stratosphere of douche canoe as my ex. He couldn't. Not even a little. Nick's kind and generous and always helping people, even when they probably don't deserve it—like me. And Maude.

And I fucked it all up.

"Now, listen here, young man, don't talk down to me," Maude says, planting her hands on her St.-John-pantsuit-encased hips. "I knew you when you were still in diapers."

Nick's mom draws to her full height and shuts Maude down immediately. "Yes, and that's when we lived in that much smaller home to the east of the golf course. If you like, we could move closer to you again. I understand the Moores to your left are selling soon. Maybe we'll just get it as an extra place for parties."

Maude physically blanches. The other folks start peeling away from the woman who has been the ringleader as well. I'm just a bystander who knows no one, and my stomach is all nervous swirls.

Nick lets out a deep sigh. "Mo-om, let's not escalate the situation." He turns back to Maude and the rest of her now-wary toadies. "I'd like to remind everyone here that I am no longer in diapers and have a law degree now, which is why I feel confident reminding everyone you are standing on private property."

"And if you don't leave," Victoria says, her tone imperious as she manages to look down her nose at Maude even though the other woman has four inches on her, "I'll call the cops and we can really create a scene."

I step forward, already digging through my purse. "Did you want to borrow my phone?"

Nick's mom looks me over, cataloging me from my slightly frizzy topknot to non-matching Rothy's that I'd thrown on in my hurry to get to Nick and apologize. Whatever she sees, it must check all the right boxes, because she flashes me a smile that is 60 percent approval and 40 percent let's-go-start-some-shit.

"You have it handy?" she asks.

"I'm always here to give the middle finger to HOA rules." I should show her—or her gardener, really—how to mow a giant SOS in her front yard. With the size of the Holloway acreage, they might be able to see it *and* her car from space.

"Ohhhhhhh, I like you." She holds out her hand. "Let's do this."

"Not quite yet," Nick interjects, stepping between his mom and me. "I'm sure Maude was getting ready to go without having to involve law enforcement."

There's grumbling, but Maude and the rest disperse. Slowly. Looking back every few steps to shoot Victoria a dirty look.

Once they are mostly down the driveway and out of earshot, Nick turns to his mom and lowers his voice to a demanding whisper. "You can still visit Limoncello in the garage, Mom."

She glances over at the car and looks at it like she's a kid on Christmas morning who got the pony she was asking Santa for. "But she looks so good out in the sun."

"Mom," Nick says. "Rules are rules, and if you didn't want to live by them, you should have bought a house in the goddamn country and not the suburbs."

Victoria and I make eye contact. I know in that instant that this woman is never going to visit her beloved muscle car in a garage, no matter how high-end it is. She's going to bring it out in the sunshine and drive it around the neighborhood fast enough that it really hugs the curves, and she'll flip off Maude every time she drives by the other woman's house. I kinda love her on sight.

"Yes, darling boy, whatever you say." She turns her attention to the retreating bunch of metaphorical pitchfork-bearing villagers. "But it does them good to have a little rebellion once in a while. My dear Maude will likely live longer from the exercise of her outrage. It's a public service, really, when you think about it."

She looks over and winks at me. It's like getting noticed by a rock star. I'm fucking giddy.

Grasping Nick's forearm, I lean in closer to him. "I want to be your mom when I grow up."

He rolls his eyes. "God help me, of course you do."

"Let's go inside," Victoria says as she turns and heads toward the massive double oak doors of the French chateau-style house that could double as a boutique hotel. "Your father no doubt has been watching the whole thing, pretending to not pay the least bit of attention to my antics."

Chapter Fifty-Seven

We follow Victoria into the two-story foyer with the double staircase and the no-lie huge chandelier in it, turn right at a butler's closet, then into a study with dark-stained wood bookshelves that go all the way up past a mezzanine level accessible by an iron circular staircase to the ceiling.

A man reading a hardback copy of *Karpov on Karpov* looks up when we walk in. He has bone-white hair, blue eyes that look like they've been dipped in the Caribbean, and what seems like a perpetually amused smile that reminds me a lot of Nick's.

"Are you done terrorizing the neighbors, dear?" he asks as he closes his book and stands up.

"Maybe," Victoria says, lifting her cheek for him to kiss, which he does. "I'll at least consider it for the moment."

He walks over to us. "Hello, son." Then he holds his hand out to me. "John Holloway, my dear. And how do you know Nick?"

Nick puts his hand on the small of my back. He doesn't try to push me forward, not even with the most subtle pressure. "This is Mallory."

I shake his dad's hand, and we all walk over to the love seats positioned facing each other in front of a fireplace big enough to do yoga in.

We sit down. Me next to Nick on one love seat that definitely looked bigger than it feels now with us hip to hip on it. It's impossible not to be acutely aware of being this near to him.

Do I shift a little so that our thighs line up? Yes. I am weak and I gave in. I'm halfway to forcing myself to readjust when he lifts his arm and lays it across the back of the love seat, his fingertips landing on my shoulder.

"I'm sure Maude isn't describing you in a kind way right about now," John says to his wife. "Are you going to put the car in the garage?"

Victoria fiddles with the full-service tea set laid out on the table between the love seats.

"She," Victoria says, "has a name."

"Fine." John gives his wife an indulgent smile as he toys with the flipped-up end of her bob. "Are you going to put Limoncello into the garage now?"

She pours a cup of tea from the pot. "I suppose." She hands it to Nick. "But I'm waiting until after dark. Maude can sit and stew for a few hours." She turns to me. "Would you like a cup of tea until it's time for dinner?"

I gulp, suddenly aware that I am about to experience something akin to the Spanish Inquisition. "Yes, thank you."

She pours a cup and hands it to me, then repeats the process for herself and John while I sit there trying to figure out what in the hell I'm doing. Here I am, meeting Nick's parents as if we're serious, when I all but shoved him two-handed out of my life—and he went—drinking tea and basking in the joy of being near him again.

Victoria adds a splash of cream to her tea and stirs it with what has to be a literal silver spoon. "So, John, I'm thinking that we could add a small track, nothing obnoxious, for Limoncello."

Nick and his dad let out matching stifled laughs at the same time. An identical sound coming from two men is kind of adorable. And I can't help but look between them to spot all the similarities. The easy laugh. The tolerant amusement at Victoria's troublemaking.

"An interesting idea," John says, calm as a cucumber slice

on a socialite's closed eyes. "I'd recommend, though, that you gift Maude a trip to Vail first."

"And a fistful of Valium," Nick adds.

Victoria sets her spoon down and sighs. "You're no fun."

"And you're completely outrageous," he says as if he's uttered those words sixty-three times a day their entire marriage and gotten a kick out of it each time.

It reminds me of how Nick looked at me when I was lying in the grass in front of my house after having my ass kicked by the lawn mower. Amused. Interested. Happy. The realization makes my insides go all soft and gooey.

Fuck.

Meanwhile, Nick's mom looks at his dad and they are having one of those married-for-a-long-time silent conversations that encompass everything and nothing in a matter of seconds. In that moment, I realize that I want that, and even more importantly, I want that with Nick. Not because I can't live without a man, but because I *need* to live with *him*. I need to be loved by him.

The truth of that has me shifting on the velvet seat, unsure of what in the hell I'm supposed to do now.

"One of these days, John," Victoria says, twining the fingers of her free hand through his, "I'll get you to join in on the fun."

"After forty years into this life with you? It's possible, I guess." He shrugs and shakes his head. "I know how you love a challenge."

Victoria scoffs. "Your life would be boring without me. You'd still be driving a Mercedes instead of the GTO."

"That's true." He leans over and kisses her cheek. "I'd have a boring life if it weren't for my very non-boring wife."

It's adorable and awful at the same time because this is the life I always wanted—the one I still want. The teasing. The fun. The in-it-togetherness, weird quirks and all.

And the thing is, I don't just want that life. I want it with

Nick because, despite how much I fought it, I've fallen for Mr. Always There and I can't imagine him not being a part of my life. All I have to do to make that want a reality is to have the guts to fight for it.

Old me would have never. But the new Mallory Martin— done with being Bach—faced down Karl and won. I've lived through finding a treasure chest of my beloved aunt's dildos. I've started a new life for myself that teenage me wouldn't be ashamed of. I'm no longer a woman who hides in law office bathrooms. I can do this.

Nick scoots closer on the love seat and lowers his voice to a whisper. "Sorry about my parents."

"They're amazing." It's true. I've never seen two people more comfortable about being themselves with each other. "Nick, we need to talk." Adrenaline surges through my veins because now that I know what I want, how I want my life to be, I want it to start now. "Can we go somewhere?"

He nods. "Sure, let's—"

Before we can make any excuses to his parents and find somewhere to talk, though, the thick oak door to the study opens and a woman in a soft gray dress walks in. "Dinner is ready."

"Wonderful," Victoria says as she stands. "Shall we?"

"Mom, you know you could have just asked me to dinner instead of staging a big fight with your neighborhood nemesis."

"True," she says with an impish grin. "But where is the fun in that?"

Nick turns to his dad.

John shrugs as he starts toward the study door, arm in arm with his wife. "She's your mother, son. She's never going to do the expected."

Nick looks over at me, a chagrined look on his face that hits me somewhere between oh-my-God-he's-amazing and how-could-I-have-missed-this-all-along. "Sounds like someone else I know."

Chapter Fifty-Eight

The Holloway dining room is huge but still manages to feel cozy. It's all soothing creams and light blues with neutral wood—everything illuminated by the sun coming in from the huge south-facing windows. We sit down at an oval table set for four. Victoria sits to my left and Nick to my right with John straight across, obviously more interested in the chicken cordon bleu than whatever intel into her son's life Victoria is about to go mining for.

I, on the other hand, am a jumble of anticipation and nerves.

"I know you two have been sparring or flirting or hanging out, whatever it is that they call casual sex that really isn't these days," Victoria says as she pours a balsamic vinaigrette over her salad. "But what I really want is to hear it all from your perspective, Mallory. Nick gives very few satisfactory details."

"Mo-om," Nick groans and sinks back against his chair.

"It's true." Victoria passes the crystal decanter of vinaigrette to John. "You're just like your father. It feels like reeling in a shark with a toy fishing pole to get either of you to give up the goods." She takes a sip of wine and turns her attention back to me. "So, tell me everything."

Everything? That's a lot to unpack, but I'm not about to turn down the opening she's given me.

I take a sip of my water and my hand doesn't even shake. "Well, it all started when he wouldn't stop harping on me to mow my grass so I would stop violating our HOA rules."

"Nicolas!" Victoria exclaims. "How could you have acted like a Maude?"

"No, he was right," I say. "I'd just inherited my aunt Maggie's house and it was in a state. Still, it was heaven compared to living with my parents while I went through a messy—and only got messier—divorce. Nick helped set up a meeting with his partner, Gina, and while I was at the office, I just sort of happened to fall into the job of being the firm's temporary office manager."

"There was no 'happened to fall into it,'" Nick says. "You stepped up, negotiated like a hostage-taker, and saved us from chaos. Once you'd been there an hour, we knew there was no way we could ever let you."

"So you liked her office-management skills, is that right, Nick?" Victoria asks, and the double entendre she's throwing down is big enough to win a prizefight.

Nick groans but says nothing else.

Breaking into the awkward silence that follows, I continue. "Between HOA issues, helping clean my aunt's house, my divorce, and Nick's office needing a new manager—well, that about sums up how we met." I take a bite of chicken that probably tastes epic, if my stomach weren't in knots. "This chicken is delicious."

"Oh yes," John says as he slices off another bite. "This is one of our chef's specialties. Nick's favorite, too."

"So is this nasty divorce behind you yet, my dear?" From a different woman, the question would have come across as bitchy. But Victoria's eyes are filled with nothing but concern for me.

I'm about to tell her the truth, that I am very much still in the middle of that shitstorm, but Nick replies first. "Mother, Mallory and I are no longer"—he waves his hand—"whatever we were before. She's the best office manager we've ever had and a good neighbor, and that's all. So let the woman eat in peace, okay?"

A hard band of regret squeezes my chest, making it almost impossible to breathe, much less eat. I turn to Nick, but he focuses on cutting another piece of chicken and chewing, completely unaware that my world is unraveling around me. The bastard. "You know, you could act like it bothers you just a little."

He swallows his last bite and slowly turns to me, one eyebrow raised. "That what bothers me exactly?"

I roll my eyes at him. "That you're not watching *Lord of the Rings* every night anymore."

He fires back, "Who's to say I'm *not* watching *Lord of the Rings* every night?"

My gaze narrows on his, the whole room disappearing except the two of us. "Are you saying, while I've been trying to sort out my baggage so that I know what I really want, you've been watching *Lord of the Rings* with someone else?"

"If you'll recall, you told me that you didn't want to watch *Lord of the Rings* with me anymore. So what business is it of yours who I watch movies with?"

I vaguely hear Nick's dad try to ask his mom what the heck is so important about *Lord of the Rings*, but Victoria wasn't born yesterday. She's crafty and she may not know exactly what we're talking about, but she knows it's not about a damn movie about hobbits.

I can't believe I've been pining away for Nick for a month, and he already moved on to someone new. The room is spinning and I might be sick, but I'm not leaving before I tell Nick what he can do with his goddamn apology now.

I open my mouth to tell him off, but nothing comes out. Not a single word. I'm too mad. No, I'm too devastated. I am shattering into so many pieces, I can't recognize what parts of me are still here.

"You planning on stabbing me with that?" Nick nods to my hand gripping my knife.

What? Dear Lord. I relax my grip and set my knife and fork down. "Of course not." I would never hurt Nick and—" My eyes go wide at where I was going with that thought. *He would never hurt me.* Not physically and not verbally. He's nothing like my ex. Even when we're fighting, he's done nothing that would hurt me. Well, except tell his mom I'm just a coworker and a neighbor. That hurt, but honestly, I deserve it. And he deserves the truth.

"Nice try, but I know for a fact you're not watching *Lord of the Rings* with anyone but me," I challenge.

"What makes you so sure?" he challenges right back.

"For starters, because you're nothing like my ex. Not even an atom similar." A slow smile starts to lift one side of my mouth—just as it does his.

"Oh yeah? You think you know me that well?"

"Yes, I believe I do." I take a deep breath and pray to every god there is that I don't mess up what I need to say next. My heart is pounding in my chest as I begin. "You are brave enough to keep giving me another chance, kind enough to help an old lady and an almost-divorced one find happiness again, and you are smart enough to know when to give me space. You love animals or you'd never have adopted that ridiculous dog, Buttercup. You loved Aunt Maggie and took care of her. And most importantly, you think I'm amazing just the way I am."

"Is that all?" he asks with an expectant look, and I know exactly what he wants to hear me say.

"I can't believe I was ever worried you might turn out like my ex. Or that I might have terrible judgment in men. My ovaries have excellent taste; I just sometimes don't listen to them. And they want you to know that they need you. I need you. Not to solve my problems but to just be there. And I'll be there for you, too."

Nick leans forward and picks up my hands, a smile twinkling in his eyes. "I told you your ovaries were smart."

I grin back at him. "They're my best feature. But to be fair, they really don't care what happens when the hobbits leave the Shire. It's sad, really." I shake my head. "They said they're having too much fun to give a damn at all."

Nick is full-on grinning now, and for the first time since we sat down for dinner, a weight is lifting from my chest, my breath coming easier with every minute that passes. He tugs me into his lap.

"What about working at the law firm being the same as falling back into old habits and reliving your old life with Karl?"

I'm going to banish that man's name from my vocabulary forever. "I was a dumbass for even thinking it."

His dark gaze is brimming with promise. "So we give this thing a real chance?"

"I'm making no promises," I feel I have to say, then add, "but yes, I would really, really like to give this a real chance."

He leans forward and his lips are on mine, moving against them with abandon. When we finally break apart, we're both gasping for breath.

I smooth his hair behind his ear. "I can't believe I ever thought you were like my ex. For starters, you're way better at kissing me—everywhere."

I blush as he chuckles and pulls me closer.

But before our lips collide, Nick's dad coughs, reminding us both we're not alone, and asks, "So, umm, should we all watch *Lord of the Rings* after dinner?"

Three horrified sets of eyes turn to John as Nick, his mom, and I all say at the same time, "No!"

Then we glance around at each other and bust out laughing.

"I don't get it," John says. "I gathered from your discussion it was your favorite movie."

Victoria leans over and squeezes John's hand. "Dear, they love it like we love Star Wars."

"Oh"—his eyes widen—"ohhhh."

"Mo-om," Nick groans. And we all break into another fit of laughter.

"I like her," Victoria says, when we finally catch our breath. "Can we keep her?"

The look Nick gives me sears me right down to my toes with all the good (and good bad) things it promises. "Only if she wants to stay."

"I do," I say, meaning it more than anything else I've ever said in my whole entire life. "I really, really do."

And so I do. And we do. And it is wonderful.

Epilogue

One year later...

The curtains hanging in the bedroom window aren't hot-pink-and-green-zebra-striped like at my aunt's house, but they still do an awful job of keeping out the sunlight first thing in the morning. The beams come in at the perfect angle to shine right in my eyes. Unwilling to give up the warmth of my bed, I try to roll over, but I'm stuck.

Nick's arm is thrown across me and when I move, he tugs me closer so I'm plastered against his muscular form. I would have rolled the other way, but nine-months-pregnant bellies and sleeping facedown on the mattress doesn't really work. I haven't seen my toes in months, putting on underwear is its own kind of balancing hell, and I get heartburn after every meal. I've never been happier.

Judging by the steady state of my contractions since the sun woke me up this morning, I'm not going to be preggo much longer, either. I'm just lying here processing all that is about to change when Nick's palm glides from the top of my belly to my breast—not that I'm complaining.

"Go back to sleep," Nick says, his words tickling the back of my skin.

Yeah. That isn't gonna happen. A baby is definitely coming. "Have you seen the sun coming in through the window?"

"I'm gonna board that thing up," he grumbles before delivering a string of kisses up my neck. "How's Happy doing this morning?"

That's what Nick has called the baby since the day we found out I'm pregnant. We were doing the whole predawn-walk-of-shame thing for months when we found out we were part of the point zero, zero, zero, whatever percent of birth control fails—not that either of us saw our happy little accident that way. We were thrilled. What can I say? Timing has never been our strong suit.

At least my divorce from Karl had been final by then. And by final I mean Gina was true to her word and made him cry—and give me half the business before I signed. He is remarried with his own child born now, and I honestly wish him all the best. I'm too excited about the future with *this* amazing man to dwell on that asshole anyway.

And this morning, so is Happy. I take Nick's hand and move it down from cupping my suddenly ginormous boobs to my round belly. Happy lets it be known that she's ready to come feel that sunshine herself.

"Did she just kick?" Nick asks.

"Oh yeah," I say with a chuckle. "Our girl's a fighter."

He kisses me again, this time on top of my shoulder. "I can't wait to meet her."

"About that." I pause, letting the moment drag out for just the teensiest bit of drama. "How do you feel about this morning?"

Nick's body freezes behind mine. "Today? Now?"

"Mm-hmm."

He stumbles out of bed so fast, he half slides, half skates across the hardwood floor but still has the wherewithal to grab my overnight bag. "Let's do this."

Never mind the fact that per usual, he is buck naked. That he sleeps in the nude is one of my favorite parts of his routines.

"While I absolutely love the view," I say, sitting up slowly and doing the a-little-this-way-a-little-that-way dance of pulling on comfy pajama pants. "Don't you think you might want to get dressed first?"

He looks down, obviously completely surprised to see his own dick. "Fuck."

He gets dressed in record time while I text Sarah, who is probably nursing her baby in the green room of Aunt Maggie's old place (now hers), then my mom, and finally Nick's mom. They'll meet us at the hospital, of course, everyone eager to meet the new addition to our family. Then Nick comes over, kneels down on one knee in front of me, and ties my sneakers.

"Let's go have a baby." He looks up at me and grins. "You're gonna be a great mom."

"*We're* gonna be great parents."

Sure, we'll make mistakes—what parents don't?—but we also have people around us who care, not because of how we could burnish their image but just because. We have family— real family. And I mean that sincerely. While things are still a bit rocky between my dad and me, we really have been working hard to have a closer relationship. Happy is responsible for that.

Nick goes ahead of me down the stairs, holding out his hand so I can grasp it for balance. Then we walk out of the house, and Nick drives us to the hospital where many painful (even with the drugs) hours later, Margaret Elizabeth Victoria is born. But you know, her daddy just keeps calling her Happy—he isn't the only one.

Acknowledgments

This book was so much fun to write, so I first have to thank Avery Flynn for making it possible. You're a fantastic cowriter and an even better person.

Liz Pelletier and Emily Sylvan Kim, for always having my back and for being the two best women in publishing, bar none.

To all the people at Entangled—Stacy Cantor Abrams, Elizabeth Turner Stokes, Curtis Svehlak, Jessica Turner. I am so lucky to work with the best, most supportive team in publishing and I am grateful to every single one of you. xoxoxo

And to my wonderful, wonderful family, who were less than enthusiastic about me diving right back into the breach but who rallied together (as always) to give me all the love and support and excitement I could ever ask for. I love you so much.

And finally, for my fans, who make this all possible. I am so grateful for all of your love and support for my books and me. It means more than I can ever say. Thank you, thank you, thank you. I love you a lot. :)

Tracy

A huge thank-you to everyone—especially the fabulous Tracy Wolff, who really is a rock star. Thank you!!! Also, to Liz and the entire Entangled team, wow, y'all are amazing, and I have no idea how I can ever repay the many, many kindnesses. I'd offer to give you one of my kids but...well, they're kind of a handful. LOL.

Speaking of kids, I couldn't do what I do without the support of all three of the Flynn kids and the fabulous Mr. Flynn. The biggest thank-you of all has to go to the readers. Without y'all, none of this would be happening. I hope Mallory's story was a good escape and gave you more than a few laughs (and okay, a couple of tears, too).

xoxo,
Avery

Turn the page to start reading the smart, hilarious look at what happens when a mompreneur tries to balance kids, work, and falling in love with the wrong guy...

RACHEL, out of OFFICE

USA TODAY BESTSELLING AUTHOR
CHRISTINA HOVLAND

Chapter One

RACHEL

"Not like that." Rachel Gibson shook her head even though her client couldn't see her. "Don't be afraid. You can't mess it up. Do it just like I showed you. Once it's aligned, then slip it right in. Boom. Done."

She glanced at the digital clock on the top corner of her laptop.

Crap, crap, crap. She was so late. A-freaking-gain.

She normally didn't take clients in her bedroom, but she'd turned off the camera, so it wasn't a big deal.

"I think I've almost got it," the deep male voice assured in a tone that was not assuring.

Rachel stilled, took a deep breath, and did her absolute best to relax the tension from her shoulders.

Perfection is not measured by degrees. It is created by degrees. She played the mantra over in her head. This particular adage was the extent of the philosophical genes making up Rachel's DNA. Seeing that most of her genetics came from a family who preferred to crack jokes at inappropriate times to deflect from thoughtful conversation, it was a miracle she'd inherited *any* deep thoughts.

That said, *this* philosophical saying was her go-to in the reality of her daily activities as the owner, manager, and only employee of her very own virtual personal assistant company. Also, as a mom to her two boys. Twins.

Anyway, perfection was within her grasp, degree by degree—if she could simply keep her shit together.

Or get her shit together. Either way.

She let out a sigh, watching her client's progress on the screen. This client was in California, so their time zones were close. Rachel was in Denver, and thanks to the beauty of the internet, she could work virtually with clients nearly anywhere. Although the new Australia client was starting to seriously cost her on missed sleep.

"Darn," he said. Once again, he fudged the design. Perfection would not happen for him with this graphic design lesson.

"Just line it up," Rachel encouraged. "Don't overthink."

Most days, her uncanny ability to find solutions to client issues was outweighed only by her inability to deal with her own crap. Sometimes she even considered taking up the joke-cracking schtick that worked so well for her brothers and parents.

"I can't get it. I'm telling you," he replied, frustration lacing his tone.

Man, she did not have time for this. She had to get out the door. They'd need to reschedule for later, which stunk because she didn't have time later.

Hell, she didn't have time *now*.

"Okay, wait, I think I did it." James sounded as relieved as she felt.

Thank goodness. She glanced at his work-in-progress on the screen of her laptop. Oh, thank, thank, thank goodness. Yes, he had it. She released a long breath.

"I can't believe I got it." He laughed, switching the video monitor from the graphic design program on the screen to his webcam. "You're the best, Rachel."

He gave her two thumbs up.

Even though he couldn't see her, Rachel couldn't help it…

she smiled. One more happy client. She'd been working with him for the past hour so he could create his own graphics for his start-up company. He'd finally figured out how to copy and paste and now he knew how to move the images around. Perfection by degrees. Her motto in process.

"I'll practice some more and then we can chat in a few days," he said, the pleased tone of his words causing that bloom of pride she adored so much in her job.

"Let me know if you need anything else," Rachel said, raising her voice into the speaker of the MacBook placed precariously on the edge of her dresser. She'd set down the computer so she could simultaneously apply her eye makeup while observing his progression on the screen.

They said their goodbyes, and she closed the laptop. Then she yawned. Last night had been another doozy. Could she get away with crawling into bed to sleep for the next eight hours? No. She could not.

Because the load of shit that needed to be done would not do itself.

That was the answer to that.

Accepting her newest client (the Australia guy) was the perfect supplement to her income. Unfortunately, she'd never been good at pulling all-nighters. Not even when she'd been an undergrad or when her twins were teeny tiny, itsy-bitsy, cutie patootie babies.

One step at a time, one project at a time, one client at a time, she was making all the things happen all the time. After all, the difference between boiling water and hot water was only one degree.

The difference between crossing the finish line in first place or second place was usually a matter of millimeters.

And the difference between "horribly late" and "let's just reschedule" was nearly always separated by Rachel's underestimation of time management.

"Rach?" her best friend Molly called from downstairs. "C'mon, hustle up. We're going to be late."

Yes, they were. But what was she supposed to say when James had needed an extra hour this afternoon? She did what she always did. Solved. The. Freaking. Problem.

"Coming," Rachel hollered, hoping her voice carried out the door and down the staircase.

"Late," Molly called back.

"Two seconds," Rachel called again. Rubbing the remnants of concealer over the dark bags that seemed to have permanent residence under her eyes, she quickly pulled her hair up into a twist, securing it with some corkscrew bobby pins her mother-in-law insisted she try.

Former mother-in-law.

The meemaw to her twin boys.

The momster who usually always got whatever she wanted, even though Rachel couldn't quite figure out how she did it.

A quick pop on the scale on her way out of the bathroom and she'd be on her way. One swift step. She could do this. Gah. She hated this part of the day.

She closed her eyes when the digital display blinked, and she considered whether the three cookies she'd eaten after lunch were going to prove to ruin her afternoon. Deep breath and she opened her eyes, glancing down.

Shit.

Damn, that thing was being a total asshole.

For the record, she'd eat the cookies again just to spite it.

Also, they were really yummy and a gift from a client. They'd arrived at her doorstep warm—with bonus ice cream— and what was she supposed to do? They were meant to be eaten warm. So she ate them…warm. That was what one did with divine cookies.

"Rachel, seriously," Molly called, but her tone sounded as though she'd just discovered the remnants of a dozen warm cookies from Heather's Cookie Co. on the dining room table, and she didn't really care if they were that late.

Double crapola.

"Don't eat those," Rachel shouted, grabbing her favorite sling-back black sandals on her way out of her bedroom, her toes sinking only briefly in the carpet because she was on a sprint.

Dammit, Molly was as good as Rachel for spiderlike senses around carbohydrates and sugar. Rachel should've put them away. Of course, her best friend would find the residual cookies.

But Rachel had plans for them—there were four left.

Two for each of her boys.

If Molly ate one, then there would be only three and that meant an argument that Rachel did *not* want to referee.

So if Molly ate one, then Rachel would have to eat one, but she'd already had plenty, and she didn't really want the scale to be more of an asshole because her best friend ate a cookie.

That made sense, right?

"Seriously, Molly, don't eat that." Rachel took the steps two at a time, skidding around the bottom of the bannister, deftly stepping over errant Legos scattered like land mines, past the corner of the office she'd set up there.

Yes, she *could* cut the third cookie in half for the boys. While that might teach them a lesson in sharing, it brought more challenges and probably the food scale to get an exact weight so things were *precisely* fair.

So it'd just be easier if—

She scooted around the corner into the dining room where the box lay open on the table.

Cookie in hand, Molly's dark curls bobbed against the exposed pale skin of her shoulder as she turned to Rachel. Rachel, who had reached the room three seconds too late.

Molly lifted her looked-to-be-recently-threaded eyebrows as she bit, her hazel eyes sparkling with the perpetual perkiness that had become her brand.

Rachel made a strangled sound.

"Wha?" Molly asked as a few errant crumbles fell from her lips.

Rachel took a breath as her cell buzzed in her pocket.

"Want some?" Molly asked around the mouthful of carb-laden goodness.

Rachel shook her head, glancing at her cell. A client. She needed to take this.

"Don't pick that up." Molly's eyes turned to slits. "We'll be even later. Not just cookie late, but client late. You know we can't be—"

"It's Cassie." Rachel stared as the number flashed on the screen.

"Cassie?" Molly asked.

"Client." Cassie had a tendency to try to do things herself that she really should let Rachel handle. "It's probably important."

"It's after hours," Molly said, totally correct in that assumption.

Rachel bit at her bottom lip. Molly wasn't wrong…yet…

"*That* is why you shouldn't pick it up." Molly clearly knew better than to reach for the phone, since she and Rachel had been friends forever. But, since they'd been friends forever, Rachel knew Molly's fingertips must itch to grab the cell and bat it out of reach. Crush it under her tennis shoe. That sort of thing.

"It is after five," Molly continued. "*We* have a Little League game to get to. Your kids and my kid are expecting us not to be late. And boundaries are important."

"What if *the call* is important?" Rachel wished she had powers of telepathy so she could reach through the signal and determine if it was something that needed to be dealt with before she picked up and made them both late. Later.

"What's the likelihood that it's not something that can wait until tomorrow?" Molly asked, her tone one of soothing comfort that usually worked for getting her way.

Molly had a knack for getting people—everyone—to bend to her will. Sometimes she used the brute force of her personality and sometimes, like now, she used a gentle touch. Molly was diverse in her manipulation techniques like that.

She'd make an excellent mother-in-law someday.

Rachel warred with herself and the decision at hand. If she answered the call, she'd be late, but her client would be happy. If she didn't answer the call, she'd be only a little late and Molly would be happy.

"My clients hire me because they know I'll always go above and beyond." Her heartbeat increased even as she glanced at her friend. The above and beyond thing was right on her business cards. In bold italics.

"True." Molly continued nibbling the cookie but kept one eye on Rachel and one eye on the phone. She also started toward the door.

"Not answering is *not* going above and beyond," Rachel declared.

"Don't make the boys wait," Molly said quietly, turning to her friend. Her understanding of the battle going on inside Rachel was abundantly apparent.

And that's what did it.

The boys.

Her boys.

Rachel wouldn't let her boys wait.

"I'll just catch up with Cassie in the car on the way." Still, Rachel had to force herself not to return the call.

Her phone immediately rang again, as it did regularly throughout the day and often during the night, too. Since she was a virtual personal assistant, she had three large clients. In three very different time zones.

This was her job. Her business. The thing that, aside from her children, brought her the most joy.

Most days.

This time, however, it was her ex calling. The father of her eight-year-old twins and the supposed-to-be one-night stand that turned into *way* more than either of them had bargained for.

Mouthing, *I'm sorry*, she immediately pressed the phone to her ear. "Gavin?"

Molly rolled her eyes, shaking her head, while making gagging noises unbefitting the cookie she still worked on.

"Rach." He did not sound like he was anywhere near the baseball field, or in a car on the way to the baseball field. No, he sounded like he was in an airport.

A slight feeling of vertigo pulled at Rachel, like the gravitational field of the earth seemed to get stronger.

No. He needed to be at the game. The boys were so excited.

She gripped the phone in her hand and closed her eyes.

Gavin's a good guy. Gavin's a good guy. Gavin's a good guy.

"What's up?" she asked, hoping her perky tone betrayed the inner turmoil swirl, willing him to say he was on his way to the game to see their boys even though she knew deep down he wasn't and she'd work her magic and all would be well. The only one who would pay the price was her.

"Dakota has a last-minute installation in Boston," Gavin said, obviously distracted because he was Gavin. Distracted. "We're heading there for the weekend. I'll be back in time to help set up for the boys' party, but we're going to miss tonight."

Yes, gravity. Her legs felt heavier by the second.

"Gavin, they want you there." *They need you there.*

"If I could be there, I would, you know that."

She did. Sort of.

He sounded genuine. Then again, he always sounded genuine. Genuine was Gavin's thing. If Gavin had a thing.

Dakota and Gavin had been engaged for a while. He worked tons of hours, in an office. Dakota, meanwhile, had carved out a name for herself as an artist who painted, and sculpted, a variety of animals in bathtubs.

Yes, this was a thing.

Dakota worked tons of hours with this gig and was, as Gavin had explained, kind of a big deal. Rachel didn't mind her. She was nice to Rachel's kids, and that's what mattered.

Meanwhile, Rachel also worked tons of hours...from her home office, so custody and the majority of childcare had been delegated to her.

Which was fine because, as she'd insisted and they'd agreed, the boys needed her stability.

"Rachel?" Dakota had apparently confiscated the phone from Gavin.

"Hey, Dakota." Rachel struggled to hold her phone and pull on her shoes simultaneously.

Dakota? Molly mouthed rolling her eyes dramatically with more gagging sounds.

Rachel nodded, ignoring her friend to focus on the conversation. Molly hated Dakota.

"Gavin and I sent the boys a surprise for their birthday. It'll be there tomorrow. I hate to ask, but would you mind—"

"I'll grab a video for you." Rachel hopped to stand, mentally rehearsing what she would say to the kids so they wouldn't feel the entire sting of this disappointment. *Your dad wanted to make it tonight, but he had to go to Boston. Don't worry, he has a big surprise for you both.*

"You're the best." Dakota's muffled voice sounded as though she'd covered the speaker before she spoke.

"Not a problem." A birthday surprise was an excellent distraction. A birthday surprise was something for the boys to look forward to. A birthday surprise was the perfect redirection for their disappointment.

This wasn't the first time she'd helped Dakota and Gavin co-parent virtually. It wouldn't be the last, she was certain of that. Gavin was not a hands-on kind of father. Then again, he hadn't really signed up to be a dad, so she did her best not to make it miserable for him.

"Bye, Rach." Gavin's voice sounded like an echo, since Dakota still had the phone.

"Bye," Rachel said, thumbing the off button.

Rachel liked Dakota. She liked Gavin, too. It wasn't his fault they'd based their marriage on one night of mediocre passion that led to their boys.

It wasn't hers, either.

It just…was.

Molly was still making gagging faces in between cookie bites. She didn't understand this part of things.

Gavin and Rachel had tried. Tried-ish.

But, despite his mother's proclivity to shoving them together, guilting them together, and offering to pay Rachel to ensure they stayed together, their marriage was as dull as their kitchen knives.

Let's just say, if their marriage were an entrée, it had no seasoning at all.

No one really understood what had happened on that one night eight years ago that had changed their lives. The night she hand-selected Gavin from a group of guys for her first ever supposed-to-be one-night stand.

The evening had resulted in one of them climaxing. (Spoiler alert, it wasn't Rachel.) He'd called her a few times after, but she hadn't returned his calls because that would've totally ruined the point of having a one-night-only curtain call.

Then—and oh boy, was it a big *then*—were the words, "Congrats, it's twins."

That part did not suck, because Rachel loved the hell out of her boys.

Besides the children, she and Gavin had shared a marriage that lasted a few months before they both came to their senses and recognized they made much better co-parenting friends and partners than co-parenting spouses who slept across the hall, because he snored like a freaking freight train on fire and she, so he told her, hogged all the blankets.

They were excellent...friends. Friends who had two kids together and eventually lived separate lives because it was just more comfortable for everyone.

"What did they want?" Molly asked, the dislike of Gavin apparent in her tone.

"Long story." Rachel grabbed the keys on her way to the door. "I'll fill you in on the way."

Where Rachel and Gavin got along fine, he and Molly despised each other. Which Rachel didn't understand.

"He's not coming to the game," Molly correctly guessed.

Phone stuffed into her pocket, Rachel flicked on the slow cooker so dinner would be ready when they arrived home. She tossed the extra cookie in a zip-top bag so it would be safe in her purse—once her boys discovered she kept tampons in the interior pocket, they avoided the thing at all costs.

"I guess that means Travis will attend instead," Molly mused.

She had been working to convince Rachel to practice her flirting skills with Travis Frank for the past four months.

The idea was so far beyond ridiculous, so off the beaten path that it didn't even show up on Google Maps.

But flirting was Molly's job, so she looked for opportunities everywhere. Rachel didn't blame her because Molly literally taught the basics of dating and had to keep her skills sharp for her clients. She used her inability to take no for an answer and her MyTube channel to teach others the intricacies.

"Dave might come," Rachel said, hoping it was Dave who would attend. Gavin had two brothers. She got along fabulously with Dave. Not so much with Travis.

For a lengthy list of reasons substantially longer than Molly's meddling.

"It'll be Travis," Molly said, a small, knowing smile teasing the edges of her hot-pink-painted lips.

"Probably." It usually was Travis who filled in when Gavin couldn't make it. Rachel started the mental prep work for dealing with him. "Do not start up about him again."

Molly bit at her bottom lip, apparently refusing to respond.

Rachel could literally feel her matchmaking friend brewing an idea to push Rachel and Travis together. Last time he'd been to a game, Molly manipulated them into sitting thigh-to-thigh on the bleachers. The time before that? Her car broke down and she asked Travis to drive them home. Then Molly caught a ride with the umpire's wife instead.

Oh, to be sure, Molly didn't *believe* Rachel and Travis had any business being together. She just wanted to piss off Gavin.

It was her way.

"I like Travis." Molly bit at her bottom lip, saying the words with the caution of one merging onto a road littered with construction. "I like it when he comes to the games."

When Gavin couldn't make a game, one of his immediate family members always showed up to—and she was quoting him here—"represent the family."

Like they were mafiosos or something.

They weren't.

They were, however, loaded beyond belief because Great-Meemaw Frank had created the first Puffle Yum and sold the shit out of the toaster tarts.

Rachel paused, setting the purse strap onto her shoulder. "Travis is a fantastic *uncle*."

She made it a point to enunciate that last word. Because any idea of flirting with Travis or doing anything beyond friendly chatter with him was an absolute nopers.

"Is that new?" Molly gestured to Rachel's bag. She may have been a black belt in flirting, but her distraction techniques could use some work.

Rachel knew how Molly operated and, in her mind, as long

as she didn't verbally commit, she would weasel her way out of an implied agreement later.

"I grabbed it at the Coach outlet in Loveland last week," Rachel said. The rose-colored over-the-shoulder bag was the last on the shelf, and Rachel had fallen in deep lust with it on first sight.

"I think I need at least two of these," Molly mumbled, examining the stitching.

"Too bad, I got the last one." Rachel grinned, nabbing the bag away with a smirk.

Molly shook her head. "There are always more online."

"Dinner's cooking, I have my keys, shoes, purse, go bag, sunglasses, boys are going straight to the field after school." Rachel inventoried everything she needed for the game.

"You ready now?" Molly asked.

"Let's go." Rachel dropped her sunglasses into her bag and held the front door for her friend.

This week was Molly's turn to drive.

Which meant Molly would be busy driving the vehicle and Rachel would spend the thirty-minute drive to the baseball field calling Cassie back and then chatting about everything but her least favorite Frank brother. So perhaps, just perhaps, Molly would leave it alone.

Maybe.

Looking for more romance?
Entangled brings the laughs.

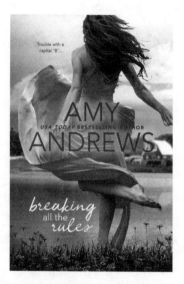

BREAKING ALL THE RULES

Determined to leave the rat race behind, Beatrice moves to a small town and is determined at 37 to break free from all of society's rules...including dating the 25-year-old cop who won't stop flirting with her.

THE REBOUND SURPRISE

Carefree bachelor Aniel is the perfect guy to have a rebound fling with after organized and predictable Libby finds her fiancé defiling her linen sheets with the maid. Except, the fine print that says condoms aren't 100 percent effective is unerringly accurate.

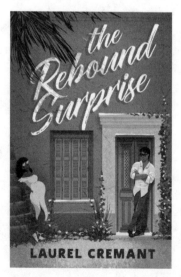

Entangled brings the feels.

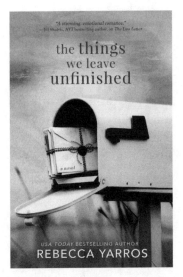

THE THINGS WE LEAVE UNFINISHED

Told in alternating timelines, *The Things We Leave Unfinished* examines the risks we take for love, the scars too deep to heal, and the endings we can't bring ourselves to see coming.

CONFESSIONS IN B-FLAT

Essence bestselling author Donna Hill brings us an emotional love story set against the powerful backdrop of the civil rights movement that gripped a nation—a story as timely as it is timeless...

Entangled brings the heat.

FOLLOW ME DARKLY

One chance encounter is all it took for Skye to find herself in the middle of a Cinderella story...but self-made billionaire Braden Black is no Prince Charming, and his dark desires are far from his only secret.

APHRODITE IN BLOOM: AN EROTIC ROMANCE COLLECTION

Brimming with romance and intrigue, this collection of erotic historical short stories is sure to excite all the senses and unleash your most secret desires.

Entangled brings the heart.

A LOT LIKE LOVE

Sparks start to fly between longtime crushes Sarah and Wes when they begin renovating the B&B her grandmother left her. But what happens when they realize each other's *real* reasons for restoring the landmark are at complete odds?

THE SWEETHEART DEAL

As enemies Tessa and Leo strike a secret marriage deal in name only to save both their businesses, they're shocked to find it not only shakes up old family feuds, but proves the old adage of never mixing business with pleasure was definitely on to something...

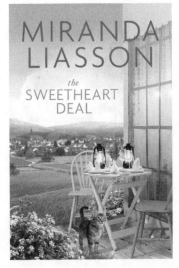

Don't miss any of the exciting new romances Entangled has to offer.

Follow @Entangled_Publishing on Instagram and join us at Facebook.com/EntangledPublishing

an imprint of Entangled Publishing LLC